The Banderman Odyssey

By Randy K. Wallace

To Susan for SAFETY!
I will remember you as
one of the many nicest nurses
on 3rd Floor!

PublishAmerica
Baltimore

March 21, 2011

ISBN: 1-4241-3346-7
PUBLISHED BY PUBLISHAMERICA, LLLP
www.publishamerica.com
Baltimore

Printed in the United States of America

Chapter 1

The sun shone brightly on the ocean side. Jason Banderman stood alone in his secret spot, staring at his reflection in the still water of a tidal pool. Mom said it was just as it used to be near the pond behind the barn when she was growing up. Jason had seen a picture of the old farm, but it was gone long before he was born.

The tidal pool appeared a bright shadowy blue; clouds drifted slowly through it. Jason walked along the beach and poked at various bits of debris with an old stick he had acquired long ago. It was his favorite stick—old and worn with time. It was the same gray color that wood gets when it's been bleached by the mid-afternoon sun for countless summer days. It was unnaturally straight for a stick (or any stick that he had ever seen before) and had the strangest spiraled pattern on one end. His mother said it was a broomstick, but he had never seen one made of wood before. The spirals were sure neat and it made a great stick for poking at things that he knew he wasn't supposed to touch. He wondered what salt spray might have smelled like, if there ever was such a thing. His mom said there had been, but he had never smelled it. Oily sludge lapped sluggishly at the shore. This was the ocean he had always known.

He poked at the steel blue water of the tidal pool and it swirled up black. He drew an outline of a house in the water. It stayed there for a few seconds before the water and sludge separated again leaving the pool reflecting the sky once more. It reminded Jason why this was one of his favorite spots. It was the one place where he could actually get down to the water. There were miles and miles of meshed fencing with loops of barbed wire lining the top. He could walk up to it in countless places, but could only look through. He remembered how happy his mother had been when he was able to point to the great weathered signs and read "DANGER." In truth, he couldn't read at the time, but his mother didn't seem to mind. She seemed so happy when he was able to point out the signs and say with a very determined child-face, "DAANNGER." She loved that.

His mother would freak if she knew he was here, but it was such a great place. The rocks came right down into the water on both sides forming a small bowl around a tiny bit of the ocean. A small cave gaped in the crag behind him where eons of waves had washed away the softer material. In the ceiling was a small hole that led up to the field on the other side of the danger-fence. It was his very own secret exit/entrance.

It truly was a hideout that no one else knew about. The entrance formed years after the fence was built, during one particularly wet spring. The scree from the cave-in formed a narrow slide into the cave; perfect for a quick entrance. Jason would often pretend to be a commando, run at full speed, slip silently over the edge and disappear suddenly from enemy view into a world of his own.

Over the years of summers, Jason had collected many special items from all around the house, village and shore to create a menagerie. He had his own collection of SPECIAL stuff. It contained some of the neatest stuff any ten-year-old could ever imagine finding. There were old radio carcasses, both glass and plastic bottles, metal containers, Barbie Doll heads, ceramics, plates, cups, and toys of every description. Jason had his special spot, his neat stick and the coolest display of "stuff" that anybody could ever imagine owning. He stood silently surveying his private paradise.

Turning back to the tidal pool, he could see himself framed against the sky in the steel blue water again. He sat down and watched the clouds drift slowly by without looking up. He poked his stick into the water and created a small black dot in the perfect picture of the shadowy sky.

Chapter 2

"Jason! Time for lunch," his mother, Sarah, yelled from the back porch. *Where is that boy anyway?* she thought. Lately, Jason seemed to be gone more. Up at dawn with a just a light breakfast, then nowhere to be seen until lunchtime. Oh, he was a good boy, but he did love to wander. The only trouble was wandering these days was dangerous; could even be deadly.

She had put up the danger signs not long after they arrived. Jason knew what they meant and usually stayed away. The fences were everywhere and the only way off the property was through a gate at the front of the house. Jason wouldn't and couldn't get off the property unless she went with him. Nevertheless, he loved to collect things and he was a truly ingenious young boy. Where was he anyway?

By the time Sarah had finished going over all the worrisome possibilities, Jason came running up to the back steps with a huge grin. She put her arm around his shoulder as she led him into the kitchen where the previous day's stew simmered on the stove. Jason's gait slowed instantly. "Oh, Mom, do we have to have this again? We had this yesterday," he whined.

"You know what I've always told you about food. Just like my mother used to say, 'waste not, want not.' And that's just what we're going to do. Wash your hands and get your bottom back in here."

Jason slouched then lumbered off to the bathroom. The water that came from the tap was a light yellow color that reeked of strange unknown odors. There were few smells that were as unappealing as the water. The stench filled the entire bathroom. When the water filled the sink and Jason added a mixture of chemicals, the smell was even worse. Jason hummed a part of a song his mother taught him, "Always look on the bright side of life."

Back in the kitchen, his mother waited at the table. He sat down, and they began to eat silently. The stew was made from rusty cabbage, and potatoes. There wasn't any meat in the "stew," but there was a slight flavor of chicken—probably from a bullion package that had expired years earlier. Jason was hungry and accustomed to eating without complaining. Any food was good food. He had gone hungry often enough to know that.

After lunch, Jason jumped to his feet. "See ya, Mom," he said and headed for the door.

"Just a minute, champ. Get back here and give a hand with the dishes. You're not going anywhere until you help out a little."

"Awe, Mom, do I have to?" Jason complained.

"Yes, you have to. Now, put the dishes in the sink and wipe off the table."

Sarah moved into the living room, which was more like a miniature jungle. Here in the largest and brightest room in the house, Sarah could nurture the plants that formed the staple for the meals. The garden was a priority for a good part of every afternoon. Sarah had every intention of having Jason grow up to be a healthy young man. For her, it was a matter of fact, not a hopeful possibility. Her garden was essential.

Jason wiped down the table, rinsed the rag and skipped to the door. Sarah caught him just in time to renew his sun block, slap his hat on his head and kiss him good-bye. "Where're you off to now?" she asked.

"Just out back, Mom. I'll be back in a bit." Then he was gone again.

As fearful as she was, Sarah admitted to herself that over the last few years the world had already begun its recovery. The widespread lack of industry had given the world its needed respite. The atmosphere, like the rest of the world, was on the mend. Sarah had begun to notice this herself. The daily precautions that she took had become ingrained. There were risks everywhere. There was absolutely no sense in adding to it unnecessarily.

Outside, Jason poked around in the dirt with his stick. If he looked carefully, there was always something new sticking out of the dirt. Sometimes it might be the sole of a shoe or a piece of broken pottery. Other times it might be a miniature figurine with "Made in China" stamped on the bottom. Either way, poking around was what Jason loved to do, and there was no other pleasure better than unearthing some new treasure to add to his collection.

He hunted around for a while, but after finding nothing of any real interest, headed to the fence. A direct route wasn't really possible. The path was obscured by a number of dead blackberry hedges that skirted the house. These were so overgrown at one time that now the dead, thorny twigs were thick and high. It created a natural barrier and forced Jason to move through a maze of prickles to get to his passage. When he arrived, he jumped without hesitation and slid down into the cave.

When he first found this place, he had to crawl and dig his way to the beach. But over the months, his sliding, first on his feet and later on his bum, helped to create a more natural slide. After countless numbers of trips up and down it, the ramp had become smooth and hard. Only the occasional rock stuck out and Jason was able to avoid most of those. Today, unfortunately, he managed to nail the largest of the stones directly. It was towards the bottom of the slide, and he had developed a lot of speed by the time he hit it. The pain left him clutching his butt in agony as he screamed silently, rolling around in the sand. Later, he would find that it left a bruise the size of a small plate on the back of his thigh, just below his buttocks.

When he was finished writhing in pain and silently cursing the world, he calmed to consider the situation. The rock had been there all along. Had he not blindly leapt through the hole in the first place, none of this would have happened. If he had removed the stone days or even weeks before, when it first emerged, this wouldn't have happened either. The solution to the problem was obvious.

Limping out of the cave and into the bowl shaped beach, Jason picked up his favorite stick and, using it like a cane, headed back to the slide. The stick made a rudimentary digging tool. He used it to begin clearing around the outside of the stone.

He hadn't worked long before he realized that the removal of the stone would also mean the demolition of his slide. It was much larger than he first thought and it became somewhat of a dilemma whether or not to continue. Once he determined that the slide was pretty much history, he decided that the new obstacle wasn't going to get the best of him. Besides, after a half an hour of steady digging, he had come to a point where he had begun to dig around the back of the boulder.

Jason struggled on. With sweat pouring down his face and into his eyes, and with the rock's face completely exposed, he sat on the stone to wipe his brow on his sleeve. It was at that very moment, the stone suddenly disappeared from under him and he followed. When he came to a halt, he found himself pinned tight in the hole with his legs sticking straight up around his ears. His arms were wedged in the hole so that he had no leverage at all. In this position, he could look up into the slide, but could not see the water's edge.

Jason laughed out loud in disbelief. First, the bruise on his leg and now this. His predicament worsened. He slid farther into the hole and became wedged even tighter. If getting out before was going to be hard, now it began to look bleak indeed. For the first time since he had found the cave, Jason realized how dangerous keeping a secret could be. His mother had no idea where he was, and he had no idea how he was going to save himself.

Jason tried calling out, but he was jammed in the hole so tightly that breathing became more difficult. In frustration and pain, Jason did the only thing left to do; he started to cry. With every tear, his energy slowly seeped away until he was completely drained. His efforts to lift himself out of the hole were fruitless. With a final heave and a sigh, Jason relaxed in utter exhaustion and disappointment. And that is when he slip-fell-tumbled further into the hole. He landed, banging his back and head on the boulder that had previously rolled into the newfound cave.

It took only a moment for a new fear to seize him. Above him, light shone dimly from the hole he had just fallen through. He was in a chamber that smelled as if a dozen rotting corpses were about to reach out and add him to their numbers. Leaping to his feet, he scrambled up the embankment and through the hole. Without stopping, he turned and continued his ascent to the surface.

Once he dreamed that he was trapped under water. In the dream, he had been vaguely aware that if he should breathe, he would die, so he swam as hard as he could to the surface. The water pushed against his face as he tore upward, but the surface seemed unattainable. Finally, when he felt he could hold his breath for not a second longer, he broke the surface. In fact, in his dream, he literally flew out of the water. Jason clamored out of his would-be grave and lay looking at the sky. He breathed deeply remembering that dream.

After catching his breath and looking at his watch, he realized that he was late returning home. Picking himself up, he ran into the house. His mother met him at the door. "Jason Dennis Banderman, where on earth have you been? I've been calling and calling. Look at you. You look like you've been dug out of the ground."

"Sorry, Mom," Jason said sheepishly and quickly slipped beneath her stare and into the house.

"Mister! Hold it right there," she ordered.

Jason froze. Sarah reached down and grabbed his T-shirt in both hands.

"Lift up your arms," she said gently, as she pulled it up and over his head.

When he had nothing on but his underwear and socks, Sarah finally let him into the house. Jason was thankful that she didn't notice the bright red circle on his exposed thigh. In his nearly naked glory, she sat him down at the table and placed a cup of water into the microwave. After a minute or so, she added a pouch of prepackaged hot chocolate and set the mixture in front of him.

"Thanks, Mom."

"You stay here and sip on that while I run you a bath. We'll eat when you're clean and then you can explain how you managed to get yourself so darned dirty."

Jason knew that some kind of an explanation was going to be a must. He didn't want to lie, but he also knew that his mother would never allow him to keep his hideout if she knew where or what it was. Jason intended to make the hot chocolate last a very long time.

Sarah went into the bathroom and began to run a hot bath. By the time Jason's hot chocolate was finished, it had long since grown cold and the bath was well on its way to being lukewarm. Sarah's temper was well on its way as well. Not normally an angry woman, she was close to reaching her threshold of tolerance and her glare told him so. Fearing his mother's wrath, Jason downed the last sip of chocolate sludge at the bottom of the mug and raced to the bathroom. While he soaked in the tub, he tossed a million explanations to his dinosaur bath pal. As the dinosaur ate the last of the throwaway ideas, Sarah came in with a towel.

"Supper's ready. Time to dry off and get your pee-jays on."

Jason ate supper silently and prayed quietly that his mother had forgotten about the explanation that she said he owed her. He gave his best "wet-cat, sorry" look hoping that she had become amnesic at some point during the last hour. He tried his best to look both miserable and apologetic at the same time, chewing every morsel twice as many times as he knew he should. The net result? He sat at the dinner table nursing his plate for nearly a full hour. It was time for bed when his mother took his plate to the sink.

"Bedtime, Jason."

Could he actually be so lucky? It was difficult to contain himself as he hurried off to his room. Almost too joyfully, he pulled the covers up to his chin. His mother looked at him with a half smile and then grew serious. Jason's heart sank.

"Jason, you know that you have to come right away when you're called. I realize you love digging up the property, but I have to know you're safe. You won't be allowed to disappear out back if you can't show that you can be responsible. If you say you'll be back by a certain time, you must. We have an agreement. You said you'd play safe and check in regularly. That didn't happen today. I was worried sick."

The lecture lasted so long that Jason felt a spanking would have been less painful. When he could hold his eyes open no longer, his mother kissed him good night. She hadn't probed him at all. Jason fell asleep with mixed emotions. Though his mother hadn't asked, Jason felt as if he had lied.

Chapter 3

Jason woke to a throbbing pain. His leg felt as if a knot had been tied in it. Massaging it didn't seem to help. He pulled down his pajama pants to get a better look. The bruise was big and black. Where the rock had impacted hardest, the skin was scraped away. The day before, it was red. Today it reminded him of the road rash he got when he crashed his bike in the driveway. He remembered picking gravel out of it for a week afterwards. His new injury combined a deep bruise pain and the searing sting of a scrape. Jason crawled slowly out of bed and dressed. As he went about the house, he hoped that he gave no sign of the pain he felt. That night, as he undressed, he found that his pants had stuck to his scrape. It took, what felt like, hours of wincing at every small advance before he finally got his pants off, his pajamas on and then crawled into bed.

During the following week, Jason stayed close to the house. His mother demanded it and Jason was happy to oblige. Although he was given many chores to do, the time allowed the bruise to heal and the scrape to become a scab before it began to peel off. It also gave his mother time to restore a little of the faith she had lost in him.

It took two weeks before his leg was completely healed and he gathered the courage to ask his mother's permission to go out back. He had finished all of his chores for the day and was wandering aimlessly around the house. Sarah responded simply, "One hour."

Jason grabbed a few things, a flashlight among them, and headed out the back door.

At the fence, a nasty, reeking odor filled the air. Jason nearly gagged peering down into the hole and the entire force of the foul stench hit him full in his face. Reeling back gagging, he stepped back and away from the hole to consider his options. It didn't take long to realize there were only two. He could either go in, or leave the hole as it was. It was clear that choosing not to explore this new discovery was out of the question.

Jason ran back to the house, checked in with his mom before disappearing into his bedroom. He threw an extra T-shirt over the one he was wearing and ran out of the house once more. He waved to his mom as he passed by the kitchen window, who gave him a warning look. Jason yelled back he'd be back in about a half an hour and was out the door.

A short time later, back at the slide, he pulled the extra T-shirt over his head and wrapped it around his mouth and nose. He stepped closer to the slide and took a few deep sample breaths. Better. Much better. This time he descended slowly, using his feet as brakes. He touched down at the bottom and rushed past the gaping hole to the beach. He ripped the shirt from his face and breathed the fresher air. A nearly imperceptible breeze coming from the ocean pushed the bad air up the slide like a chimney. He stood downwind and could not detect the bad smell from the cave.

Recovered, Jason dug out the flashlight, re-wrapped the T-shirt around his face, returned to the cavern and stuck his head into the hole. Even with the T-shirt over his face, the smell was almost unbearable. He flipped the flashlight on and peered inside. Subterranean water had washed the rock away and formed a deep cavern about four feet high. It stretched back far enough from where he lay that he couldn't see the back and could not tell what was causing the stench.

Part of the musty smell was caused by soil that never gets dry, a kind of damp swampy odor. But there was more. There was a rotten smell that only comes from something when it is decomposing slowly. Jason's imagination began to take control of him. Frantically, he backed out of the hole, scrambled up the slide for the second time that day and ran home without looking back.

He walked through the door and his mother noticed that he had come in earlier than they had agreed on. Chalking it up to his trying to make a good impression, she let him disappear into his room again.

Jason closed his bedroom door and rolled onto his bed. Staring at the ceiling, he let all the possibilities of his new discovery run through his mind.

What could possibly be in there? Maybe there was a pirate's treasure, or an underground city. Was there an immense maze of tunnels, that when he mapped them, he would find that they went on forever? What was the best way to go about exploring this new discovery? He might need string, just in case he needed to retrace his steps back to the cave entrance. He would definitely need a flashlight. He lay there and his list began to grow. In his mind, a plan began to form.

Chapter 4

Before it was time to sleep, Jason had completed his list and had a systematic plan for exploring the cave. The following day, after he'd finished his chores and morning studies, he put a few exploring supplies into his backpack. His gear included a coat, rubber boots, an extra pair of socks, a knife, a flashlight and a ball of twine. He waved good-bye to his mother. She asked where he was going.

"Just exploring," he replied, and then he was gone.

At the beach, he emptied his pack. Underground it would be cold and wet. He slipped on the extra socks, rubber boots and put on his jacket. He donned his T-shirt facemask, held his ball of string in one hand, firmly grasping the flashlight in the other. Determined and with the empty pack on his back, he strode to the entrance, flipped the switch on the flashlight and crawled into the opening.

Once inside, Jason found that he could almost stand up. The sides of the cavern were solid stone. Though water was not dripping from them, they were wet and cold to the touch. He peered around the small enclosure and noticed a fissure toward the back, near the floor. He took one end of the ball of string and formed a large loop. He threw the loop over the stone that had tumbled down weeks earlier, and pulled it tight. Holding the flashlight in one hand made unraveling the ball of string difficult. Traversing to the back of the cave, he had dropped the string three times. Although Jason's excitement and fear were nearly overwhelming, he forced himself to move more slowly and deliberately.

At the small crack in the wall, he had to get on his knees to look down into it. The passage was small and dipped down before turning up hill again. Jason could see no more than a few feet into the tiny cave. There was nothing left to do but hunker down and start crawling.

He wriggled into the gap and began the short descent. The passage narrowed even more and turned sharply upward. Too late, his back could not bend backward far enough to allow him to be able to continue on his stomach. Coming into the tunnel downhill and headfirst, backing up was impossible. The empty pack caught on the close rocky ceiling making him feel claustrophobic. Jason panicked. He couldn't breathe. It was impossible to move forward and he couldn't wiggle back.

The best course of action was to leave the pack behind. The coat hadn't been such a good idea either. In this close space and working so hard, Jason began to sweat. His frustration grew. Rational thought fled until something his mother had said came to mind. "Whenever you're doing something really difficult, slow down and think; take your time. Frustration only makes things worse." There were countless times that this little saying had helped him.

He took a few deep breaths and slowly began to relax. Getting out of the pack proved to be more difficult than he expected. He couldn't maneuver to get his arms free. He took more deep breaths and then it occurred to him that there was another way to get the pack off.

Against his chest were adjustment straps. The straps could be shortened or lengthened to fit just about anyone. The clips could also slip right off the ends. Jason rolled to one side, and pulled back and up on the clasp. The strap slipped easily and cleared the end of the clasp. He rolled to his other side, repeated the process and the pack lay loosely on his back.

His coat was more of an obstacle. With the pack in the small opening with him, it seemed there was even less room to move around. He had begun to relax and his body began to cool off. He decided not to worry about the coat after all. He made a silent pact with himself to try and anticipate problems from now on and his best to avoid silly mishaps like this one.

He rolled over on his back and wriggled down to the bottom of the dip. From there, he inched his way up the embankment using his feet as leverage. Progress was slow particularly because he could not see anything except the ceiling, which was only four inches from his face. Being both curious and afraid made clear thinking harder. Both of those feelings made it that much more important. Earlier Jason had imagined a walk in the park as he traveled down high passages in search of his underground city. Now he realized anything would have been better than this.

Jason moved forward slowly and ascended about two feet along the passage. It began to level out and widen slightly. The new development allowed him to roll over once more and look ahead into the passage. He shone his flashlight into the pitch-black darkness. The cave continued on in much the same way. He looked back. The light from outside had disappeared altogether. Jason felt as if he were in a tomb. He turned his thoughts forward and commando crawled down the tiny passage. Even if he had wanted, there was no room to turn around.

Fifty feet later, the passage suddenly opened up into a large subterranean chamber. Small pools of water were scattered about on the floor. Jason considered the possibility that he was standing at the same level as the ocean outside. Against the far side of the cavern, no more than thirty feet away, was another cave-in. It was much the same as the one that Jason used as a slide. In one significant way, this one was different. Besides all of the loose dirt that had fallen, there was also a large pile of cardboard boxes at its base. Some of the boxes had tipped over and had spilled their contents. Old wet paper littered the cavern floor.

Jason worked his way slowly and carefully around the outside perimeter of the cavern. He examined the walls. He could see at least half a dozen openings of various sizes leading deeper, away from the ocean. Debris that had fallen from above already blocked some of them. Others disappeared into the darkness, and still others ended abruptly after only a few feet.

Jason moved to the piles of boxes and looked up into the area they had fallen from. The source of the caustic odor that filled the cavern was coming from up there. Beyond the boxes, a jumbled mess that consisted of every kind of disgusting decomposing material imaginable would not be long before tumbling down also and joining the papers. Jason pulled at one of the boxes. Something rolled into the darkness. Jason screamed and ran back toward the cavern's entrance. His heart pounding in his ears, he sat down near the exit and stared at the ground between his feet, too afraid to look up. He wasn't sure, but the thing that had rolled out was about the size of a human head.

Digging deeply, his summoned his courage. He stood and directed the light back across the cavern. There it lay, half submerged in one of the pools of water. From where he sat, it was impossible to tell exactly what it was. Jason was pulled along by his morbid curiosity. He had never seen a human skull before.

He inched his way forward, never taking the light from the head. It was as though he half expected it to roll over and stare up at him. He continued forward. Even as he stood directly over it, he could not identify what it might be. He hadn't brought his stick with him and was thinking how great it would be to have it right now. He would never know what it was unless he touched it.

He used his boot to roll it over slowly. It was round and the same disgusting black color all over. His courage grew. He prodded it with a finger. The surface had a soft, slimy and mushy feeling, but was firmer underneath. Jason picked the melon size ball up in both hands. He began to pick at the black outside layer. When he was finally able to identify the object, he burst into a fit of laughter. He tossed the head of lettuce aside, laughing uncontrollably. His legs felt weak and he sat down on a nearby rock. Adrenaline coursed through his body. His limbs shook uncontrollably.

He sat there until his courage was restored before making his way over to the piles again. He pulled at the boxes on the bottom of the heap and they tore apart easily. A gray glop oozed out of them. He pulled at one of the boxes a little higher up. It was damp, but not entirely soaked. He dragged one down where he could get a closer look. On the outside of the box, in big black letters was stamped, VANCOUVER SUN. Below this, it was stamped January 1, 1999—December 31, 2001. Jason lifted the lid and reached inside. The newspapers were too damp to be separated, so he began to pull at more of the boxes even higher up. As he worked his way further into the heap, he found the boxes there were in better shape. The ones toward the center were much drier.

After a half an hour of pulling down box after box, Jason found one that contained papers, which were quite dry. He picked one out from the center to have a look at it. The picture on the front drew his attention. In the photo a huge crowd of people stood, supposedly, on some street in Vancouver. It looked as though they were fighting amongst themselves. The paper was dated January 2009. There were three distinct groups of people in the picture. The most obvious group was the people running around screaming and breaking windows with sticks and rocks. A second group of uniformed men held clear plastic shields, wore helmets and wielded clubs. A third group consisted of a number of bodies that lay at the feet of those who were still standing. Jason couldn't tell whether these people were alive or not. The headline made things clear, "Robson Riot Claims Thirty."

Although the image was quite shocking, Jason had never seen so many people in one place in his entire life. One question was clearer than any other, "Where are all the people now?"

Jason checked his watch. He had been gone longer than he planned. He tucked the newspaper into his jacket, and made his way out of the cave.

Getting out was much easier than going in. Where the tunnel narrowed and turned downhill, he rolled onto his back and slid backward down the little hill. When he reached the bottom, he used his feet to push himself up the embankment and into the first chamber. He stood up, crossed the chamber and exited through the hole in the slide.

He arrived home and slipped into the house, out of his dirty clothes and then into his room. On his bed, he pulled open the old newspaper. More pictures captured his attention immediately. Even the ads were interesting. Again, he was struck by how many people there were. He noticed the pictures of the burning buildings and the overturned trucks. Another picture showed a group of people holding placards. Some of the signs had sayings like, "We Want Jobs" or "What About Our Kids." He was surprised at that. There were pictures of products that various stores were trying to sell. Jason's thoughts turned to all of the abandoned buildings with broken windows and empty shelves. There were still stores that he and his mother frequented that hadn't been raided completely. These offered many useful items. It was at these stores that his mother renewed the products she used to grow the plants and purify the water. Were they…department stores? Or…no, hardware stores. The department store was where his mother could get cloth and clothing.

In the back section of the newspaper, Jason noticed a section of comics. He read this section over carefully. He especially liked *Garfield*. He never had a pet before and wondered what it might be like to have a cat of his own. He sure wouldn't want one like Garfield.

After the first time through, he started from the front again and read the headlines, being sure not to skip a single one. Most of them had a picture that went along with it. The more interesting ones were in bigger print. Soon he began to read individual stories. It didn't take him long to tire of this activity. Most of the stories seemed like isolated incidents. Some of them seemed caught in the middle—an ongoing investigation of premier so and so, or forest workers continue to demonstrate in front of the parliament buildings. Other stories merely stated that certain events had taken place. Such and such apartment burned down, or so and so was found in an alley behind a downtown pub.

Jason didn't spend a lot of time reading the paper. The stories were about problems he couldn't understand, people he didn't know, in a time that didn't exist. He laid the paper down beside his bed and rolled over to stare at the ceiling. He was still thinking about all that he had read and seen when his mother called him for dinner. He ate his meal in silence and went to bed with no fuss at all.

Sarah noticed Jason's silence. Normally, he would have come in chattering about something new he had found or something that he'd seen. He'd have questions to ask. "What's this, Mom? Did you ever see one of these before? Isn't this neat?" Something was going on. She decided she was worrying over nothing and let him alone for now. Tomorrow she would try and find out what was on his mind.

The morning sun rose and Sarah began her daily task of tending her garden. She was working quietly away when Jason came up behind her. She worked silently, oblivious to the fact that he stood watching. He startled her with a question.

"Mom? Where are all the people?"

Sarah's eyes suddenly widened in shock. She had time to half turn and face Jason before she collapsed to the floor.

Jason staggered back in fright as his mother tumbled to the floor. His first thought was she had a heart attack or maybe an embolism. He read somewhere about a woman who suddenly dropped to floor. She simply died.

"Mom? Mom!"

He fell to the floor beside her and wrapped his arms around her. "Mom, Mom, Mom," he whispered over and over, tears streaming down his face. With his head buried in her chest, he noticed that his head was rising and falling. She was breathing! He stood and ran to the kitchen. From the counter he grabbed a cloth and from the fridge a pitcher of chilled water. He poured water onto the cloth and raced back to his mother's side. She lay on the floor with one leg tucked awkwardly under her. If she were sitting upright, it would have been underneath her. Jason helped to straighten her leg and reached for a sofa pillow to put under her head. He applied the cloth to her forehead and silently prayed that she would be okay.

When Sarah came to, she found herself lying on the floor, a damp cloth on her forehead and a couch pillow beneath her head. Jason knelt close by; the worried look on his face made him almost unrecognizable. "Mom! Are you all right?"

Sarah didn't respond at first. Her gaze circled the room as she tried to orient herself. When she did, she burst into tears.

"What's the matter? Why are you crying?"

Sarah tried to respond to Jason, but she was heaving and shaking so badly that she couldn't speak. She couldn't staunch the flow of tears.

Eventually, she struggled to her feet. She used the wall and then the coffee table for support as she made her way slowly to the sofa. Once there, and through the sobs, she beckoned Jason to come and sit beside her. He slowly got to his feet and sat next to his mother.

"Jason, why did you ask me that question?" she asked through eyes red with tears.

There would be no more secrets. Jason told her about the paper he had found. He told her about the cave and the beach. He told her about the tunnels. He was careful to leave out the more frightening details of his latest experiences. He told her about the pictures of the hundreds of people fighting, of the demonstrations and the accidents.

In horror, Sarah listened. She was torn with guilt, realizing the dangers that Jason had been exposed to without her knowledge.

Jason was surprised that his mother didn't blow her top. Instead, she sat thinking quietly for a long time. Her eyes seemed deep set somehow. Jason noticed lines on her face that he was not accustomed to seeing. She would have called them worry lines. They were caused by the way her tense muscles held her face at night when Jason was sleeping. They appeared on her face just before it was mealtime when Jason was nowhere to be seen and he hadn't answered her call. They came in secret, in the darkness of the night or in the gray light of the hardware store when she prodded around looking for things she had run out of at home. Jason rarely got to see what made them, but now he hardly recognized the old lady before him. She seemed to be struggling. But this struggle came from deep inside. Finally, she turned to him. "Jason, I think that you are old enough to know."

And so, Sarah related the sad story of her own childhood and her premature induction to adulthood.

Chapter 5

Eight-year-old Sarah helped her mom in the kitchen. They were making tomato soup and tuna fish sandwiches. Just as the last sandwich was being cut her mom sent her on one last errand. "Go and get the boys for lunch, love."

"Michael! David! Lunchtime!" Sarah yelled from the kitchen table.

"Sarah! I said, go and get them!"

Sarah trudged off to find the boys. She heard a commotion coming from the barn, so she headed in that direction. The boys were in the loft playing. Far enough, she thought. Sarah hollered again.

A few minutes later Michael and David came running into the house. It was the first Monday of summer vacation. The three children waited in their seats while Mom brought the soup from the stove top to the table. It was then that Sarah's father appeared at the door. He was home from work early. Unaware of it at the time, he was coming home from the last day of work, from the last job that he would ever hold.

A few weeks later, with Employment Insurance run out and the city's population up in arms about the lack of jobs, and the rising cost of living, James Masterson joined the hordes protesting in the province's capital, Victoria.

The following week, the late James Masterson was buried in a cemetery a few miles from his home just outside the city of Vancouver. If one looked closely at the story on the front page of the *Vancouver Sun* on the previous week, Masterson could be seen among the hundreds of protestors lying on the trampled grass in front of the parliament buildings. His name appeared in the same paper in small print in an obituary column that had begun to double weekly.

His wife, Susan Masterson, knew the world was falling apart. When she was at university she had taken what they called doom and gloom courses. There were predictions that by the year 2012, taking into account the current rate of population growth, the use of fossil fuels, and the pollution of the atmosphere, the world would forfeit its ability to sustain human life on its existing scale. People would die. She remembered hating those courses. They were pessimistic and uninspiring. That was how she felt when she was at university and known then as Sue Mendenhall. That had been years before she got married, and at a time when raising a family seemed that most natural thing to do.

She stood looking out of the kitchen window at the rain that Vancouver was famous for. Now, in retrospect, she had nothing but regrets. Her husband's death had been only the first of a series of tragedies. Following the massive rise in unemployment, the government was unable to support the jobless and was forced to renege on its insurance policies.

When unemployment reached a staggering forty-eight percent, businesses began to fold. In an effort to recuperate some of what was bound to be lost, they began to offer their products at ludicrously low prices. While the prices of luxury items hit rock bottom, those necessary services skyrocketed. The price of fossil fuels doubled overnight. The electric companies quickly followed suit. The entire world was locked in a deadly downward economic spiral.

As people's needs rose, so did their discontent. Soon tempers flared. Riots were taking place regularly. Eventually, stores were vandalized, ransacked and eventually cleaned out completely.

If anyone could be counted among the lucky ones, Susan was one of them. Perhaps "luck" is not the best word to use. She was aware of the predictions. Early on, she could tell where things were leading. Following her husband's death, she immediately began to stock up. She filled her basement. She stacked it full of every kind of non-perishable food that she could find.

Months slipped by. Outside the world had been raging. Inside Susan had managed to maintain some sense of normalcy. But now, even with all of her planning and preparation, she along with most of the rest of the population had begun to starve.

No one had realized just how dependent the city had become upon the rest of the world. With transportation systems at a stand still, goods were simply not coming into the city. Every day, the streets became increasingly violent. Food was rapidly becoming next to impossible to find.

Then one day during another sadly memorable lunch, Sarah's mother collapsed as she prepared the last of the canned food to be found in the house. Unsure what else to do, Michael and David helped her to her room. It was there that her awful secret was revealed.

Without their knowledge, Susan had begun to ration food for her children. She had begun to ration less and less for herself. Now with nothing left in the house, there was nothing the boys could do to nurse their mother back to health. Although they scoured the community and did everything that they could, two days later, Susan Masterson was conscious for the last time.

Chapter 6

"David, where's Mommy?" asked eight-and-a-half-year-old Sarah as David entered the room.

David didn't reply. He walked past her and grabbed Michael by the arm. Even though he was the younger of the two, he hauled Michael through the front door and onto the porch. "Listen, you've got to tell her. Someone's got to tell her," he said frantically.

Michael sat down on the steps with his head bent to his knees. His shoulders hiccupped as he wept silently.

Sarah appeared at the front door. She stood between the boys and put her hand on Michael's shoulder. "What's the matter, Michael? Are you okay?" When she got no response, she turned to David. "What's the matter with Michael, David?" Still, she waited for a reply, but got none. Sarah dismissed the boys and went into the house.

Neither Michael nor David realized that Sarah had gone until they heard her voice from upstairs. "Mom…! Mom…! Something's wrong with David and Michael. They won't talk to me."

They turned simultaneously and screamed as they tore up the front steps and through the house. "Sarah! Nooooo!"

When they got to the top of the steps, they found Sarah inside standing by the bed at their mother's side. She knelt crying quietly as she held her mother's lifeless hand. The boys joined Sarah and held her as she wept. Eventually, she fell asleep at her mother's side and the boys slipped out of the room. They quietly descended the stairs and began to discuss what they would do. Their mother would want them to hold the family together. It was clear that if they didn't do something, they would not survive. Together they left the house. It was the first of the many hunting expeditions to come.

The next few years were quiet ones for Sarah. It had been agreed that the boys would be the breadwinners while she took care of the house. Hiding became her routine. It was safer than moving around outside. There were new dangers now and the boys didn't want to place Sarah at any unnecessary risk. Her job was simply to wait for them to come back. They left each morning and were usually gone most of the day. Almost every evening they came back with something to eat. In the years that followed, they never explained to Sarah the details of how they provided for the family each day. Sarah never asked.

Chapter 7

The sun continued to rise earlier each morning as spring approached. The days were getting longer and the winter rains were finally beginning to let up. For the most part, the previous year had been uneventful. Boredom was now the flavor of the day. Sarah found that it was extremely difficult to find things to keep her busy. She had long since lost interest in the old toys that she had been so fond of before her mother's death. Any dreams she might have had were as far away as the sun in winter.

Sarah sat at the breakfast nook that overlooked the front yard when she heard the commotion from behind the house. Her first thought was that it was the boys, but it was much too early for their return. She slipped out of her chair and tiptoed to her bedroom located at the back of the house. She parted the curtains slightly and peeked into the back yard. She could see five members of one of the many gangs that roamed the streets these days. The leader wore matching black leather pants and coat. Silver studs lined the sleeves and legs. He wore bright silver rings in his ears, eyebrow, nose and lower lip. A gold chain connected his lower lip and one of his ears. Sarah had seen this group before, but always at a distance. She let the curtain close, turned her back to the wall and slid down to the carpet. She listened in fear. With her heart drumming in her ears it was difficult to concentrate on what was going on outside.

"What was that? Did you see that?"

"Yeah something from that room over there."

"Hey, I bet there's someone in there!"

"Let's check it out."

It was impossible to tell who was talking. Sarah sat against the wall paralyzed. They would come in. And when they did, they would find her. The boys had told stories about gangs like these. What would they do if they found her? The sound of the voices grew nearer. The light from the small space between the curtains illuminated a small patch on the far wall. As Sarah sat mesmerized by it the small strip of light suddenly halved. Someone was looking into the room. There was only the space of the wall separating them. It was easy to imagine the window steaming up with his hot breath against it. Sarah's heart rate doubled, pounding in her ears.

After torturously long moments, which felt like hours, the patch of light widened again and the voices moved around the house to the garage. Sarah gathered all of her willpower and scurried along the floor towards the door and out of the bedroom. In the hall, she turned to the stairs and moved as quickly as she could into her parents' second floor bedroom. She raced into the closet and closed the door behind her.

The gang moved noisily through the house without a care or worry. She could hear "leather man" as she came to think of him, ordering the group around. He systematically sent them through the house looking for anything out of place. They were looking for her. Leather-man made certain that every inch of the house was covered! A girl yelled from the room that Sarah had just been in, "She's not in here!"

"Did you check the closet?"

"Of course I did! Do ya think I'm a greener or somethin'?" the other responded with disdain.

Sarah crouched in her hiding place. She was trapped. It would be only a matter of time before she would be discovered. What then? The racket continued to grow louder as the search moved to the second floor. Sarah waited, sick with fear.

The bedroom door swung on its hinges. She heard the sheets of the bed as they were flung aside. There was a grunt. Someone was checking under the bed, she thought. The door on the shower slammed against the wall as they combed the en suite. The only place left to inspect was the closet. The door opened and there was an audible click from the light switch. Nothing happened. No power. He cursed himself for forgetting…again. Some habits are hard to break. There was more racket as clothes were thrashed from one side of the closet to the other on their hangers. A few moments later, the door slammed hard enough to leave a ringing in Sarah's ears. A voice yelled out in disgust to someone in another part of the house, "Nothing up here!"

Sarah released her breath slowly and relaxed a little. He didn't bother to look up to see her perched on the top shelf. Her body had begun to ache; she slowly turned so that she could lie on her stomach, hoping it would be a more comfortable position. Without warning, a shoebox slipped from the shelf and plummeted to the floor. Sarah's arm snaked out and followed the box through its descent. It tumbled in slow motion. Her fingers closed on it just as her arm reached its full extension. Saying a silent prayer of thanks, she hauled the box back up. The top slipped from it and fell to the floor. Sarah held her breath as it fell, like a dried leaf in the fall, to the floor. In the hallway, a dopey looking boy stopped briefly. He listened carefully for a moment and then moved on. Footsteps moved away, and faded into the distance. Sarah exhaled.

For the next few hours, the house was ransacked as the gang looked for anything that might be of value. They collected their loot in the living room and spent the rest of the day going through it. Meanwhile, Sarah waited patiently in her place on the top shelf of the closet. She had no concept of time in her small dark place. Eventually she fell asleep.

When she woke, it was to the sound of her name being called. Groggily, she rubbed her eyes and listened. She recognized the voices of David and Michael and called to them.

David was the first to hear her. "Mom's room," he yelled to his brother. Sarah could hear them pounding up the stairs. By the time they crashed through the door, she managed to climb stiffly out of the closet.

The boys wrapped their arms around her thankful she was all right. Another successful day had passed in the new world. Family had taken on a new meaning since their mother had died. They were still alive and still together.

***

Had her parents been around, they would have discovered how remarkably bright Sarah was. The long quiet days left her little to do. She began to read the storybooks that her mother and father had purchased for the children. She read those until the covers fell off.

Sometime in her twelfth year, bored and thirsty for something else to read she began to take a closer look at other books her mother and father collected for themselves. She started with the encyclopedias. They were filled with interesting tidbits of information. She found them fascinating and eventually she began reading the others.

Her thirst for information was limitless. Countless hours of boredom with nothing to do but wait silently made it easy to become engrossed. The books were wonderful. What's more, her mother and father had cherished them. It made her feel closer to them somehow. It was easy to imagine her father sitting beside her on the couch with his arm around her as he read one of the countless fairy tales he had collected. She learned about the environment from her mother's old textbooks. She learned about basic construction and home repairs from her father's do-it-yourself books. There were craft books and first aid books. Although she couldn't read everything at first, her knowledge grew steadily and with that so did her understanding.

The years passed slowly and Sarah looked in the mirror one day to discover she had grown into a young woman.

She had begun to keep a small selection of plants around the house. Most of them were useful for one thing or another. She even had a strawberry plant that provided a special treat now and again. Meanwhile, her older brothers continued to leave the house on their daily excursions. Every day they came back with something for the small household. They also came back with stories to tell. They told about the cruel people who took what they wanted from anyone they pleased. There were those who would do anything to survive. Sarah was never entirely sure that the stories they brought home were always about others.

She never knew how they always managed to provide for the home. The boys said very little about that. In these times, scruples were as scarce as food. It was easier for Sarah to think of them as the valiant princes in the fairy tales that she so often read. They were the heroes who would go to the ends of the earth for their sister, and she for them. With thoughts like these, a smile was never far behind.

Then one evening, during Sarah's eighteenth year, she waited patiently, but the boys didn't return.

Chapter 8

Days passed and her worry grew. Most of the plants she had grown were edible. She began to rely on them solely for her nourishment. A week later, she broke down in tears. Her grieving lasted for days. She ate little. Her new ritual consisted of going to the front window in hopes that her brothers would arrive just as she pulled the curtains aside. Each day she coped with the disappointment anew.

Although she had developed quite a garden, it was not enough to sustain her permanently. The lack of food was becoming a matter of survival. Like so many times in her short life, Sarah found herself contemplating her future. What should she do? Where should she go?

Although she had read books from almost every genre, she knew that she had few practical skills. One morning at sunrise, she filled a backpack with what she considered to be necessities, walked out of her house and made her way west toward the city of Vancouver. On her way, she passed one vacant house after another. Many, like her own home, had the useless carcass of a car parked in the driveway. She looked at a license plate, "Beautiful British Columbia." *Maybe, once upon a time,* she thought sadly, as she read it.

That night she made her bed in an abandoned warehouse just outside the city center. Her sleep was disrupted by continuous city noise, much different than the old familiar noises. The night was filled with high-pitched screams, explosions and gunshots. After many restless hours, she fell asleep wondering, *What on earth am I doing here?*

Like her neighborhood, most people had moved on. If they didn't survive, it was impossible to tell. Only their refuse was left behind as evidence of their existence. She thought hard about what Vancouver might have to offer as she looked at the empty back yards. A screen door bounced idly in its frame and it occurred to her that it was a place people left from and not a destination at all. There was only devastation here. One thing was painfully clear; the city of Vancouver was a place to stay away from.

The following day, Sarah turned north and began to skirt the city. She stayed away from tall buildings and hid whenever she heard a noise. The sun was high overhead when she heard the metallic hollow sound of a garbage can tip over a short distance away. She leapt behind a nearby fence, hid and listened carefully. From around the corner of an adjacent house a medium sized grayish brown dog sniffed its way in Sarah's direction. It lifted its head and saw her. Its ears perked and it hunkered down on the grass.

The company of a dog would be perfect. A dog could offer protection as well as company; something she had begun to crave. She called to it. "Here, dog. Come on, boy." If the dog remembered having ever been called before, it didn't show it. Instead, it looked intently at Sarah; not with the curiosity she hoped to see, but with a look that frightened her. The dog inched forward and became more agitated. Other dogs appeared behind it. No longer a single menace to worry about, the pack saw Sarah and a moment later they charged.

She ran to the front of the nearest house and threw open the storm door on the front porch. She was able to wedge herself between the doors before the dogs leapt at her senselessly, slamming her between the two hinged slabs. She frantically turned the knob. It was useless. In desperation, Sarah pushed against the window in the center of the door, but her weight alone was not enough to break the glass. She would have to do more than push. Summoning every ounce of her strength and courage, she pushed back as far as she dared and took a step away from the window. She threw her full weight against it. It shattered inward and her body followed the shattering glass into the foyer.

With Sarah no longer there to keep the dogs from ripping open the storm door, they clawed it aside and were at the main door, leaping at the new opening. Sarah staggered to her feet and ran to the stairs, the dogs on her heels. Blood trailed behind her as she ran to an upstairs bedroom, giving the dogs reason to linger. She slammed the door behind her. An instant later the dogs were yelping and scratching at it.

In pain, Sarah collapsed to the floor and then clawed her way to the bed. The sleeves of her shirt were already soaked with blood, but she hardly noticed. It was her side that was screaming at her to stop moving. She used everything left in her to reach the edge of the bed. She rolled over and propped herself up against it.

For the moment, the door held the dogs at bay in the hall. Sarah examined her bloodstained shirt. Her sleeve was streaked with blood from the shoulder to her wrist. The bulk of the pain came from her side. She lifted her arm to look and winced at the searing pain.

The window hadn't shattered into small, harmless pieces. It had turned the window of the door into a gaping mouth full of countless dagger sharp teeth. When she leapt through it, her arm was laced with numerous minor cuts. Her torso followed and most of her weight landed on the sill. A long shard had been poised vertically there and did not break off until it was lodged deep inside her belly. Looking at a puncture wound she could see the shard poking through her shirt. She could feel it slicing at her with every movement.

Blood loss began to take its toll. Sarah struggled against her shock and fear. Was the shard fairly short, or would it turn out to be so deep that it would be lethal? She had read about bleeding caused by such wounds and knew that when she dislodged the glass she might begin to bleed even worse. She briefly considered the possibility that she might have what the books had called "deadly bleeding." She reached behind her to see what kind of bedding might be there. There were no blankets, but a fitted sheet still remained on the mattress. She turned as much as she could to try and remove the sheet and immediately felt a searing pain from somewhere deep inside. She winced.

Following a brief struggle and with tears streaming down her face, Sarah managed to remove the sheet from the bed. The bleeding from her side had increased. She gingerly lifted her shirt to survey the injury. Thankfully, the piece of glass that protruded was large enough to grab hold of. Mustering her courage, she took the piece of glass between her fingers and thumb. She expected it to slide right out. Instead, her fingers slid from the slimy surface. She screamed in pain as her arms ripped free causing a new wave of pain in her side. She was sure that she was using all of her strength, but the shard didn't budge.

She needed the glass to be dry. Taking a hold of the sheet, she wrapped it around the exposed glass. Sarah leaned back against the bed, hands trembling. She could hear the dogs just outside the door. They were less aggressive, but they were still hounding around on the upper floor. She could hear their paws drumming up and down the hallway.

"Focus, Sarah! Focus! You're bleeding to death," she warned herself. She forced her attention to the piece of glass protruding from her side. She took a deep breath and with everything she had left in her, she yanked on it as hard as she could. The glass pulled free and instantly, blood began to pour from the wound. She was ready with the bed sheet. Taking the corner, she pressed it firmly into the wound. The cloth turned red, saturated. Rather than release the pressure, Sarah added more fabric to what she was already holding against the wound. Using one hand to hold the sheet in place, she removed her belt with the other. She slid the belt around the back of her and placed the buckle where she could operate it with one hand. After some fiddling, she managed to arrange the belt so that it would tighten directly over the wound. She cinched it as tight as she could. Later, she would say that the pain was unbearable. She managed to buckle the clasp before she slipped into unconsciousness. Her last coherent thought was that she was too late.

When she came to, she lay on her side in a congealed pool of blood. She was shocked by the size of it and she began to reel. Her face grew cold and white. Consciousness left her once more. The next time she woke, it was night and too dark to assess her wound and she couldn't help being grateful for that. She was alive and hungry and that was enough for now. She tried to move into a more comfortable position, but the sharp tearing pain in her side convinced her to stay still.

Careful, to keep her body stationary, she reached into her backpack and took out some of the provisions she had stowed there. Afterwards, contemplating her situation, her thoughts became random and soon turned into dreams.

During her third wakeful period she was vaguely aware of the silence that filled the house. The light coming through the windows indicated that it was early morning. The bleeding had stopped and her bandaging needed to be changed. She eased the pressure off of the belt and removed the sheet. The wound was lightly sealed and she was careful not to stretch her side. She brought the sheet around in front of her and dug into her pack for a pocketknife. She cut off the blood soaked portion of the sheet and discarded it. The rest, she torn into large squares, but not before she placed a cloth over the wound, replaced the belt and pulled it as tightly as she dared. The first of the squares, she folded into a smaller square that consisted of about eight or so layers.

Afterward, she sideslipped out of the mess she'd made and again opened her pack to find something to eat. The cuts on her arm were mere scratches by comparison to her other injury and she didn't bother to deal with them. By the way that they had begun to heal a number of days must have passed.

Her clothes were matted with blood and she needed a change. Although she was afraid to open the wound, she knew that she had to get moving. She needed to clean up and find some food to replace what she had eaten. Maybe the house had some useful items lying around.

She rose to her feet and inched her way around the room. She searched the closet and the dresser that were left behind. There were a few pieces of unwanted clothing but only big enough to fit a child. It was apparent that who ever left this house behind took only the essentials. In the closet on the floor and on the shelf, were dozens of toys and games. There was even some bedding left behind. Maybe there were useful items elsewhere in the house.

She opened the door and found the house silent. Her bravery slowly returned and she edged into the hall. The blood on the steps was lapped clean. Sarah warily looked up and down the hall, but the dogs were nowhere in sight and the house remained eerily silent.

Sarah kept her movement to the upstairs and investigated each of the bedrooms in turn. In one of the rooms, she found some clothes that were a bit too large, but they would do. At least they were clean. As carefully as possible, she changed and added a few of the clothes to her pack, just in case there was an emergency.

She started slowly down the steps being careful to lead with the foot on the same side as her injury. In this way, she managed to keep from stretching the healing wound. She searched every nook in the house and scattered her salvage on the coffee table in the living room.

Apparently, the owners had packed lightly when they left. The house was almost completely furnished. In the garage, there was gardening equipment, tools and a variety of other hardware that would be useless to a family on the move. Sarah spent most of the day looking through the house and resting often. By mid afternoon, her side demanded that she take a break and she took that time to sift through the things that she had chosen from the house.

Of the various miscellanies that lay on the table, a bottle of disinfectant was among the items. She had done her best to keep vigorous movements to an absolute minimum. But even so, the task of going through the house had taken its toll on her. She sat down for a much needed rest with disinfectant in hand. It was a nasty and painful business, but there were no doctors to administer antibiotics if it became infected. She struggled through the painful process with clenched teeth.

Her selections were too numerous to keep them all. She could carry only a small bag and there would be countless houses just like this one along the way. She began to set aside what she considered to be the absolute necessities and even then, realized that she would have to prune the pile even more. She still needed to take some bedding, food and something to keep her injury clean. When she was done, she left behind much of what she pulled together on the living room floor.

After the attack she considered finding some sort of a gun, but there were a number of reasons why a gun would be impractical. She had no experience with firearms; she didn't think she could hit anything anyway. A firearm meant that she would have to find and carry ammunition as well. Pepper spray was something she would be able to wear on a belt or carry easily in her pack. There was nothing like that in the house so that would be a priority as soon as the opportunity presented itself.

With a fresh dressing and a pack reduced as much as possible, Sarah once again braved the streets of the Vancouver suburbs. She kept close to front yards and continuously scanned the surrounding neighborhood for possible escapes. Her injury made it impossible to move fast. Staying close to building entrances was essential. She looked like a silly movie spy moving from one doorway to the next; always ready to duck inside at the slightest indication of danger. Instead of a cane, she armed herself with a crowbar that she could use on any door, or on a dog for that matter, should the need arise.

She spent the night in a borrowed bed, with borrowed blankets. The day's journey had been hard on her and the wound had begun to weep. She cleaned it as best she could, put some ointment on it and donned a new bandage. She lay down in the half-light of the evening and fell into a dreamless sleep.

The morning sun poured through the window illuminating near microscopic flecks of dust that floated around the room. Her stomach had ceased to beg for food and was now demanding it. Today she would try and solve the problem of finding nourishment in a city where there seemed to be nothing. She wished she had asked about the secrets that her bothers never shared. She was becoming weaker as her body fed on itself. She would be willing to do almost anything to stop the screaming demand from her gut.

Sarah left the house and turned toward a small community shopping center. The direction was clearly marked with the too-numerous-to-count billboards and signs that were so common to such areas. As she drew nearer, her fear and apprehension rose. What would she do if she met someone? What would that someone do?

At the shopping center, she went directly to the hardware store, and from there she went to the sporting goods center. The store had been cleaned out. At one time guns stood chained together in a row. Now the chains now hung loosely on empty shelves. Below, the cupboards, where the ammunition was once held, were open and bare. The glass counters were smashed and empty. Broken glass littered the floor. Sarah surveyed the area and moved to the receiving area. In the back room was a large bay door; she was at the loading dock. Inside, there were cases of goods that had arrived but had never been opened. Somehow, this grab bag bonanza had been overlooked. Some were stacked neatly on shelves while others cluttered the walls of the back room. She began systematically examining the boxes. There must have been more than a hundred.

Many of the boxes were cases, but more of them were labeled "pre-pack." They were identified by a piece of tape with the word "pre-pack" printed on it. Inside each of these boxes was a wide variety of products. There was no clear indication to Sarah what might be in each one. Unlike the cases, there were no useful markings on the boxes. Because she couldn't tell what might be in each box she was careful to open them all. Finally, her search was rewarded. Inside one of the pre-packs was a shrink-wrapped pack of six bear mace containers. She also found some holsters to strap them on. Sarah took three of the mace containers and one of the holsters. She put the holster on and placed a bear mace canister into it. She also found a pair of small, but powerful binoculars and a multi-tool that contained a knife, screwdrivers and a pair of pliers. She put this on her belt and discarded the pocketknife she had been carrying. Redundancy was not a luxury she could afford.

With one hand on the bear mace container she felt her confidence rise. She felt sufficiently armed. Sarah left the hardware store and the shopping center. It was time to head back into the suburbs in search of a place to rest, and something more important...she needed to eat.

The bear mace helped calm her fears significantly. She knew that it was stronger than regular mace and that alone boosted her courage. She wandered into the suburbs. Making her way slowly from one vacant community to another, she investigated every possible location where someone may have left behind a candy bar, a bag of chips or anything that might take the edge off her hunger. Every grocery store she walked into was completely devoid of edible products. She could not even find a stick of gum.

In desperation, she decided to check out some of the vacant homes that she came across. At her first stop she went first to the cupboards. Nothing. Then she went directly to the refrigerator. She pulled it open and discovered that her hunger problem was solved almost immediately. In fact, she could image never eating again. The fridge was packed with a multitude of disgusting containers bursting with mold. Sarah covered her nose and left the house as quickly as her wound would allow.

House after vacant house revealed the same phenomenon.

Ideas exhausted, she wandered aimlessly for hours until she came upon a school. More out of curiosity than anything else, she used her crowbar-cane and broke through one of the windows. A twinge of guilt passed through her as she considered for a moment her act of vandalism against public property, and vanished as quickly as it came.

Still favoring her stinging side, Sarah lifted one leg and slid it through the window. She stood surveying a vacant classroom. The walls were bare and the desks were neatly stacked in one corner. The black boards were wiped clean as if ready to start fresh in September. She turned to the teacher's desk. Unlike the rest of the room, this was piled high with various papers and books. A computer sat dusty and silent beneath the clutter. Sarah crossed the room to the door and began to investigate the rest of the school. Most of the doors were locked. These were classrooms and were of little interest to her.

She passed the office, the maintenance room, the sick room, the gym and finally, the cafeteria. She stepped behind the long stainless steel counter and into the kitchen area. Ignoring the large refrigerator, she made her way directly to the pantry. Cautiously, she opened the door and was greeted by a scurrying sound in the dark. She pulled the door open and leapt back.

A momentary flash of movement caught her eye as a half a dozen mice scurried for cover. *Good sign*, she thought. On some of the shelves were the deflated remains of bagged goods that had been long since pillaged by the fury occupants. On closer examination there were cans and some jars that had been used for storage. One contained what looked like flour and another that could be sugar. There were also various other containers that might contain spices of some kind.

Sarah reached into the pantry cupboard and began to haul out anything that looked like it might be of use. The tops of the jars and cans were littered with the last ten years of mouse shit. Her hunger was far beyond screaming at her. A week ago she would have been disgusted at the thought of eating from any of the tins. She did not hesitate. Snapping out a dusty towel, she cleaned off the loose stuff the mice had left behind, pulled out the tins and continued to dig into the pantry. She stopped when she came to something she recognized, a number of cans of tuna fish. She darted to the kitchen counter and scoured the drawers for a can opener. After a brief search, she found one and began to open a can. It hissed in a familiar way but before going further, she bent over and smelled the contents. The fish smelled good. She completed the opening and dived into the can with her fingers. She couldn't remember tasting anything so delicious. She quickly finished off the tuna fish and opened another. It wasn't until she had downed three quarters of the third can that she began to slow down.

After she had eaten all the tuna fish that she could, Sarah turned again to her surroundings. As far as the school was concerned there was nothing of importance left behind, but for one starving girl, there seemed to be enough to last her a lifetime, certainly enough to save her life.

She stood in the semi darkness gloating over her newfound treasures. Somewhere in the back of the kitchen, an automatic fan of some sort kicked on. She jumped in surprise. It took her a moment to register the meaning of it. Everywhere else there had been no electricity. Why would a place like this be different?

Realizing the implications, Sarah looked around for a light switch and found one. The entire kitchen area was instantly flooded in light. Sarah turned her attention to the large white doors at the back of the kitchen. It was apparent that they were the refrigerator and the freezer, but *which is which?* she thought. She didn't really want to open the refrigerator. Even though it had been working all this time, there was no telling about the condition of the food inside. They looked identical. Being unable to come to a conclusion, she resorted to the old fashion method of making her choice. "Eeny meeny miny moe," she started, first pointing to one and then the other. She knew that when she was finished she would still be faced with the dreadful task of actually opening the door, so she proceeded slowly, "catch a..." Then she stopped. Staring right back at her was the solution. Beside each of the doors was a thermostat. She chided herself for not seeing it sooner. The first thermostat was set just above the freezing mark. The second was set well below. The mystery had been solved.

Sarah flipped the light switch and walked into the large freezer. It stood mostly empty except for a few small packages wrapped in brown paper. These were completely covered in frost and impossible to identify. Sarah looked over everything and then stepped out and closed the door behind her.

After all of the searching and the days and days of fasting, she had found food in what she thought would have been the most unlikely place. Feeling satisfied from the fish, she walked back to the office area. Adjacent to the office was the sick room. In it was a bed. For bedding, it had on it an old woolen blanket and a pillow with white and gray stripes. It was stained and coverless. Exhausted and with her aching side she lay down on the cot and was asleep almost instantly.

Chapter 9

For the next weeks, Sarah stayed at the school. She took this time to heal properly and investigate the building thoroughly. The staff room turned out to be a gold mine of information. The coffee tables were loaded with pamphlets about every imaginable topic. There were newspapers and magazines. There was a publication called "Teacher." Teachers were concerned about their careers months before the school shut its doors to students. They wanted to know what was happening and what they could do about it. Sarah organized the papers according to the date and feasted on the new information. She read how the economy had collapsed. There had been other depressions, but this had been much more severe than any at other time in history. She considered the possibility that the economy might be bouncing back in other parts of the world, but British Columbia had become one massive ghost town the size of three medium states.

While many homes were dark and without power, she discovered that in some areas service was still being provided…well, maybe not provided. It was more likely that when the building was abandoned the power had been left on. She thought about why this might be and the obvious explanation was that the power company did not disconnect services to public operations. If the school still had power then it was possible, even likely, that there was power in places like hospitals too.

Sarah's spirits rose. Her basic needs were met and her body was healing nicely. She was left with the time and energy to think about her future. One thing that she wanted more than anything was to have a home once more. Even a home without a family would be better than a life of continuous wandering. Her home had once been torn from her. She would replace it…somehow.

Sarah had always dreamt of living near the ocean. When she was well enough, she restocked her pack, prepared in mind and body, to brave the dangers of the world outside once more. She turned her attention deliberately to the west coast, specifically on the Sunshine coast. She began her journey toward the small town of Gibson.

Many years earlier, Gibson was a small isolated community known for a television show called, *The Beach Combers*. Back then the only way to and from the community was by ferry, but now a small road wound through coastal forests making it possible to get there by road. Even with the new access, Gibson always had the flavor of a small resort town, never developing into a large community. Sarah felt it was the perfect place to start her new home.

Though Sarah had never been out of the Vancouver area, she still remembered her family excursions to the sunny beaches and the beautiful waters. As it turned out, Sarah's memory for direction had been good. She did, at least, leave the city going in the right direction. It wasn't long, however, before she was at a loss for where to turn next. It was difficult to find her way in the suburbs. The communities had been planned to make high-speed travel difficult. The streets twisted among the homes. There were numerous cul-de-sacs and playgrounds connected by trails that passed from one to another. There didn't seem to be any streets that went straight through in the direction that Sarah wanted to travel. She would give anything for a map.

It wasn't just old department stores that could be useful. Many other old businesses had treasures to share as well. She found useful items on nearly barren shelves. Even gas stations with not a drop of fuel still had a treasure or two to share. She sat on the curb studying the map from the rack beside the rusted till.

That evening she found herself in a sparse area of town. She had reached the outskirts. The distance between houses was beginning to grow. Once again, she relied on an abandoned home for shelter. It had become a routine. She began by casing the entire house, checking at every window and door. This one had been left unlocked when it was abandoned. It didn't matter anyway. Locked homes were usually broken into anyway. She needed one that had as yet drawn little attention. Often, it was off the beaten path and had not been a target of vandalism. A home that had been undisturbed for years would probably be safe for just one more evening.

Night came and went, chased away by the rising sun. Progress seemed slow. Away from the city, there were new, unfamiliar dangers to face. Every strange sound brought her to a halt. Her ears perked and her legs readied to take her to safety. It was hard to maintain a sense of emergency when every alarm was false. Once it was a stray cat, another it was a bird flitting from one branch to another, still another was a rodent looking for its next meal.

It took days, but slowly Sarah began to relax as she became more familiar with this new environment. She became accustomed to the sound the wind makes as it rushes through the trees, a chattering squirrel protecting its stash and the eerie sound two trees make when they rub together. Although her guard was always up, she was finding she could see the beauty in the forest around her. After all, there was more to the world than the dangers it presented. Allowing her mind to wander, she even found herself whistling a pleasant tune. It seemed that life was less threatening the farther she got from the city.

The city noises were far behind. Houses were sometimes kilometers apart. Her whistling faded away as she approached a crossroad. She reached into her pack and pulled out her trusted map. Gibson lay many kilometers ahead, but there was a small community, maybe only a gas station, ten kilometers aside. It would take her the rest of the afternoon to get there and the whole morning the following day to return to this point. Deciding that it wasn't worth detouring for, she continued down the road.

Evening found Sarah still hiking along the road. She had hoped to, but had not come across an old roadside hotel, an abandoned home or a broken down barn. As the last of the daylight began to wane, Sarah hoped that the next corner would reveal something new, something useful, but each turn revealed the same, another corner, another hill, a bit of a straight and then another corner. Sarah trudged on.

When the light was completely gone and it was only possible to tell where the pavement was by the feel of it beneath her feet, she began to lose hope of finding shelter. Without strength to carry her further, she left the roadside and found solace beneath the overhanging branches of a large spruce tree. She wrapped herself up in every piece of clothing she carried, rolled her pack into a ball for a pillow and lay down in a pile of dead, brown spruce needles.

***

Morning came and went, while Sarah slept dreamlessly. Although the sun was high in the sky, the stranger cast no shadow in the dense forest foliage. Sarah was aware of a presence before she was fully awake. She lay perfectly still with one hand on her canister of bear spray. The other was poised to push herself up and roll her over at the precise moment. Sarah breathed shallowly as the stranger moved closer.

In her imagination, the approaching figure was huge. A dozen different possibilities of what he might intend to do to her coursed through her mind, none of them good. Suddenly, in a single swift movement, she attacked. She hoisted herself over, popped the safety mechanism and let loose with the full force of the aerosol spray into the face of her would be attacker.

There was a flurry of movement as the stranger's hands flew to his face. He dropped instantly to his knees wheezing and screaming, "My eyes! My eyes! Oh, God, my eyes!" His voice trailed off as he struggled to breathe.

The stranger stumbled to his feet, removed his hands from his face and stared at Sarah with sightless eyes. He spun on his heel and turned back in the direction he had come, stumbling out of the trees toward the road.

The ditch was nothing more than a shallow trench between the forest and the road. The figure did not step across the ditch and onto the road. Instead, he stepped into it expecting to take a step onto solid ground. The sudden drop threw him off balance. He stumbled. Unable to check himself he fell forward slamming his head into the pavement. He lay there motionless.

Chapter 10

A long time ago Travis used to like to whistle. He generally did it everywhere he went. But that was before. A person couldn't go around letting his presence be known. No one was safe these days. Silence and stealth were his new way of life. Just as he had never been prone to silence, Travis had never before been a loner. But nowadays, a person was better off alone.

At one time he led a group of teenagers who had banded together to help each other to survive. They called themselves the Castaways. Travis had never intended to lead anyone. It just happened that way. He had certainly never intended that anyone get hurt. It just happened that way. Part of surviving meant taking. And part of taking meant hurting. It was a mad circle and Travis found that he could no longer abide by it.

In the beginning, the Castaways were a close-knit group of friends who had gone through school together. They had lived under similar circumstances and had become closer still as their adventures bonded them. But as time went on and one tragedy seemed inevitably followed by another, Travis eventually found himself a leader of a group of strangers, wondering how he got there. One sleepless night, he took what few belongings he had, and walked away from the city.

He was surprised at how good he felt, walking away from the rot and filth of the Castaways and breathing freely for the first time. There was something better out here and he was going to find it.

He had been on the road, traveling west for the better part of a week. He wandered in whatever direction suited him at the given moment. The idea developed from the thought that everywhere was likely to be just as bad as the next. Sometimes he might flip a coin. Another time he might choose the road less taken. He was determined to go forward, never back.

It was early afternoon when he saw the colorful bundle in the shadows of a giant Sitka spruce. Scavenging was a way of life and coming across anything of interest warranted further investigation. Travis left the roadside, crossed the ditch and made his way carefully toward the pile of clothing.

He was no more than two meters away when he recognized it for what it was, a human form. The body lay face down in the dead spruce needles at the base of the tree. On its head was a hat that completely covered hair and face. *It* lacked the normal stench of decay Travis expected to note. No part of flesh could be seen, so Travis was sure of nothing.

He inched forward.

Without warning the figure suddenly rolled over and emitted a stinging mist directly into his eyes. He fell to his knees cursing and screaming. His eyes burned in their sockets. He looked around him, but he could see nothing. Afraid that his attacker was not finished with him, he struggled to his feet. Tears streamed down his face. His throat was clogged and breathing was almost impossible.

The blurry form in front of him began to fade. He estimated the direction he had come from and turned to flee. Light was coming from where the road should be and he stumbled toward it. Suddenly, the ground disappeared from under his feet and his body was flung forward.

He was unaware of the sickening dull thud of his head crashing against the pavement. Luckily he would not remember it.

Chapter 11

Sarah scuttled away from the man, pushing with her feet. She didn't stop until her back was up against the tree. She sat panting and sweating as the figure lay on the pavement no more than ten meters away. A pool of red was beginning to form on the pavement beneath his head. She watched it spread in horror.

If only her brothers were there to tell her it would be okay. If only her mother was there to remove her grip on the canister of bear mace so that it would stop spraying into the air in front her. Her fear gripped her. Her body vibrated in shock.

By the time she recovered her wits the canister was empty at her feet. Using the tree branches, she stood up and took a step closer to the prone figure lying helpless by the roadside. The pool of blood had grown. The man must surely be dead. Cautiously, she stepped closer.

The man was still breathing. She knew from the warnings on the bear spray canister that the product could be extremely hazardous to people. Blindness could be a permanent condition and directions had been to rinse thoroughly and seek medical attention. If the man regained consciousness, he certainly wasn't going anywhere.

She rolled him over onto his back. There was a gash in his forehead that stretched from his hairline to his eye. Blood poured steadily from it. The man was probably in his early twenties. In his unconscious state, his face was slack and emotionless. Sarah was aware that though he looked peaceful now, a mere moment ago who knows what was on his mind.

Sarah wondered what to do…bandage him up and lead a blind man around, just so he could get even with her when the opportunity presented itself? That didn't seem like a sensible solution. But then, leaving the man here to suffer was not a humane thing to do either. In order for her to be safe, she would have to finish the job. He was unconscious and would feel nothing.

She reached behind her, unsnapped the leather pouch holding her multi-tool and pulled it out. She flipped the knife open as one who has been accustomed to using it and placed the knife blade just below his left ear. It was sharp and a simple slice into his artery would let the blood flow freely and allow him to pass into unconsciousness and eventually death.

The only evidence of the struggle within her was the tremulous shaking of her hand. How could she take a human life? Is this what she had grown up to become? Was this the way the new world was meant to be? Knowing that it was a mistake, Sarah replaced the knife in its scabbard, took one last look at him then turned to walk away.

She gathered her belongings, hopped the small ditch and continued west. She had gone no more than a hundred meters away when the moaning began. The cursed moaning! Why couldn't anything be easy? She stopped when the moaning grew louder. Should she run away or return to the young man's side? Disgusted by her own weakness she slowly turned to face him.

The man lay on his back staring blindly up at the sky. He had regained consciousness and was now calling out for help. Filled with guilt and shame she slowly walked back to him.

Putting her pack on the ground, she rummaged through it for her makeshift first aid kit. She removed compresses and a strip of cloth. Without cleaning the injury, she covered it with a compress and tied the strip around his head. The stranger looked up at the sky blindly, unaware of Sarah's presence.

She dragged him off of the road and laid him down in the grass beside the ditch. She used water from her canteen to rinse his eyes. She put her pack under his head.

The man wore a large trench coat that was matted with pockets, which contained a variety of items. Among these was food and water. There was also a rudimentary first aid kit. What a good idea this coat was. It contained many different compartments and removed this man's requirement for carrying a pack. The coat would supply warmth at night. Sarah replaced his belongings and covered him with it.

It wasn't until the following morning that the man regained consciousness. His eyes watered profusely when he opened them, but they lacked that blind stare Sarah saw when she first sprayed him.

"Do you know what happened to me?" he asked Sarah.

"Shhhh," she replied, avoiding the answer.

"I can't see."

"Stay calm and rest. Here, how about some breakfast," she encouraged.

She helped the stranger to sit up and put a little of what she had in his hand. He sniffed it and then took a bite, chewing gratefully. Once finished, he lay back down and was quickly asleep again.

Through the days that followed, Sarah learned that the man's name was Travis. And though he made many inquiries, she avoided giving him any explanation for his predicament. He offered his own history freely and Sarah continued to care for him. Together they made their way along the highway with Sarah helping him avoid the numerous potholes. He was happy to go in whatever direction she desired as long as it wasn't back toward Vancouver. Ridden with guilt, she felt obligated to take him along. With each passing day her guilt grew.

The days passed slowly and painfully for Travis. Although he didn't say much about it, he was used to being in control and hated feeling dependent. He bathed his eyes regularly hoping that they would recover. At first, he could only see the bright outline of the sun when he was facing it. But during the last few days the world around him had begun to take form again. Today he could even make out the faint dark spots that were potholes. He was happy that he could now avoid them on his own.

Travis couldn't remember anything from the day of the incident and he was plagued with almost debilitating migraines as a result of his collision with the asphalt. When he wasn't concentrating on keeping his footing, his thoughts were of his strange benefactress. There was something familiar about the color of the coat she wore and he was sure she knew more about what had happened to him than she let on. Unfortunately, whenever he had asked about it she had avoided the question altogether. And though she was gentle with her refusals, she did not elaborate on any of his questions.

Days passed. Travis opened his eyes. Today the sky was more than just light blue. He could distinctly make out individual clouds. He was elated. He turned to look about him. Images were still hazy, but he could easily make out most detail. He turned to Sarah.

"I'm going to be okay. I'll be able to see perfectly soon. I know it."

The guilt that haunted was too much to bear. She looked at Travis sadly. "There's something I need to tell you. I know you've asked about it many times and I've always said nothing. But you need to know that I am the one who did this to you."

"I know," Travis, replied matter-of-factly.

Sarah was stunned. "You know?" she managed.

"I suspected. But I still want you to tell me everything."

Sarah explained how the events unfolded that day. She apologized over and over, as she retold the story. She explained to Travis how horribly scared she had been. Finally, she explained how close he was that day to losing his life. Travis smiled. "I don't think I was nearly as close to death as you'd like to believe."

"What do you mean?"

"I don't believe even for a moment that you are capable of such a thing. I have seen the way that you value life and I know that had you stumbled across me, you would have stopped to help me. You would have helped even though it meant risking your own life. In fact, that's exactly what you did."

"You mean, that's exactly what I'm doing," she said with a mischievous smile.

Travis laughed. "I suppose so."

They gathered what they had and set to the road once more. His improved eyesight allowed them to make better progress. Sarah explained to Travis where she was going and why. Her logic seemed solid, so he remained her traveling partner. Sarah was secretly glad that he had decided to come along. She had missed the company of someone since her brothers' disappearance and truthfully, she felt safer when Travis was around, blind or not.

One sunny summer day in the early afternoon, the two of them walked under the arch that marked Gibson's town limits. The trees grew thick, close to the ditch and shaded the narrow highway. The town was located among the hills along the ocean side. The main road followed the curve of the shoreline and other roads branched off of it, winding their way in other directions.

They decided to explore the little ghost town. It was a scary feeling. On one hand, the community seemed completely abandoned, but on the other hand, both Sarah and Travis were consumed by a feeling that they were being watched. One empty street after another slowly slipped by as they wandered through town, hand-in-hand.

Travis and Sarah decided to make a home close to the original downtown area. It turned out to be easy for them to pick one they both liked. It seemed as if they owned a little piece of heaven. They were able to find everything they needed and between the two of them, they were able to manage any problem that arose. Months passed by.

Later, as things go, and Travis and Sarah realized their love for one another. One day the two of them welcomed a son into their lives. They named him Jason. They loved each other infinitely. And if it is possible, they loved Jason more.

It was not difficult to care for Jason as an infant. Keeping him within the confines of the house was an easy task. Furniture was sparse and Jason had all kinds of room to crawl and then run. Even so, neither Travis nor Sarah wanted a life of confinement for their son. Their home was becoming less and less appropriate for the little family.

The community wasn't as devoid of inhabitants as they first suspected. And over the years, they learned that though the people who remained in Gibson had a deep desire for privacy they also had a strong sense of community. It was an odd sort of comfort, because the community was still a place of danger. Every now and again, some new stranger would stumble into the little town. And often, it was for no good.

Once the decision to move was made, Travis spent each day looking among the houses for one that would provide a suitable environment. One day he came home triumphantly. The new home was located on a flat piece of land adjacent to the ocean. Although the ocean had become so polluted it was not safe to swim in, it was still pretty to look at. There was a tall wire fence that surrounded the property. The front yard could be seen easily from the house. The driveway was closed off by a large gate that matched the rest of the fence. This place was perfect. Travis brought Sarah to the spot. She agreed and they moved in immediately.

Life ran smoothly for the next years. Jason was five years old when Sarah and Travis decided that once again they would need to find a new home. Their livelihood depended on what little Sarah could grow and what Travis could gather from the surrounding area.

One early spring day, Travis left to find a better home for the family. He would return to take them to their new home. Sarah waited patiently, but Travis didn't come back.

Chapter 12

Sarah's story didn't end there. It was where it ended for Jason on that day. The hardest part of the story to retell haunted her dreams. It haunted her in the face of her son, who was growing to be more and more like his father every day. Every contour, the color of his hair and the color of his eyes were each a wonderful and painful reminder of the man who had walked out of their lives with her blessing. The act of remembering was overwhelming.

Her tears flowed, and the story continued to play on in her mind. She remembered her growing feeling that she had made a horrible mistake. She knew she would never be able to make it up to her son.

Days, weeks and years slipped by and still Travis had not returned. The first year was the hardest. It was nearly impossible to answer Jason's daily questions of, "Is Daddy coming home today?" or "where's Daddy?" without breaking into tears. The stories that seemed to help them both the most were the ones that depicted Travis as the hero who was fighting against all odds to find the perfect home where they could all be safe and happy. She wanted to believe it so bad that it made the telling easier and soon enough it was easy enough for her to believe too.

Nothing could have been more painful than that, yet there was something. It could not be marked on a calendar to remember and mourn over, yet it must have happened at some point. Like footprints in the sand that are washed away by the incoming tide, slowly, the waves begin to gnaw at the prints until at some undeterminable moment they cease to exist. At that moment, all evidence that anyone ever passed by is gone and only a memory is left to mark the passage. It was that way when Jason stopped asking about his father. It felt as if he had given up and forgotten Travis.

Chapter 13

It seemed like minutes, but hours had passed since Sarah had begun her story. Jason sat in silence pondering the gravity of it all. The few memories that he had of his father were pleasant but now he was engulfed by a strange pang of longing. Sarah got to her feet and went into the kitchen. She made a small snack and the two of them ate in silence.

In the days that followed Jason was allowed nowhere without his mother. He showed her his slide and small part of the beach that he called his own. She learned about his collection and discovered the caverns below the property. In the end, there were no secrets left for Sarah to discover. It was no longer a secret place, and some of the magic had disappeared forever.

As fall approached, the weather began to turn. Cooler weather was accompanied by strong winds and torrential rains. Though there were no weathermen to tell the world about the variations from one year to the next, things naturally reverted back to the older method. One neighbor talked to another and they would kibitz about how hot it was the year before. Did you ever see so much snow? Why, two years ago, the wind took the roof right off the old watchtower. And so on and so on.

This year's weather wouldn't be analyzed until next year. But when it was, it would be described as horrific, especially for the town of Gibson. Normally the winds and waves that lashed at the shores were held at bay by Vancouver

Island, which stood between Gibson and the open ocean. It took the brunt of the abuse and slowed the winds down significantly. This fall, none of that seemed to matter. The rains poured down and the winds threw waves and sludge high over the fence to leave the house and its windows splattered with black sludge. Jason and Sarah lay under siege within the walls of their tiny home. Little had been done over the years to preserve the home and rain poured in freely.

Long ago, Travis had reconnected power to the house by throwing the switch at the top of the service pole at the end of the driveway. Somewhere north, turbines still turned out power as the water continued its cycle, oblivious to the fact that the world was falling apart.

During the strong winds, a tree fell across the line, something that had never happened in previous years. The seemingly endless source of power abruptly ended and at the worst possible time.

Without power, the house was cold and dark. The leaks that seemed to be everywhere flooded and drenched everything. They moved their important belongings into the one dry room and set up house there. Sarah had always maintained stores of supplies that included clothing, food and clean drinking water. All of these were now in short supply. It was impossible to dry anything once it got wet. Food and water were beginning to dwindle. She would have collected water from the roof, but the water from there was tainted with seawater and oily sludge. The days passed and Sarah feigned a smile as the stress and worry continued to strip away her youth.

And so it is with bad situations. When endurance is no longer possible, another day comes and goes. The sun rises. One impossible day has passed and another is begun. The weeks were slow and painful.

Six weeks had passed before the sun broke through the clouds and the winds finally let up. Sarah and Jason carried jugs to a runoff stream that meandered its way to the ocean about a kilometer from the house. They filled the jugs and began the arduous journey home. The windows were opened and Sarah began to reclaim the rooms that nature had borrowed. Life began to return to normal. No longer housebound, Jason had the incentive to be outdoors as much as possible. He would help his mother clean for the first half of the day and then outside for the warm afternoon sun. The ground was drying and the weeks of solid rain had uncovered numerous treasures. He had no urge to go back to the caves. There was a lifetime of discoveries to be made in his back yard.

Unknown to Sarah, the earth had begun to change below ground as well.

If Jason had returned to the caves, he would have found a whole new world forming below. Decades earlier the old landfill had been reclaimed. A conservation officer once occupied their home. The fence had been erected to protect government property. Now years later, somewhere below the house the muck from the dump began to shift from the old landfills to the ocean caves. It began to move slowly toward the sea. New, unstable, caverns were beginning to form under and around their home.

The weather remained mild, but like all coastal environments, winters are moist and dreary. The house was old and dilapidated when they first moved there. Sarah was accustomed to the annual shifting of the house. It always left doors hard to open, which in turn made the winter drafts much worse. Winter slowly slipped by, and the danger beneath the house grew.

Once again, March knocked on the door with the fury of an angry landlord. It held the family captive and eroded their spirits. Trapped inside and with little to do, Sarah began to lay plans for the coming summer. Spring, and the hope it contained, were just around the corner. The long days of winter had given Sarah plenty of time to think. Her home was no longer an acceptable safe haven for the two of them. The fence may have suggested safety, but she recognized it for what it was—a pleasant façade. Like the pitcher plant, sooner or later, the apparent safety would prove to be the demise of the unwary visitor. When the weather was warm enough, they would leave, head east across British Columbia and then into Alberta.

She included Jason in the planning process. She told him stories of where his father had gone and why. The prairies had always been less populated. The ground was flat and easy to till. The plains had once supported herds of buffalo and deer. Maybe they would again one day. Travis would have come back if he could but she never shared with Jason what she had once suspected and had long since come to believe. She knew well, the dangers of travel and so did Travis. They were well aware of the risk he was taking, but Jason had been too small for that kind of journey. Now that he was older, it was time to find a place to build a real home rather than to stay and wait for the house to deteriorate around them. Someday the earth would reclaim its own. The coastline would return to the way it once had been. Only the ruins among the giant spruce trees would be left to tell the story.

Sarah planned to be gone long before that. She and Jason planned carefully together. By the end of April, Sarah had gathered the maps and the supplies she would need along the way. There were numerous rivers and a mountain range to cross in order to get where she was going. They would need

to make it through the mountain pass before the winter snows began in October. If everything went well, she would be in Alberta before then.

On an early morning in May, Jason and Sarah stood outside their home looking at it for the last time. Each of them had on a warm set of clothes and footwear that would last the Journey. Though Jason was smaller, he carried everything that he would need. Each of them had a load to bear. Jason was excited about doing his part and shouldered his pack with determination and pride.

Sarah looked back at the home with an uncanny feeling that she was leaving something behind but couldn't put her finger on it. Her hair was pulled back into a ponytail to keep it out of her eyes. She looked over at Jason and made note of the hat that he wore and she glanced up at the morning sun. Then it came to her. HER HAT. It was in the house on the kitchen counter. Of all of the belongings she would need, her hat was one of the most important. It would keep the rain and the sun off of her as well as help her to keep warm on cool nights. She turned to Jason. "Just a second, hun. I'll be right back. I forgot my hat in the kitchen." She ran inside.

Sarah felt the front step give a little as she entered the house, but she paid it no mind. After all, she would be turning her back on this heap for the last time in just a moment. The floor shifted under her feet as she made way through the living room, passed the garden that she would soon leave behind. Ignoring the tilt of the kitchen floor, she grabbed her hat and turned to the door.

The house first began to moan and then to screech as if in pain. Sarah recognized what was about to happen and dashed back through the living room. She managed a couple of steps before the floor disappeared beneath her. She clawed at the snapping floorboards scrambling up, but tumbling plants and furniture rained down on her.

From outside, Jason heard the house groan. He had no time to feel a pang of worry. The house gave a tremendous lurch and fell in upon itself. He could hear his mother screams over the sound of snapping wood. The power line that was anchored to the house snapped free and lashed back at Jason like a giant tongue. He leapt aside. The wire whistled past him and then lay lifelessly in the driveway. The house let out a final sigh as it came to rest in a heap at the bottom of a hole in the old landfill site. Jason stood alone shocked and dazed.

Even before the wreckage settled, Jason stripped his pack and ran toward the house. If his father would have been there he would have grabbed Jason by the collar and ordered him to stay back. His father would have recognized the danger. But he wasn't there. Jason ran blindly towards the collapsing structure.

The roof sat close to where the floor had once been. Jason could hear the shifting mud and creaking wood as the building continued its downward path. The exterior door lay heavy in its frame. Even if Jason could open it, it would no longer lead into the house. Jason scanned the wreckage for a way in.

The living room window had shattered and its empty frame was lined with shards of glass. It gaped like the open maw of a sleeping giant. Jason scrambled across the wall without a thought and crawled in through the window. The interior walls had been transformed to broken timbers and slabs of plaster lying in all directions. The floor angled deeply into the ground and was cluttered with what remained of the walls, the roof and the old furniture. On hands and knees he moved deeper into the wreckage and called for his mother. No sound returned to him. He listened carefully hoping to hear the breath of her. Nothing.

He crawled on his hands and knees deeper and deeper into the debris of the broken house, where little light penetrated. He continued to call and search for his missing mother. Hours passed. Jason worked himself down into the muck the house had settled into. He crawled on his hands and knees. The thick mud was nearly liquid. It was as though it had reached some critical point and ceased to be solid ground. It sucked at his arms and feet refusing to let him go, clamoring at him to join his mother. He hunched over and tried to move among the shards and splinters. It was then that he saw what he would have mistaken for a mud covered glove had he not brushed it with his foot. He felt as though his body was going to explode when he realized that he was standing right on top of her. His weight was added to the weight of the wall that was holding her submerged in the mud. He called to her repeatedly as he pulled at her arm to free her.

Most of the material was too large and heavy for Jason to move. Eventually he cleared away enough of the mud to expose her face. He could not accept that she had not survived. Tears ran freely down his face and landed on hers. He wiped the mud away as gently as he could, staring into her lifeless face. He called to her over and over, "Mom!" He pleaded with her to wake up. Eventually his voice grew quieter and quieter until he finally fell silent.

Jason held his mother's hand as he wept in the darkness. He lay in the cold muck as the sun began to sink outside. The rain started up again and tiny rivulets streamed down around him. Still he held on. She was the only person he had ever really known. Long after his hands and feet felt as cold as the lifeless stiffened hand of his mother, he lay there next to her, shivering in the dark. Even when the morning sun created clouds of rising steam, Jason lay underground next to his mother. He thought dreamily that his underground caverns would be a grave for him after all. Jason lay with vacant eyes as the hours passed.

Maybe it was the beetle that scuttled across his leg and disappeared into the muck beside Sarah that finally snapped him back to reality. He looked dazedly at it as it burrowed its way into the mud. It filled him with disgust. Maybe it was the strength and will to survive that had been bred into him that made him finally move. With the afternoon sun pouring down on him, Jason once again clamored out of the ground and up into the world of light and the living.

The May sun broke the evil spell of the spring rains, but it was still not enough to warm Jason. He stood looking at the wreckage. Everything that once looked like a house and yard was abolished. The fresh wet hole had opened up a new world of rot and decay. The only things missing from the picture were the big machinery used for moving garbage, the crows and the seagulls. Jason found himself facing what could no longer be mistaken for what it was…a landfill.

He turned away. Behind him, there was nothing. In front of him, the ancient, crumbling blacktop stretched, first to the town, and then to unknown points beyond. Just outside the fence that had surrounded his yard was a squat dilapidated shed. It would never make a home, but for now, it was a place to sleep. If he had any emotion at all, his face did not show it. He didn't break out in tears or sob. He neither thought of himself, his father or his mother. Jason made his way to the shed and without forethought found a dry, dark corner. He put his back to the wall and sat paralyzed. Eventually he let gravity take over and his body rolled over to the ground.

Darkness fell and he didn't notice. The sun rose the next day and still, he lay motionless in the shed. Through the days that followed, the sun moved in slow motion across the sky and the moon followed its path at night. Animals crept in and out of the shed. Some were looking for shelter, others a meal. A rat edged his way up to him. It noticed that the body was still warm and moving. It crept away, disappointed. It would be back later to see if there was any change. Maybe there would be feasting later. It disappeared into the shadows.

A fly lit briefly on Jason's eyelid. It had found some moisture there, looking for a place with plenty of nourishment for its young, but Jason's eye twitched imperceptibly and the fly moved on.

Eventually he could no longer ignore the pain and the weakness that had begun to set in. His body was slowly taking what it needed from him. Though he was incredibly sad, the helpless and hopeless feelings were beginning to subside.

Sarah's survival pack waited indifferently in the driveway. It contained many of the same elements that Jason's pack contained. It also contained a few other essential items. Jason went through the familiar contents and separated out what he needed.

There were few personal effects in her pack. She had planned to travel light. Jason scavenged the objects that would help him most and left the rest. In one pocket he found a butane lighter, his mother's multi-tool and a compass. In another, he discovered a wax candle some paper and a pencil. At the bottom of one of the smaller pockets was a gold locket studded with fine diamonds. The case was worn where Sarah had spent countless hours holding it in her hand, stroking it gently with her thumb. The chain was formed with an intricate design of multiple links that made the metal look rope-like. There was a small metal button on one side. Jason pressed it and the front of the locket popped opened slightly. Although the locket had an antique look about it, the hinge was surprisingly stiff. He pried it open with his thumbnail.

Inside were two pictures. They were of poor quality and had been taken with a Polaroid camera years before. The old Polaroid instant pictures were thick. All the chemistry for the picture was trapped between two layers of thick paper. The pictures in the locket had been split apart so that only the sheet with the picture on it remained. They were of very poor quality and time had obliterated most of the images. Still, it was clear who each person was. On one side of the locket was a picture of a man. Jason had a vague recollection of his father and recognized him. The second picture had much less detail, partly because the image was much smaller. It showed a woman cradling a newborn in her arms. Even as small as the picture was, it was easy to identify Sarah. Jason assumed that he was the child in the picture.

In an instant, it occurred to him that everything that happened was his father's fault. He tore Travis' picture from the locket and threw it to the ground. He snapped the locket closed, put the chain over his head and threw his pack on his shoulder. Whether or not it was his intention, his foot came down squarely on the discarded photo. As he turned to leave, his foot squashed it into the dirt. What was left of the image was much less than it had been and now it also included a tear through most of the face. It didn't matter much, Jason's back was turned and he was already rapidly leaving the ruins behind.

Surprisingly his pack wasn't much heavier than it had been. Even though he was still chilled to the bone, a brisk walk would warm him up in no time. He maintained his quick pace in time with the turmoil he felt. His face was shrouded by the dark thoughts that haunted him. Even though the sun was getting higher in the sky, the trees that grew close to the road provided shade that matched his demeanor.

At first his sadness and anger were so great that it was impossible for him to discern one angry thought from another. They came rushing in one after the other, each one overlapping the next. The scenery rushed by.

In time, his mind began to slow and with it, so did his feet. It was true that if it hadn't been for his father none of this would have happened. His mother would still be here and they would be one happy family.

Jason couldn't remember very much about his father but he must have been the most selfish man that ever walked the face of the earth. Jason's thoughts seemed to move in diminishing circles. Each revolution seemed to be winding down to one unavoidable conclusion. It seemed like only moments ago that he and his mother were about to set out on a journey to find a new home and hopefully the man that his mother loved, his father. The locket swung and knocked lightly against his chest making him acutely aware of it.

Jason's pace continued to slow.

There were so many things that his mother valued, but it was the locket she chose to bring. Now that she was gone—Jason still couldn't come to think of her as dead. He suddenly realized that he no longer had a purpose or a goal. Would he travel to Alberta, build a house and plant crops to live on? The idea was as preposterous as it sounded. Without his mother there was no real reason to leave home. But without his home, he had no reason to stay. Where were his roots now?

His gait continued to slow and falter until he was hardly moving at all. It was akin to a steam locomotive coming to rest beside its platform. Each stride moving slower and slower until finally the trailing foot did not surpass the one in front, coming to rest beside his leading foot.

Jason stood motionless in the middle of the highway with one foot on either side of the faded yellow line. There, a battle went on inside of him. Only the features of his face were any indication of it. Until that battle was won or lost there would be no going forward or back.

As suddenly as the emotional storm had come on, it was over. Jason wheeled and turned back toward the ruins of his old home. He had already traveled more than a kilometer but that didn't matter now. His muscles were warm from his hike. He broke into a dead run.

He maintained his speed most of the way back and covered the distance in less than half the time that it took him to make the journey in the first place. By the time he got back to the driveway he had slowed to a fast jog. He ran straight to the spot where his mother's pack was strewn.

He bent down ignoring the litter. He found the spot where he had been at the moment that he turned to leave. He knew that the picture had been there at his feet. He scanned the area looking for the small photo. It was much smaller than it had seemed when it was framed in the locket, about the size of a dime. Jason got down on his hands and knees and ran his fingers through the dirt. Maybe he had inadvertently buried it when he turned to leave, but it wasn't there.

Jason stood up and faced the ruins. The stench rising from it was as bad as he had remembered when he first discovered his cave. Beyond the heap lay the dark ocean with its layer of oily smelling sludge. Jason considered how impossible it was to get upwind of the ocean. He smiled inwardly. That wouldn't happen unless the wind changed.

Then it struck him. "Yes! The wind." Jason turned so that the wind and the ocean were at his back. Again, he stood over the spot where his mother's pack laid, its own kind of carnage. He scanned the area once more and moved away from the spot keeping the wind at his back. He moved slowly in the direction the wind might have blown the picture. He walked slowly scanning the ground from side to side. He had gone about ten meters when he saw a small rock in the driveway. There, pinned under the edge was his father's picture. Jason picked the remains up and carefully brushed it off. Besides the tear in it, there were scuffs across it as well. Still, the features of Travis' face were discernable. He held it carefully. It was the only remaining evidence of his lineage.

Jason brushed it off as best he could without adding to the damage and carefully replaced it in the locket. He turned once more to look at the house he grew up in. The backpack laying crippled in the driveway, suddenly seemed wrong. It reminded Jason of the ravaged and looted buildings. It was simply not fitting.

He gathered his mother's belongings and carefully put them back in the pack. Each of the smaller items he put into the various compartments. He rolled the extra clothes and repacked them as much like his mother as he could. When everything was back in the pack, he picked it up and carried it to where the front steps of the house had been. Timbers stuck up in various directions. Jason picked one and hung the pack on it.

He wasn't running away this time. He slowly turned to go. His heart was heavy with sadness, worry and regret. As he walked away, the house began to creak. The ground below it was still shifting and sinking. Jason could imagine his old caverns filling up with liquid mud as it made its way slowly to the ocean. The board that held Sarah's pack began to tilt and then slowly it fell into the pit. It seemed fitting to know that those things would rest with his mother. He walked away.

Chapter 14

Through the days that followed, Jason walked mindlessly. The route was laid out by his mother weeks earlier. Alternate crossings for rivers were marked out, but for the boy who had never been out of his own back yard, the distances were too great to imagine. He woke with the first rays of the morning sun, took enough nourishment to stave off hunger and then walked on. He marched until the sun touched the ground, made camp and slept. Morning arrived and he repeated the pattern. The days crept by.

Jason had learned much from his mother. The woods had grown up along the roadside and provided everything that he needed. He recognized most of the edible plants and gathered what he could whenever possible. Towns, he treated with caution and respect. He took what he could use and passed through as quickly as possible. The days crept by.

At times, he found himself reminiscing about a happier life. He dreamed of creating the home his mother had often described. She told stories of the time before he was born when, the only two people in the world seemed to be Travis and her. She often imagined what it would be like when all three of them were together once again. Whenever she talked about his dad, there was always a smile to accompany it. She often spoke about how they had planned to find a wonderful new home and make a fresh new start. Even though he could barely remember his father, Jason had always harbored a secret dream that the two of them would someday be reunited.

There are lessons that children learn that help them grow into adulthood. Under normal circumstances these lessons are mercifully spread out over the course of a lifetime. But even in the best of times, Jason never really enjoyed what anyone would consider a normal childhood. His had been brought to an abrupt end. Unlike most of us, Jason, already knew happiness couldn't be found in the objects that can be accumulated. Those were fun, but not a source of real happiness.

Tragically, Jason would never recognize how much he had truly lost. It would always affect the way that he would make decisions. Other children his age would play in a way he may have once been familiar with, but in no way that he would ever understand again.

The road he traveled was out of use by vehicles and was slowly being reclaimed by nature along with everything else. Trees had begun to grow close along the edge of the asphalt and saplings were beginning to take root in small crevices that the frost had made in the hard surface. In many places the pavement was so broken it looked more like gravel. Grasses and flowers grew thickly wherever they could.

The road wound its lonely way through the wilderness, unlike the more populated areas, where the maze of roads needed to be carefully navigated. For the time being there were no decisions to make. The trees and plants crowded in. Looking ahead, the highway looked more like a narrow part in the trees than a road. Onward he plodded, sure of nothing.

The local wildlife had found its own way back into the world as well. The first animals to return were the deer, moose and elk. Neither the encroachment of man nor the constant pressure of hunting and poaching threatened them. Fields and parks that had once been a haven for children now grew lush green grass that had never seen the cutting blades of a mower. First, the herbivores, the grass-eaters, returned followed by the animals higher up on the food chain. A new population was taking over, one that was not human, but in ways, more humane. Jason's quiet footfalls did not alarm the wildlife and he found himself stopping to watch in amazement the habits, antics and behaviors of the new inhabitants.

The sun had passed its highest point in the sky and Jason's feet were hot and achy from the long day's walk. He sat down at the foot of a big spruce tree and opened his pack to choose from the meager stores he had there. While he ate his meal silently, he listened to the sounds of the world around him. He learned quickly that the forest was never truly silent. There were constant rustling sounds—a light breeze that caused two trees to rub together creating a living, shrieking sound. Now and then, a cawing came from far away. Was it a crow or raven? The awesome sound of wind being pushed rhythmically beneath great wings of a bald eagle could be heard long before it was seen swooping down in front of him, no more than thirty meters from the ground.

Out of the corner of his eye he saw movement between his bent knees. Without moving his head, he cast his eyes downward. A mouse peeked out from the grass, oblivious to the fact that Jason sat just above it. It picked and poked its way through the grass to investigate anything that might make a meal. Jason thought for a moment, *So this is how mice behave like when they're not frightened.* He closed his eyes and napped with his head against the tree.

A half an hour later, he woke with his legs rested but his back stiff from the tree. He stretched and limbered up before jumping the ditch and walking back out on to the road. It was impossible to imagine traffic ever having been heavy along these thoroughfares. In some ways, it was as if time had reversed itself. Life, in the world had slowed down. Only the hardy people stayed to eke out an existence in the new wilderness. They had to learn to contend with the ever-changing seasons and to live through long hard winters along side the wildlife. Those who could not learn the necessary skills quickly either perished or they picked up and went south to a warmer drier climate. The new Canadians were limited to their small day-to-day world. It was a simpler but harsher world too. It meant, for Jason, a long and friendless journey. But he was used to spending time alone and did not long for the company of others. He longed for his mother.

With his thoughts inward and his feet determined, he marched on. There was no telling when he might come across another living soul. He knew there was possible danger if that were to happen. He had gone over the procedure he would use a hundred times. The scenarios came from talks with his mother. She had always said, "You can never be too sure about people. Sometimes they're looking for companionship; other times they're more like predators. You can never really tell the difference."

The solution was quite simple, avoidance.

Chapter 15

He could tell he was entering a hamlet before he arrived. Houses appeared at the roadside and became more frequent as he progressed. Besides the increased number of dwellings, somehow, some of them seemed more kept, more used. It could have been the change in sounds. These were different than the ones he was familiar with, out on the road. Whatever the clue, Jason became more cautious. He began to stay closer to the edge and to stop frequently to listen carefully.

He heard the mooing of a cow. A little later he heard the squeaking of a hinge. Then another strange sound came to his ear. Could it be children laughing? He strained to hear, but the sounds were still too far away. The wind was growing louder. He had been on the road so long. Part of him wanted to run ahead. He wanted to stop by every house, wave and say, "Hello! How are you today, Mrs. Smith? Isn't the weather beautiful? By the way, your flowers sure look lovely!"

It's what every fiber in his body longed for. It's what he craved. Even if he dared, these emotions were not in him to share. The little man inside him was not about to let the boy come out to play. There could be dangers here that he could not foresee. He kept to his plan. He did not run headlong and unafraid into the village. He stayed quiet and watched from a distance, not unlike the animals that watched him warily from afar. There were people here.

He could see them at their normal daily activities, the activities they were bound to, that were dictated to them by the changing seasons. This was the planting and growing time.

As Jason had passed by a number of houses and saw some of the people, already. His confidence began to grow. He could hear his mother's voice in his head warning him to be careful. Secretly he wished to be seen. His deepest desire was that the town would reveal itself to be warm and welcoming. May it be filled with wonderful people who would embrace him and invite him into their homes? It was a secret wish though, and not one that he would ever dare to articulate. Instead, he walked a little more boldly, less concerned about being as silent and invisible as he could have been.

To his left a woman knelt amid ankle high plants arranged in rows. It was impossible to tell what kind of plants they were…food of some kind. His mouth watered at the thought. She was pulling and picking something and putting it in piles next to her. She already had several small heaps along the row she was kneeling in. The woman wore the old familiar blue jeans that seem to have always been a farmer's staple for clothing. These ones had been patched at least once too often, another sign of the times.

She seemed older…older at least than his mother. It was difficult to tell her hair color. It was covered with an old bandana. As she straightened up to stretch her back and to wipe the sweat from her eyes, Jason moved quickly to the edge of the road and out of sight.

Chapter 16

Hannah caught sight of the young boy peering at her from the edge of her broken down picket fence. He wore grungy set of clothes of a nondescript nature. Mostly they were the colors of the earth. In fact, as she looked more intently it seemed as though the dirt that covered the boy from head to toe might be the stuff that held his clothes together. He cowered when she looked his way as if he were about to bolt. She smiled inwardly and went back to pulling weeds.

Hannah had made a lot of adjustments over the past twenty-five years. She had survived her own bad luck as well as the looting years. And, she had also survived the mistakes she made along the way, learning to survive. She could grow what she needed and to make use of everything that God provided. She was a teenager when things began to fall apart and like so many others, the best years of her life had been spent finding ways to stay warm and keep living. She wasn't much for waiting for things to get better. By God, she would make them better.

Her community was home to a scant thirty people. Although there were numerous homes to choose from, they chose to live in a close-knit group. It wasn't how they had planned it. Each had gravitated to another. These were not like the old homestead days. There were threats everywhere and few people had the skills that their great grandparents had grown up with. It wasn't a perfect community, but it was Hannah's community.

She was instrumental in some of the major changes that had taken place. There was a time when the people who lived there did nothing more that live in borrowed hovels. Hannah had begun to rebuild the town. When the banks foreclosed on almost all of the homes in the area, most people packed up and left in the hopes of finding employment and a new start somewhere else. Unfortunately there wasn't better luck anywhere else…just more of the same kinds of problems. Now the people who had once lived in them were long gone. Surely, somewhere was a vault that contained all the documents that proved ownership of billions upon billions of dollars worth of property. These were relics. Even the buildings that contained those documents were no more than catacombs, time capsules for a way of life that was as extinct as the dinosaurs.

Eight years earlier, Hannah had decided that it was time to clean up the community and the surrounding area. It wasn't that she didn't have enough to do as it was; it was just that she hated to see all that was there go to waste. She had lived through so many hard times already. There were buildings that were being destroyed by the elements because the windows were broken during the early years of looting. It wasn't that she intended to fix any of them up; she just wanted to slow the decay. Many of the houses had been ransacked. Some of them had been burned. There was so much cleanup to do. She started one do-it-yourself project at a time.

When she wasn't working to make sure she had winter supplies of wood and preserves, she was busy trying to restore some of the more useful buildings in the community. Some were unsalvageable and those, she burned and cleared away. There was still equipment that had been used to build roads and haul garbage. There was no way to repair the equipment once it broke down, but that didn't bother Hannah too much. There was so much of it. When a machine stopped working, she towed it to a kind of graveyard she started. It was a gravel pit that grew more thistle than anything else. She sometimes thought it would be interesting to see the place in a hundred or two hundred years from now. She wondered what kind of story it would tell.

The fuel and oil she needed came from an old card-lock fuel station that had been put in place to service the logging industry that once flourished in the area. She rigged a system for pumping what fuel remained. Already, she had pumped out thousands of liters and hoped that there were still thousands left.

Somehow, and certainly not intentionally, she had become a figurehead in her town. She had no official designation nor did she did have a particular job description. When something needed to be done Hannah was the kind of person that would get to it and do it. It was not in her nature to ask for help or complain. It was as if her example was enough to make all of the difference. As the other remaining members of the community saw the work that she was doing, they began to pitch in. It didn't really matter whether it was because they felt guilty or because the felt inspired. What had grown as a result was a small, almost thriving community. Like all towns, people come and people go. This one was no different. There weren't any particularly unseemly characters hanging around and those who stayed, stayed because they wanted to. They worked because that was what made sense. It was necessary.

In truth, Hannah wasn't nearly as old as she appeared to be. She was only a couple of years older that Jason's mother. She would be forty in the coming fall and had long since stopped worrying much about wayward travelers or what they might think of her. Had she been wearing cleaner clothes, or if her hair was pulled back, she would have indeed been an attractive woman.

She was comfortable with her qualities. But she was long over worrying about what others thought of her. Mostly, those who came found that there was little here for them and left.

Truly, there was not a wealth of riches to be plundered. It was a small, old and broken town, being rebuilt by a small group of weary and somewhat broken people. They were fixing each other and the community, but it was a slow process. The careless wanderer would never notice such things and Hannah was beyond worrying about it.

She watched the boy from the corner of her eye, as he slowly worked his way along the fence. She wondered where he had come from and after toying with the idea, decided that it didn't really matter. By the look of him, he couldn't be more than ten or eleven years old. She kept her head down and focused on her work. She waited until he was directly to her side, almost to the point of passing her, before calling casually to him, "Hello!" She turned to him and smiled, "Welcome, stranger." It was the kind of welcome you might hear from a corny old western movie but it was like magic to the boy.

The boy stopped and looked at her incredulously. It was evident by the face he made that he had not expected this. Had she frightened him? He reminded her of a wild animal that was about to bolt. His dark half-squinted eyes followed her every move. She ignored him and continued to pull her weeds.

The boy watched her for a long time. She gave him no reason to stay or go.

Hannah wanted to find out what he would do of his own free will. When she had nearly given up that he would respond at all, he did.

"Where am I?"

"This place used to be called Harrison. Now, well, we haven't really decided what to call it. I call it home. What brings your little self all the way out here—in the middle of who knows where?"

She spoke in a way one might be expected to speak to a young boy. Jason was unfamiliar with the tone.

He stood motionless for a long time. It was difficult to tell whether he was pensive or stupid. He was not afraid, but his behavior created more questions than answers. After the uncomfortably long pause became even more uncomfortable, he finally answered. "I'm looking for my father."

"Hmmm…we don't see many visitors around here. I don't recall anyone coming through here that I would think might be likely to be your father. What makes you think he came this way?"

The boy stood there silently.

Hannah changed the subject. "Hey, you look like you could use a bite to eat. How about it?"

Still the boy stood silently. She could almost see the argument he must he having with himself. He looked thin as a rake. What would cause him to hesitate? Interesting.

The boy shrugged.

"Well, I'm going to go inside to make some lunch. You're more than welcome to join me. I think I'm going to make some chicken soup and sandwiches. The flour, and the chickens are home grown too…one hundred percent organic."

Hannah shoved her gardening spade into the soft black soil and stood up. Her back cracked audibly. She smiled over at the boy as she walked to the house. She had to pass close to him to get through the gate and she half expected him to break into a run. He didn't.

The house was a country style home with a covered porch. There was a small upstairs area built into the roof part of the house. There was a dormer on each side with a small window in the gabled end. On the main floor, the door from the porch led directly into the kitchen and dining area. Hannah swung open the screen door and went into the kitchen. It slammed shut behind her and bounced against the frame once before settling onto the latch. She watched through the kitchen window to see what the boy would do. He was standing by the fence. Well, if she was going to get the meal on she had things to do. She turned her attention to the task at hand.

The best way to keep food fresh was to eat it fresh. What she didn't eat fresh, she canned for the winter. Two days ago, she butchered one of the chickens. She had chicken dinner twice with some beets she had preserved and a few of last year's potatoes that she brought up from the cellar. Last night she had taken the bones and remaining meat and put them on the stove to simmer. This afternoon the smell of the soup filled the house.

She used an old wood stove to heat the house and to cook with. She stoked it with kindling and in a short time the broth began to boil. She looked out again to check on the boy and noticed that he had inched a little closer. Smiling, she reached into the cupboards and pulled out two of everything.

She heard the steps creaking outside and knew that he was climbing the front steps to the porch. She waited until his face was nearly pressed against the screen door before inviting him inside to lunch. "Have a seat at the table," she indicated with a motion of her head. Her hands were busy. "Lunch is just about ready. I was wondering what I was going to do with all of these leftovers," she added with a smile. "What's your name? Or should I just call you boy?"

"Jason," he replied shyly.

"Well, Jason, I'm so glad to have a little company. My name is Hannah," she tacked on as she poured a glass of water for each of them.

Jason barely looked up as he scarfed back the food that was put before him. He couldn't remember the last time that he had eaten so well. It must have been at least eight months ago, prior to winter. It made him think of his mother, which saddened him.

Hannah was surprised at how quiet the boy was. She had tried a few simple questions, but getting anything out of him was nearly impossible. Evidently, he did not feel like talking. When he was finished with his meal he politely asked to be excused and offered to help with clean up. Hannah declined and invited him to sit while she took care of it. The sofa looked so comfortable Jason could not bring himself to say no.

He faced the hardest thing to do, saying goodbye and walking out the door. When Hannah was finished cleaning up and put the last dish away, he could think of no reason he should stay. Reluctantly, he got up from the sofa and turned to Hannah. "Thanks so much for everything," he told her. "I really should get going."

"Don't be silly, Jason. Why don't you stay for dinner? You could rest here tonight and then be on your way after you've had a good breakfast."

Jason's mouth watered at the idea. He turned the idea over in his mind for an instant before smiling broadly. "Thank you so much!" he said with enthusiasm.

The rest of the day Jason helped Hannah in the garden and around the house. When it came time for dinner his stomach was more than ready. He ate hardily and helped with the dishes afterwards. By then he was nearly falling off of his feet with fatigue. Hannah escorted him upstairs, showed him the bed he was to sleep in, and the bathroom. She gave him a towel, said good night and left him to his own devices. Jason cleaned up and slipped into bed. The blankets were warm and heavy, but before he had time to reflect on the day, his eyes deceived him and closed on their own.

It was almost eleven o'clock in the morning when he finally awoke. Downstairs he looked for Hannah, but she was nowhere in the house. He looked in living room, kitchen and the bathroom on the main floor. When he came to her bedroom, the door was ajar. He peeked in briefly, but could not see her there. After exploring as much of the house as he felt comfortable, he went to the back door and on to the porch that overlooked the garden. There she was, working away at tending to the plants. She looked up when she heard the screen door swing on its hinges. She smiled, stood and came towards him.

"You must be about ready for breakfast," she said happily. "I didn't think you would ever get up."

Jason looked down at his feet shyly.

***

One invitation followed another and Jason never found it within him to turn them down. Every part of Hannah's home and the village seemed to offer him everything he had longed for. With each passing day, Jason felt more like a member of the community. Through the weeks and months that followed, he was introduced at one time or another to everyone in town.

The summer days trickled by slowly. With Jason's help, Hannah continued to tend her meager crops. The garden that once contained only sprouts had become corn, tomatoes, carrots, peas and potatoes. At harvest time Jason joined Hannah on his hands and knees, gathering the fruits of their labors. Preserving the vegetables followed. There was much to do. By mid-October the last of the potatoes had been cleaned, dried and stored in the root cellar below the house.

Hannah cut a hole in the floor a few years earlier. With a spade and bucket she had removed enough dirt to create a small hole below the house. When it was finished it was about two and a half meters long, two meters wide and a meter and a half deep. She made a makeshift ladder to get down into it. The dirt walls were shored up with rough pieces of lumber. Along one side of the cellar was a series of wooden bins about a meter deep. A large heavy wooden shelf was set against the opposite wall. The potatoes and carrots were put in the bins, while the preserves were stored on the shelves. The natural heat of the ground kept the food from freezing on the coldest days but kept it cool enough as well, to keep the vegetables through the winter months.

When harvest was over and the winter rains began to pour, the townspeople kept to tradition. They gathered in the building that used to be city hall. Each family brought something from what they did best. One family brought freshly baked chicken. Another brought potato salad. A third family brought fresh green salad. The food was laid out on old tables set in a row. Everyone brought enough silverware, cups, plates and bowls for themselves and Thanksgiving was celebrated. The party could not be compared to the gatherings the older folk had been used to having in the old days. Although simpler, this was much more gratifying. It was an opportunity to get together, share stories and be honestly thankful that the hardest part of the work was over. It was a time to celebrate the full stores that would hold them through the long winter to come.

Boasting was a natural part of the event. It was a chance to hear how much of the kind of produce each family had harvested. Over the years, a kind of trade had begun to emerge. Hannah hadn't grown hens for laying or butchering, but Edna McLeod did. Their method for exchange was simple, a week for a week. Hannah traded a week's worth of eggs for a week's worth of potatoes. She tried to produce lots of carrots and potatoes so that she would have enough to get the things she needed from those who produced it. She knew that Edna would never see her in need, but it was important to Hannah that Edna be paid fairly. The spring months were sometimes scant, but for now, it was feasting for all.

The colder, wetter winter months were a time of hibernation. Hannah tried to do the projects that could be done inside and around the house. Drafts were stopped up as they were found and Jason helped where he could. He learned a lot about keeping house. He was not just a young child to be taken care of anymore. He was a boy who could be useful. In the process, he learned lessons that would serve him well as a grownup. It was as if Hannah had taken over where his mother had left off. It saddened Jason to think that the longing for his mother was lessening with time. He couldn't help feeling guilty about it.

The winter crawled by and Jason had almost given up thinking about him. There were those times it gnawed at him, but they were short lived. His warm blanket and the smell of a hot breakfast always seemed to get the best of him. He made excuses for himself. It was impossible for him to know where his father went anyway.

One early spring night, when there was nothing much to do they sat and ate a quiet dinner together. Hannah asked Jason about his father. Jason didn't know much about his father. It was memories of his mother that came flooding back. Every day was easier, but now and then he would find tears streaking down his face at his last memory of her. As he spoke, he became caught up in all the wonderful things that they used to do together as a family. He tried hard to remember everything he could about his father, but his memories were sketchy. He had fleeting memories of being tossed in the air and jumping on his father's back for a horse ride. Most of the story, however, involved him and his mother. Finally, he pulled out his locket and showed Hannah. She tried hard to look through the rip and the scratches. Even in its poor condition the face looked familiar. By the end of the evening, Hannah was positive that she remembered the man called Travis. If she was correct, then she not only knew where he was going, she also knew a great deal about Sarah as well. For now, she kept it to herself.

Travis had indeed come through town. Like Jason, Hannah was the first person to greet him. She remembered that it hadn't started out quite as smoothly as it had gone with Jason, but maybe that was because she didn't see a young boy as a threat.

At the time, Travis told a story from the point of view of a proud father. He told about the brightest five-year-old he had ever seen and felt blessed that he could call him his son. Hannah couldn't remember seeing anyone glow the way Travis had. She even tried to convince him that he and his family should come to Harrison. She remembered being vaguely jealous. Travis was only a year or two younger than she was. He was handsome and intelligent. Fear did not seem to be in his vocabulary. She remembered being attracted to him. She remembered having mixed feelings as he talked about his family. Why couldn't anything like that happen to her? Now she found she was listening to the same story all over again, this time from the mouth of a ten-year-old. It was amazing how much the story hadn't changed, even though it was coming from a different point of view and years later. Looking at him more closely, she could see the contours of Travis' face in his.

It had been six years since Travis arrived in town. How could he possibly be alive after all of this time? Would he remember his son even if Jason were able to find him? Would Jason remember his father? The scratched and torn up picture certainly wouldn't be of much use.

Jason slept soundly that night. His warm memories brought him some comfort. And for the most part his dreams were filled with pleasant images. Hannah, on the other hand, spent a restless night. It was difficult to imagine Jason finding success with his crazy plan to find his father. Not worst of all, but certainly something that weighed heavily on her mind, was the fact that she would have to live with the guilt of sending this boy out into the world and then never knowing what had become of him. With the morning sun Hannah had come to a painful resolve. This boy was everything any parent could possibly wish for in a child. She felt the unbelievably strong need and duty to provide a home for him. When she weighed the pros and cons she finally decided regardless of Jason's hopes about finding his father, she could not allow him to continue his journey. There are times when children do not know what's best for them. In Hannah's mind, this was one of those times. She would not tell him outright that he could not go; she would simply not empower him or provide the opportunity.

Chapter 17

For better or for worse, fate has its own plans. The conversations that she and Jason shared only served to bring Jason's own dreams and plans to the forefront of his mind. Hannah had imagined that she would be able to turn his thoughts away from his quest. She knew he longed for a home and she intended to offer her home as a substitute. But the next few days only proved Jason's obsession was far stronger than she imagined. Something awakened in him. He talked incessantly about nothing else. She tried to change the subject as often as she could, but Jason was relentless.

Eventually the day came when Jason stated that he was planning on leaving. He spoke to her as one adult would speak to another. He informed her that he knew that his father had headed east and he would go in that direction. He felt confident that he would come across other people just like Hannah, who would help him along the way.

Hannah did not know what to do. She had never had a child of her own but at the same time she felt absolutely confident that what Jason proposed would only lead to disaster. She could not allow it. In her frustration, she did the only thing she could do. She refused to allow him to leave.

It was all right that he was mad and frustrated. It didn't really matter that he ran upstairs and slammed the door to his room. This was something children did some times. It was even something adults did at times. He would eventually forget about his dream to find his father. There were all kinds of ways to keep his life busy and full.

That was the plan. No matter how good a plan might be its success is often determined by outside factors. There was no way that Hannah could have predicted how driven Jason would be or how grownup and independent he had become.

Jason came down from his room, and it was as if the old Jason had ceased to exist. The new Jason was hostile and resentful. He continued to help out in the ways that were expected of him. It was not in him to be a lazy lay about. The home he had once felt welcomed in had now become his prison. The stalemate lasted less than a week. He could tolerate it no longer. Eventually, he made up his mind and he approached Hannah directly.

"I'm leaving," he said simply. "You cannot keep me here if I don't want to stay. You can lock me in my room if you choose, but I will still leave."

There had been no conversation. There was no chance to talk him out of it. Jason turned and left the room. Hannah stood dumbfounded.

Back in his room, Jason rolled his thoughts over and over in his mind. If Hannah had stopped him and tried to make him see the nonsense of it, it might have been more than he could stand. It was for this reason that he said what needed to be said and turned away. He had hoped that she would not force the issue and she hadn't. If he had been more than eleven he might have added that he loved her and that she had become so much like a mother to him that it was painful. He would have said how much he had appreciated her warm house, comfortable bed and cozy blankets. If only his mother had been here with him, they might have been able to make this town their home. But Jason was only ten and the only words he could think of were "good-bye."

Hannah didn't lock him in his room. In fact, she didn't say anything at all. She was horribly torn and felt backed into a corner with no way out. She was out of choices. Since there was no good decision to make, she made none. She would sleep on it and maybe in the morning she could explain things to Jason. Maybe she could change his mind then.

But sleep didn't come easily to Hannah that night. Terrible images of what might happen to Jason kept replaying over and over in her mind. She knew that he spoke truthfully when he said that he would run away. He had made it this far on his own and he could probably make it a lot further. The hours trickled by. The night sky turned a dark gray and then warmed. Slowly the sun rose.

In his own room, Jason spent an equally restless night. He knew full well the significance of the wonderful gifts Hannah had given him already. She had never offered, but he knew that if he wanted, this could be his permanent home. He understood completely that it was not out of meanness she wanted him to stay. Though he wasn't yet a man, already he carried his pain as if he were one. In the deepest part of him, he felt that to stay would mean that he would have to give up on finding his father and regaining his family. How could he make it clear to Hannah that the costs of staying were just too high? He knew that it was something he could never hope that she would understand. With silent tears rolling down his face, he packed his clothes.

Chapter 18

Almost six years earlier, Travis left Sarah and Jason with horribly mixed feelings. He knew that the location they had chosen was not at all as safe as it seemed. Living on a landfill held too many dangers to consider staying permanently. Sarah had grown up living in secret and hiding. For her, staying was a better choice. On the other hand, Travis spent his young adulthood, as a migrant. He went wherever it suited him best.

He did his best to make it clear to Sarah all the dangers there were. The supplies in town were running out and the ocean would not be a viable source of nourishment for generations to come. They could not afford to wait.

After months of deliberation they decided that Travis would be able to travel quicker and more safely than they could as a family. He would stand a better chance of being able to avoid any of the new dangers that might be waiting. They discussed the kind of location that they might need, and decided on two things. He wanted to find a home where there was a lot of space, a long growing season and an area that was relatively unpopulated. He would find them a suitable place to live and then he would return. Once the decision was made he did not delay. He kissed the only two people who meant anything to him and walked out of the door. Jason was five years old at the time.

Travis had an idea about where he wanted to travel. He knew quite a bit about western Canada and decided that Alberta might provide the kind of environment that the two of them wanted and needed for their little family. He expected to pass through many small towns and would try and keep an open mind about whether or not they would meet his needs. He wanted to get back home to Sarah as quickly as possible. When they decided on the move it would be quick and direct. Sarah had dismissed the idea of becoming a nomadic family who would eventually settle down when they found the right place.

Travis traveled for three days before he came to the small community of Harrison. If he had been able to see what the little town would be like in five years, he would have turned around immediately and went back to get his family. Unfortunately, the little town of five years ago resembled a ghost town. The stores like many others had been looted. The windows were smashed and the doors were broken down. It was raining when he walked down the streets that day, which gave the town an unwelcoming feel. While looking for a dry place to spend the night he noticed a glow coming from a window and decided to investigate.

He peered into the dimly lit room, and noticed a woman sitting near a burning candle reading a book. He glanced around the room trying to assess any hidden dangers there might be. He employed the tactics he developed years earlier. The woman looked harmless enough. He wondered if there were others. It did not seem likely to him that a woman would live alone. He tried to see if she was armed but could not see any weapons close by.

Travis went to the front of the building and rapped lightly at the door. Without warning, the room went dark. Travis called out again, but there was no response. Then he heard a small clicking sound. It came from behind him. He was about to turn when a female voice said firmly, "Don't even think about moving."

Travis froze.

"Drop the pack slowly. Now step away from it. Put your hands where I can see them."

She tickled him as she frisked him and he jerked. The dark hid the smile on his face. When she was satisfied that he carried no weapons she demanded, "What do you want?"

"Well to tell you the truth, I was looking for a warm dry place to spend the night. I saw your light and I came by to ask for your help."

Hannah looked at him skeptically. She bent down and scooped up his pack. She motioned him into the house.

Travis could have overcome her at any moment if he had chosen to. He sensed that she was only concerned about her safety and had no real desire to hurt anyone. It was that way with so many people these days and they had every right to be cautious. He allowed himself to be directed into the house and waited patiently while she relit the candle. She went from one candle to another and lit each in turn. Then she turned so that he could see her face. She was a good-looking woman. But like so many others, the new harder life had taken its toll. The deep lines in her forehead and in the corner of her eyes told their own story of hardship. He stood uncomfortably as she eyed him trying to satisfy herself whether or not he posed a threat. She went through his pack compartment by compartment. When she was finished and sure that there was nothing sinister about it, she threw it back to him.

"There's the couch. Leave in the morning." She went upstairs and he heard a door lock.

Travis slept dreamlessly and woke rested with the sun beaming into his eyes. He thought about what the woman had requested and packed his belongings. He decided that he would say thank you in his own way and so he began to make breakfast. The smells slowly worked their way upstairs and eventually were enough to wake Hannah. When she finally came down the stairs, he was ready with a pack to walk out of the house.

She didn't know whether to be furious with the stranger or to be thankful. He had invaded her privacy. He had gone through her cupboards. He had been through her private belongings. She smiled inwardly admitting to herself that silverware and dishes weren't exactly private. By the time she reached the bottom of the stairs and saw Travis with his backpack slung over one shoulder and ready to go, she couldn't help but smile. She couldn't remember a time when someone else had made her breakfast...or anything else for that matter. She hadn't realized that she had taken the time to make herself as presentable as she could. There was a brief awkward moment when he tried to say thank you and goodbye at the same time. The moment was made more difficult by the fact that she wanted him to stay.

"Why don't you sit down and have some breakfast with me? You look like you've been traveling a long time and could use a bit of a rest," she invited.

Travis barely hesitated. He was glad of a chance to spend a moment with someone who was offering to be hospitable. He decided to take her up on her offer.

Even the night before, in the poor light of the candles, Hannah couldn't help but notice that he was a handsome man. She fantasized briefly, but squelched her thoughts.

He stayed the evening, that night, and the following day. They sat through supper. She asked him about himself and sat patiently as he told her about his life with Sarah and Jason. An artist could have painted a picture of Travis' family based on his descriptions. Hannah listened attentively without interrupting.

A few days later Travis decided it was time to move on. Even though she begged him to stay a little longer, he was insistent that it was time for him to go. He had a hundreds, maybe thousands of kilometers ahead of him that needed to be traveled.

She packed him a lunch and threw in various staples that he would need for his journey including some homemade deer jerky. He thanked her sincerely and was gone.

***

Travis left Gibson and his small family behind with a detailed plan of where he would go. He would head east towards Alberta. He would start his journey by traveling to Hope. There he would connect with the Transcanada Highway. That route would take him through most major cities as well as countless small towns. Somewhere along the way he hoped he would find a suitable place to call home.

Sarah was well aware of the plans. She hoped that if something went wrong, and she and Jason were forced to follow, they might hear news of his progress along the way and find out what had happened to him. Although she tried to explain it to Jason, she could not expect him to get anything but a rudimentary understanding of the world beyond the fence. Without the help of his mother's knowledge, Jason had no hope for finding his father.

Chapter 19

Hannah and Sarah were remarkably similar in so many ways. From Travis' stories, Hannah understood this. She knew that as long as there was one road coming into town and one road leaving Jason would be okay. The moment he made a wrong turn and got off of his father's trail there would be no hope that Jason would ever find Travis. This was Hannah's private knowledge and it filled her with a gnawing guilt and worry.

If she told Jason nothing, he would leave anyway. On the other hand, if she did tell him what she knew of Travis' plans he would be filled with hope and leave also. She was absolutely sure about one thing. Jason would not survive for long on his own, and that is why, when Jason came downstairs with his pack strung across his shoulder he was met by Hannah who was completely set with her own traveling gear. This was not the first time she had been on extended camping and hiking trips. She was completely prepared for survival. Included with her gear she carried a high-powered rifle.

"What are you doing?" Jason inquired.

"I believe you said you were looking for your father? I guess we're going to find him together."

Jason was elated. A moment ago, his spirits were down, armed only his determination and loneliness to drive him onward. Now he had a companion who knew his father too. He knew they would find him…together.

***

Hannah left her house with mixed feelings. There were so many things she was unsure of. Even today, her memory of Travis was as vivid as if he had just been there. She remembered her feelings of jealousy after she had gotten to know him. She remembered thinking how lucky Sarah was to be with a man like him.

She was torn as well. She had spent a lifetime building her own roots and now she was giving them up for the sake of a wild-goose chase. Would she ever see the threshold of her own house again? "I must be insane!" She said it out loud. All of this for the sake of a child? She closed the door and turned the key in the lock, and looked at the beaming boy beside her and thought, *Absolutely*.

A few short years ago, it was still not uncommon to see vehicles traveling the roads. A few short years before, was a lifetime ago. Once oil ceased to be delivered to these areas and the economy collapsed, other businesses rapidly followed. The large motor vehicle companies had advertised plans long ago to build and sell electric cars, solar cars and even hydrogen powered cars. But they had been unprepared. The economic collapse came too quickly. Even if a product had been in place now, no one could afford the new vehicles. Currency had lost its value.

For a long time people were able to utilize unused reserves at abandoned fuel stations. It took no time to deplete those reserves. Roving gangs had destroyed many of the local fuel supplies. The evidence of a mechanized world was all around them, but only as a monument to the way the world once was. Hannah and Jason traveled by foot. If she could find an alternate form of transportation, she would. In the meantime, they would have to rely on their own two feet for locomotion.

The highway to Hope had been used mainly as a trucking route. There were few communities in the Fraser Canyon and so there were long stretches of road with only the pavement and trees for company. There were many areas where the road dipped close to the Fraser River. The beauty was breathtaking. Mountains lay directly ahead. Hannah explained the basic route. There were two main mountain ranges between them and the prairies of Alberta. Nestled between the two was a small valley that could boast of British Columbia's most pleasant climate and best producer of fruits and vegetables. After that, they would have to cross the treacherous Rocky Mountains. She didn't think they could traverse the entire province in a single summer season. They would need to cross the Rockies the following year. Once they started that leg of the journey there would be no turning back. They would have to reach the other side before the snow began to fall. To add to their challenges, there were many sections of the route where winter-like conditions could be found all year long.

Route number one was well marked and easy to follow. They were on the same path that Travis had hoped to take. The closer they could stay to it, the better. He wouldn't have changed his plans if he didn't have to. It was likely they would come upon any obstacle that Travis might have stumbled upon. Hopefully they could deal with it in much the same way.

They arrived in the quiet town of Agassiz. If there was anyone here, they were laying low. That was just as well for Hannah. She was never sure whether there was going to be a conflict. Sometimes it was easier to keep to yourself. As they left the seemingly deserted town, Hannah kept an eye open for one of the few crossings along the Fraser River. According to the map, there should be a bridge to her right as they moved along the river.

For all of history most of the runoff water in British Columbia came down this raging river. Some of the longest salmon runs in the world led to places deep within the interior and all from this single source of water.

Hannah remembered that somewhere in the canyon was a place called Hells Gate. There, the riverbed narrowed to less than thirty meters across while the river raged two hundred meters deep. Looking ahead, maybe the entire canyon should be called "Hell's Gate." Historically the canyon had been one of the biggest obstacles in opening up the province for transportation and commerce. Hannah shuddered at the thought of traversing it. What might they expect from a place so wild and untamable? She looked to the southeast where the bridge should be. The river spilled through. The only remaining evidence was the odd concrete pylon sticking out of the water.

Even if the bridge had been intact Hannah would not have crossed it. She knew that Travis had headed toward Kamloops and that he wanted to use Route One. If the bridge was still standing it would have been a good indicator about what to expect from other bridges further along the road. There were no choices. She led Jason past the ruins saying nothing to him. In this case, the less he knew the better off he'd be. Besides, it might mean nothing at all.

They rested the night in Agassiz and the following day hiked out early toward the east. For the most part, the hike was uneventful and they made good time. They were approaching a large concrete structure as the day came to a close. It looked like some kind of bridge over the road. Jason had never seen anything like it before. There was a weathered road sign attached to two galvanized posts indicating that the highway split and the one they were on, ended. The options were to travel east or west on Route One. Without hesitating, they rounded the corner to the left then up a small incline and into a merging lane, of a two way highway. Hannah had never been here before but she expected for a road that was supposed to cross the entire country of Canada, it would be more…substantial. Inwardly she shrugged and carried on saying nothing. Jason wouldn't know the difference anyway. For him, all roads were the same.

They made camp a kilometer or two from the giant concrete dinosaur. On the southwest edge of the highway, stunted grass grew in the predominately harsh environment. After the meal, they laid out their bedding and fell asleep looking at the stars twinkling in the clear night sky. An owl hooted eerily, but Jason was already asleep. The long walks were beginning to take their toll.

Chapter 20

Hannah was deep in thought when Jason suddenly became excited about something ahead of them. She had been trudging, head down, staring at the ground. They came around one of the innumerable corners. A large hole gaped wide in the side of the mountain. A concrete face surrounded the opening. The entrance was a perfect half circle with its sides extended to the ground. Jason ran ahead to read the plaque that was printed with the name of the tunnel…"Yale." In many places, the concrete had begun to flake off. A small pile of gravel had formed at the base. Inside the tunnel, there were several places the water trickled down the sides leaving the walls damp. Jason was amazed at how much cooler it was on the inside. It was a short tunnel. The dead lights above, hung in steal cages. The paint had pealed off of them long ago. Already they were red with rust.

Jason held his breath as he ran all the way through it. When he got to the far end of the tunnel, he turned around and ran back through again. Hannah took the opportunity to rest a bit while Jason played. It had been a long time since she felt youthful and it was wonderful to see Jason behave like a boy. She forgot how enjoyable the simplest things could be.

"Hey, squirt, there are six more of these and this one is nothing compared to the ones we'll be going through. There's no electricity, so you might even get a bit of a scare." She grinned wickedly, realizing that she was excited too.

"Awesome!" he yelled as he skipped ahead. "This is so great."

The mountains hemmed them in from every side. The sheer rock faces were their own works of art, painted in grays, blues, reds and pinks. Like all tourists, it wasn't long before they became complacent to the beauty and one sheer rock cliff began to look the same as the next. The next tunnels were big brothers to the first one they had gone through, but did not excite Jason the way the first one had.

The constant roar of the river lay somewhere unseen to their right. Jason noticed that the sound of it was growing louder. Hannah explained that they should come to a crossing soon. Less than an hour later, the road turned sharply to the right and the river came into full view straight ahead. Jason raced to examine the concrete pilings that looked like the fingers of a giant hand poking out of the water on either bank.

Hannah studied the ruins trying to decide what was likely to have happened. It was not an important mystery to unravel. It was more out of curiosity than anything. The fact was the bridge was gone. There would be no crossing the river at this point. From what she could surmise, it looked as though part of the rock face had broken off and fallen into the canyon. As the rocks fell they may have tore away some of the steel and concrete that supported the bridge. With those gone, the bridge had collapsed into the water and was probably swept away. The debris from the mountain filled in a good part of the original waterway creating a new waterfall.

The level of the water was well above any high water mark that had stained the rocks in previous years. There were numerous trees along the water's edge that were half submerged. The water was a muddy brown. It carried as much debris as the river could carry toward the ocean.

Jason approached the edge of the road where the broken concrete ended abruptly. He looked up and down the canyon. The river was swollen and running wild. The sight was a spectacular one-of-a-kind that Jason could not appreciate. Unknown to them, five hundred kilometers away, Kenny dam had finally given way. No one was around to regulate the flow of the dam, and high levels of spring runoff had overflowed it. Being an earth dam it quickly collapsed. On that day, there had been a twenty-foot wall of water that swept through the canyon. By the time it reached the bridge, it was carrying anything that would move in its current and anything that would float. It had hit the bridge with all of its force.

Jason peered into the water and realized its significance. He was heartbroken. If this were the only way across the river, how would they carry on? Would Hannah decide that there was no other option but return to her home?

Chapter 21

It had been one week of hiking since the two of them left Harrison. In that time, Hannah had begun to get to know Jason in a new way. She always knew that he was helpful, intelligent and independent, but his character was stronger than that. He had strengths that she admired in a person. A few short days ago, she had been thinking about what she would do if a time came when it seemed futile to carry on. She would need to make Jason understand that their effort had come to nothing.

As she searched her soul, she couldn't help wondering about her own motivation. Was she hoping for failure? Did she really want to see Jason succeed, or was she just going along for the ride? And what if....What if they actually succeeded? These were just a few of the questions that kept turning over in her mind. Not so long ago she would have been more than happy if the journey came to a sudden halt, so that they could return home to her own sanctuary. That was a mere three days earlier.

She thought about the adventures the two of them had shared in brief time they had been traveling together. Two days ago, Jason had come across a dead skunk. He had never seen or smelled anything like it. Though it was enough to gag over, the two of them knelt beside the carcass and examined it. She explained to Jason about their way of living and their defenses. Jason listened attentively. He wondered how it might have died. It was so decomposed that Hannah couldn't tell, but she did go on to say that she thought that skunks had no natural enemies. They laughed together about the importance of staying clean.

That evening she had pulled a sliver from his hand that began to fester. While she waited for the sun to set, she made a makeshift walking stick. Jason wanted one too. She picked a straight piece of willow that was easy to work with. After making the stick she cut a short piece off of the narrow end, about four inches long and made a whistle from it. She trimmed it so that it had the look of an ancient flute. When she had the mouthpiece looking just right, she scored the bark all the way around, then she took the piece of wood in both hands and twisted it so that the bark came off like a little tube. She explained to Jason that this would only work in the springtime when the sap was flowing freely. It was the perfect time of year. After that, she grooved the wood to control the airflow, slid the bark back over the stick and handed it back to Jason to try out. She explained that she could adjust the hole in the wood to improve the sound. Jason thought it was the coolest thing and spent the entire next day making music…okay, maybe not music…noise! He played it until the bark dried up and it wouldn't work anymore then he spent hours making his own.

As the days passed, Hannah thought about her own loneliness. She began to realize how lifeless her life was before Jason walked into it. She realized she had settled into a routine that revolved around survival and nothing more. She had forgotten that there was more to life than merely living it. One should live it well. She had given up on the idea of ever having a real family or friends. She had settled into the life of conquering hardships.

Today, she faced the obstacle in front of them. She was oblivious to the concern that covered Jason's face. She scanned the river up and down to see if there was any other way to cross. She knew that there was another old bridge just up the river. It had been on its last legs years ago and she wondered if it might still be there. Hannah stepped out as close to the edge as she could and looked up river. Unbelievably the bridge seemed intact. It had been built at a much lower level that the second Alexandra bridge. The concrete column on the west side of the bridge could be seen jutting out of the water. The cables stretching across the river seemed to be in place, though they only appeared above water in a couple of spots. The rest of it was submerged in the mucky water. There was no way to tell if the bridge was passable unless they got a closer look. She turned to Jason. It was then that she noticed the distraught look and the tears streaming down his face.

"Hey, bud…what's the matter?" she asked with a smile.

"It's no use. We're never going to find him. We may as well go back," he managed to get out between hiccupping sobs.

"No. We're not going to give up. There's still hope. The way I figure, he may have passed over this bridge long before it fell into the river. Even if he didn't, there are lots of other ways to cross. We just need to go downstream a ways."

Hannah knew that there was a crossing in Hope. She prayed that they would not have to go all the way back to Vancouver. They sat where the pavement ended with feet dangling towards the roaring water as they ate their lunch. Even on a day such as this, the Fraser Canyon was a remarkable sight. The lower elevations were covered in trees that gave way to steep slopes of multicolored rocks higher up. Besides the normal grays that one would expect to see, there were greens, purples and pinks streaking across the rock faces. Above that, there were snow-covered peaks. Those peaks were formidable and they would have to cross them if they wanted to reach Alberta. It was both an awesome and foreboding sight. The journey had just begun.

With the meal over and the bugs beginning to find them, the two stood up, stretch their arms, cracked their knees and searched the area for a path leading further upstream. Hannah pointed out the ancient bridge. Jason's excitement was unbounded and he scampered from stone to stone looking for a trail of some kind.

They found no path to speak of, but picked their way through the rocks toward the old Alexandra Bridge. They hadn't gone far before they arrived at another impasse. The trail ended abruptly. A sheer cliff disappeared into the water. They stood with the perfect view of the old bridge. The water was so high that the bridge looked as though it might be floating. There was just enough space between the bridge and the water that logs and other floating debris could pass under it. How it had survived, but not the newer one, was another mystery.

For the second time that day, their spirits were pounded down by disappointment. Without discussion they started the trek back. In no time they were on the road again, this time backtracking.

Jason's thoughts were interrupted when a squirrel ran squeaking to the middle of the road. It first ran one way and then the other, scolding them the entire time. After the brief moment of indecision, it scurried into the woods on the opposite side.

By the time they reached the overpass and the highway that led to

Agassiz, Jason was tired and sore. Hannah explained that Hope was just a few more kilometers down the road and that if the bridge was washed out, they would rest there tonight, otherwise they would cross it and spend the night on the other side in Hope. It was enough of an explanation to placate Jason and they trudged on.

The last hour seemed the longest. In the dark, he trees that grew up thick on the edges of the road looked like great black walls. The road was invisible in the dark. It was only by looking at the horizon and the lighter sky above that the walkers could tell where their next footfall should be. Their feet felt their way on the hard surface of the road. They could feel their feet leaving the road when they felt grass or gravel beneath them.

The moon had risen by the time they rounded the last corner and were once again standing, facing the river. The water was high on the bridge, but it still spanned the great river. They crossed without mishap.

Chapter 22

The sun rose on the two companions as they rested in an abandoned furniture store. The building was once an old apartment complex, each room converted into a show room. It was the first building the newcomers stumbled into upon arriving into town and Goldilocksed in one of the rooms still containing furniture.

The building was uninteresting with a large, square, flat roofed. A bed hung from one end as if thrown through the side of the building. At one time, it was an interesting and fun way to advertise but Jason only looked at it curiously. The statement was lost on him.

The two of them hiked down Water Street with the town of Hope on the left side and the Fraser River on the right. The river was high enough that the water threatened to flood the road. Abandoned gas stations and fast food restaurants lined the highway. Once they reached the other side of town the highway split, providing three choices. They could head south to Vancouver, east to Penticton or north along the mountain ridge to Kamloops. Jason looked up at Hannah trying to see if she had already figured out which way might be best. Hannah shrugged her shoulders at Jason giving him an opportunity for some input. She pulled out the map to discuss a strategy.

"This road is called the Coquihalla," she said, pointing to the four lane highway that wound its way uphill. "It's a big highway that bypasses the canyon. We could choose this route and drop into Kelowna here or Kamloops just a bit further on. Kamloops is where we were originally trying to get to but Kelowna is further along the Transcanada highway. That would probably make more sense if we just want to get to Alberta. If you want to try and track your dad, it might be better to try and pass through as many towns that he may have went through," she said as she pointed out the various places along the map.

"What about this other way to…Penticton?" inquired Jason.

"Well, if we cross here, we'll be off of your father's planned route for a lot further distance."

"Well then we should head into the mountains, right?" Jason prompted.

"I'll tell you what, Jason, how about I give you what information I have and then you can make the final decision? Sound good?"

"Okay."

"The main problem that I see using the Coquihalla is that it was meant to be an express route. There are no towns up there for kilometers. Even in the summer, there are usually winter conditions. We would have to be prepared for some pretty tough going.

"On the other hand, to travel towards Penticton we'd be going away from the last known destination of your father, but I don't think we would be up in the mountains very long and there should be smaller communities along the way. We might find it easier to find food and shelter.

"If you think your dad made it out of British Columbia, then we should go to Penticton. If you think he might still be in or around Kelowna, then we should hike up there and see. Either way, I think the safer bet would be to travel to Penticton. Once we're there, we could decide whether to continue on into Alberta or stay in British Columbia. We have to cross this mountain range in front of us either way."

Jason turned it over in his mind. He wanted to get on the way and make the most of the morning, but he also knew that it was an important decision to make. He knew that Hannah would follow him either way.

After deliberating the pros and cons Jason replied with conviction, "I think that it would be best to go to Kelowna. We need to get back to the route Dad was on as soon as we can. I know it may take longer, but if we miss him we will lose all chance of finding him again."

"Then let's get on the road. We need to get over these mountains."

They turned left and walked up the hill. The road was a huge big four-lane highway. Harsh winters had begun to destroy it. Frost heaves broke up the pavement and grass grew up wherever it could find a crack.

Between the dips and turns, the road climbed steadily. They gained altitude, but there were few places to look back over the landscape. They had imagined that they would have a beautiful valley view, but whatever view there might have been was obscured by hills and trees.

Up and up they climbed. The higher they went the colder the ambient temperature became. It felt like they were traveling in a trench. The hills and trees engulfed the sun much earlier. Once it disappeared behind the trees and hills, the warmth was lost and the temperatures quickly fell below freezing. For warmth, they huddled together and pulled their clothing tightly around them. It was late May. In their minds, it should have been much warmer. At this high elevation, when the wind blew it always felt like it was coming from the north.

It was imperative to make short work of the journey ahead. There was no way to predict whether the temperatures would begin to warm up as they traveled or cool down. To make the most of their time, they kept their days long and their nights short. The evening routine began by finding a large spruce tree with a soft needle bed and low lying branches to protect them. It made for an instant shelter where they could hunker down for the night, wake up with the morning light, share a small breakfast and continue on their journey. Their muscles grew strong and their skin dark and leathery.

Chapter 23

The rain began just before dusk. Hannah estimated there was about another good two hours before it would be too dark to travel. Dark clouds cut down the natural light, making it seem later than it really was. It wasn't nearly as late as it seemed. If it started to rain harder, it could be disastrous. She kept an eye out for a place that would make a good shelter. She looked to Jason. He was doing the same.

Rain drizzled. They walked hard, keeping a fast pace. They were far from the summit. The highway led them persistently up hill. The cool rain fell on their sweating bodies. Jason became more energetic. He even tried to catch small drops in his mouth. They hadn't seen rain in days and it was refreshing.

However, the water fell relentlessly. It slowly began to penetrate their protective clothing. Water from the grass slapped against their legs and wicked down into their boots. Jason's toes were getting uncomfortably cold and they were still nowhere near a place that would make a decent shelter. Darkness began to consume the grey backdrop of the storm.

"Hannah, don't you think we should stop soon? It's getting kinda cold," Jason suggested matter-of-factly.

His voice was wavering and she knew he was much colder than he was letting on. They had been traveling across a large open area and so far, she had been unwilling to leave the road. She expected to come across something suitable, earlier. The sky grew darker and darker. "Hey, Jay, hang in there, buddy. If you see somewhere that would make a good place to stop just let me know. We need to get out of this weather."

As night fell, the rain began to change, first to wet flakes and then finally to snow. To make matters worse, the temperature had dropped and the snow began to stick.

The situation was rapidly becoming dire. She had no idea how cold the night might get or how much snow would fall. It would be no surprise if the wind picked up. Even in these conditions, it would be hard to survive. Moment by moment her fear began to grow. Hannah's feet were no longer aching. They were now stinging in pain. Her hands were in no better condition and her soaking wet gloves had already pruned her fingers. She tried to zip her coat up further, but she couldn't grip the zipper hard enough to pull it. She worried about Jason who trudged along beside her without complaint. She noticed him rubbing his hands vigorously together and shuffling his feet in an effort to keep them warm.

At least the thin covering of snow made the road more visible. Rocks and trees lining the road appeared black, while the road was a light gray strip stretching out in front of them. The contrast between the snowy road and the mountains helped her distinguish objects in the near darkness. She pointed this out to Jason.

Improved visibility meant that it was more likely they would be able to find a decent place to hold up for the night before it was too late. They increased their speed, which helped improve circulation. They became more alert and each began pointing out possible campsites to one another. They were desperate and redoubled their efforts to find a place appropriate to spend the night. Scrambling up small slopes continued to draw warmth to their extremities. Though water sloshed in their boots, the act of focusing on the problem at hand increased their chances of surviving.

A dark spot that looked like it might be a cave or overhanging rock was nothing. A tree turned out to be a scrubby pine offering no protection. Undaunted, they searched on.

Looking ahead Jason saw another small dark area that looked worth investigation. Part of the rock face had collapsed and created a jumble of gravel that started at the rock face and ended about halfway across the road. Just above, a boulder that had not fallen protected a small part of the hillside from the falling snow. It wasn't a large area, but maybe it would offer some protection.

The two scrambled up the embankment as best they could. Their feet were numb with cold. Like Hannah, Jason could no longer feel his toes. The protected area just below the rock did not have a conveniently level floor. The rock was part of the remaining rock face. The debris from the landslide sloped away at an uncomfortably steep angle.

"I think this is the best we're going to be able to do tonight. What do you think?" Hannah asked Jason.

Jason was already under the overhang and pushing his back into the big rock and trying to push some of the gravel out of the way so that there was a place he could prop his weight without sliding down the hill. Hannah saw immediately his excellent idea and did the same. Using their feet, they pushed enough gravel away to level out a small area and create a ledge large enough to spend the night.

Unfortunately, finding a place to spend the night was only the first part of the problem. They were both wet to the bone and freezing cold.

"Jason, we have to get out of these wet clothes and we need to get warm."

The clothes inside their packs were dry. The downside was that they were only a light set of spare clothing. The raingear was saturated. They changed into what dry clothing they had and then covered up with the raingear once they had wrung as much water from it as they could. Although the outside layer was wet, there was not enough moisture in it to soak through the dry layer beneath. Their boots were completely soaked so they put on an extra pair of socks over their feet and set their boots aside. Together they cuddled as closely as they could, beginning an uncomfortable and sleepless night.

The morning came quietly. Heavy cloud cover still subdued the light and around ten centimeters of snow covered the ground. To the right and the left, the mountain road wound away and out of sight. The slope continued below them with only the flat section of the road breaking its descent. The stores in their packs had dwindled and they snacked on what uninteresting fare they found inside.

While they ate, they discussed their situation. Even though their journey was still the main goal, they had some immediate needs to meet. Though the day was cold, it was warming up enough to melt the snow. They would wait for the snow to melt and then use the rest of the day to try to find a place that would make a more suitable temporary camp. They needed to get a fire going, warm up and dry their clothes.

The drizzle started up again, even before the snow had completely melted. The travelers huddled together and waited. The sun passed the mid point in the sky before it finally broke through the clouds for the first time. Hannah did not feel they would survive another night without the heat of a fire.

"Well, kid, I think it's time we made some tracks. How about it?"

"Sounds good," he replied.

Jason leaned back to pull one of his boots on and winced in pain.

"What's the matter?" asked Hannah with concern.

"Nothing," he replied.

"Jason, you've got to tell me what's going on."

"I don't know. I haven't looked. My foot stings."

The worst thoughts ran through her mind as she carefully slipped one sock off after another. She expected to see black frostbitten toes or worse. What she found wasn't as bad as she feared, but it was bad enough. She carefully peeled the sock away from the blister that had become an open wound.

The skin was torn away from the ball of Jason's right foot. The blister was soggy and raw. The skin that had once covered it was just a flap. His whole foot looked old and wrinkled.

"Is it bad?" inquired Jason.

"It's bad enough. This must have really hurt. Why didn't you say anything about it last night?"

"I didn't feel anything until this morning. I was hoping it wasn't bad. It didn't really hurt until I tried putting my boot on."

"It's bad alright. You need to be able to walk. We need to get out of here," she said, while digging into her pack.

She pulled out bandages, gauze and ointment. It was worrisome looking at Jason's foot. She cleaned the lint from the wound and used a pair of fingernail clippers to get rid of as much of the dead skin as she could. Afterward she applied some antibacterial medication and wrapped it up as best she could with bandages.

The experience punctuated the need to find a suitable shelter so that they could get warm and dry, refresh supplies and reevaluate the situation.

When she was finished, Jason was able to get his boot back on. It was tender and he favored it cautiously. He would not be able to hike for a full day, but they would need to find a good camping area soon. They hadn't thought to bring materials that would provide emergency shelter. Hannah expected to be able to find many vacant houses along their route. She had not realized how void of civilization the mountains of British Columbia were. The hours wore on. Jason's limp worsened.

On a more pleasant note, the drizzle had given up and the sun was shining.

Eventually, it warmed enough that it became necessary to tuck their rain gear into the straps of their packs. Their damp clothes began to dry. These were the lightest clothes they carried with them, which would not protect them when the evening temperatures began to drop.

They were gaining elevation continuously and Jason found it interesting that no matter how high they got up into the mountains, it always seemed as though they could look up and see more mountains. He wondered how much higher they would have to go before they would finally begin their descent on the other side. Would there ever be a place where they could look out and see the remarkable green valleys that he had imagined?

They gained a lifetime's worth of knowledge about outdoor life in yesterday's unfortunate developments. They were beginning to develop clear ideas about what they would be necessary to be successful getting across the Rocky Mountains. Unfortunately, they were in the middle of a different mountain range that provided its unique challenges. They only had what they brought and they would have to find ways to make due. They would need to make better progress. The summer would soon come to a close. They could not afford to be up in the mountains when the real snow began to fly.

Jason had limped along for the entire day without complaint. Although he was in great pain, he trudged along stoically. Maybe it was because he was afraid that if he became a burden, she would choose to turn back. It occurred to Hannah that maybe he was so quiet because he was a driven young boy who wouldn't let a little pain get in the way of something that was far more important to him. Either way, she respected the fact that he showed such inner strength.

It was nearly dark when they finally came across an outcropping of overhanging rock next to the road, partially hidden by a thick grove of trees. Among the living trees were numerous dead falls as well as dead standing wood. It was perfect. The rock would make a good shelter and there was plenty of wood for a fire.

Hannah picked a location about two meters away from the stone face to start a fire. The previous day's rain had saturated the outside bark of the dead wood. With a small hatchet, she cut a piece of wood about a foot and a half in length. Holding it upright so that the point of one end rested on a log she started to make splinters. The first chips were wet, but the inner wood was sound and dry. Once she amassed a small pile, she used the hatched more like a knife and made much thinner shavings. When she was finished, she had a small pile of dry tinder that would work very nicely to start a fire.

She collected some larger material and stacked it close by so that she could add it as the fire grew. The kindling lit easily and soon the rock wall grew warm as it began to absorb the heat. Later, during the night, the wall would continue to provide warmth for hours after the fire had died down, even if there were only embers left. Jason kept the fire going strong while Hannah fashioned a way to hang the clothes to dry.

The campsite served them well in the weeks that followed. Jason's foot slowly healed. Hannah woke up early each morning to do a little hunting. Rabbits were abundant in the area and provided a good source of protein. Although she didn't have to go far to harvest rabbit, she had hoped for bigger game. It would be perfect if she came across a deer or possibly a mountain sheep or goat. If she could bag larger game, she would be able to use the time to dry some meat and replenish the non-perishable supplies that would be essential to continue their journey.

Jason's foot continued to heal and any large game there may have been steered clear. It wasn't until his foot almost healed and he began making short hunting expeditions with Hannah that she finally came across a number of mountain sheep grazing at the edge of the road less than a kilometer from their camp. She took careful aim and dropped one of them with a single shot. She removed the hide. It looked like it would be warm. Tanning hide would be a valuable skill, but there was no point wishing for the moment. She did not know how to preserve the hide. The next time the opportunity arose, she would add that skill to her repertoire. In the meantime, the two of them took the meatiest portions from the carcass and left the rest. Even before they finished, a bald eagle came to rest on a nearby treetop surveying the spoils it was about to enjoy. Laden with as much as the two of them could carry, they walked back to camp.

They spent the remainder of the afternoon preparing an area where they could fillet and dry the meat. The rock face made a perfect place to dry the meat. The smoke from the fire would add a bit of flavor to it as well, though it would be nothing like the pleasant taste of hickory.

After they laid the meat out to dry, they stoked the fire and kept it going through the night. Once finished, it more closely resembled leather than meat. They wrapped it up in the same material that Hannah had used to store the deer jerky she often made.

She asked Jason how his foot was feeling and whether he thought he could travel on it. His foot was still a bit painful to walk on, but he was anxious to get moving, so he told her he would be fine. Hannah made him promise to let her know as soon as it started to bother him so that she could do something about it—BEFORE it became a problem again! He promised he would, so the two broke camp and began their journey afresh.

The sun was shining once again. The cool mountain air was not nearly as biting. The world is a beautiful place when a person is comfortable. She would make a better effort ensure that was always the case. It was too long a journey to risk disaster and tempt fate a second time.

The day passed uneventfully and Hannah stopped regularly to check Jason's foot. It showed no sign that it was getting worse.

***

The big cat watched from an overhanging rock. It stood perfectly still, camouflaged in the dry brush.

***

Hannah knew they were being followed. She hadn't become aware of it all at once. Among the noises of the wilderness, there were always the normal rhythmic sounds of the woods that followed them along their path. The trees rocked and swayed in time with the breeze. It created its own continuous, predictable and monotonous symphony. Now and again another noise, out of place with the other sounds, not loud or scary, but different enough to draw their attention had become a periodic addition to the music. It would have been easy to dismiss as her imagination playing tricks. A pebble bounced down the slope from above, Hannah swung her head in that direction, nothing. She looked over at Jason to see if he showed any indication of having seen anything. He smiled back at her.

Her feelings of foreboding grew. Sometimes a sound seemed to come from the left, other times it seemed to come from the right. She was beginning to feel silly and paranoid then a sudden movement caught her eye. A brush was swaying, but it was out of time to the rest of the forest movement. Had it been a squirrel or a bird? The hours trickled by.

Then, "Jason, did you see that?"

"You think we're being followed," Jason responded.

"I'm not sure, but yeah, I think we are."

Fruitlessly, they watched the roadsides more carefully for the next hours. There was no further sound or movement. The feeling of tension eased as time dragged on.

105

Then something was different. The hairs on the back of Hannah's neck stood on end. She felt primitively in tune to her surroundings. Jason could feel it too. They picked up their pace.

The sun was beginning to set, but there were still hours before nightfall. Regardless, they decided to pitch camp earlier than usual. Jason saw a suitable area that provided and abundant source of dry wood and an area open enough to give them some pre-warning if something were to appear out of the woods. It was the first time that Hannah felt herself in real danger and she wasn't quite sure how to deal with it. Jason worked diligently to ready the camp area. "What do you think it is?" Jason inquired.

"I'm not even sure we're being followed. But I think it would be wise if we were careful," she said with a smile, hoping he'd believe it.

Jason could tell that she was feigning confidence. He too, felt uncomfortable and unsure. He had always thought of himself as a man. His confidence waned and he slid naturally into the role of the child. He found himself looking to Hannah to make decisions. She suggested they needed to gather enough wood to last the night. He set to it immediately.

Since wood was abundant, it didn't take long. There were still a couple of hours before dark and so they gnawed at homemade jerky as they thought about ways to make good defenses for the night. Hannah chose a spot that would provide good protection from behind. It would leave them nowhere to run to, but it would force any predator to approach from one direction only. Hannah hoped that fire would be the biggest deterrent. Jason thought that it might be useful if he encircled the camp with dead branches. He was excited about the idea of making some kind of an alarm. It would keep him occupied and couldn't do any harm.

"That's a great idea," she said.

Waiting was the hardest thing. It was still too early to try to sleep. They kept the fire going and maintained a watchful eye. As night fell, it was decided that they would keep watch in shifts. One of them would stand guard while the other rested. Jason offered to keep watch first but Hannah would have none of that. There was no arguing with her so Jason settled in while Hannah watched the fire and fed it.

Somewhere beyond the light of the fire, an occasional glint from black glassy eyes flickered on the other side of Jason's stick barrier.

The hours passed and Hannah's eyes grew heavy and glazed. She drifted off to sleep. The fire began to die. Soon there would be nothing left of it but charred embers.

The beast sat watching and waiting from its own resting place. When the fire was no more than a faint red glow, it began to rise on its haunches. Hannah and Jason slept on. The coals grew colder.

The beast silently rose to its feet, crouching. Its body hovered inches from the ground. It stepped silently forward while Hannah and Jason slept deeply. The glow from the fire was barely visible. Hannah's body shivered with cold and then she stirred. The animal froze, its eyes fixed on its quarry.

Oblivious to the danger, Hannah awoke to the chill of the cold night air. She turned to Jason. He lay curled in a tight ball in an effort to keep warm, sleeping soundly. How long she had dozed? She glanced at the sky. Was it graying up preparing for sunrise? It seemed a little brighter. Maybe it would be light in an hour or so. With a nearby stick she poked at the embers and a cloud of sparks rose into the air. She drew a pile of hot ash together and added a couple of smaller pieces of wood. Before long, the fire leapt to life and began to devour what she provided it.

The warmth increased and Jason began to unfold like a flower in the early morning sunshine.

The cat lowered itself to its belly and settled down to wait once more.

Hannah looked up at the sky often to try to decide how much longer it would be before the sunrise. An hour ago, she thought it would be at any minute, but two hours later and it seemed that the sky still looked the same as it did when she first awoke. Another hour had passed by and still there was no change. She wondered if she had slept at all. She shook her head, thinking how tired she would be later. She threw another stick onto the fire and noticed a faint reddish glow from the east.

Hannah tended the fire as the sun rose slowly. The temperature dropped overnight encrusting the world in a sparkling white. Jason woke a little later unaware that Hannah had been awake all night. He was curious about how his barrier fared and made his rounds to inspect it. He interrupted Hannah's thoughts a moment later when he called her name.

The morning sun was already starting to take the chill out of the air and in a matter of minutes, the leaves that were now frosty, would look coated in dew. Hannah came running and stood beside Jason. The image before them was obvious. The grass was matted in an oblong shape. The area was devoid of the frost that covered the ground everywhere else. Hannah reached down to touch the earth. It was still unnaturally warm. She looked back to the fire only twenty meters away and shuddered.

They scoured the area for tracks but were unable to find a clear imprint.

The tracks they could make out suggested that the animal might be a small black bear or possibly a cougar. After a quick breakfast, they broke camp and were once again on their way.

***

Neither Jason nor Hannah noticed, but somewhere along the way, their path began to lead imperceptibly downhill. It would be days before they noticed the difference in the weather. For now, they breathed white mist and shuffled their feet to warm them.

By mid morning, the sun had warmed the ground and the frost disappeared. Except for the foreboding feeling that haunted her, it was a perfect mountain morning. The contrast between the blue sky and mountain peaks was stunning. Birds seemed to be everywhere and were constantly surprising them as they exploded out of the grass in front of them. Occasionally a ground squirrel sat chattering and then barked angrily as they approached.

They stopped for a brief lunch when the sun was at its highest. "I've been watching all day long and I haven't seen or heard anything," Jason stated.

"I've been trying to keep a lookout as well and haven't been able to see anything either. Maybe whatever it was just bedded down for the night and that was all. There's probably nothing to worry about."

Chapter 24

A month ago, the big cat's fur was sleek and thick. Back then, she had her winter coat and didn't notice the cool night temperatures. Now, her coat was mottled and sick as her warm winter coat began to fall out and make way for summer fur.

She rose from her resting place as the woman at the fireside began to stir. It wandered away some distance before it stopped to sniff and paw at a field mouse hole in the ground. One small rodent scurried into the open. The heavy paw came down swiftly and there was an audible crunching noise. She went back to the hole to dig out the remaining inhabitants completing her morning snack. Afterwards she made her way up among the rocks and sat perfectly camouflaged eyeing on the travelers.

She sat silently as the two packed hurriedly and broke camp. The road ran east and west along the north side of a wide gully. The cat backtracked east and then headed northerly up the slope. She made her way silently among the rocks as the travelers meandered along the road some times ten or fifteen meters below.

Throughout the day, she was a shadow—silent, constant and unnoticed. The sun grew hotter as the day wore on. The cat continued her pursuit. Her quarry stopped to rest for a small bite to eat, and her mouth watered as it watched unnoticed. In synchronization, the three—woman, boy and cat—

lifted themselves from their resting spots and slowly moved east.

They were less cautious now. It would not be long before she would catch them unawares. The big one looked like it might have some fight. She was not interested in this one. She was interested in the little helpless one. She would wait for an opportunity. Patience, she reminded herself.

***

The shadows lengthened and the warmth of the sun slipped away with the light. Hannah and Jason made camp and lit a fire. Night creatures drowned out the other sounds. Hannah and Jason slept through it.

The cat's hunger and desperation were beyond control. It had not actively hunted since it began following Hannah and Jason three days ago. Its hunger drove it on. Soon the hunger would be so strong that it would overpower the cat's fear of humans and it would strike. It was only be a matter of time. It stared at its quarry, unblinkingly in the night.

That night the hunter and the hunted entwined in a strange kind of dance orchestrated by the fire. In the dimming light of the dying fire, it raised its body and prepared its slow crouching advance. Hannah awakened, stoked the fire and watched it carefully as its warmth and brightness grew. The cat settled to its belly once again and the dance replayed as the fire died.

On the fourth night, the clouds parted to reveal a full moon. Eerie light bathed the trees and rocks. The firelight did not reach into the night as far as it had on darker nights. The cat rose. It no longer looked with longing eyes at the small boy. It no longer cared about the danger of the burning flames. These, it no longer perceived as risks. The cat was a survivor and it was time to feed.

Hannah and Jason lay sleeping in the light of the fire. Flames sparked and the wood snapped covering the sound of the cat as it crept nearer. Occasionally a twig snapped beneath the heavy cat's paw, but the crackling fire drowned the sound. The weary pair slept on.

Silently the cat crept forward, stopping now and again at the sign of the slightest movement. It crept closer, moving nearer, preparing to pounce. The muscles in the cat's legs tightened and rippled. Without sound, it launched itself into the air. At the same moment, Jason's body stirred. Perhaps he felt the breeze caused by the cat as it jumped. He rolled over, eyes gaping in time to see the cat's face and open maw framed in the firelight. He instinctively kicked, scuttling away from the cat. His feet pushed at the loose dirt as he back peddled away from the cat. He kicked Hannah in his efforts and she woke up with a start. It diverted the cat's focus. It locked on the soft flesh of Hannah's neck.

The cat came down on four paws and reared up on its hind legs. It twisted its body and came down hard on her. Hannah brought her arm up to stave off the attack. The cat's huge mouth clamped down on her forearm. Hannah did not feel the cat's teeth sink deeply into her flesh. She only felt the pressure and the brute strength of the cat as it tore her arm free of its intended target.

Hannah rolled sideways but the cat was quicker than she imagined. It batted at her. The five centimeter claws shredded her jacket and ripped into her skin. Her adrenalin flowed. Instead of pain from the tearing flesh, she felt only a tug on her arm. Using her feet against the cat, she pushed herself away, but again, the cat was on top of her tearing at her throat. Hannah spun sideways under the weight of the animal. The cat missed its target and she felt its teeth sink into her shoulder.

Though the battle had begun just seconds ago, Hannah's strength was quickly slipping away. She was bleeding from a half a dozen wounds. The cat repositioned itself to attack again. Hannah wheeled backwards, warding the cat off with her feet as best she could. The cat worried her from side to side, preparing for a final assault. When Hannah's position was perfect, the cat made its final lunge. There was nothing she could do to stop it. The cat flew through the air at her.

Jason swung a large branch across the cat's path. He managed to check its motion. The cat landed awkwardly and turned immediately on its attacker. Jason brought his stick around and positioned it between him and the cat.

The cat batted it out of the way, but Jason moved quickly, keeping it between them. Hannah was recovering quickly. Her left arm was nearly useless. She reached to her belt and took out her knife. She struggled to her feet and stood beside Jason.

The two of them faced the cat screaming. Jason smashed the log on the ground in front of it over and over yelling, trying to disorient it. Jason's arms were beginning to tire. He was finally able to bring the branch down hard on the cat's shoulder and neck. The cat stumbled back and shook its head to clear it. As silently as it came, the cat turned on its haunches and disappeared into the darkness. Hannah fell to her knees. Jason rushed to her side.

In the dim light of the dying fire, congealed blood from Hannah's wounds was everywhere. Her torn clothing was saturated and it was impossible to tell how badly she was injured.

Jason began to panic. Even in the subdued light of the fire, he could see how pale she had become. He tried to talk to her but her words were slurred and her sentences made no sense. He tried to think clearly but it was so hard. Images of his mother clouded his vision and destroyed his judgment. The possibility that Hannah might not survive, made the task almost too great to bear.

Jason frantically searched for the area where the greatest part of the bleeding was coming from. Blood seemed to be everywhere. Every tear in her shredded jacket oozed. He pushed her into a sitting position. She almost fell over. He righted her and unzipped her jacket trying to avoid cutting it off her. She would need it to keep the cold at bay. He raced, feeling like he was stumbling and wasting time. Hannah was slipping away and he was too slow to stop it. He fought panic.

Her right forearm was injured. Using his knife, he slit the coat from the cuff to the elbow. There were a number of clean puncture wounds. Although the coat sleeve was completely saturated, the wounds seemed to be closing. There was not a great deal of blood loss here. The worst must be coming from elsewhere. Jason was sick with the fear. Already too much blood had been lost.

He told himself that the punctures on her arm didn't matter. This didn't look like a wound that could kill her. The cat had focused its efforts on Hannah's upper body. He continued to search, pulling at the coat, balancing Hannah's body, fighting against time and despair.

He pulled the coat from her shoulders. His hand came away covered with fresh warm red liquid. He worked quickly to cut and tear through her clothing so that he could get a clear view of the wound. The cat bit Hannah more than once in her shoulder area. Some of the puncture wounds were clean and neat while others had torn deeply into her flesh. Jason worked quickly.

One of the cat's attacks had begun high on Hannah's shoulder, at the base of her neck. Blood poured freely, drenching him as he worked. He spun around and grabbed Hannah's backpack. She kept the first aid supplies there. He pulled at the extra cloth and compresses. He folded a compress tightly and pushed it against the wound where it was bleeding the worst. He let it rest there while he positioned the sling. He slipped it around her back and under her right arm. He pulled the two ends together, tying them near the wound. He positioned the compress over the wound and placed the sling so that it would put pressure on the wound as evenly as possible. He cinched it tightly and tied it off.

Jason moved to the other wounds he had found and began putting bandages on them as quickly as possible. He checked her legs and lower torso for any signs that he might have missed an injury.

He finished dressing Hannah's wounds without resting. He was cold and she must be cold too. He made her comfortable where she sat and helped her into a prone position. He took what warm clothing remained and covered her as best he could. Then he began to build up the fire. Jason stood by helplessly. Her chest rose and fell slowly. The fire blazed and Jason kept watch.

Chapter 25

It was well into mid morning before Hannah began to stir. She opened her eyes slowly, squinting in the bright sunlight. She tried to move, but she winced in pain. Jason had been watching her carefully and was waiting for her to wake. He supplied some jerky for her to chew on. She took it from him weakly. She tried to tear off a piece but didn't have the strength to do it. Jason took it from her. He tried to pull it apart with his hands but the jerky was too dry and tough. In the end, he took it between his own teeth and bit off a chunk and gave it to Hannah. She took it from him and began to knead it slowly in her mouth. She slowly broke it down and began to swallow it. She was able to get down a few more bites before laying back again. Exhausted she fell asleep.

Jason was keenly aware of the crisp mountain air. Under normal circumstances, brisk walking would have kept their bodies warm. It had a biting quality that gnawed at them continuously. He spent the day keeping the fire burning, and made sure there was enough food and water available if should she wake.

By mid afternoon, he was so exhausted he could no longer stay alert. He made sure the fire was burning well and had lots of fuel and decided that he would take a short nap. He promised himself he would wake up with the slightest noise. He sat down close to Hannah, closed his eyes and was asleep almost immediately.

The hours slipped by, the sun sank slowly.

Jason bolted upright to a sudden popping sound. It was dark except for the blazing fire. He spun his head to the left to look over to where Hannah had been resting. She was not there. Startled he scanned the area. He was overwhelmed with a sick feeling that something terrible happened. It sucked the air from his lungs. He fell forward on his hands and knees wrestling against vomiting.

He sat back on his haunches, taking a gulp of air, willing his stomach to settle. Obscured by the flames, Hannah sat crouching on the other side of the fire. She fed it gingerly with her right hand. The other she held motionless next to her body. She smiled weakly at him.

"Hey, kid, I don't think I could have done a better job myself. Thanks," she said with a faint smile, indicating her bandages.

"You shouldn't be moving around," he said, his voice thick with concern. He moved toward her quickly, assuming a mother's role. "I'm sorry I slept for so long. You need to get some more rest."

Hannah laughed lightly. "Jason, I couldn't sleep right now even if I wanted to. My back is killing me. Tell you what, I'll keep the fire going and you get a bit more rest."

Jason relaxed visibly, pulling his jacket tighter around him. She had given him permission to be the child. He returned to his rough bed, lay down and closed his eyes. He woke with the morning light in his face. Hannah had already cleaned her wounds, reapplied her bandages and was working at mending her torn jacket. The big cat had not come back.

Her jacket was beginning to look like something from the fourteenth century with its large stitches of thick material. The lines of stitching crisscrossed here and there, as she connected the material in any way she could in order to hold it together. She hoped that it would still be somewhat water repellant. When she was finished, the stitching did hold, and for the most part her coat did the job that it was intended to.

Jason and Hannah stayed and maintained the camp for several days as Hannah's wounds healed. They kept a careful watch and made sure the fire was always burning brightly during the night. If the cat had bothered to stick around, it never showed itself again and the feeling of being watched evaporated along with the cat.

When Hannah was strong enough the carried on. Every now and again, they came across old weathered signs that had long since been left to the whims of Mother Nature. Some had rotted and fallen among the foliage.

Others wait patiently for another winter or two before they too would succumb to the ravages of the mountain climate.

They marched on and it seemed like it had been a thousand years ago since they passed the dilapidated sign that stated they were at an elevation of a thousand meters above sea level. They continued to travel up one steep hill and then down another, dipping and rising, turning and twisting. Even on the sunniest days, at this high altitude, the chill of the mountain air was like a cold fall day. Mid summer struck but who would have guessed. Hannah and Jason plodded on, their food stores depleting.

It was difficult to postpone their journey for the preparation of food. The time it took to hunt took them away from their main focus of getting out of the mountains. Preparation took precious time as well. The road they traveled, neither of them had been on before. On the map, it looked like an easy hike that would only take a few weeks. There were numerous areas where spring floods had either entirely washed away the road or left it flooded. Still other portions of the road were obliterated by avalanches.

Their clothing was beginning to lose its effectiveness. It was beginning to wear out. The fact that Hannah's clothes had been shredded and repaired didn't help matters. As the days passed, the never-ending stresses on garments not meant to withstand that kind of use and abuse, was causing them to deteriorate. Hannah's coat was a rag and Jason's knees had been peeking through his pants for weeks. The shredded material stopped inches above his kneecaps and didn't start up again until it was part way down his shins. In the old days, he would have been hip for his attire.

With trepidation, Hannah decided they must stop again to make a semi permanent camp, replenish their food supplies and try to repair their clothing as best they could. The mountain had taught its lessons well. They understood keenly what might happen if they didn't plan ahead and prepare for the worst. They would have to stay healthy and warm if they were going to complete their journey.

To pass the time they played a game of looking for kilometer markers. It helped keep their minds occupied and had another very useful purpose. They needed to gage their speed to figure out what kind a pace they were keeping. They also needed to know how much farther there was to go. Hannah had kept a rough calendar in her head as they journeyed east and was trying to keep track of how much farther they had to go against how much time they had left before the weather began its turn into the winter months.

Hannah estimated that they were able to make ten to fifteen kilometers each day. Unfortunately, there had been many delays along the way and there had been many days where traveling was slowed down tremendously by conditions out of their control. From what she could tell, it had been about forty days since they began their journey. With the delays and backtracking they averaged, a deplorable, kilometer a day. They needed to pick up the pace if they were going to reach Kelowna by winter. If they didn't make the journey in time, they wouldn't make it at all.

Weariness was another factor and it was beginning to have an impact. Wild game proved to be scarce at these high elevations and there never seemed to be a decent place that would make a good campsite when they needed it. They trudged on eating the last of the mountain goat.

Their supplies continued to dwindle and their spirits continued to fall. They stopped to rest, basking on a south-facing slope and eating quietly when a small herd of mule deer walked into a clearing just below them. It was fortunate that they were upwind of the deer. A light breeze blowing in their direction, brought sound with it as it came. The grass rustled as the hooves moved through it. Without taking her eyes away from the deer, Hannah popped what remained of the jerky she was holding into her mouth. She reached casually for the rifle that lay beside her. Jason sat unmoving, his mouth watering.

A deer looked up periodically to check its surroundings, but the wind held its direction and the hunters remained undetected. Hannah operated the bolt that would allow her to slide a shell into the chamber as silently as she could. There was a slight click when the round popped up from the magazine. To her ears the sound of metal against metal, as she slid the bolt forward, seemed loud enough to startle the herd. For that matter, so did beating of her heart. The bolt slid forward as far as it would go and Hannah used the palm of her hand to rotate it down into its position, simultaneously cocking the gun. The deer continued to feed unaware.

Sitting on the slope, Hannah slowly raised the rifle to her shoulder and used her bent knee as a rest. She leveled the gun and brought the deer into the cross hairs of the scope. She was just uphill of her target and less than a hundred yards away. She did not compensate. The gun had been sighted for this distance. The light breeze would be of no consequence. The target held its position. Hannah squeezed the trigger. Jason jolted as the thunder erupted next to him. Hannah slammed another round into the chamber as the herd bolted in every direction. Her focus remained steadily on her target.

While the other deer scattered her target remained. The impact of the bullet had jolted the body. She knew that it was hit. The animal staggered and then fell, rolling sideways in the grass. It bounded to its feet momentarily as though it had tripped and leapt away in the direction of the rest of the herd. Hannah hoisted the rifle up ready to send another bullet in its direction, but the deer's body became limp in midair and it fell into the grass motionless.

Leaving their packs, Jason and Hannah raced down the hill. There was no moment wasted contemplating the lifelessness of the beautiful animal before them. There was no remorse. Animals were a source of food. They were sustenance. It was a different kind of harvest.

Hannah quickly moved to the throat of the deer. She slid her knife through its skin and flesh, and with one motion cut through most of the soft membrane of the neck. Blood began to flow freely and Hannah moved to the lower part of the animal. With Jason's help, she made an incision that looked like a capital "I." The top of the "I" was created by an incision that connected the front hooves. The bottom of the "I" connected the rear hooves. The center cut ran with the length of the body and connected the two lines.

Within an hour, the hide was laid out flat with the hair down. On it they placed as much boneless meat as they could salvage. Hannah had not chosen a particularly large animal. They needed to be able to carry what they harvested and she did not relish the idea of waste. She had chosen a medium sized animal and by the time they had gutted and de-boned it, there was less than half its original weight.

Hannah glanced around. There had been no time to consider how she would prepare the meat or where they would have to move it. She needed to make a fire and create the materials she would need to dry it.

Looking directly up the hill from where they stood were the packs that they had left behind. Beyond that, out of sight from where they stopped for lunch, was a protected area nestled among the trees. There couldn't have been a more perfect environment for the chores that lay ahead.

Already she had ideas about what she would do with the raw hide. Each of them grabbed a hold of two corners and lifted. It made a makeshift sling for the meat and they carried the whole thing up the hill towards the rock. They laid the hide down among the rocks then Hannah sent Jason back for the packs. She began immediately to prepare the meat for drying. When Jason had finished collecting wood for the fire and started it, he went to work helping Hannah cut the meat into thin strips that would dry quickly. The makeshift working area came together quickly. Jason took green boughs from the surrounding evergreen trees, threw them onto the fire to create the smoke they needed. They used nearby willows to create lattices to support the meat so that it would dry flat.

Tired from the long day's work, that night they feasted on fresh, mouth-watering venison. They maintained the smoky fire and dried the meat through the night. Hannah wasn't particularly worried about the recipe. Her main goal was to get as much moisture out of the meat as she could. It had to dry enough and cook thoroughly enough so that it would keep. That was simply all there was to it. All the effort would be for nothing if the meat rotted in their packs. It would be even worse if they ended up sick from the bacteria that might grow on it. They worked through the night to prepare the meat.

In the following days, Jason's main job was to tend the fire and take care of the jerky as it became dry enough. Hannah turned her efforts to the clothing that was in much need of repairs. She knew that there were ways that a person took care of hide to turn it into leather, but she also thought that she might be able to use the hide raw just as well.

While the hide was still moist, she cut patches from it for the knees of Jason's pants. She poked holes along the edges less than a quarter of an inch apart. The hide would shrink so she took her patches and laid them out to dry. She worked at them periodically to try and keep them from turning rock hard. It didn't help much.

She pegged the hide down in the grass on the slope. It was amazing how much warmth was in the sun. A few days later, the hide was mostly dried.

Hannah carried rolls of thread in her pack. She first doubled and then quadrupled long pieces. Using the largest needle she had, she sewed her new patches onto Jason's jeans with the deer's hair on the inside. When she finished these, she asked Jason to trade with the pants he was wearing and began working on a second set of patches for his other pants.

In the beginning the new patches were stiff and hard. He was thankful that Hannah had put the hair on the inside. As active as he was, it wasn't long before his natural movements slowly softened the hide. Soon, he forgot about them altogether.

It was during the chore of repairing clothing that Hannah noticed for the first time how much Jason had been growing. The clothes that once fit nicely were now beginning to ride up high on his ankles. His shirtsleeves were beginning to look as though they were intended to be three quarter length. When she first met Jason he had come up to her chest. Now his head came to her chin. It was even easier to see the contours of Travis' face in Jason's. He was quickly growing into a handsome young man.

Wood was plentiful. Unpredictable spring weather had long since given way to more dependable midsummer weather. The days slipped by too quickly. When the hide was finally as ready as it could be and the meat stored safely, the companions donned their packs and left their camp without looking back. They had burned another week of summer and both recognized the need to make good time. Already dark clouds settled on the mountain peaks behind. Clear blue skies accented the eastern skies. They were in a race that their lives depended on to win.

They made good progress and each day seemed no different than the next. The sun rose warm in the sky in the morning and that warmth in turn, soaked into them all day long. There seemed always to be a light breeze in the mountains. That, and the fact that they were always on the move, was enough to keep the bugs away. The evenings seemed warmer and the days were long. Places that would make an acceptable camp were abundant. They pushed the daylight as much as possible.

It was late summer when they stood at the top of a hill that seemed as though it dropped into oblivion. There were no longer rises to break their view. The downward trend lasted for as far as they could see. Hannah and Jason looked at each other and then at the giant hill. It was too early to tell, but from where they stood it looked like they were standing at the brink of the end of their journey. Were they on the last of the path that would lead them down into Kelowna? They fought the urge to run. It was likely that they were still days away from the closest settlement. Involuntarily their pace quickened.

Chapter 26

The raggedy pair wandered into the ghost town of Kelowna in the early fall of that same year. They had spent more than three months in the mountains. The weather had not yet turned cold in the valley and the days were still long and warm. The hills were still scattered with apple orchards and produced the Macintosh apples that British Columbia had been famous for. The season was over but Hannah and Jason were able to find the odd late blooming fruit. Their bodies were craving a diet that contained some kind of fruit or vegetable. They took the best they could find and carved away the parts that were inedible. They feasted before continuing their slow march towards what they hoped would be civilization and a warm welcome.

The streets were not as deserted as they had been in so many of the communities in the lower mainland. The echo of children playing in the back streets danced on the wind. It was a good sound, a sound of hope.

They walked cautiously through the streets. This town was just like all others these days. While there was evidence of habitation, it only sported a portion of its original population. Without the roar of automobiles, the streets were silent. Caution was always the best practice and they were becoming experts.

Hannah and Jason moved slowly, believing they were undetected when, as if a switch was flipped, and all the lights were suddenly turned off, the community became silent. Jason and Hannah stopped abruptly. The warm welcoming sounds were gone. The too familiar silence of a town long devoid of people was overwhelming. Their hopes of a warm welcome were suddenly destroyed. Along with the sudden silence, their fears were compounded and the potential for danger seemed to double.

They must have been spotted. A message must have swept through the town. It was easy to imagine children being rushed indoors by their fearful mothers. A new and deadly threat had just entered their secluded community, one worth hiding from.

If Jason and Hannah had been able to look at themselves for a moment, they may have had some understanding of the response to their invasion. The pair looked as though they had stepped out of time. Their clothes were ragged, torn and patched in the oddest ways. They looked more like a combination of animal and old world. Their hair was matted and dirty. Instead of individual strands, Hannah's hair had long since become dreadlocks. Jason's was no better. The dirt on their skin gave them a filthy Cro-Magnon look. It would have been easy for them to understand their welcome had there been a mirror to look into. They may have even laughed.

Instead, their spirits fell as quickly as the noise in the streets. Hannah was acutely aware of the pain in her shoulders from the long haul and the extra load their provisions had added. Jason had been doing the work of a man and carried his share of the food as well as his share of the responsibility. It was more than either of them could bear. It was as if a vacuum filled every space in their bodies. Jason collapsed onto the sidewalk of an old department store and let the carcass of his backpack fall beside him. Hannah joined him and they sat motionless in the shade of the awning.

After sitting for what may have been hours, Hannah reached for her pack. She unzipped a side pocket and pulled out a water bottle. She took a swig and passed it over to Jason. He looked at it indifferently at first and then casually accepted it. Although his body craved the moisture, he had no desire to relieve it. He took a small gulp and passed the bottle back to Hannah.

"What do you think, big guy?" asked Hannah.

Jason glanced from one end of the vacant street to the other. If he hadn't been there to hear the noises of the children playing, he could have easily imagined that the town was empty. "I didn't know it would be this hard. I thought that it would just be a long walk. Now that I think about it, if I hadn't been for you coming with me, I would have been dead ten times by now."

"Easy does it! I know that big cat would have been the end of me if it hadn't been for you. This was never a trip anyone could have done on their own."

"That's my point, Hannah! I can hardly remember what Dad looks like. It's been so long since I've seen him. It seems a lifetime ago that I met you. How can we ever hope to find him? Why did I even try?" Jason burst into tears.

Hannah pulled her pack from between them and slid over to Jason's side. She wrapped an arm around his shoulder and pulled him closer. He let her, and closed his eyes with the familiar smell of her smoky dirty clothes filling his nostrils. "You don't have to wonder what he looks like, Jason. You're his spitting image."

Jason's chest heaved as he rested against her.

Chapter 27

A skinny little whisker of a man ran toward a second man. The second man was the size of a mountain both in height and girth. He was a good foot taller than the little man who ran towards him. The little man was yelling frantically.

The big man put his hand out to slow the little man, but he was running too quickly. Instead of coming to a halt in front of the big man, the little man slammed into his open palm and crashed to the ground. Even then, his mouth continued to fly. "Two men just came into town. One is as big as a mountain. He's here with a shorter one. They're walking down the streets as if they own them! Ya gotta hurry, Harry. Come quick!"

"What are ya goin' on about Fidjitz," demanded the big man. He reached down and using the collar of his shirt, hauled the kid-sized man to his feet.

"I swear. I'm telling you! Two of the ugliest looking no-good-down-n-outers just came out of the mountains. No one comes that way! Hurry up Harry. They're almost right in town."

There had been a number of other people standing around Harry and now many of them had begun to scurry off. Harry let Fidjitz drag him by his shirtsleeve toward the main street. Eight or ten other men joined them. The small group split in two. One group disappeared into the shadows and the buildings. The other stealthily made its way to where Fidjitz had seen the intruders.

When they arrived at the place, the strangers were where Fidjitz had left them. They were still sitting on the sidewalk. From where Fidjitz and Harry stood, they could see a half a dozen other town folk looking silently down on the intruders. They certainly did look the pair. The bigger of the two was clearly armed and if judging by the clothes they were wearing, they weren't the most savory of people. Harry hunkered down and put a finger across his lips to Fidjitz. Fidjitz nodded back and looked seriously on.

For the longest time they stood studying the strangers. Below, the two intruders sat motionlessly on the sidewalk. The watchers were posted silently around the scene in a kind of stalemate.

From where Harry stood, it was impossible to tell much of anything about the two. If what they carried with them was any indication, they were wearing every stitch of clothing they owned. The brimmed hats on their heads covered their features. They sat in the shadows and that made it even more difficult to assess them. They were hulks waiting for…what?

***

Of course, if Hannah and Jason had been able to see themselves they would have been running and hiding as well. Each of them was filthy. There was enough dirt on their faces to hide every indication of their ethnicity. They hunkered on the sidewalk dressed in hides and cloth. Their packs were black and hammered by their journey. If they had ever seen or had been a part of civilization, they didn't look it.

Hannah appeared twice her size in the clothes she wore. They had become all one dark color at some point during the journey. None of this occurred to them. They were too tired, lonesome and dirty to consider their presentation to the community. The stalemate lingered on.

***

Harry watched from above. Suddenly the big fellow moved his pack aside and scooted across to the little man. The little guy leaned against the big man.

Fidjitz elbowed Harry and pointed. Harry's eyes had already begun to narrow. He had begun to look past the bulk of their clothing and the dirt that hid their faces. And as he studied, understanding slowly began to dawn on him. What was that glistening on the little guy's face? Were those tears? Harry looked closer. *Damn this is stupid*, he thought.

125

Harry stepped out into the sunlight ignoring Fidjitz who tugged at his sleeve frantically trying to prevent him from going. Harry shrugged him off.

***

Something caught Hannah's attention. She was sure that she had seen movement from across the street. The moment that they entered the town, Hannah had suspected that it was likely that they were being watched. After all, wouldn't she have done the same? She scanned every door, window and the corners of every building she could see. There were brief fleeting movements among the shadows. Jason noticed that Hannah was beginning to tense. He too sat up and became more alert. He followed her gaze. Suddenly Hannah stood up and walked to the center of the street.

"What is it with you people? Have you forgotten what hospitality is? Are you all a pack of cowards?" Her voice cracked with the strain. If her emotion hadn't been riding so high, it might have been comical. In an instant she demolished any doubt that she was a woman and Jason was a boy. In disgust, she turned to walk back to where Jason sat on the sidewalk.

An incredibly tall stout man in his late forties was already standing beside him with Hannah's rifle resting comfortably in his hands. "No, lady, we haven't forgotten about hospitality, but please don't confuse caution with cowardice. I'll just hold on to this for the time being if you don't mind. And by the way, welcome to MY town. You might recognize it…it used to be called Kelowna." He drummed the rifle stock with his fingers.

By the time Harry had finished his brief monologue, Hannah stood eyeing the big man, wondering what was going to happen next. In a way, she recognized herself in him. She also had fashioned her own town and even back home, she would have never taken wandering strangers lightly, unafraid to put the safety of her town ahead of their sensibilities. She didn't expect any different from these men. She supposed that they were blind to the fact that she was a respectable woman who deserved to be treated with dignity.

Before her thoughts were complete, the big man was joined by a sly looking squirt of a man. Then, at almost the same instant and from every doorway, a body appeared and began to advance upon them. When the movement stopped, they were surrounded by almost twenty menacing-looking figures.

The group of men circled them with Harry standing the closest. Hannah looked from one face to the next trying to determine their intent. The blank stares that were returned gave no clue. Hopefully she was looking into the eyes of a group of concerned citizens who were only worried about their community. Finally Harry spoke. "What brings you two all the way out of the mountains and into Kelowna?"

"Actually, we're just passing through. We were hoping to get some rest, clean up, replenish our supplies and get on the move again. We've been traveling for weeks," Hannah stated simply.

"Where you comin' from? We ain't seen nobody come from the mountain pass in years," the weasel threw in.

"We started out from near Vancouver. Do you know where Harrison is?" Jason added.

"Never heard of it," the weasel bit back. He was a nasty little man.

"Like I said, we've been traveling for weeks. We probably made a big mistake taking the route that we did, but that's just the way it goes I suppose. I'm surprised we made it this far. We've been in more scrapes than I can count, and to tell you the truth I'd be more than happy to tell you all about it if I had a full stomach," pressed Hannah.

Harry smiled inwardly. He liked her feisty nature. Already he had given her the once-over and was thinking to himself that she might clean up pretty nice. "Well, I'll tell you what. I still don't know what to make of you so if you don't mind, I'll just hold on to this rifle of yours."

Without a pause Hannah answered, "I probably won't be needing it any time soon anyway. I've already got this wonderful warm feeling swirling around inside me. I can tell what a wonderful cozy little town this is. I can hardly imagine ever wanting to leave." Hannah's voice was thick with sarcasm. She continued with hardly a pause, "It seems to me like you can do one of two things. You can either hold us prisoner, or you can act like there is still a little hospitality left in this godforsaken country and offer us something to eat and maybe a place to clean up."

Harry smiled unkindly. "I guess that's almost exactly what I was trying to decide. The truth is, lady. There's one other option I was thinking about exercising. We could take everything you're carrying with you and send you packing on your way."

"That would suit me just fine. We made it this far. I'm sure we can keep taking care of ourselves…without your help."

"I can't help wondering how you're going accomplish that. Have a look. Everything for as far as you can see belongs to me. I guess you could help yourself to anything, but then…you'd be stealing from me," stated Harry.

"I'm not used to having my integrity questioned." She could feel her face warming. The tension in the air was electric. "Just hand me back my rifle and I'll forget I ever set foot in this stink hole. We'll be out of here so fast, by supper time tonight you'll have forgotten we were ever here."

Jason knew that Hannah would never back down. In desperation, he jumped in. "Listen, mister. We're more tired, dirty and hungry than you could ever imagine. We just want to sleep where it won't snow on us."

A switch flipped and Harry's face softened. "We'll you sure as heck must be one tough pair to be travelin' on those high roads. The fact is we've *never* seen anyone walk out of those mountains. I'll tell you what. Our little community isn't nearly as hostile as you seem to believe. I'll lend a hand to a couple of fellow Canadians. Heck, I'll even invite you to my own home for dinner. By the way, everyone in these parts calls me Harry."

Hannah put her hand out for her rifle.

"I don't think you'll need it while you're in town. I think I'll hold on to it for a bit. We'll see how things go." Harry turned to walk up the street toward the center of town. The small crowd parted and the three headed up the street together. Fidjitz followed along behind, not dissimilar to a dog.

The crowd stayed with them until they mounted the steps of Harry's home. As he opened the door, he turned to the crowd with a look that seemed to say, "What on earth are you still doing here?" It was enough. Everyone except Fidjitz scrambled away. He stayed on Harry's coattail even as they walked up to the door. Without acknowledgment, Harry closed the door, leaving Fidjitz standing alone on the other side. Fidjitz looked blankly at the door for only a moment before sitting down on the steps to wait.

Inside, Harry led Hannah and Jason to the kitchen. He offered them a chair. Hannah was surprised to see him pop a couple of mugs of water into a microwave oven, punch a couple of buttons, and then turn it on.

"Hey, Maggie, come down here and meet our guests," he called, apparently talking to the house.

Hannah heard movement above them and a few moments later the familiar pounding of footsteps on a staircase echoed through the building. A gaunt looking woman in her late forties, wearing too much makeup and a bright red dress overloaded with frills, poured into the room. She reminded Hannah of an old saloon hostess from a western movie. By the sound of her hurried steps on the stairs, she expected the person making the noise to be excited and happy. Instead, her eyes were cold and lifeless. If nothing else, maybe a hint of fear could be detected in them.

By the time introductions were complete, the timer on the microwave went off and Harry pulled out the steaming cups. He opened a cupboard and brought out a container of instant coffee and a package of hot chocolate. Jason's mouth began to water immediately.

Hannah wondered at the show of it all. A cup of cold water would have been great. But still, she was surprised to see so many of the old familiar conveniences that she had been accustomed to in her childhood.

"Your curiosity is obvious. Why don't you let Maggie show you the bathroom and you can freshen up. Later you can ask all the questions you want. I'm quite proud of our little northern treasure. I would be happy to tell you all about it over dinner."

The house more closely resembled a mansion. There were several bathrooms on each floor. Maggie first took them to where Jason was to clean up.

Hannah tried hard to hint to Jason to keep his belongings with him. Something was up with Harry and until she figured out what it was, she wasn't going to trust him at all. She glanced back at Maggie as she closed the bathroom door. There was only one word to describe Maggie's getup...bizarre. Hannah left the clothes that she had been wearing on the bed, but took the rest of her belongings into the bathroom with her. She hoped that Jason would have some forethought as well. She need not have worried.

The water from the shower was absolutely heavenly. She turned it on as hot as she could stand and let it flow over her head across her face and down her body. She put a generous amount of shampoo into her filthy hair. Although it did not work up lather the first wash, she still felt it doing its work. She washed all over savoring every moment. It was more than a cleaning she was looking for. She needed a spa treatment.

A half an hour later, she emerged feeling new all over. She returned to the bedroom to complete her grooming at the vanity that was there. On the bed beside her old clothes was a complete fresh set. She had been supplied with undergarments, a tee shirt and pair of denim shorts. Not the cutoff kind either. On the floor, there was a pair of real leather sandals.

They were taking a bit of a chance thinking that she might like this style. She smiled inwardly anyway. It was perfect. It was warm in the valley. The warm summer sun was absolutely inviting and she felt totally refreshed. It was a great start.

When she brought her bag downstairs, it was so disgusting she didn't want to touch it. She hadn't noticed it much before, but now she was keenly aware that it reeked of campfire smoke and old sweat. It was not a pleasant combination. The pack was more dirt than fabric. There was no one waiting for her when she got out of the room so she made her way back downstairs.

There were kitchen noises coming from somewhere below. On the way through the main living area, she noticed Jason's pack in a corner and sat hers beside it. Always cautious, she listened carefully and gave a quick inspection of the main living area. It was furnished with beautiful solid wood pieces. Artwork covered the walls. Other than the fact that the room had a very rich feel to it, there was nothing of interest.

From the great room, she passed through an extra wide opening into a luxurious dining area. There was an antique solid wood table that looked as though it had never been used. Tucked underneath were a series of matching chairs. They were absolutely magnificent. In the center of the far wall were two large ornate swinging doors. The voices were coming from behind them. She listened, but Jason's voice wasn't one of them. She could definitely hear the voice of Harry and the woman he called Maggie. She chose the door on the right and it moved freely as she put her weight against it. It opened into a large kitchen stocked with everything a professional chef might need.

Harry and Maggie stood beside an island counter in the center of the room. A third person that Hannah had never seen before was busy preparing a meal. Hannah half expected there to be an air of tension in the room but there was none. Her concern rose. Jason was nowhere in sight. Hannah's heart began to beat a little faster, but she kept her composure and hoped her agitation wasn't noticeable. If Harry or Maggie noticed, neither of them showed it.

"Where's Jason?" she asked with a smile.

"My goodness, don't you look absolutely marvelous? Doesn't it feel good to get out of those old dungarees?" Harry chimed in, avoiding the question.

Maggie, who had been happily carrying on a conversation only moments ago, was now silent. Stepping around the pleasantries Hannah responded, "Thank you so much. Has Jason come down from the bathroom yet?"

"Isn't he just the most precious little boy you've ever seen? Harry said, directing the question to Maggie.

Maggie's lips turned up into something that was supposed to be a smile, but the lack of emotion made it painfully clear she was only smiling because it was expected of her.

Harry ignored her and turned back to Hannah. "Maggie and me never could have any kids. We tried and tried."

"Yes, Jason is very special." Hannah was doing her best to try and imagine why Harry was trying so hard to avoid answering her question. Before she could press him further, Harry continued with his own agenda.

"Where's his father? A boy and his mother shouldn't be out travelin' all alone. I'm surprised a pretty thing like you would even dream of such an unbelievable adventure."

Hannah was becoming quite distraught and there was no way she could hide it. Harry stood, watching her reactions. It was clear that he was getting some kind of satisfaction from it, but she couldn't figure out why. She looked back over her shoulder towards the main floor bathroom. As if reading her thoughts he added to end the suspense. "Jason's just out in the back yard. Come on. Let's go see what he's up to. I thought he might prefer to play in the back yard while he waited for you."

From the kitchen, they went through a mudroom. The back door opened onto a porch. The porch overlooked a huge back yard. There must have been more than four acres back there. Near the center was a large tree. Hanging from it was an old tire swing. Jason was swinging happily back and forth. He seemed mesmerized by his surroundings. He looked up when the screen door slammed shut and the noise caught his attention. The moment he saw Hannah, he leapt from swing and made a beeline towards her, running straight into her arms. She hugged him tightly. Then she held him out at arm's length to get a better look at him. He had been provided a shirt, jeans and a brand new pair of running shoes. He was so excited that he spun in place with his arms out to show off his new apparel.

"Hannah, look at these. Have you ever seen anything so great? I wish my mom could have been here to see this. She would just flip!"

Harry raised his eyebrows. "And all this time I thought you two were mother and child. Were you being sneaky, Hannah?"

This time Hannah had no doubt about Harry's smile. There was no warmth in it at all. She may as well have been looking into two black beads. They reminded her of a rat's eyes. She did her best to give the impression of confidence. "I guess if you had asked and I told you that he was my son, you could say I was misleading you. As far a sons go, this young man is more a family to me than anyone ever will be."

Hannah's tee shirt exposed the injury on her arm the cat made. The scar was still a deep red. It ran from her elbow and disappeared beneath the sleeve of her shirt. Hannah indicated to it now. "If it hadn't been for Jason I'd be out there somewhere instead of standing here getting the third degree from you."

The conversation was interrupted as the maid came onto the porch. "Dinner's ready."

"Now that is perfect timing. Let's all relax while enjoying a great meal," Maggie added, trying to break the tension.

Hannah kept Jason close as she followed Harry and Maggie into the dining room. Something wasn't right. She couldn't understand why the host and hostess were acting so strangely, but until she could figure out what was going on, she would try and stay as close to Jason as possible.

By the time the meal was over the sun had set. The sky was a beautiful red and purple color burst that lit up the horizon in the west. Under other circumstances it would have been picture perfect.

Over the course of the meal, Hannah suggested several times she and Jason should finish up and see about finding suitable accommodations. Each time, as though he didn't hear, Harry carried on with whatever conversation he was leading. With the sunlight, nearly gone Hannah was again becoming more agitated. Jason could feel the tension as well.

She needed to make herself understood, but she wanted to find the right words. She wanted to be forceful, but not confrontational. How could she manage that? She felt like a fly in a spider's web.

Normally she wouldn't have put up with the mind games that Harry and Maggie were playing at, but she couldn't help feeling that if she pushed hard she and Jason could end up prisoners. In fact, she felt as if they were already.

Fidjitz came bursting into the room as the meal came to an end. He ran directly to Harry and began to whisper something into his ear. Harry listened intently. His face was a dark mask. When Fidjitz had finished speaking, Harry turned nonchalantly to Maggie. "Maggie, why don't you show our visitors where they will be sleeping tonight? I'll be back in a bit."

Hannah noticed that Harry had given her no choice. She made sure to grab her bag as Maggie led them upstairs. Jason followed her lead. He was shown to his room first. Maggie motioned him inside and closed the door behind him. She continued down the hallway. On the opposite side of the hall, she opened a door for Hannah.

"Sleep tight, deary," Maggie said as she turned to leave. Hannah began to look over her surroundings when she heard the ominous clicking of the door's lock. She ran quickly to the door to try the handle but it was locked tight. She could hear Maggie's footsteps as she moved down the hall. There was a pause. The woman was too far away for Hannah to hear but she figured she was probably stopping to lock Jason's door. Her fears were confirmed a moment later when Maggie cackled as she descended the steps, "Sleep tight all."

Hannah listened as her footsteps disappeared down the stairs. It didn't take Jason long to realize what had happened. She could hear him banging and kicking the door, making as much of a racket as he could. Perfect. Maybe he would keep it up for a bit.

Hannah surveyed her surroundings. The windows were barred. It took her only moments however to see a much easier way out of the room. Though the door had been modified so that it could be locked from the outside, whoever had engineered it had overlooked a very important aspect of the door. The hinges were on the inside of the room. Hannah dug through her pack until she found what she was looking for.

The multi-tool she always carried was where she left it. She opened it up and found the awl. Using the tool, she slammed it up into the hinge to drive the pin out. A couple of hits with the palm of her hand quickly told her painfully that it was a bad idea. She needed something with a little weight to use to strike it. Without hesitating, she walked over to the dresser and using her foot, she broke off one of the legs.

Using the dresser leg as a mallet, she made short work of the pins. Moments later the door was off its hinges. She retrieved her bag and left the room. Before going down the hall to help Jason, she propped the door back into place. At a glance, it might look as though everything was where it should be. She quickly ran down the hall towards Jason's room.

Jason was still hammering loudly on the door. It took several moments to get his attention. Hannah's worst fear was that he would start screaming as if she was Maggie, which would draw unwanted attention. "Jason," she hissed. "It's me. Calm down," she said urgently.

"Hannah, she locked me in! Help me get out of here. We've got to get out of here. Hannah. Hannah. Are you still there?"

"Jason. Shhhh. I'm right here. We've got to move fast. Get your things together. This will take me a minute."

This time she used a screwdriver to pry the doorjamb away from the doorframe. It was held on by only a few small finishing nails. She wasn't concerned about getting it off in one piece. She was only worried about getting it off near the latch. In moments, she was jamming her knife behind the latch, pushing in the latch allowing the door to swing open. She threw the bits of doorjamb onto the bed.

Jason was already out of the room waiting for her in the hall. He kept watch in the hall in the direction of the stairs, making sure that no one was coming. Hannah carefully closed the door and together they moved toward the stairs.

Quietly they made their way to the main floor. The lights were still on all over the house. It was impossible to tell where anyone might be. Everything was silent. The living room was empty, which was a bonus. Light was coming from beneath the dual swinging kitchen doors. Hannah took Jason's hand and pulled him to the left side of the door. They stood with their backs against the wall listening carefully. Again, they could hear nothing. With her left hand stretched out flat against the door she pushed against it, opening it just a crack. She could see about half of the kitchen. That much was empty and silent.

Hannah let the door slip back into its original position and then shifted to the opposite side of the door. She opened it and could see the rest of the kitchen. It too was empty. With relief, she turned to Jason and motioned him to follow.

Jason heard footsteps coming up the hallway off of the main living space behind them. He pushed Hannah the rest of the way through the door and slid into the kitchen. Without hesitating, they ran to the outside door. They slipped through and Hannah held the knob so that there would be no clicking noise when the door closed. She guided the screen door back into its place.

Chapter 28

Jason and Hannah slipped into the dark, while nightlights flooded the fields surrounding the prison that still functioned a few kilometers outside of Kelowna.

Each of the prison cells was part of the original structure, but there had been many additions and modifications made since it was originally constructed. At one time it was a maximum-security prison complex that housed some of central British Columbia's most renowned criminals. Its function wasn't significantly different although it no longer contained criminals.

The prisoner stood facing the bars with his face pressed between two of the cold, hard metal cylinders. A normal-sized man would have stood there with his cheeks resting, one on each of the adjacent bars. But this prisoner was a lot skinnier than most men and had paid for it with a lifetime of being teased, taunted and tormented. He could feel the cold metal far back on his face. Only his cheek bones stopped him. Like a ring one size too small, it felt as though only his skin prevented him from being able to slide right through the bars.

This was not the first time that he found himself at the brink of despair. Uncountable weeks had passed since he was first introduced to the cell. It had become equally impossible to count the number of times he had tried to get out of his cell in this way. It could never be said that he was a fast learner, but he was persistent. He twisted his head one way and then the other. He pushed as hard as he could. The cold rusted metal scraped against the sides of his face. Although the pain was terrible, he could feel his progress. It encouraged him to continue to work his way forward.

He pushed harder.

His cheekbones cleared the bars, and then his face suddenly passed through. His ears quickly followed. Unfortunately, his triumph was short lived because he realized immediately that he was now in a terrible fix. He could neither go forward nor back. His injured face had begun to swell. And now his head was acting somewhat like a fishhook. He tried to pull back into the cell, but his ears and the bones of his face kept him from being able to pull free.

In a panic, he began to yell.

His cellmate came from behind him. They had been through this before. In the past, the cellmate had tried to calm him. He had tried to find something that would act as a lubricant to help his stupid friend slide his head back into the cell. There was nothing he could do to make the situation better. The man was a fool and understood little.

The cellmate barely hesitated. He took a short step back. He swung his leg forward. His foot came to an abrupt stop against the idiot's tailbone. The air instantly went out of the trapped man's lungs and he slid to the ground in pain with his head still trapped on the other side of the bars. He lay there motionless, whimpering quietly, clutching his ass.

"I bet you licked a frozen metal pole when you were little," said the cellmate. "What the hell do you think you're doing screaming like that?" Part of him wanted to leave it at that. He may have as well, if it had been the first time the idiot had pulled the stunt. "You know what they'll do if they see you like this. They'll solve your stupid problem all right. They'll come in here and take your head right off." He snapped his fingers loudly to make his point. "Are you so stupid that you can't figure that out for yourself?"

From down the corridor a heavy metal door swung on its hinges. A bright light spread across the floor. The elongated shadow of a guard filled the hall from one end to the other. The normal din of the block was replaced by silence as all breathing was temporarily suspended. For a long, time the guard stood looming in the hall and then as quickly as he came, he turned and walked away. The door swung slowly closed leaving the prisoners in the dark once more.

The idiot whimpered. He looked like a cow ready to be milked with his head in the feeder. He only needed a feedbag and a milk bucket to complete the picture. He certainly wasn't going anywhere anytime soon.

There wasn't much to talk about in a cell shared with a man who was unable to speak. And there certainly was no point in carrying on a conversation alone. The idiot had pulled this stunt one too many times and this was all the excuse the cellmate needed to go on a verbal rampage to no one in particular. He ranted unceasingly for an hour at the man trapped between the bars. In disgust, he left the idiot with one last parting thought before returning to his own cold corner.

"Shut your trap and stop your damn whining."

The idiot continued to whimper softly between his clenched teeth.

"Shut up! Otherwise you can stay there until breakfast comes."

This time the idiot followed the directions that were given and closed his mouth. If nothing else, it proved he had some understanding of the language although he almost never used it.

As the hours passed, the idiot continued to kneel stupidly on the floor with his mouth gapping. The other inmate paced slowly back and forth as the hours crawled by. A small puddle of drool had begun to form in front of the idiot who paid no attention to it.

The night wore on, and the temperature in the cells dropped steadily. It was cold at the best of times and now the idiot's teeth chattered audibly. Out of necessity, the two prisoners usually huddled together at night to keep warm. The clothes that were provided them were not intended to do more than provide only the most basic protection and a little privacy. Any of the prisoners could drop dead and there would be no human that would mourn. Those who died were the lucky ones.

The idiot continued to grow colder and colder. It had been a part of a plan. When he was cold and tired enough it would prevent him from making such a fuss for what had to happen. It was what the cellmate had been waiting for. There were no sedatives here. He would have to do what he could. Exhaustion and near hypothermia were the best substitutes to be found. He walked up to the idiot and emotionlessly stated, "Be still."

The idiot was too cold and tired to move. The cellmate lifted the idiot's head and squared it to the bars. He pressed the idiot's ears hard against the side of his face and began to feed them slowly between the metal rods. The idiot whimpered quietly in response to the pain. Somewhere in his near unconscious state, he knew how precarious his situation was. Pushing hard and steadily, the Good Samaritan slowly forced the idiot's face back through the bars. His beard slowly peeled away and with it came plenty of skin as well. There was no ceremony or rejoicing. The Samaritan left him by the bars and retreated to his own space to get some rest.

Outside of the prison gates, the sun was rising for the rest of the world. Inside the cells, there was no hint of sunlight in the dark hallways. Without warning, the door at the end of the hall clanged open and light flooded in. It was a familiar occurrence. Three burly figures lumbered down the hallway. Except the occasional glint of light reflecting from their eyes, the guards were silhouettes. For the idiot, it seemed as if only minutes had passed since he was freed. Still, he raised himself from the floor and scrambled to the darker corner of the cell.

It was too early for the regular morning routine that was used to move prisoners to the worksites. This was a separate activity used to keep prisoners frightened and well behaved. A large brass key had been inserted into a square lock that was set into the barred door. There was an audible clicking sound inside the lock as the key did its work. The door swung on its rusty hinges.

A few moments later the three guards passed by a second time, traveling in the opposite direction. The guards held a reluctant figure along between them. The two hundred men and women who remained in the cellblock collectively sighed in relief. It had not been one of them.

The idiot scooted closer to his cellmate and they huddled shoulder to shoulder against the back wall. They used each other's body heat and that was enough to keep them alive for the time being. A small metal door slid open in the wall just above them. Another daily event that they had become accustomed to, took place. A wet gooey slop came through the hole and landed in a disgusting heap on the floor. It wasn't that the glop had landed on the floor that made it disgusting. It was the fact that it was a gooey thick white sauce of the most disgusting consistency. The goop landed in a pile on a part of the floor that was sacred. It was a place that was never walked upon. It was kept as clean as the prisoners could keep it. There were no utensils provided. The floor, the goop, their hands…breakfast, lunch and dinner. When the last of the stuff fell through the small opening the steel door slid closed with an audible clang.

The cellmate thoughtfully fondled the ivory colored bone he wore around his neck. There was another cellmate before the idiot had come along. That one left him the bone as a souvenir. One day he had reached up into the hole as the food was coming through. He had intended to try and hold the small door open. Unfortunately, he lost two of his fingers in the process. They were delivered neatly with the next meal.

It hadn't taken the long for the man to become sick and weak. His hand had become infected and useless. Soon his own uselessness matched the uselessness of his injured hand. Not long after that, two guards came at dawn to take him away. He did not return.

The bone seemed to give him strength somehow. It reminded him that life was short and dangled by a thread. It was worn shiny from constant rubbing. The inmate wasn't sure how long ago it had been. It might have been years. Time was a difficult thing to keep track of when there was no way to mark its passing.

Each morning, after the goop was served, the guards came down the hall to release the prisoners into the sunlight. They looked neither right nor left. There was no hesitation. The prison doors along the hall opened as if they were one and the prisoners entered the hallway. Once in the hall, the guards did a quick pass-by, glancing into the cells. The idiot stayed low, hidden in the darkness of the cell. He had barely eaten his share of the meal and had not slept the night before. The guard walked up to him and shook him. When he did not get a satisfactory response, he backhanded the idiot into unconsciousness, slammed the cell door closed and left him behind.

The rest of the prisoners marched out of the cellblock two abreast up a short flight of stairs, through security gates, the exterior doors and into the blinding light. They stopped only briefly to meet with prisoners from the other cellblocks in the prison. It was a hodgepodge group of men, women and children.

The group followed the fenced area around to the east, a few miles behind the prison to a plateau. On top of the plateau was an old open pit coalmine. The guards led the prisoners to the mine where they worked until dusk.

The ore was taken to the west of the coal mine to where it was refined and stock piled. It was the fuel that provided heat and electricity for the town. The stockpile was already large enough to supply the town with power for decades.

For the prisoners it was grueling work. Folk who worked the mine did not have a long life expectancy. Without the heavy equipment that would have been used to move the ore, it had become more beneficial to sink individual mineshafts. The shafts brought their own kind of dangers that included gas pockets and cave-ins. Death at the mine was a daily occurrence.

The idiot's cellmate looked up and down the ranks. Most of them were frightened and bewildered. Their faces wore a broken look that he had long since grown accustomed to. A stench of fear filled the air. It was a disgusting display of broken human flesh. Most of the people who stood around him were already corpses waiting to be buried. They were devoid of any personality to speak of. There were few prisoners who could look up and meet his eyes, but they revealed themselves to be no more than human husks more closely resembling fearful animals.

A noise came from somewhere behind him. He turned in time to see one of the members of his group throwing up. He had once thought about forming alliances and friendships but had decided not to bother. What was true then was still true today. There was no point introducing himself to anyone. It didn't matter at all that his name was Travis Banderman.

When he had first arrived, like any inmate, he was stripped of everything that he owned. What they left to him were only the rags that he now wore. When or if it was decided that his clothes should be replaced, then like his food, they would be thrown unceremoniously into a clump on the cell floor. The only belonging that he could really call his own was the bone that hung from his neck by a cord he had fashioned from the hem of his shirt. He found himself stroking it gently as his thoughts wandered. What kind of man had he become? There was no chance to finish his thought. The group was moving and he could not afford to fall behind. It had proven fatal for many. He still had some will to survive; some hope of escape.

Chapter 29

What would have taken a half of an hour for a free man to hike took the prisoners nearly twice as long. They dragged themselves to the crest of the plateau and looked into the seemingly bottomless pit that gaped before them. They braced themselves for the knee pounding descent that would end in front of their respective mineshafts. Most of the prisoners were seasoned and were no longer emotionally and physically affected by the routine. New prisoners were wide-eyed and nearly paralyzed with fear. There may have been a third group of those biding their time and hoping for an opportunity to flee, but they were either too small in numbers or too wise to be visible.

Travis had often toyed with the idea of flight, but looking at this broken group reminded him of what he had always known. They would be of little help when or if an opportunity presented itself. He stood among them and wondered what he might look like in their eyes. No, he was not a pinnacle of strength himself. His cell had been his home for so long he could hardly remember life before it. Before long he would stand before his own mineshaft looking into the depths of it. For now, he found himself longing to be home. He wondered what had become of Sarah and Jason. Facing the daily task assigned to him was one thing, but when the memories came flooding back it made the idea of carrying on almost unbearable. He shook back the tears that were already welling up in his eyes. For now, his cell was his home—and his life.

Thinking of the cell brought his mind full circle, where it came to rest back on the idiot. There had been so many times when he would have liked to have seen them take him out of the cell and away. He was utterly exasperating at times. It wasn't always easy to remember to be patient and kind.

Through all of the months, they had shared the cell he never seemed to be able to get a firm grasp of the spoken language. Travis had never really taken any time to try and understand why that might be. It seemed pointless. When he considered it, he could have had worse company to be sure. The idiot would usually respond correctly when he was spoken to, which proved he had some understanding. In many ways, he was more similar to a mongrel dog than a human being. In the last months, Travis had become both his teacher and his protector. There had even been the odd tender moment. It occurred to Travis that the idiot had become something to him as well—a friend. Not so long ago he had finally given the idiot a name, Al.

Enough of that, he thought. His cellmate had been a gibbering idiot without the sense to keep his head in his cell. There had been countless times when he had pulled Al's wedged head free from the bars. He counted back briefly and came up with at least a half a dozen. He shook his head with a faint smile. As futile as it might seem to anyone else, one thing could be said for good ole Al, he never gave up.

Travis looked around at his own impossible plight. Maybe he had learned something from the idiot after all. The group had wound its way down the spiraling roadway of the mine. They were being released and set to their individual tasks. The moment for thought, hope and dreaming had passed. It was time for the real work to begin.

The prisoners broke into smaller groups and made their way silently to their individual shafts. The mineshafts wound this way and that following the thin veins of coal ore wherever they ran. In intervals that were spaced too far apart, makeshift coal-lanterns lined the rock walls.

The mining was accomplished with the most rudimentary tools. There were other dramatic solutions available, in the form of explosives, but they were never employed unless there was no other alternative. The workforce was expendable and the value of explosives was very much higher than a human life.

Travis looked at the crew around him. It consisted of nine other men. There were no women or children among them. It was their job to sift through the ore and select the best of it. It was impossible to determine its quality in the dark depths of the mine. Although the guards were ruthless, even they understood that. Sometimes a few of the stronger boys were sent into the mines. In many places, the shafts were small and tight. There were places where a boy's small body was the better tool for the job.

They hiked until they reached the very end of their tunnel and then the group of ten broke into two groups of five and their tasks were divvied. One of the men took hold of a pick while Travis reached for a shovel and began to fill the buckets with ore. As soon as he finished filling one, one of the other three men picked it up and began the long hike out of the mine. Throughout the day, they switched their assigned jobs as necessary. It was backbreaking no matter what position was worked, but the long walk out of the mine gave the miners a chance to stretch their legs, if not their backs.

The day wore on and the wagons were slowly filled. There were two wagons for every group of ten. Each team of five was responsible for its own wagonload. The day was over when the wagon was full. No point in finishing early either. The day was long enough as it was and the miners were forced to work through all of it. They were digging for the full duration whether they made their quota or not. The payoff was to finish on time and avoid the penalty. Work steady, work hard and fill the wagon before dark. It took approximately three hundred buckets of ore to fill each wagon. No time for talking. There was only time enough to load the wagon before dark.

Travis had started his tour working with this very group. He could still remember his first day. There had been no warmth from the other prisoners. They were all too tired and too overworked to care…unless he didn't pull his weight! Then they cared. Then they cared plenty.

Of the original group there were only two members left and he was one of them. The other was a hard man who Travis felt sure hadn't yet resigned himself to his fate. There would be hell to pay if the crew failed to meet quota. First, there was hell to pay the guards, but then there was still the payback to this man afterwards. Travis couldn't blame him. There was nothing worse than being saddled with a couple of greeners and then have to follow them around all day and wipe their noses. It was worse still to fail to meet quota because of them.

Today was one of those days. There were three new men assigned to the crew. One of them had replaced Al. They looked fit enough, but they looked more scared than anything else. Why shouldn't they be? If it had happened to them like it had happened to Travis, they were lulled into a false sense of security before being captured. They were wined, dined, and then showed what a wonderful little town they had stumbled into. They were given a hot bath, fresh clothes, a hot meal and a comfortable bed. Unfortunately, for Travis the bed hadn't last the night.

These new men were probably exhausted from the long trek that had brought them to this Godforsaken hole. They had closed their eyes and had fallen asleep to visions of sugarplums. They were rudely awoken to find that they were tied hand and foot. They were dragged to a wagon and eventually dropped in a dark cell with nothing to look forward to but a hard day's work and eventually a bullet to end it all.

Now that he thought about it, it was what was likely to happen to the idiot. There was no point feeding what couldn't earn its keep. If Travis made it through the day, he'd find out if there was a new cellmate waiting for him when he returned. Another bucket was full. He had ten more to fill before rotation. His turn on the pick was next...a harder job by far. The crew could only fill the wagon as fast as a man could dig.

Although the newcomers looked to the old-timers to see what was to be done, no encouragement was offered. It was just that way in the mines. At least these newcomers knew enough to get their asses in gear. They'd learn the rest as time passed.

The day wore on like every other day had done before it. The wagon was loaded and the crew hiked back to the prison in the dark. Although it still took hours, the hike back always seemed to pass more quickly as the way it is with repeated long journeys. Travis absently wondered about Al. It was highly unlikely that he would still be in the cell.

Chapter 30

Outside the prison, the sun's position in the sky indicated it was near noon. Inside the cell, it may as well have been midnight when the idiot regained consciousness. He sat crouched in the dark corner nursing the growing lump on his head. "Idiot" was just as good a name as any for this man. He was hardly a man at all, really. Everything that he had demonstrated in his limited life proved that he was a poor specimen of a man. He had no memories of his parents or the home he must have had when he was a child. He once had parents. That fact was inescapable, but he had no recollection of them or any name they may have given him.

The first time he'd been greeted as if he was anything other than a beast was by Tavs on that first day when he was thrown into the cell. Over the months that followed, he had come to recognize two names. Sadly, they too would eventually fade from his memory, much the same as everything else, but Tavs had given them both to him. The first was Al.

Travis had come to understand that Al had very little understanding of the world around him. Whatever ailed Al made it next to impossible for him to learn anything new or remember recent events. He had only the most rudimentary knowledge and understanding of the English language. When Travis first decided to name him Al, he did not expect to begin the arduous task of teaching it to him.

It wasn't long after he gave Al his first name that Travis gave him his second…"Idiot." It seemed to make no real difference to Al. He didn't know what an idiot was anyway. Travis was certainly nicer to him than anyone else had ever been. What frustrated Travis most about Al was his inability to remember anything. He came to believe that Al's short-term memory lasted only a few minutes…just short of the time it would take to put those thoughts into the way back part of his mind. The part that would allow him to remember the lessons that he learned, the experiences he had or even that the day had passed.

For no reason other than his own personal optimism, Travis was convinced that if Al was brought up in a normal household he might have, one day, overcome some of the challenges that faced him. It was an important belief to hold. If Travis expected to help Al, he needed to believe that his work would come to some good. And, in some ways, it had. Progress was slow and hard, but if Travis could compare Al's abilities today with the first day he arrived in the cell, there was really quite a significant difference.

If Al could talk, he would tell Travis that he always impressed him. He would say that he was sure he could always remember how strong and smart he thought Travis was. There was a time when he was afraid of Tavs as he was of the guards.

From the beginning, it seemed very important to Al to communicate with Travis. It was difficult to understand the many strange sounds of the English language. He knew that he could never hope to understand the world the way Travis could.

Al wasn't an idiot at all. Under the severe circumstances of his birth, he was deprived of oxygen for just a few moments too long. The resulting damage that occurred to his brain caused him the difficulties that would last his lifetime.

In frustration and despair, Al's parents had left their teenage boy to fend for himself. These were years lost to Al and for that he was blessed. He would never remember the daily horrors that were a normal part of his life. Each new morning brought fresh questions, but never any answers. Scars he would never be able to explain covered his body. Al did grow up but he grew up oblivious to all but the most basic skills.

Travis ran into a number of insurmountable problems when it came to Al's education, the biggest obstacle being his physical disabilities. Al had never really spoken. Travis believed that he never learned to speak. He could make out some simple words but the noises that came from his mouth were akin to hushed whispers. Maybe he was embarrassed to try or maybe he was unable to mimic the sounds that Travis tried to teach him.

Although learning was slow and difficult for Al, there was one thing he knew without a doubt. Captivity was a harsh and unpleasant way of living. He rediscovered almost every day that if only he could get his head through the bars, maybe the rest of him would follow. It was simple enough; the only way out of the cell and the prison was through the bars.

Chapter 31

Al waited until after the guards were gone. It would be a long time before the hall door would open again. He walked up to the bars and placed his face firmly against them. He began to work his cheeks from side to side forcing them forward all the time. Part of him was familiar with this. His cheeks were still raw from the previous night's ordeal. He could remember being this far before and knew he could progress further. Again, he worked his ears through and the rest of his head followed easily.

He rested.

This was as far as he'd ever gotten in the past. Tavs had always been there to help him out when he had grown calm. Tavs wasn't here this time. Al was alone.

When his body had recovered, he stood up and turned his body sideways to the bars. His head was naturally narrower than normal, but that went along with his slim frame. He started first with his arm and then his shoulder. His shirt added too much thickness so he removed it and laid it close by. Using the same technique as he did with his head, he slowly forced his upper body between the bars. He exhaled as much as he could and forced his chest and ribs to flex as he forced himself through the narrow opening. With each painful moment, and not unlike birth, he pushed his way further between the bars. Al took shallow breaths. There was no room for his chest to expand to allow for the expansion necessary to allow his lungs to fill with air. It wasn't until he felt sure that he could stand the pain no longer that the last of his ribs passed between the bars. His stomach moved aside to make room for the bars. He collapsed on the floor, half in and half out of the cell.

He was dozing quietly when he heard heavy footfalls drawing closer. The sound was coming from somewhere on the other side of the door, far down the hall. Al began to panic. He was pinned to the floor with little mobility. There was no going back. He could not push with his legs as he had the previous night. The most he could do was wriggle his lower body while pushing with his hands against the bars.

Al twisted his body and cocked his hips. Instead of working his entire hip area as he had done with his face, he focused on just one hipbone at a time. He could feel the skin peeling away as he made slow progress, but adrenaline and fear were more than enough to counteract the pain. The sounds of the guards' steps grew closer. With an audible pop, the ball of his other hip cleared the bars and the rest of his body followed quickly. At the last possible moment, he grabbed the clothing that he had shed earlier. He ran towards the door.

Just then, the doors swung open and the guard appeared. Al stood behind the door with less than a foot separating them. Al held his breath. The guard completed his brief survey and satisfied that all was well, turned and left the cellblock. The door swung closed behind him.

It was impossible for Al to tell exactly how long he stood behind the door and waited. He had learned to keep important ideas in his head by replaying them over and over. The image he now replayed was of the guard walking down the long corridor. In Al's mind, he kept walking over and over from one end of he hallway to the other. When he could hold on the image in his mind no longer he ran to the door and looked through the little window. He was a very small man, but when he stood on the tips of his toes, he could see out. The hall was clear. The guard was nowhere in sight. He slipped through the door as quietly as possible.

Even though it had only been yesterday that he passed through the corridor on his way to the mines, none of it was familiar to him. He could remember that he needed to get out and that it wasn't going to be easy. He couldn't even remember what he was supposed to do in the mine until someone put a bucket in his hand. He was on his own today and already the urgency to leave the building was fading. He was having trouble remembering why he was in this unfamiliar place. Ahead of him were empty corridors. Behind him? He turned to look. There was a large metal door with a small square window in the center. Curiously, he went to it and opened it and then the memories came flooding back. He was sure that someone from inside the cellblock hissed at him to go, but it was only one of his own thoughts rattling around his skull. It was such a unique occurrence that he didn't recognize it for what it was. He listened to the voice and went.

Somehow, Al's feet managed to lead the way for him. He had learned long ago not to trust his memories. They were quiet shadows that seemed more like dreams than reality, but it was those dreams that he relied on now to help him. As if some inner instinct had taken control, he followed his intuition. He did not second guess or waste time wondering which way was the correct path. He trusted the ghosts in his head. He stayed low and left the building as quickly as he could.

Most of the guards were out looking after the prisoners while they worked at their various tasks at the mine. The few who remained had the easy task of looking after a nearly empty facility. There was never anything going on and mostly they slept or played cards.

Once outside Al headed towards the trees. In the brush, he found a safe hiding place and there he rested. The prisoners returned, chains clanging, but Al slept through it.

Chapter 32

Maggie came into the living room and found the door to the kitchen still swinging back and forth on its hinges. She immediately thought of their guests and ran to the foot of the stairs. She could see the first bedroom where she left Jason. The door was closed. Instead of going directly upstairs to check the rooms, she turned to the kitchen. She slammed through the door only to be greeted by the silent stainless steel appliances. She ran immediately to the exterior door and yanked it open. She was just in time to see the gate swing lazily into its original position.

Maggie spun on her heel, raced back upstairs, and unlocked the door to Jason's room. She saw the molding lying on the bed. Jason was nowhere to be seen.

As quickly as she entered, she turned and ran up the hall towards Hannah's room. With key ready in hand, she put one hand on the doorknob. The door overbalanced and fell into the room. Maggie's face paled. A thousand thoughts should have been running through her head. Instead, her entire face slackened and lost three shades of color beneath her heavy makeup. Like a sleepwalker, she stumbled to the bed and slowly sat down on it.

When Harry returned, the house was unnaturally silent. He went from the kitchen to the other rooms on the main floor. The house seemed empty.

Emotionlessly he reached into his pocket and produced a metal object about four inches long. With a flick of the wrist, he transformed it into a knife. With his back to one wall, so that he could either look up the staircase to the hall, or down into the living room, he worked his way slowly up the stairs.

He wondered casually if he had underestimated the woman and the boy. He scanned the rooms as he passed by them until he found Maggie sitting solemnly on the bed. He did not acknowledge her, but left her sitting there as he walked downstairs, turning off the lights as he went.

Chapter 33

Hannah and Jason ran into the street and away from the house. An occasional light illuminated a window, but otherwise the streets were black. The pair raced silently towards the outskirts of the city.

There was no time to worry about choosing their next destination. It was more important to get to a safe location that would allow her and Jason to take some time to think and get reoriented. Why was it necessary to make the hardest decisions under the most adverse circumstances? It had become a way of life for her. She discovered long ago that it was a skill that could be developed and honed.

Together the fugitives scurried through dark back streets. They ran for an hour without stopping, before slowing to an effortless jog. Regardless of the fact that there was no evidence that a search party had been formed, she wanted to be a safe distance from Harry and Maggie before she looked for a place to rest.

The streets formed a standard grid. It was easy to keep track of the general direction and distance that they had traveled. Hannah knew that they were at least a couple of kilometers away from where Harry lived and that suited her just fine.

It was now time to worry about the numerous, apparently vacant houses. It would have been nice to have been able to slip into one of them, but she had no idea how populated the area had become. She would not risk entering a dark house. They stumbled through the unfamiliar streets, past what appeared to be uninhabited homes and then beyond. After an eternity, the city houses began to thin.

Tired, worn out, and nearly collapsing they stumbled into a barn. Feeling her way into the dark interior she found her way to a supporting post in the center of the building and the attached ladder. It creaked and moaned as they warily climbed up. Although the loft smelled musty, remains of hay still littered the floor and seemed dry enough. They drew enough together to make a soft cushion and lay down to sleep. It was long after dark. It wouldn't be long before the morning sun would begin to shed its warm glow on the surrounding countryside.

The moment her head touched the hay, Hannah began to turn over the evening's events in her mind. She could hear Jason's deep breaths above the rustling noises of the mice and other rodents that inhabited the barn. Questions filled her mind. The day was lost in a flurry. There had been no time to become acquainted with the town. There was no time to develop allies. By morning, their bellies would be telling them it was time for breakfast but they had little food. It would be hard to choke down the deer jerky after the feast she could still taste in her mouth.

Questions haunted her thoughts. Why had they been deceived with false hospitality and then locked into their rooms at night? Why had the townspeople, at their first arrival, surrounded them the way that they had? What were they planning on doing with them once morning came? Where did their power come from while everywhere else hydroelectric dams were slowly breaking? The province was slowly shutting down, but from what she could tell, Kelowna still enjoyed the comforts of the old world. There were so many riddles to unravel. Too many.

The morning sun rose on the old gray barn. Birds began their morning search for food and the world began its ageless routine oblivious to the changes around it. The adventurers slept through it. Hannah awoke first. She took the opportunity to survey their surroundings. The barn was an ancient old style one with a loft above and individual stalls below. At the front of the building there was a large opening in the loft that used to load hay through. Above the door was a block and tackle. There was no longer a rope to hoist whatever was necessary up from the ground below. Along the side, where the roof and floor met lay an old hay elevator. It looked like a conventional conveyor. There was a motor attached to one end that once drove the chain that once moved hay from the truck to the loft. Hannah could imagine the farmer's children or a hired hand waiting to stack it neatly.

Other than the old elevator and the hay, the loft was empty. The roof was made of ancient shakes. Each year it rotted a little more. She could see the sky through the multitude of holes in the roof. In one section, a beam had given way and part of the roof littered the floor where it caved in.

Hannah walked to the ladder they climbed the night before. She was amazed that they made it safely up. The rungs of the ladder looked ready to fall off. Some kind of animal had eaten almost all the way through many of them. In her days, Hannah's parents had kept horses. It had always been hard to keep the wooden fences in good repair. The horses continually gnawed at the wood forcing them to replace the boards one by one. That's the way these rungs looked, as if some kind of an animal had been chewing at them. She thought about the bale elevator. Later she would throw that down and use it instead to get to the ground.

Among the many possessions in her pack, Hannah carried a pair of field glasses. Sometimes she considered taking them out all together. She rarely had need of them, but today she dug them out of the bottom of her pack and headed to the loft opening. They were high enough off the ground that she could see a little of the town and surrounding area. It looked as though they were south of the city center by several kilometers. They were also uphill quite a bit. The view was good. Across the valley on the opposite hillside, Hannah could see the even rows of trees that signified an orchard. There were other flat areas that looked like cultivated fields. Some might be corn while others looked like they might be some kind of grass crops. There was even evidence of livestock grazing on higher slopes.

The organization that was evident was amazing. Her amazement was punctuated by the rumbling in her stomach, but she would have to ignore it for now.

Even with the binoculars, the city was impossible to evaluate. From where she perched the city streets were invisible. Except for the wind rustling the leaves of nearby trees, the whole world was silent. Out of the north, from somewhere in the hills, a black plume of smoke rose silently into the air.

Something about this place was extremely odd. Someone, she couldn't remember who, had noted that no one had come out of the hills in a very long time. If they had tried to capture her, maybe there had been others. She went back to the hay where she had made her bed. Jason was still asleep. By the look of the sun and the feel of its warmth, it seemed to be about mid morning. She lay back down to try and piece the puzzle together. She must have been more exhausted than she thought. Before long those images became dreams.

Chapter 34

A clamor from below snapped Jason out of his deep slumber. It must be Hannah. He was about to yell down to her when he saw that she was still asleep beside him. He rolled towards her gently placing his hand over her mouth. Her eyes flew open. A shocked look appeared on her face, lasting until she heard the shuffling from below. Jason removed his hand and the two lay motionless. At least two men from below were talking.

"I don't know why we're here! It's not as if they're going to hang around. They're probably long gone. You see anything back there?" enquired one.

"Nope, nothing," reported another.

"Check out the loft and we'll get outta here."

"Are you joking? You get up there yourself. Take a look at that ladder. It's not worth it to me."

"Listen, you useless sack of crap. Get your ass up there and check it out or I'll end this argument with a bullet here and now!"

The second man grunted. There was a pause and then the sound of his weight on the lower rungs. He slowly climbed the twelve-foot distance between the two floors. Hannah and Jason sat motionless, afraid to breathe. The distance continued to close until Hannah was able to see a shock of hair peek through the hole in the floor. She would give him only a moment more. When he looked up she would jump quickly to her feet and knock him backward through the hole. With any luck that would disable him and it might give them a bit of a chance to escape. Either way they would go down fighting. Every muscle in her body tightened as she readied to leap, a tigress preparing to spring.

The man's hand reached for the last rung. He clasped it firmly and began to draw his weight upward. The rotten wooden rung gave way. His arms flailed as he fell backwards. He managed to get a hand on the next rung down, but the momentum of his body was already too great for the rotten wood. He continued to break his fall against consecutively breaking rungs as he tumbled down the ancient ladder. He landed in a heap on the ground with the only way up into the loft in ruins.

The man standing below got the man to his feet. There was a brief huff of disgust followed by the sound of retreating footsteps. A few seconds later, Hannah and Jason crawled to the edge of the barn. They watched as the men disappeared into the brush. Jason smiled with some satisfaction. One of the men was favoring his leg, evidently in some pain.

"Jason, this couldn't have worked out any better. They'll move their search somewhere else and as long as we stay low and out of sight we'll be fine."

"What about food, Hannah? I'm sure getting hungry," added Jason.

"Take a look on that hillside over there. What do you see?"

"It looks like a bunch of fields. I don't know about those rows of trees on the right."

"This whole area used to produce quite a few different crops, including fruit. I imagine that's what keeps fat-cat-Harry eating like a king. How about we check it out?"

"I can taste it already. Let's go." Jason was already moving towards the bale elevator.

"That's the thing, isn't it?" frowned Hannah. "We need to get across the other side of town without being seen by any of the locals. From the treatment we got earlier and by that search party that was out for us, I'm suspecting that it might not go as easily for us if we're caught again."

As Hannah spoke, Jason scanned the city below. His fear of being caught wasn't an issue at all. Simply, they would not be caught.

On the valley floor a river ran. A number of bridges spanned it. They could get to the river, but they would still have to cross it once they got there. Some of his questions could only be answered once they got closer. Then Jason's eyes fell upon what might be a partial solution. Behind the barn and far up into the mountains a ravine began. In the early spring, water would fill the gorge with rushing water as it flowed to the river. It looked like a jagged cut through the city, a dark green swath of trees snaking its way toward the river. It was a continuously forested area that would offer cover as they worked their way toward the river. It was broken in only a couple of places where the road crossed it. He pointed this out to Hannah when he saw it.

Through the course of their journey, they had spent countless hours together and it was beginning to show. Sometimes it was as if they were able to think as one. By the time Jason's gaze met Hannah's they were already thinking the same thing.

"Perfect! That will definitely get us down to the river," Hannah said.

Getting to the river was only one part of the problem. On the other side of the bridge, the entire area was fenced and one field bordered the next up and down the entire length of the valley. There were no trees to offer sanctuary. It was getting late and it would be dark before long. "If we leave now, we should be able to cross near dusk," Hannah continued.

They hauled the bale elevator to the edge of the loft and pushed it out. It teetered for a moment and then they controlled its slide to the ground. Within minutes, they were entering the gully that led to the river. The undergrowth was thick and dead trees littered the ground. It made progress slow, slower than they anticipated. The old trails that children made had long since overgrown. What remained were game trails that zigged and zagged through the brush leading downhill towards the river. There was the occasional carcass of a shopping cart lying with weeds choking every hole made by the crisscrossed heavy wire. A little bit farther along they looked into the creek to see an old baby stroller without wheels, tossed there years earlier. It was rusted through in numerous places and the cloth seat the infant would have sat in was long gone. Only a few small tattered remains of cloth were attached to the rivets. Even after people were long gone from the face of the earth there would be evidences of some kind of strange culture, artifacts that would serve more to confuse than to enlighten.

The evening came and went and the sun began to sink in the sky. It was hard to tell if they were making good progress. Now and again, they saw the remains of a broken down old fence through the brush, but that was all. The sun sank lower and lower. Soon objects became darker shadows among shadows. They rested briefly and considered stopping for the night when Jason noticed an open clearing just beyond them. They were just a few meters from the graveled edge of the road that blended into old broken pavement. The road turned to the left and then onto a bridge that spanned the river ahead of them.

Secretly, Hannah was half worried that the bridge would be brightly lit or even guarded. It was neither. The sun was gone and it was almost completely dark. The great gray expanse was only slightly brighter than its surroundings. The bridge disappeared into the darkness on the other side and it was impossible to tell how far below the water swirled on its path to the ocean. They stopped to listen carefully. Even their breathing seemed too loud. Hannah could hear Jason's long exhausted exhales, each making room to draw in another deep breath. Everything else was silent and the way seemed clear. Hannah knew that once they got onto the bridge there was probably not going to be a chance to turn back.

Cautiously they stepped out into the open. Hunkering down they scrambled across. They neared the halfway point when they stopped and turned, paralyzed by the sound of voices. There must have been dozen people maybe more, moving towards them. Besides voices, there was the distinct sound of shuffling feet and the occasional clanging of metal. The soft glow of torches joined the sounds. The torches looked like poorly hung Christmas tree lights as they bobbed along the road drawing nearer and nearer to the bridge. The group moved quickly and with purpose. Hannah and Jason stood motionlessly in the darkness.

In panic, Hannah ran to the edge of the bridge and looked over. A slight shimmer showed only that the surface of the water was far below, but told nothing of its depth. It was late summer and there was no guessing whether it was safe or not. The distance between them and the lights was closing rapidly.

"Jason, get ready. We need to move quickly if they turn onto the bridge," Hannah spat in a harsh whisper.

The noise and lights swung momentarily away as the group rounded a small bend just before the bridge. Jason stood frozen. If there had been enough light for Hannah to see more than just his silhouette, she would have been greeted by a stark white face filled with fear.

She did not wait to see if he was coming or going. She grabbed him by the wrist and they moved swiftly along towards the opposite shore as quietly as possible. A moment later the party of men stepped from the road onto the bridge. The sound of their footfalls on the pavement changed pitch though the rhythm of their steps remained constant.

"Time to swim!" Hannah stated. She turned toward the edge of the bridge but Jason remained frozen in place behind her.

***

Some swimmers fear that below the surface of the water there are weeds waiting to entangle feet, body and arms, waiting to pull the swimmer slowly down if they could. The swimmer could struggle to get free, but the more he struggled the tighter the tendrils would hold. The swimmer's next breath would not be clean rich air, but the dark cold water.

Another fear is that the water is full of eels or sharks lurking just below the surface. Once the swimmer begins rhythmically moving his feet, legs and arms, he has suddenly become more than just a swimmer. He has become a giant lure. The creatures of the water sense the movement and come rushing in. A short frenzy of movement would follow and the water would turn a deep red.

These are fears that some swimmers have.

Jason's fear was much deeper than this. In his mind, those fears would have had form. Jason's had none. In the world he grew up in, there were no pools of clean wonderful water to learn to paddle in. In the world Jason grew up in, not even the water he washed with was safe. He did not see escape in the direction that Hannah was pulling him. He saw most certainly and without a shred of doubt that to leap from the bridge would be the same as suicide.

When Hannah ran to his side and grabbed a hold of his hand to lead him to the edge his body had already become as rigid as steel. Hannah walked toward the rail with his hand in hers. Suddenly she no longer tugged at his arm. It had become a cable. She looked back surprised to see that he had hunched down and braced himself with both feet. Hannah's body was yanked to a sudden halt, forcing her to take a step backwards.

In the moments of indecision, the torches gained on them significantly. The lights were moving quickly and would soon be on them. The halo of light grew closer and closer. Hannah looked from the approaching men to the opposite end of the bridge. There was no time to hesitate. There certainly wasn't any time to discuss the issue with Jason. She grabbed his arm with the expectation of lifting him clean off his feet. Simultaneously she whirled and hauled him away from the approaching lights as fast as she could move. Jason didn't have time to brace himself this time, but it didn't matter. They weren't headed toward the water. Within a couple of steps, he took over the use of his own legs and together they ran without looking back.

Once across the river the distance between the ground and the bridge closed quickly. As soon as it was possible, they leapt over the side and slid down the embankment. Without hesitating, they scrambled into the shadows under the bridge. Stomping feet pounded overhead. The sound of the footfalls changed once more as they moved onto the road.

After the rabble had passed, Hannah and Jason edged quickly up to the road. They were just in time to see a group of people, flanked on either side by armed men, disappear into the darkness.

There were questions for Jason to answer. She would try to remember to ask him about this later. In the meantime, there were other more important things to consider. The answers were marching away into the darkness. Hannah was up and moving staying just beyond the light of the torches.

Chapter 35

Harry arrived at the worksite as the sun began to rise. He stood overlooking an ancient open pit coalmine. It was the key element to his empire, the one he spent the last ten years creating. He stood on the edge looking out. It stretched a full kilometer across and three hundred meters deep. A lake had formed at the bottom. There was no telling how deep it might be. There was no method available for pumping the water out or draining it, so Harry employed traditional strategies. Wherever there was evidence of a coal vein, a shaft was dug into the rock. Workers milled about like ants. Some moved in and out of the shafts carrying buckets of ore. Others manned the horses and periodically brought wagonloads of low-grade coal ore up the spiraling roadway. There was activity all along the trail from the lakeshore to the surface where Harry stood surveying his accomplishment. The work force below was impressive, but the greatest concentration of the workforce was invisible. It was far beneath the surface where rudimentary tools were used to dig and haul the ore.

The raw material was first brought out of the shafts where the ore and rock was separated as well as possible. The tailings were dumped into the lake at the bottom of the pit. Already a huge pier had been constructed. Anyone who had any background in geology and mining would be able to see clearly that the mine would not produce ore for very much longer. Harry knew this all too

162

well, but he didn't care. It didn't matter. He wasn't community building. His goals were baser than that. The electric grid that the coal powered had its own limited lifetime. It was a toss up which one would last longer, the coal or the power plant. Soon electricity would truly be outdated.

Harry stood proudly overlooking the industry and found himself reminiscing. Before the collapse of the economy, Harry had been a successful entrepreneur. He had started several small businesses, brought them to fruition and sold them for handsome profits. His intent had been to play his game of real life monopoly until he had enough to retire on. And he had finally reached that point.

Then the bottom fell out for the whole world and prospects turned for the worse. Even that was okay. At first, it had not been a huge setback. As long as money had value, he was in good shape. He used his nest egg and maintained his lifestyle for as long as he could. There was a brief in-between period that had been very difficult, but he quickly remedied the situation. Harry smiled at that thought. He was still remedying that situation. He lived as he never before imagined and the power he wielded and the control that he had over the lives of those below him was intoxicating. He positively glowed. In his world, there were two casts. There were those who enforced his rules and there were those who lived by them. It was his job to make the rules.

Today he had a particularly enjoyable job to do. He had two of them really. He turned to Fidjitz who stood drooling beside him. Harry would never describe Fidjitz as his right-hand man. He didn't trust anyone that far. It just wouldn't do to let anyone have that kind of power. It wouldn't be worth the risk of a challenge for leadership.

***

Fidjitz was a nervous little man who both feared and adored Harry and Harry's way of life. His job was simple. It was to deliver information. He did his job well and with enthusiasm. He loved nothing more than to see Harry put into action. This singular ability made him feel more powerful even than Harry, at times. In Fidjitz's mind Harry was his gun and Fidjitz was the man behind the trigger. He too, was particularly happy today. It was a very good day. Today he was going to do more than just point Harry. He was going to use him to kill someone who he had come to hate.

Fidjitz's mandate was to identify any potential threat to Harry or their way of life. Often the threat was as simple as someone who had contrary ideas too willingly shared. If the threat might eventually create an undercurrent, it was a risk too large to take. Fidjitz gathered information; he gathered his evidence.

When he had enough evidence to share with Harry, he loaded the Harry gun. He fed the information to it and the Harry gun always made the same predictable decision. There was no trial, no publicity, no ceremony, no proclamation, no lecture AND no leniency. Fidjitz pointed and a man of his choice disappeared. It was his game of solitaire. Harry was his pawn and he loved it.

A week ago, Fidjitz had picked just such a target. He had been contemplating it for a while. He played back the events that led up to today with a sick glee. She would have made a nice one. It was supposed to be natural. She was supposed to fall in love with him. Granted no one else ever had, but that was the "old" Fidjitz. This was the new one. Now he had an important and prestigious job. Now he was the second most power man (if not the first) in the entire community, maybe even the second most powerful man in the whole entire world. She would be pleased to be with him. He was sure that she would be. How could she not be?

With his chest puffed up and his ego stoked, Fidjitz confidently approached the woman. He went to her and looked into her eyes. He could already hear the words as they flowed effortlessly from his mouth. In a moment, he would start a new life with his new companion. They would live happily and contented.

That was the way it was supposed to happen. There was no chance it should have gone any other way. There are those times in a person's life when everything falls into place perfectly. Fidjitz had been sure that this was one of those moments. It was his moment.

It could have been his scruffy mat of filthy hair that he didn't seem to care much about. It could have been the fact that he had a bad posture and his back was slightly hunched. It might have been that the few remaining teeth in his head looked like small black pebbles and that when he smiled the stench was toxic. It could have been that he was just a skinny runt of a man and that every piece of clothing, no matter what size, seemed to hang off of him making him look a bit like a scarecrow.

In the woman's eyes and the number one reason that she was completely repulsed was that he was a rotten corpse of a man who lacked even the smallest sense of humanity.

Fidjitz, who was the second or maybe the first most powerful man in the entire world, recognized the obvious immediately. It was undeniably clear that the woman found him thoroughly repulsive. His mouth gaped. The words that he had only moments ago rehearsed were gone without a trace. He uttered no sound. Thoughts about a future with this woman vanished just as quickly. It was as if they never existed. Fidjitz turned away. The woman would pay for the way she made him feel. She would pay for thinking she was better.

Fidjitz stood at the brink of the coalmine standing next to Harry. He had aimed his gun and his gun stood poised ready to fire. It was with satisfaction and pride that he now handed the high-powered rifle to Harry. Shells were hard to come by and they were never wasted.

The woman walked out of the mine carrying a bucket load of ore. Without warning, her body flew backwards and landed motionless on the ground. Those who stood around her had had no time to react. They merely gawked. They heard the report from the rifle a heartbeat later. A few people may have looked up toward the sky to try to see where the bullet had come from but Harry was too far away and besides, he was already walking away. It was going to be a busy day today.

The woman was of no consequence really. She was probably lucky. Had she managed to have hidden her disgust and made a move from the mine to Fidjitz's side, it would have been a different kind of hell, not necessarily a better one. Her name is lost.

Fidjitz had felt sure she would want him. She worked below with the slaves. She was in the lowest cast. They were all expendable. Fidjitz offered the world to her. Even as he followed Harry, he had already forgotten her. Far below, workers carried her corpse to the end of the pier and threw it unceremoniously into the water. Work continued.

According to Fidjitz, the woman was a disruptive force. There were countless replacements waiting. Every day, they wandered into town or demoted from other ranks. Labor was in greater supply than coal. One less worker would make no difference.

Harry wondered at times about the information provided by Fidjitz, but it really didn't matter. Fidjitz would never dream of breaking the golden rule that Harry had given him. Fidjitz's rule was simple…make no mistakes for the worse. Simply put, if Fidjitz did not provide information in a timely manner and if some kind of uprising took place as a result…Suffice it to say, Fidjitz would only make that mistake once. The fact that he was still breathing attested to his infallibility to date.

Harry's next stop was the fields. He had an assessment to make and a decision would follow. He rode to the cornfields in the horse drawn wagon with Fidjitz riding in the seat beside him. He pulled the reins to bring the young paint to a halt along side the barbed wire fence. On the other side, a crew of men and women harvested corn while guards looked on. Harry had come to have a look at one of the slaves in particular. The slave in question was a tall man who wasn't heavily built, but his muscular body rippled in the sun. Harry noted that he was working separate from the others, which suggested that he had removed himself socially from the group.

Harry watched him work for a long time. The slaves were given a water break during the day and it was this that Harry wanted to be around to watch. There was large drum of water with a spigot on the bottom. Hanging from a small chain was a single dipper, a dipper everyone shared. The workers lined up. There was a rudimentary pecking order. Today a shorter stockier man raced ahead to the barrel, disrupting the order. He filled the dipper with water and was poised to take a drink. He put it to his lips, but already the tall man was beside him, yanking the hand that held the dipper, spilling the water. The dipper bounced to the end of the chain and hung there. Effortlessly he squeezed the hand that held the dipper. There was an audible grating of bone against bone before the shorter of the two dropped to his knees massaging his aching hand. The taller man picked up the dangling dipper, filled it and drank. He filled it a second time and drank it down again before letting it drop for the person behind him.

The shorter man's hand was not broken, just badly bruised. When the last of the workers had their drinks, he gingerly picked up the mug and drank his share. The guards hustled them back to work and the day carried on as if the events that had just taken place were nothing out of the ordinary.

Harry nudged Fidjitz, who immediately crawled through the fence and crossed to one of the guards. The guard and Fidjitz exchanged words and then Fidjitz walked briskly back to Harry. He picked his way across the rutted field, looking up only occasionally. Harry was getting impatient. He broke into a jog not wanting to upset the big man. He tripped in the dirt, jumped up, brushed himself off and hurried on. When he got to the fence, he pulled the barbed wires apart and quickly slid through. The wire above him snagged his shirt while the bottom wire caught hold of his pants on his inner thigh near his crotch. He let go of the top wire so that he could focus on detaching the bottom wire when more barbs entwined in his shirt. He looked up worriedly. Harry's face was not softening. His look drove icicles right through him. Fidjitz grabbed the top and bottom wires again, spread them apart and stepped through. He ignored the sound of ripping material and winced when the barbs from the bottom wire tore into his leg. He ran to Harry looking apologetic and climbed into the wagon. Harry ignored him, clucked the horse into motion and the two of them were gone.

Chapter 36

The next morning Harry got up some hours after the sun and gorged himself on a lumberjack's breakfast that consisted of eggs, milk, bacon and fresh buns, compliments of Maggie.

Maggie stood motionless against the wall behind him. Though she looked vacant and forlorn, she moved as if she could read his mind. She cleared dishes and provided second helpings without any direction. The concealer did not cover the scar on her cheek Harry had given her. The wound had intended to be a lesson. It served to add another enemy to Harry's almost infinite list.

With breakfast finished, Harry sat nursing his coffee. There was a knock at the door. He gestured to Maggie and she showed two men in. One was the guard from the previous day and the other was the taller man who had ruthlessly crushed the hand of a man for taking his place in the water line.

Maggie showed them into the dining room. He didn't bother to look up or acknowledge them as they entered the room. He drank his coffee slowly and even ordered Maggie to provide him with a refill while they waited. He added sugar and fresh cream, and then deliberately stirred the coffee while the two men waited like statues.

There was an occasional slurping sound from Harry as he sipped his hot beverage. It was thrilling to exercise his power over others. He wanted the visitors to feel as if their lives were at the whim of the man they stood before. The guard was not in danger, but it was impossible to tell when Harry was going to make an example. The guard had no intention of becoming one of those.

After twenty excruciating minutes, Harry looked up at the slave, ignoring the guard who brought him.

"What's your name, slave?" he asked with contempt.

Although the man did not cower to Harry, he wasn't nearly the terror that he had been in the field the day before. He was smart enough to know that the tables were turned and he was no longer at the top of the pecking order.

"Sterg," he replied without embellishment.

"Well, Sterg, you are at a serious crossroads in your life. You've got two choices. I'm going to give you a chance to step up in the world. You can go back to the fields or you can work for me, personally. I've been watching you and I think I might be able to use you."

At those words, the prisoner's demeanor changed. Though he stood taller, he was far from the man of only a few hours earlier.

"What's the difference?" he more stated than asked.

"Attitude will get you killed, boy, and that is absolutely the only warning you will ever get from me."

Sterg recognized that Harry's reply as nothing more than the statement of a simple fact. His body adjusted itself once more making a visible change in his attitude. His stance shifted and his face softened. Harry ignored the uncomfortable feelings he had produced, and did nothing to give any indication that he preferred or appreciated the attitude shift. He simply carried on.

"The difference is simple. You move from the hole you are kept in and you move into one of the houses I provide for you. You go to work each day and you do the job I give you to do…any job I give you to do." His eyes were a dull lifeless gray that showed as much emotion as a shark's. There was a long uncomfortable pause. Neither the guard nor the prisoner dared to utter a sound.

Then, as if someone flipped a switch, Harry's eyes softened and his face relaxed into a broad smile. It was the kind of smile that was intended to say, "Don't get too close because I'll bite your hand right off."

Harry motioned to a chair. "Sit down," he said to the slave.

To the guard, he nodded toward the door. "I'll let you know when I need you."

169

As far as the guard knew, Harry didn't even know his name. He was grateful for the dismissal and needed no second invitation.

The guard stood silently outside. He grew up the son of a businessman never learning much of anything except how to run the cash register when his father was out. When the bottom started to drop out of the economy, it destroyed his family. It began when his mother left his father. It ended a few weeks later when his father stepped off the roof of one of the taller buildings. His short journey ended on the pavement below, which left the guard an orphan. He was sixteen at the time.

Those first few years were tough ones. He had committed crimes he would have gone to jail for in another life time. Now he worked for Harry. There was food on the table. He had a wife and a family to go home to. Now he committed crimes as a part of his job for Harry. He was ashamed. He felt evil. His job was eating at his conscience but in Harry's world, they weren't crimes at all.

The woman he lived with didn't care for Harry either, but she was happy she had a roof over her head and somehow she found a way to believe that deep down the man she was with was a good man. She could excuse him for things he was forced to do when he was away from the house, as long as he was a wonderful man once he walked through the door. Maybe one day he would be able to be the good man she knew he was. This is the story she told herself while he was gone and it was the dream that filled her nights. What about reality? She kept that locked safely outside the front door. The world was an ugly place.

Chapter 37

Hannah and Jason followed the chained prisoners for the better part of an hour. There were both men and women of a variety of different ages. All of them looked tired and defeated. Their clothes were no more than filthy rags. She hadn't seen many hardened criminals, but these didn't fit her image of what they might look like.

Hannah was vaguely aware of the river off to the left. The river and the road were like parallel ribbons winding along the valley floor. The shuffling feet of the prisoners was enough to drown out any sound they were making but they were cautious anyway.

Without slowing, the prisoners made a sudden turn to the left and continued uphill. They walked for another kilometer in the darkness before lights began to peek from over the hill ahead. The lights illuminated the grounds of a huge compound of some kind. There were high fences surrounding it with loops of barbed wire strung across the top. At one end of the compound, was a large open space devoid of buildings and brush. In the corners were towers that reminded Hannah of rooks in the game of chess. On the other end was a series of concrete buildings, each with barred windows.

They could go no farther. The lights in and around the compound were so bright they lit up the prison, its yard, and the entire area around it as well. The lights were blindingly bright and there was no way of telling what kind of security measures had been taken. She did not want to risk getting closer to the compound tonight.

Jason stood staring after the prisoners until the entourage disappeared from view. A few moments later they heard loud metallic sounds like heavy metal doors clanging shut, but they were far away and deep in the bowels of the complex.

Fatigue was beginning to get the better of both of them. It had been a long hard day already and they were both painfully aware that it was not likely to be going to get any easier in the days to come. Hannah tugged at Jason's arm and the two of them returned to the shadows of the trees where there was little risk of being spotted from the prison complex. They stripped their packs and sat down against opposite sides of a large spruce tree. Hannah was fatigued and aching. She wondered how Jason must be feeling. He had been a real trooper and had not complained at all. She thought back to the instance on the bridge and then decided to let it drop altogether. With her back to the tree, she rolled her head towards Jason until she could feel the rough bark against her cheek.

"Hey, Jay, my boy. Can you remind me again why we're sitting dangerously close to a prison that is still functioning, in a town where we've had nothing but troubles, when a meal was easier to come by out on the road?"

Jason didn't respond for a long time. At first, she thought maybe he had already fallen asleep. She wouldn't have blamed him.

Then…"You know I was wondering that awhile ago. I thought about saying something but then I realized if my dad came this way, he could be here. He could be right under our noses and we could walk right past him. I don't know what they're doing here, but I think when we were back at Harry's we were very close to finding out the hard way. I think if we had been in Harry's house any longer we would be in there by now," he said, pointing to the prison with a nod.

"It's your call, kid. What do you want to do?"

"If there's any way that I could know for sure what happened to my dad, then I just got to. We've come so far for so long. We can't just stop now!"

"That's what I thought. I just needed to know where your heart was. I'd love a chance to plant my boot right up Harry's…" Hannah trailed off without finishing. She had already made her point. On the other side of the tree, Jason's mouth curved up into a small smile.

Hannah continued, "It looks like we're going to be hanging around for a little while. We'd better get some sleep."

Jason didn't need a second invitation. With one hand, he pulled his pack around and with practiced ease pulled out those bits and parts that would turn the hard ground into a passable bed. Hannah did the same. She wondered if she would hear the deep breaths that would tell her Jason had fallen asleep, but she had not fully formed that thought before she drifted into a deep dreamless sleep.

Chapter 38

By the time the sun was streaming through the leaves and was bright enough to wake the sleepers it was no longer morning. They had slept through the prison's morning ritual. Hundreds of prisoner slaves had filed out of the prison gates and marched down the road just as they had a thousand times before, a broken group of raggedy spent human shells. Once out of the gates, the main group split into several smaller groups and trudged off in different directions. Some went to harvest apples, others a vegetable crop of one kind or another. Another group would harvest the hay that would feed the animals through the winter. Yet another was responsible for slaughtering the beef to be consumed that day. The prisoners would taste none of it. Had Hannah and Jason been awake they would have seen all of this.

Chapter 39

At the mine, Harry smiled at his accomplishments. It was easy to justify after all. He had created a community, a way of life. Where would these people be without him? In Harry's mind, it took less time to ask than to answer. It was simple. Without him, they would be nowhere. He looked at the sheer number of people milling about below—both free and slaves. Mentally, he patted himself on the back. He thought of Hannah and the kid, but only to dismiss them. They were nothing. The horse he sat on gave its head an impatient shake. Harry took the reins and turned it towards town.

He didn't go straight back to the house. Regardless when he arrived, he knew that dinner would be waiting because Magee knew that he held her very existence in the palm of his hand. Magee had wandered into town years ago and was brought before him. At the time, she was feisty and beautiful. It was his nature to make quick decisions and when he saw her, he knew she would be his. Lately he couldn't figure out why he kept her around. She was a broken shell, a remnant of the woman she once was. She had never relished Harry's dream. She had never fallen in love with him. And she had never spent one happy moment in the house that had been her home for the past decade.

Chapter 40

Hannah woke with a start. Jason was tugging at her sleeve. His eyes were hardly more than narrow slits. His face still had that just-woke-up groggy look, but he wasn't looking at her. He was looking further into the brush staring wide-eyed. Hannah followed his gaze. Sitting on his haunches, looking more like an animal, was a skinny rake of a man. He looked as though he might have come straight out of a horror movie. His hair was a tangled shock of leaves and dirt hanging from everywhere it would stick. His clothes were no more than rags. The holes in them were so large that if he ever took them off he might not be able to figure where his legs or arms should go. More skin was showing than cloth.

Although his appearance and attire were shocking, it was not nearly as fearsome looking as his face. His eyes held a vacant, either retarded or insane look. Hannah leaned towards insane. Large chunks of skin and beard were missing from his face revealing oozing flesh. The scrapes began at his temples, and then worsened as they progressed along his cheeks to his jawbones. Blood that had run from his face had saturated what was left of his shirt. Wherever there was a hole in his shirt, an injury showed through. Hannah expected him to attack or bolt at any moment. What actually occurred was a standoff of sorts.

The man's eyes were like an animal's, but it was his stare that seemed to hold Hannah and Jason in check. The three formed a strange triangle.

Chapter 41

Travis returned to the cell that night and found it empty. There was more blood on the floor than there had been when he had left. He was alarmed but then he saw that the bars were more stained. He could visualize Al forcing his way between the bars as he had done so many times before. With the previous injury to his face unhealed, the blood would obviously be more. Once he managed to get his beaten face through the bars once more he would have been tired and in pain. Most certainly, he would have rested his face on the cold floor, probably a comfort to his hot and swelling face. The puddle of blood on the hallway side of the cell door seemed to go along with this scenario. Travis shook his head in disbelief. It was impossible to conceive that Al would be able to get very far once he escaped from the cell. He would be lucky to remember the way out of the building much less have the knowledge and forethought to be able to avoid the guards and find a safe place to hide.

The door clanged shut and only a few minutes later, the small metal door slid sideways unceremoniously delivering the goop that was the evening meal. Travis ate in the silence and solitude of his cell while his thoughts returned to Al.

No matter what happened and no matter where Al was, Travis hoped the best for him. Anything would be better than merely surviving in this cell; sometimes even a bullet would be better. He lay down in his corner and considered the tenacity of it all. During the years that he had spent with Al, some of the stupidity that he had witnessed was amazing. Those moments stood in shadowed obscurity compared with the strange respect that Travis had come to regard him. Travis found his eyes drooping from the hard day's work. He fell asleep. His parting conscious thought was *Go, Al!*

His dreams allowed him to return home to Sarah. During his grueling days, he often wondered what had become of his wife and son, but his dreams replayed the pleasant sunny times on the coast. Images of the love that he and Sarah held for Jason as they watched him slowly grow up and discover the world around him filled his dreams.

Although the dreams always started with warm and wonderful images, they did not usually end that way. As dreams sometimes do, the events would often unwind to reveal a story of tragedy rather than hope. Travis tossed on the cold concrete floor. In his sleep, he struggled to save the lives of his loved ones. He woke with burning images of disaster, shivering in the darkness. With each passing night, the weight of guilt and regret grew heavier.

Chapter 42

Al woke up in the underbrush that he had fallen into on the previous evening. As the early morning sun peeked over the horizon and began to illuminate the underbrush, it poured into his eyes. He looked around briefly at his surroundings. The memories of the day before were already no more than a mist in his mind. Although the memories were gone, the feelings associated with the prison were not. He looked up and the fences instantly filled him with a terrible sense of foreboding. His sense of dread was awakened; his first impulse was to run as fast and as far away as he could. At that moment, he turned and saw Jason and Hannah sleeping peacefully in his hidey-hide.

Anyone else would have wondered where the strangers had come from or who they were, but in Al's world, it never occurred to him. Each day was a brand-new dream and in his world, his dreams often seemed more vivid than reality. Today there was a boy and a woman. There was no way for Al to know if they had always been there or not. Al adopted the first explanation that came to his mind—all of them were traveling companions. He stood staring and waiting. The reason for his presence in their lives would be revealed, eventually. If he had learned anything, it was to wait and see. For Al, nothing was ever familiar.

"Familiar" was a concept as impossible for Al to fathom as the concept of color might be to a man born blind. Although next to impossible to imagine, Al woke every day without recollection of events from the previous day or even the previous week. He lived without memory of family and home. Under his circumstances, it was a blessing. It was best that he had forgotten the events of the world's last decade.

Al stood in front of Jason and Hannah staring, waiting for some indication of what was to come or be given some context of why these people were in his life. He could not remember the cause of the wounds on his face and body. Yesterday was a lifetime ago. He was vaguely aware that his face was inflamed and in pain.

Chapter 43

The sun crept slowly into the sky. It was turning into a beautiful day. The sun was already warm and the sky was cloudless.

Hannah looked fearfully at the raggedy man. He had a wild look about him. He might attack at any moment. They stood locked in a staring contest. His eyes were open wide as if they were propped open with toothpicks. The man looked crazy and unpredictable.

"Through the eyes of babes" has so often been said that it has become more cliché than poetic reality. In the world of adults, there is often no room for the thoughts or the perspective of a child. However, there are those times when a child's view can add the needed twist to show a completely new reality.

Unlike Hannah, it did not occur to Jason that the man had a crazy look. Odd, yes. Even Jason would have had to admit that. But crazy was not Jason's first impression. In Jason's eyes, the man's look contained child-like elements. He saw a man filled with mixed emotions. His face was, expectant and hopeful all at the same time. Seconds ticked by and Jason became convinced that the stranger was no real threat. Hannah's reaction to the man was more puzzling to him. He couldn't understand why she seemed paralyzed. He broke the silence with a single question. "Who are you?"

The newcomer did not respond immediately. His eyes turned to Jason and his mouth turned up into a broad smile, a smile so broad that his eyes became nothing more than thin slits. Warmth covered his face instantly. It reminded Hannah of a dog greeting its master after a hard day's work. The fact that the man said nothing accented the strange situation. They waited patiently for him to answer.

After another long and uncomfortable silence, accompanied by the steady surreal gaze from the man who Hannah and Jason began to believe was a lunatic, they wondered where he had come from and what caused his strange injuries. Hannah glanced up at the prison. By the looks of the man's clothing he certainly could have come from there.

Hannah pointed to the man and the pointed to the prison. She tried to show him that she wanted him to tell her where he came from. She asked very slowly, pronouncing each word carefully and pointing up the hill. "Did you come from over there?" The newcomer followed her gaze to the prison and back, the silly grin never leaving his face. Hannah repeated the question. She pointed to her own eyes with two fingers to gather his attention. He followed her fingers and looked directly into her face. "Did you come from the prison?" she stated slowly once more. She got no response.

"Maybe he doesn't speak English," suggested Jason.

"It's possible, but I don't think that's the problem. You would think that he would at least try to communicate or show us that he understands," countered Hannah.

"What should we do then?"

Hannah turned her gaze away from the newcomer and faced Jason. There wasn't time to consider a new addition to their duo. A third man who offered more as a liability that as an asset would change everything in a way that couldn't be positive. Though any threat from the man seemed highly unlikely, the risk of having him tag along was too great.

"We need to look after ourselves right now. He seemed fine before we arrived, I can't imagine why he wouldn't be fine once we're gone. If he came from there," she said, indicating the prison, "he must be more resourceful than he looks."

The moment the words came out of her mouth, she knew the logic seemed terribly flawed and the statements seemed ludicrous, but for now, it was the best that she could come up with. There was really no other option. It was equally unimaginable to think that they could care for him, and at the same time do the things they needed to do.

Jason turned to the man. "You have to stay here. Don't follow us. You need to stay where you are. Stay here. Stay." He said each word slowly and deliberately hoping that some understanding was taking place. It seemed to be working. When Jason and Hannah walked away, they looked back every once in a while to see that the stranger stayed where he was. The man stood in the brush smiling and waving stupidly as he watched them leave. They crossed a barbed wire fence tangled with willow, poplar and other shrubbery. They looked back one last time and there was no evidence that anything might be out of the ordinary.

Chapter 44

From their vantage point in the barn the day before, they could see that a variety of crops covered the western facing slopes. It was getting on towards fall and there would be vegetables and possibly fruit if they could just get to it. The growing season was fairly short. There might still be corn to gather and who knows what else. They could only hope. They moved south along a lower ridge overlooking the valley.

No more than an hour passed when they began to hear noises of industry. There were the sounds of horses, the creaking of wagon wheels, the grunts of workers and the periodic snap of a whip. They were in a hay field covered in short sharp shards of grass. Not too long ago, workers must have been harvesting here. Jason was surprised at how the stubble cut into his knees and hands as he knelt down. His focus was on the activity that lay over the knoll. He ignored the discomfort.

They inched closer to the crest of the hill. First, the leaves and branches from the trees came into view. It was impossible to tell how many workers there were. They were scattered throughout the orchard. The wagons had flat beds with short six-inch sides. Pickers came and went in a steady stream. Loaded wagons were hauled away and replaced with empty ones. Regardless of what the horses and wagons were doing, the workers kept coming with full baskets and leaving with empty ones. There was always a guard ready to prod anyone who seemed to pause or who was not moving steadily along.

Looking at the bounty in front of them was almost more than either of them could stand. Hannah glanced at Jason in time to see him swallow the saliva that had filled his mouth. The workers had just begun to work in the orchard. Every tree was loaded with fruit. The space between the rows of trees was too narrow to allow for the passage of wagons. As they worked farther and farther into the orchard, the wagons grew farther away.

They inched back away from the hilltop. If they could just move around to the other side of the orchard, they would be able to collect as many apples as they wanted.

The hills above them to the east appeared to be void of human presence. Just behind them was a shallow ravine, dry through the summer months. It was the kind of cover that they needed to allow them to get to higher ground without the risk of detection. The hillside offered a much better view of the valley as well. They wound their way up the ravine until it petered out near the ridge of the valley. Below, the orchard looked like a small field of berry bushes planted in tight rows and the workers looked like ants. Beyond the orchard was the town and Hannah was able to recognize the building that served as Harry's home, the one that would have been used to hold them prisoners. Even from this distance, she could distinguish the trees that were in the back yard. Shivers ran down her spine.

Scrambling along the hillside was the easy part of the task. Driven by hunger it took only minutes to skirt the orchard. Once they were out of danger of discovery, they jutted directly to the trees. Many of the ripe apples were hanging heavy on lower branches. Jason hoped he might have to climb for them, but some were so low that even he had no problem reaching them. They filled every space available in their packs and clothes.

It took only a matter of minutes to gather as many apples as they could carry. It was gratifying to be able to feel the weight of the heavy load of food in their packs. To avoid discovery, they turned again to the hills. The farther they could get away from people, the better. They came across a small outcropping of rocks that offered cover. Sitting behind it, they began to feast on the delicious apples they carried in their hands. Jason couldn't remember tasting anything so wonderful. He ignored Hannah's reminders to ration himself and not to eat too many. He would pay for it later.

With their hunger satiated, they shouldered their packs and continued south along the ridge. The lack of activity in the town was like the other communities they had been through. Only a skeletal population existed which was centered largely in the area that they had already left far behind. The absence of people was a relief.

Jason led the way along an ancient path. They had been hiking without much concern for over an hour. Ahead of them the path wound around a large bolder that perched on the downhill side of the trail. Jason ran to it, and slapping both hands on the rock, he vaulted around it landing on the other side. He was shocked and surprised finding it necessary to backpedal up the hill as the rocks and turf he tore loose with his feet tumbled down the hill.

He turned his body and scrambled up the hill. His hand found a buried rock that seemed as though it would hold his weight, but it slipped free and he began to tumble down the steep slope. He felt a sharp tug on his arm and his body came to a halt. He looked up to see Hannah's fingers wrapped around his wrist. She pulled hard and helped him scramble up and onto the safer ground.

The two of them sat on the trail panting, afraid to look down. No sooner had they regained their breath than they heard the sound of voices from below. Jason leaned forward and looked down the slope. Three men, armed with rifles, stood below. Binoculars hung on straps from their necks and they were looking up at the dust cloud created by the falling debris. Jason knew they had heard him, but he prayed that Hannah had pulled him back before they had seen them. Jason's body and curve of the hillside obscured Hannah's view. She looked at Jason with an expression that asked "What's going on?" and then she too heard the voices. They sat paralyzed, frozen in space and time.

Chapter 45

The men turned at the sound of the falling rocks, probably caused by a rabbit or something like it, probably nothing of any significance. During the long inactive summer months, they had taken to playing cards with an old worn out deck that one of them always carried. Now and then, someone new wandered into town, but it had been months since that had happened. If the diversion had seemed to be something other than falling rocks, it might have piqued some interest from the trio.

A few rocks and some dirt tumbledown from a large bolder just above them. By the time they lazily turned their heads upward, the dust had already settled. The game was interrupted briefly as they discussed the matter. The consensus was that the mini landslide was a natural occurrence and not one for concern. Their focus returned once more to their card game.

Whoever had planned the defense of the community had placed the outpost in an excellent location. They had positioned it on a flat section of the hillside, skirted by boulders similar to, but smaller than the one Hannah and Jason were now hiding behind. Their location provided cover, as well as an excellent view of the main road leading into the city. Anyone entering the city by this route would be visiting with Harry.

It had been good fortune that prevented them from detection. It was a miracle that they weren't noticed when first approaching the large rock. It is not often that one walks head-on into a hornet's nest without getting stung. Now they were pinned.

Jason was tired of being afraid. He was tired of being chased. He had had enough of being imprisoned and the thought of sneaking around to avoid these men was more than he could stand. Before Hannah could stop him, he braced his feet against the side of the hill and pushed hard against the boulder. He wanted to crush these hornets and clear out the nest. Though it was his intention, he was surprised when the boulder gave way and began its descent. Hannah sat in utter shock as their only cover crashed down the hill.

Below, the cards forgotten, the men had only time to rise from their seats. The boulder gathered speed. On its third bounce it shattered into a number of smaller pieces, knocking other rocks loose and transforming it into a landslide. One of the men saw the two intruders above him, too late to do anything about it. The first of the debris took him off his feet. A larger rock struck his chest, crushing him instantly. He was buried with any thoughts that he might have shared with the others.

The two other men were quicker. Each of them dove to the side. By the sheer size of him the larger man should have been slower, but as it turned out he was the quickest of the three. He leapt clear to avoid the bulk of the threat, turning in time to see the second man swept away by the falling rubble. There was no time to contemplate his companions. The rocks had not stopped falling.

As the last of the boulders passed by him, he stood alone in the settling dust. He was amazed to find himself alive. He looked up to see where the slide had originated. It was then that he saw Hannah and Jason standing above him on the hillside. The cause of the slide was obvious. He raced back toward what was left of the outpost. The cards were now scattering in the wind, but that was not what he was looking for. There, exactly where he had left it was the rifle he had dropped. He ran towards it hopping from one rock to another.

It hadn't occurred to him that the rocks would not be stable. He planted his weight and the rock twisted beneath his body. He lost his footing and his feet went out from under him, launching his body into the air. He tried to use his agility to save himself, but his feet were already above his head. He reached out to try and break his fall, but there was no flat place for his hand. It snapped beneath him as he came down on it. Hannah and Jason both heard the audible snap. His breaking arm did little to slow his descent. The back of his head was the second point of impact. When his body came to halt, it remained twisted at an odd angle.

Jason and Hannah waited for a long time to see if the man would get up.

There seemed to be no movement. It seemed clear that they were out of danger. They carefully picked their way through the debris down the hill to the man's side. Blood poured from a wound on his head, but he was still conscious. His arm was bent and twisted out of place. He was wearing a long sleeved shirt, but it did not hide the bone that was sticking through it.

He looked at them almost apologetically. "I can't feel my legs. Please, help me."

Jason's stomach lurched. He turned away and threw up.

The man was bleeding from his head and nose. He had a back injury and Hannah knew that she should not move him. She couldn't provide medical care and this man would spend the rest of his days in a rusted wheelchair—if he lived at all.

Before she finished her thought the man suddenly began to choke. Hannah didn't know whether he was choking on blood or his own tongue. She wanted to help, but before she could react the man lost consciousness. Hannah reached for his good arm to feel for a pulse. It was there, but it was weak. A moment later it was gone altogether.

Twenty years ago, he might have survived. He might have even recovered. But they lived in a harsher world than they used to. Hannah and Jason stood to walk away. Jason stopped for a moment to bend over and dry heave once more. He was not sick to see the blood and gore. He had scars on his body from his own accidents. He would have to live with the fact that in a fit of anger he had killed three men. He doubled over. His retching echoed across the hills. He stood up with tears in his eyes. There was no time for nurturing. They moved on.

They hadn't gone far when it occurred to Hannah that Harry might want retribution. Harry was looking for them and he would love to capture them if he could. They were unarmed, but these men had not been. They had been prepared for anything. Hannah stopped. "Wait here! I'll be right back."

"Where are you going?" demanded Jason.

She didn't want to stick around any more than he did. She scrambled back to the outpost ignoring his pleas not to go. The men hadn't had time to pick their rifles from the ground. One of them was snapped in two. When Hannah picked up the second one, she was surprised to see that it was her own. The scope was busted off, but other than that, it seemed to be in good shape. There was no ammunition with it. Driven by necessity she picked her way through the rocks to the first corpse. She quickly rifled through the dead man's pockets but found nothing that she needed. She moved on to the second who had been carried further down the hill. The first large boulder that struck him had pulverized his entire torso. The shells she had once carried in her pack she found strung on a makeshift bandoleer, now soaked with the man's blood. Although she was filled with disgust, she unclipped the buckle and pulled on it until it slipped free. She couldn't bear the idea of strapping the thing to herself, so she removed each shell and put them into her pack. She had almost finished when she heard the rocks shifting behind her. She turned swiftly, ready to scramble to safety but was relieved to see that it was only Jason who was joining her.

He looked down to see tears streaming down Hannah's face. "It was my father's," she said, trying to explain why she was robbing from the dead. She put the last cartridge in her pack. They returned the way they had come and were forced to walk passed the man they watched die. Jason looked down at him and noticed the butt of a revolver jutting from his jacket. He stopped to look closer. Impulsively he reached in and pulled it out of its holster. If the man had bullets for it, he could keep them. The gun was probably loaded anyway. Hannah didn't protest.

Since there was one outpost, it was likely that there would be others. They were probably set up at each of the entrances to the town. How many would there be? Three? Four? Ten? There was no way of knowing. Better to be cautious. Now that they were aware of the outposts, they might be able to avoid any others they might come across, hopefully with less bloodshed, hopefully not their own.

Chapter 46

Bradford came crashing through the door and into the kitchen. He yelled at the top of his voice as he came. "Harry! Harry! Come quick! There's an emergency!"

In Harry's world, there were no emergencies. Everything could be taken care of in due course and there was never anything that couldn't be taken care of. Regardless of the apparent urgency, he took his time.

Evidently, Bradford was agitated. Harry walked slowly in the direction that Bradford led him. Like an overexcited dog, Bradford ran ahead a ways and then back to Harry just as quickly. Then he ran a ways ahead again and back. If he hadn't been afraid to, he would have grabbed Harry's sleeve and tugged at him to move faster. Instead, he kept trying to urge him along with his antics. "Ya gotta come quick, Harry!" His voice was almost cracking.

The glare in Harry's eye was enough to tell the man that it was time to stop with the demands. Still, he kept ahead of Harry leading him along as fast as he could get Harry to walk. Behind Harry's house was a lane that bordered his back yard. They passed through a latched gate into the alley. There, a team of horses and a wagon waited. The horses were tied to the top rail of the picket fence. They reached the wagon and the man stood silently waiting for Harry to do or say something. The back of the wagon was covered with an old tarp. Whatever the man wanted to show Harry was beneath it. He walked forward and pulled the tarp back to reveal the bodies of three men. Harry knew all of them. The big man had been a good friend of his.

He turned to Bradford and demanded, "Explain this!"

"Wuh, wuh, we don't know what happened. When we got to the post, it looked like some kind of landslide fell on 'em. We found 'em in the rocks when we went to relieve 'em."

"Who's up there now?"

The messenger had expected to be grilled and he prayed that he had all the right answers. "Bert and Danny stayed up there. They sent me back with the bodies. They sent me to see you, Harry. They said to be quick, so I was quick. I came as fast as ah could, Harry. I hope—"

Harry cut him off. "Alright, alright! So shut up why don't you!"

Bradford's mouth snapped shut and he swallowed the sound that was about to escape. His whole body contracted inwardly.

"Did you bring all of their belongings back with them?" Harry enounced these words slowly and carefully.

The man nodded dumbly.

Harry poked through what had been brought back in the wagon. If he noticed the empty holster or the missing rifle that his good friend always carried with him, he never showed it. He turned and walked back into the house.

"Harry?" the man asked meekly.

Harry turned with contempt.

"Harry...what do you want me to do with the bodies?"

"Dipstick! What do we always do with the bodies? What the hell do we ALWAYS do with the bodies?" Harry turned away once again ignoring the bewildered look in the man's eyes.

Bradford hated these sorts of responsibilities. Harry was known to fly off the handle as often as not. If he dumped the bodies as he was ordered to, Harry might change his mind by morning and Bradford could find himself feeding the worms along with these unlucky sods. He couldn't ask clarification from Harry either. That would definitely seal his fate. Damn!

Bradford untied the horses from the fence and climbed into the wagon. He clicked his tongue and slapped the horses' backs with the reins to get them to move. This was not good at all. He shook his head and repeated his thought. Not good at all.

Chapter 47

Hannah and Jason crossed the main road that led into town. They came across another bridge and crossed it without mishap. Instead of sticking to the road, they headed into the western hills. For the duration of the trek, they kept a careful watch for any other outposts.

Jason was not handling the trauma of the day very well. He spent the day walking with his head down, brooding. They had traveled several kilometers since they left the outpost. It was beginning to get late. Jason had spent the day fondling the weapon that he had taken from the dead man. He should have been watching for danger. She felt the need to find a place to hold up until morning so that she could to talk to Jason and try to help him deal with his feelings.

None of the houses on the outskirts of the city was inhabited. Knowing what she did about Harry, she wondered whether this was by his choice or not. She suspected that in this town there were no real choices.

They stood in the empty yard of a beautiful home that had done a good job of withstanding the harsh winters. The city stretched out below them. As the sun began to sink slowly over the hills, lights blinked on around the city. The effect was a visual picture of where the free population was centered. She thought about the prison and wondered about the people held there. Which was greater? Could the prisoners be counted on to fight if the opportunity arose? Would Harry ever be challenged?

Other lights appeared. They could see firelight from the outpost they had visited earlier. It prompted them to look for evidence of the other outposts. They were able to identify three other probable sites. The road entering town from the west was a dark gray ribbon that wound its way into the light.

There was another red glow where they first met Harry. It was probably that outpost that had detected them in the first place. She remembered that they were not recognized as a woman and a boy at first. Well, enough of that, she was guessing, but the locations of the fires were good to know.

Together they walked to the front door, turned the knob and went inside. As it turned out, the house was not abandoned. There was a terrible rancid smell coming from everywhere. Jason had no idea what it was, but Hannah recognized the stench immediately. It was the stink of a packrat nest. By the smell of things, there was more than one nest and the rats had been there for quite a while.

They moved from one room to another checking each one carefully. Jason fondled the gun he was holding, trying his best to look prepared for anything. He scanned the room carefully while Hannah quickly inspected the rest of house. Jason could hear her moving around somewhere deep inside the building. Suddenly there was a scurrying noise. It was coming straight at him. In the darkness, the object looked the size of a football and was racing straight at him. Jason pointed the weapon at the thing in front of him and fumbled with it. By the time he managed to get the gun into position, the object had already scurried between his feet and disappeared through the door. Jason pulled his forearm across his forehead to wipe away the sweat that stung his eyes.

In his panic it did not occur to him that it might be an alarm to the town's people who were looking for them. How many angry townspeople might the shots have brought? Jason silently counted his blessing and stowed the gun in his backpack.

Hannah came back from her rounds. "Looks good. We can spend the night here."

"Here?" protested Jason. "How can you say that? This place is filthy. It's infested with RATS!"

"It's perfect!" she stated with a smile that Jason couldn't see in the dark, but could hear.

"How can you say that?" he protested.

"Look around you, Jay. When do you think anyone has ever set foot in here? Even if they came in for a quick look, how much of this place would they explore?" These were rhetorical questions and as she expected, she got no response to them. "There's a fairly clean room in the back. Follow me."

They passed a couple of large nests. One was spilling out of the closet and onto the floor of the room. The nest was made mostly of mattress stuffing. Over the years, it had grown to more than three feet deep. It was not the only one that size in the house. There were two others on the main floor and there were probably more upstairs.

Hannah led him into a back bedroom that was not nearly as filthy as the rest of the house. What was left of the mattress was no more than a deflated rag filled with holes. It had obviously made some quality nesting material. With Jason on one end and Hannah on the other, they grabbed the mattress and flipped it over. There were a number of holes on the bottom side, but it was in much better condition than the top. The moving air renewed the stench the rats left behind.

They put down their belongings, and sat down on the bed for a much needed rest. It had been a shocking day for both of them and she felt a need to determine how badly shaken Jason was. His normal upbeat demeanor was absent. His head hung down and all she could see was the locks of brown hair on the top of his head. "You want to talk about it, Jason?" She was answered with silence.

Hannah could almost hear the wheels of his mind turning. It was uncharacteristic of Jason to refuse to talk about what was bothering him. He was usually a very up-front kind of kid. Maybe he was trying to get his thoughts together. She decided to give him the time he needed and waited patiently for him to get his thoughts together.

Painfully long minutes passed before he began to talk. When he did, his feelings came out all at once. In the time that she knew him he had never ranted, but she listened intently and did her best to process what she was hearing.

"What are we doing here, Hannah? What are we risking our lives for? I killed three men! We left that man behind at the prison even though we knew he was probably just lucky to have escaped. If those wounds on his face aren't taken care of, they could kill him. Even I know that! I pushed a boulder off of a hill because I was mad. I didn't think about the consequences! I don't even remember where we've been. I couldn't get back to the prison if I had to. I saw a rat running toward me and tried to shoot it. I didn't even think what would have happened if the gun had gone off. Two days ago, we crossed a bridge. You wanted to jump into the water and I couldn't do it. I knew what the risks were. I knew that we just couldn't let ourselves be caught. I killed THREE men today, Hannah. I killed them. That rock looked like I could push it and I wanted it to crush them. I wanted to destroy them. I did it too. You didn't do it, Hannah. I DID IT!" Jason's tears were flowing freely. He wiped his face on his sleeve. He was finished talking.

It was Hannah's turn to respond, but for the life of her, she didn't know what to say. Jason was growing more dependent on her. She had no idea that he felt that their reason for being here was gone. His confidence was crushed. What could she say that would make it better? What did he need? He was a tough kid. He was nearly a man. He had done things most men couldn't have dreamed of doing. Hell, he was more of a man than most men she knew. Not knowing where to start, she followed her instincts. "Are you finished feeling sorry for yourself, Jason? Anytime you want to be done with all of this whining about how horrible you are…well that would be great! Now that you've told me how you feel, let me tell you how I feel. You're right…about some things. We need to see what we can do about that. But you are so wrong about some other things. Let's be realistic.

"First of all, we've all done some very terrible things out of anger. Most of the time we are very lucky and nothing bad happens because of it. But you need to see it for what it was. It was an accident. And that's not all. If you had not been able to move the rock, what do you think would have happened? A strong wind could have knocked that rock loose on any stormy day! Come on, Jason! How strong do you think you are?

"Secondly, we all have fears. I knew something was going on when we were on the bridge. I was hoping that you would talk to me about it sometime. If I had to guess, I would bet you've never been in water over your head. I would bet that you don't know how to swim and that it was just too hard for you to deal with it that night. That's what I think. Whatever it is, Jason, you can work through it.

"You're also right about the man we left behind. I'm worried about him too. I truly hope that nothing bad has happened to him. It's been bothering me ever since we left this morning and I had already decided that we should make our way back there and see if we can find him.

"You are a good young man and I am very proud of you. If you don't mind me saying, Jason, we have an impossible job ahead of us and we're going to have to be damn tough if we have a hope to live through it. You feel like getting some sleep? We're going to need everything we've got tomorrow."

196

Overwhelmed, Jason crawled onto the bed and scooted to the wall. Hannah lay down beside him. The moon rose and created an eerie light in the room. A rat moved slowly across the room staying close to the wall. Hannah hissed at it and it scurried away. She closed her eyes and the next time opened them it was to the morning sun shining into the room hitting the wall where the moon had the night before.

The travelers started their morning by eating an apple. They continued up the hill once again. By mid morning, they had come full circle and were standing outside the barn where they had spent the night three days earlier. Their travels had taken them past most of the farming industry, the main reason the town was alive. The mystery of electricity in the community was yet to be solved. For now she assumed that there was still power coming from the Kitimat power plant. She wondered about that. If there was an unlimited supply of power, why were more lights not used in the city? It didn't matter at the moment. She could only deal with one problem at a time. She changed her course and walked toward the ravine. At least it was a familiar path that they had already been down and traveling would be quicker because of it.

Long before midday, they were once again facing the bridge they crossed only a few days earlier. There was no one near and there seemed to be no real danger. The biggest concentration of activity happened when the prisoners were moved to and from the worksites. Otherwise, except for the epicenter of the city, Kelowna more closely resembled a ghost town.

There was no sense staying out in the open any longer than was necessary. No one was on the road or within hearing distance. It looked safe enough. They ran as quickly as they could across the entire expanse, not attempting to hide or hunker down. Their strategy was to get across as quickly as possible. If they were spotted, they could deal with it later.

A horse whinnied from far away. The travelers ignored it. Although they were in relatively good physical shape, the sprint left them panting with pangs ripping into their sides.

They didn't stop when they reached the other side. They ran to the underbrush that lined the road on both sides. They collapsed in the tall grass to catch their breath. A dog barked, probably a stray.

When they were calm and their breathing had returned to normal, they continued their journey toward the prison facility. Hopefully the man they encounter the day before would still be there. They feared that he had been recaptured. It was not far to the prison. It was mid afternoon by the time they got there and went directly to the grove of trees. Hannah and Jason split up and searched the brush for some sign of him. They called to him quietly hoping to get some kind of response. Nothing.

The trampled brush indicated he had spent a significant amount of time in the area. There was no evidence that he was taken by force or that he had left the area on his own. Jason's shoulders weighed heavy with a deep sense of guilt. He hung his head and returned to the spot where they made their bed the last time they were here. He pulled an apple from his pack and rolled it around in his hands. He had no desire to eat it, but the smooth red skin was soothing. He toyed with it a little longer before returning it to his pack. His hand fell on the butt of the gun that was stowed there.

He took it from its hiding place to look at it. It was a large caliber pistol that employed a revolving cylinder to hold the shells. There was also a release lever that allowed the cylinder to flip to one side for loading and unloading the bullets. Jason operated the mechanism and the cylinder fell open to reveal a series of brass circles. All the holes were full. He put his finger on the side of the cylinder and pulled down quickly. It spun freely. A series of audible clicking sounds followed. He snapped the cylinder closed and admired the weapon from one end to the other. It was the first revolver he had ever seen and the feel and weight of it in his hand was magic.

He had an unbearable urge to experiment with the weapon so that he could understand how it worked. He noticed that when he pulled the trigger slowly back a small lever moved up and forced the cylinder to turn. It was evident that it would stop when the next bullet aligned in the barrel. He also noticed that the top trigger (it reminded Jason of a small hammer) moved back as well. He could see that when the cylinder was in the right place, the hammer would release and slam down on the end of the bullet. Jason was mesmerized. He continued to pull the trigger and the hammer continued to move slowly away from the bullet.

Suddenly, a hand came across his and squeezed lightly. She didn't know how familiar he was with the weapon he held and had assumed he had some understanding of it. She knew he was comfortable with the rifle she carried. Watching the fascinated look in his eye told her everything that she needed to know. She sat down next to him.

She examined the weapon for only a moment before she found and released the catch that held the cylinder closed. She turned the barrel up and let the shells drop into her open palm. She held them over Jason's hands. He clasped them together and opened them so that she could let them fall in to his open palms. She turned the pistol so that it pointed away from her and looked down the barrel to see that it was clear. She then used her thumb to click the cylinder into place.

She turned the weapon first one way and then the other. It was as if she were giving it a good looking over to decide something about its personality, then she pointed it away and slowly pulled the trigger. It was as if her finger hardly moved before the hammer was released and slammed into place with a loud clicking noise. Hannah followed that by pulling the trigger back slowly. Jason could see the cylinder turning and the hammer moving back. Hannah continued to pull the trigger. When the cylinder clicked into its next position, the hammer released almost instantly, repeating the same clicking sound.

Hannah spoke quietly, as if they were having some kind of secret meeting. "These weapons are much more dangerous than a rifle in a lot of ways. Somehow, they're also more fascinating. Look at how short the barrel is. A weapon like this is easy to hide, but it is also very easy to point in unexpected directions. It's important to be extremely careful. The best place for this gun is probably with the man you got it from." Hannah's tone was not one of reprimand, but her whole demeanor gave Jason a sense of reverence and respect for the weapon.

Hannah continued, "I saw earlier that you found the safety. Did you notice that even the previous owner used it?"

Jason nodded silently and Hannah carried on.

"I took the bullets out of the cylinder so that it would be safe to show you about the gun. You should never handle a loaded weapon unless you plan to shoot it. This particular pistol is called a forty-five. It gets its name from the caliber. Look on the back of the bullet."

Jason took one of the shells in his hand and rolled it over. He could see some writing printed near the primer. One of the markings was the number forty-five.

"These guns are famous for the amount of damage that they can cause. They are also amazingly loud. In the old days people would wear hearing protection when they used them." Jason watched her carefully. He wanted to remember everything that she said.

"Did you notice that the trigger has two positions?"

Jason shook his head.

"When the hammer is pulled back, the finger trigger is set. Watch how when I pull the hammer back the cylinder turns, but look. The finger trigger is moving back too."

The hammer clicked into position and the finger trigger clicked into position too.

"Watch my finger as I pull the trigger." Hannah had just begun to put pressure on the trigger when the hammer was suddenly released. It came to rest with a loud click.

"As second way to fire the gun is to pull steadily on the finger trigger. The hammer is pulled back steadily until the cylinder is in position. Then the hammer is released and the weapon fires. Watch my finger."

This time when Hannah pulled the trigger, he noticed that the amount of distance that she needed to pull was far greater. It seemed like she pulled for a painfully long time before the hammer suddenly changed directions and slammed down.

"Jason, you can think about the best way to use the gun. It will probably depend on the situation you're in. I don't see a problem with you keeping it, but I suggest you put those shells in one pouch and the gun in another. We haven't needed it so far and we probably won't ever need it."

Hannah put the weapon on top of the bullets already in Jason's hands as if to punctuate that the gun was too much for him to handle.

The visual statement she was trying to make was lost when from behind them came the sound of breaking twigs and brush. Jason instinctively grabbed for the gun, but instead of pulling it up and pointing it, he ended up juggling it from one hand to the other like a bad circus performer. In the meantime, the shells that were in his hands fell in the grass and underbrush at his feet. He hadn't had time to look up to see what kind of imminent danger might have presented itself. Hannah was already standing and facing the direction the sound came from. By the time Jason managed to get the gun under control and stand, he found himself, pointing the empty weapon with the cylinder flopped open to one side at the man they had come to find.

Under other circumstances, it would have been funny. As it was, every ounce of strength Jason had left in his body drained. He plopped to the ground completely spent. He looked up to see the stranger mimicking his expression. As a smile spread across his face, the man followed suit.

While the man stood there dumbly, Hannah pulled a fresh apple from her pack. The man looked thin before, but if he had spent two days and a night here alone, he was probably hungry. The man took the apple without hesitation and began to chew on it. In a flash, he was finished with it, seeds and all, and Hannah offered him a second one. There were plenty of opportunities to fill their flasks with clean water so Hannah offered the man some water as well. He took it and began to drink deeply. He drank so fiercely that Hannah thought he might choke himself. To save him from himself she pulled the flask away. He followed it thirstily with his hands but made no attempt to take it back. Hannah offered him a third apple and he took it. This time he ate more slowly.

When the man was finished with the apple, he went over to where Jason was still sitting in the grass. He crouched down in front of him and studied his face intently. He shifted his weight to look at Jason from one side, and then he changed his position again, so that he could get a good look at the other. He studied his eyes, his ears and his nose. Jason allowed him to stare for as long as he wanted and even when the man reached out to touch his face like a blind man might, Jason let him. When the man seemed satisfied he sat back still gazing at Jason. He said one word. "Tavs." He took another bite from his apple and repeated the only word he had uttered up to that point. "Tavs."

Chapter 48

At the house, Harry paced in the front room. A new fist-sized hole adorned the wall. Harry hadn't considered the possibility he might slam his fist into a stud instead of the space between them when he punched it. Luckily for him, he hadn't. He rarely lost his temper. Lacking scruples, did not mean that he lacked patience. He paced back and forth, fuming as he went.

Harry was once the dead man's best friend. He hadn't built the community on his own. Ten years ago, he had a partner. The town was almost overrun with people moving across the province looking for greener pasture. Many came, looted and left. Others stayed, but not always to be useful members of the community. Often, they were parasites that came more to leach the community dry.

There was much to do to rebuild the community and little manpower to accomplish it. The prison was the perfect facility to control the transients. Once he began to round them up, they were an obvious solution to the shortage of manpower. They were human waste and it was without regret that they were forced to work or die. At least there was value in their remaining days. When they died, they died useful citizens.

The community was more important than anything else. It was difficult to believe that the world was ever going to develop any kind of organization. If the community were going to grow, then the people who lived there would have to make it happen…regardless of the cost.

There were many down-and-outers who were hoping for nothing more than an easy lifestyle and a place to spend time to end their days. These were rounded up.

Other transients had no intention of falling into the same types of traps that history was famous for. They were not about to be told what to do and when to do it…especially not by the likes of "some self-appointed psycho leader" as it was sometimes put. Those people had already caused enough pain for the community and they deserved the sentence that was handed to them immediately.

They were escorted, although somewhat forcibly, to the local penitentiary. Once there, life began brand-new. The transients became useful members of the community whether they wanted to or not.

Originally his policy was to educate the transients and bring them back into useful service in the community. Once he gave them back the humanity that they lost, he would give them back their freedom and they would become positive members of the community. That was the plan.

With his friend lying in the burial pit, Harry found himself thinking back to those old days. He couldn't think of one person that had ever been sent to work from within the prison that ever developed any kind of attitude change. If anything, they tended to become more like animals than they were like people. Those who started out lazy and complacent became angry and resentful. They hated the community and everything it stood for. Those released had gained a new position by proving a lack of compassion. These men and women were generally given positions of authority over the very people they had worked with side-by-side.

The ex-prisoners tended to be ruthless and short-sighted. Once released, they perceived their new life as rich and rewarding. He needed them to maintain order, but they changed the flavor of the community as well.

Harry's dead friend had always loved the outdoors. He had been a huge supporter of the movement and wanted very much to organize and protect the community. As the policing and administration workload increased, he lost his desire to work so closely with the law making and punishment issues. He contented himself with rounding up those negative elements of the community and bringing them to Harry. It was a good system and worked well. He lived in a world where he enjoyed the freedom to do the things he believed in and the respect from the town's people was partial payment.

He knew that he was feared more than he was respected. Respect wasn't something that he was willing to sacrifice. He was happy to enjoy the benefits the community offered. Through the years he was never able to see that the happiness and contentedness he enjoyed was only experienced by a few.

Of all the people that controlled the community, only a handful of men and women could be truly held accountable for the way that the community functioned. They were blind to the fact that a large percentage of the people were driven and haunted by fear. These few "leaders" could not see that the political climate in the community was collapsing. The world was about to crumble around them and they could not see it. Their shortsightedness would be their own undoing.

It seemed obvious to him that the death of his friend had not been an accident. Someone else had been there. Someone else had probably staged the whole thing. The missing guns were evidence of it.

Had there ever been an attack on an outpost before? Ever? Harry thought hard about it. He thought back to all the conflicts that he could remember. In all of the past years, there wasn't a single instance where an outpost had been caught off guard and decimated.

People came into the community all right. They came looking for an easy meal and a soft bed. They came to loot and to steal. They did not come looking for a fight unless they could win at no cost.

The outpost was placed high in the hills overlooking the main highway that led into the city. Any travelers who came into town from that direction would never have come over the hilltops. They would have stuck to the easiest path to travel. They would have been unprepared to be accosted by Harry's outpost.

He played the different scenarios in his head and in each one there was one constant. He could visualize that boy and that woman sneaking down from above. He could see them poised behind the rocks. He could see them creating the avalanche. The image was infuriating. But the scenario did not end there. The intruders had come down to the outpost. They walked among the bodies and had gone through their possessions. They were murderers and thieves. No! Worse still, they had robbed from the dead. They had robbed his best friend. And worst of all, they had the power to turn *his* town upside-down.

Harry continued to work himself into a furry. Without warning, he slammed his fist into the wall, punching another neat hole beside the last one. His "maid" winced from inside the kitchen but was not about to leave the sanctuary of her haven on account of the man she feared and hated, ranting on the other side of the wall. In his current frame of mind, he was dangerous and that made her afraid.

Another part of her enjoyed every moment of his rage. The man that had caused her so much pain was experiencing a little himself. She had no idea what was creating these feelings for him, but she wished nothing more than to see his pain increase.

By the time she finished cutting the tomato for the soup, Harry had ceased pacing in the living room and resumed sitting in his favorite chair staring out the window into the street. His mind reeled behind his blank stare. Those troublemakers had been wandering freely around his town for days. They had been using *his* town to their advantage, and worst of all they had been plotting against *him*. It was just a boy and a woman! How could they do this to him? He had done everything he could for them. He had offered her the world and she had spat it back in his face. She was a hateful evil woman!

With the sun setting over the city, a plan formed in his mind. A thin smile formed on his pursed lips and he yelled for supper.

After the meal, Harry called out to Maggie. She returned without hesitation, ready to comply in any way that was demanded of her. It was a relief that the request was simple...to pass a message along. She nodded her head slightly and left the room as soon as he finished talking. The door swung silently closed on its hinges behind her. Although Harry had not said the word "now" every part of him indicated that his orders should have been carried out yesterday.

Less than fifteen minutes later, she returned with a woman who joined Harry immediately. The woman was older than Maggie, but in better condition. She was more muscular. Her skin looked as though she had spent a lifetime in the sun. It had gone through a variety of stages of tan and now had a permanent plastic look. The sun was stealing what was left of her youth. Beneath her tanned skin were deep wrinkles. Although her body was well proportioned and she was beautiful by any man's standards, her face had the look of a ferret. Her eyes were narrow calculating slits.

Her arrival erased any doubt that she was the right person for the job. The rest of the evening was spent discussing his plans. They covered every detail of the plan and she would begin to execute it in the morning. Her success would lead to his reward. The woman stood to leave and smiled back at Harry with her conspirator's smile. It fit her naturally.

Chapter 49

It was late in the evening when the woman named Faydra left Harry's home. She went straight home to her closet and took out some of her older, raggedy clothes. She picked through her outfits, matching them as she went, in a way she might have done if she were going to a formal ball. She picked the pants for the occasion and then she began to modify them. When she finished the work, she donned them and went to a full-length mirror. She turned around several times, examining herself from every angle, top to bottom. Passable, she thought.

She was exhausted when she was finished and decided to get a few hours of sleep before starting her assignment.

Chapter 50

Jason loved to let the sun wake him. He always slept as long as he could. Between him and Hannah he was never sure who woke whom first, but it seemed as though they were never more than a few seconds apart. He looked at the blue sky and was thankful that there was no evidence of clouds. They breakfasted on apples again and went down to the river to freshen up. Jason was still trying to figure out what he could about their new companion. Hannah, on the other hand, had resigned herself to accepting the responsibility of taking care of him.

It was accurate to say that the new addition to their troop was childlike. In size, he wasn't much larger than Jason. He was thinner and only a bit taller. The man was extremely thin. He looked almost sickly. By mid morning, he still had said nothing more than, "Tavs." Jason decided that should be his name. It would at least give him something to call him while he tried fruitlessly to communicate.

"So you like the word Tavs," Jason pointed out more than asked.

In response, the man became quite agitated and began to repeat the word over and over excitedly.

Maybe Tavs was not a good name after all. It might not work very well if every time he tried to get the man's attention he responded by repeating it over and over. It would be even worse if he needed the man to be quiet. Maybe he better come up with something else.

He spent the morning trying to think of an appropriate name. He studied the man carefully. Jason thought that when the man sat still he had a look as though he was about to spring. In some ways, he resembled some mystical forest creature. He wanted to work his personality into the name he would choose for him. It never occurred to Jason that the process might be inappropriate. He was trying to name the man as if he might name a pet. He needed something to call him and he needed something that would work. The man was certainly not going to help him.

"I've sometimes wondered what an elf would look like. I bet they look just like you. How about Elvin? I think that sounds good. From now on you're Elvin."

Al smiled dumbly. Maybe it was because his new name sounded familiar in some way. He may have smiled because the tone in Jason's voice sounded so friendly. Either way, the man seemed to accept his new name. Jason liked the sound of it.

"Hannah! I've decided on a name. We should call him Elvin!"

Hannah looked up from what she had been doing. "Elvin…hmmm. Did you ever think that he might already have a name?"

"I've thought about that, but do you think he's going to tell us what it is? I think we need to call him something. Calling him 'Hey-You' isn't going work very well."

"Elvin sounds totally fine, Jason." Hannah smiled. "We'll call him Elvin."

Chapter 51

Faydra went to the site where Harry and his crew were killed. Another crew had already taken their place. The new lookout point was set up about twenty meters below the original.

If they had moved the lookout because they didn't want to be too near where people had died, it didn't stop them from thoroughly investigating the area. In the two days since the accident-slash-murder, the entire area had been polluted with tracks from every goofball who felt the urge to test his Sherlock Holmes' skills.

The rocks that had fallen from above created an area of loose scree beginning just above the outpost and ended where the slope leveled about thirty meters below. In the main lookout area, cards were still scattered about. Faydra scanned the debris where the card game had taken place. It hadn't rained yet and several of the rocks were splattered with brown, dried blood. Here and there, cards were strewn about. A lunch that had never been eaten had become rank after spending days baking in the sun. There was nothing at the site that might indicate that it was anything more than an accident. It was her job to solve the mystery and locate the culprits…a boy and a woman, but it occurred to Faydra that she might be on a wild goose chase. Had Harry finally lost his wits? There were numerous rumors flying around over the past few months. Essentially, the consensus of the rumors was that Harry had lost his touch, his vision and his good sense. Faydra spent another few hours at the site but found no evidence here that it had been anything other than what it appeared. She needed to find evidence that someone else had been here.

Faydra skirted the area searching for any sign that there had been another presence besides those of the dead men. The portion of the trail leading up to the outpost was the most recently disturbed. There was still clear evidence of the horse and wagon. There was also a second set of tracks that overlapped the first. The path from the main site to the wagon was littered with footfalls and scuffmarks. These seemed to be caused mostly from moving the bodies out of the rocks. It was impossible to determine if there had been any other people. It was a tracker's nightmare.

Faydra moved up the slope to where the rockslide had started. It was steep going and there were traces of foot traffic going both up and down the hillside. She could tell the difference between those going up the hill and those coming down by the way that the toes or heels dug into the soil. They moved the soil in specific and predictable ways.

She continued up the slope looking for the origin of the rock. When she reached the trail and found where the rock had been seated, it was evident that the rock had never had a firm seating on the hill to start with. It was amazing that it hadn't fallen sooner. Faydra was an excellent tracker, but even a master could not have made sense of the mess she was now looking at. Those who had come earlier had destroyed the evidence in the entire area.

From what she could glean from the outpost she slowly began to form an opinion about what had happened. The information she gathered from the tracks that led up to the rock and back to the outpost seemed to confirm her thoughts. Up until now, there were two possible solutions. The more likely of the two seemed to be that it was an accident as the first report had suggested. The group of men who found the bodies had probably taken what was valuable before reporting the deaths. Of course, they wouldn't admit to taking the weapons. They would have hoped that Harry wouldn't notice. As far as they knew, he hadn't.

What of the woman and the boy? They probably hightailed it out of the valley as quick as they could. What would possess them to stay? They were lucky to have gotten away the first time. Faydra decided to look no further for them…for now. If it became necessary to track them, she would. Otherwise, there were more likely scenarios than this one.

Harry would never approve of a half-baked investigation. She didn't have anything more than guesses and Harry would not appreciate hearing about the guesses. He could easily come up with those on his own. He wanted more than that. He wanted to be sure. And, if he couldn't be sure, then someone's head would no doubt be on the chopping block. It wasn't going to be hers!

For Faydra, there would be no wild-goose chase after the woman…yet. One thing was certain; the solution to the problem was in the missing guns. When she found the guns, she would know what had happened to the men. Faydra was glad that she decided to go after the crew instead of the woman and the boy. Even though trying to hunt down the woman might become necessary, it meant too that she would end up doing some bushwhacking. It wasn't the direction that made the most sense at the moment.

Faydra made one more, quick pass around the site looking for anything that might provide more information. Nothing presented itself so she headed down the hill following the same path the wagons used. Too bad they rotated the crews so frequently. She could have interrogated yesterday's crew right here and now. Oh well. Time to get on it. Faydra hiked out.

Chapter 52

It took a couple of hours of walking before she ended up back in town. She made a note of the orchards and the corn crops as she passed them on the way. Harvest was in full swing and the crops represented the easiest meals available. If the woman and the boy were still around, they would probably frequent one or both of these places. These would be Faydra's aces in the hole for later.

She headed to the building that became known as Central Appointments. The old city hall had been taken over for this purpose. As in all large operations, the need for organization couldn't be escaped. Central Appointments was the organization used to make sure all the most important needs of the community were being met. These included providing scheduling for personnel throughout the city and shuffling prisoners when necessary. There was also a small militia that was made available for emergencies. These men maintained a strict training regime and provided a kind of boot camp for those who would eventually fill the ranks. Trusted manpower was a commodity as much as anything else.

Central Appointments had records about where each crew was and its members. She walked to the counter, looking from one end to the other. The office appeared to be vacant. And there was no sign posted suggesting where the lineup began.

She reached the counter and peered over. There was a woman sitting disinterestedly at a desk, thumbing through some papers. When she heard Faydra's fingers drumming on the counter she looked up with as little interest as she showed her work. Her demeanor transformed instantly when she recognized Faydra. She donned a smile and almost ran to the counter. "Faydra! I'm so sorry! What can I do for you?"

"Tell me where I can find the crew that was on the southeast ridge the day before yesterday," she demanded.

The receptionist almost fell over herself running to a beat up filing cabinet that was missing most of its original paint. It looked as if it had been scavenged from a dump. If the contents of the drawer were any indication of the amount of work there was to do, it was no wonder that the secretary had little or nothing to do. Inside were a couple of file folders, each containing a number of loose-leaf sheets. She flipped through the folders and pulled out the one with the words "Outpost Duty" scrawled across the top in pencil. Inside were a number of loose sheets. The first was simply a list of names. Some had been crossed out and others had been added to the bottom.

The big man who had once been Harry's friend had been in charge of scheduling the entire group. It had been his job to determine when and where each crewmember would be assigned. Most of the men were given specific postings. There were other assignments that involved roving detail. Each was given a predicable rotation.

The woman at the counter thumbed through entries and found the schedule entitled "Southeast Outpost." She followed the rotation until she found the entry she was looking for. She read the names for Faydra. "Cornwallis, Dempsey and Bradford should be the men you're looking for."

Faydra waited somewhat impatiently as the receptionist looked at her blankly. She became alarmed as the seconds dragged on.

What is it that Faydra wants? Am I supposed to read her mind? the secretary thought.

Faydra continued to wait in silence. There was nothing more frustrating to her than dealing with visionless peons who were good for nothing more than preening and smiling. This receptionist was one of these people.

Suddenly, it was as if the lights went on. The receptionist flipped through the remaining pages and pulled out another schedule. This one was not a list of names, but a list of places. The receptionist located the words "Southeast Outpost" and looked at the line just below it. "They're roving on the northeast side of the city today. They've just started their tour."

Faydra swore under her breath and turned to leave.

The secretary continued, "They're scheduled to be at the northwest outpost in three days." It came out more like a question than a statement.

Faydra continued out of the building without looking back or acknowledging the woman's last statement. She looked at the sun, estimating the time of day. It was late enough to head over to the old community center and check out what was on the menu for lunch. After that, she could take a bit of a siesta. There wasn't much more to do until evening. She certainly wasn't going to wait for three days to talk to Cornwallis.

Faydra walked down the familiar streets towards the city center. Although many of the buildings were in use, they were not particularly well kept. They were beginning to take on an ancient look as the sun and rain beat the paint and stucco from them. Even if someone had wanted to do any upkeep on these buildings, finding materials to do it would be next to impossible. Already, so many skills were lost. Faydra wondered what the world would be like in thirty more years when these buildings were nothing more than fallen down carcasses of rotten wood. It didn't matter anyway. If the rule "those who live by the sword die by the sword" applied to Faydra then she didn't have too many warm summer days left to enjoy anyway. She didn't care.

She walked into a building that was more dilapidated than others around it. An old sign hung at an awkward angle. Most of the letters had peeled off it. Now it just said "B ng." There was part of an "o" left at the end, but it was so obscured that only close scrutiny would reveal it for what it was. Faydra wasn't about to invest that kind of time. She knew it was the old bingo hall and that was enough.

The smells of cooking that came from the hall could never mistakenly be described as "momma's kitchen," but for the hungry man it was good enough. It was still early and not everyone had come in for the rush. Soon there would be huge lineups of people waiting for a meal. It was never intended to be any kind of social service. Its main purpose was to make the distribution of food much easier. The harvests were brought to various central locations and then had to be prepared so that they could keep over the winter. Rather than try and make sure that all the people got their fare share, mass meals were prepared. There were groups of older children who where responsible for delivering meals to those who could not leave their posts to come into the hall.

It all worked out very well for Harry. The community meals had been very popular. It was another way to provide an occupation for the less aggressive and talented members of the community. It was enough to make them happy.

There were still many people who had even smaller roles in the community—each one important to make the community work. Some of them had never even set eyes on Harry, and for many of them Harry was a celebrity. He was their savior. It was his foresight that allowed them to have one easy winter after the next. There seemed to be always food on the table. To some people, Harry was a saint.

Faydra knew better. She smiled inwardly wondering what the cook would think if he knew half of what people had gone through to make sure that he had flour in his barrel in the back room behind the kitchen. There was blood in that flour! *Eat up, cookie*, she thought as she piled on a helping of stew with some unleavened biscuits that were heaping on a giant sized platter.

Outside, the day remained sunny. The air was calm and it had already begun to get stuffy inside. She walked towards the door. One staff member, a young cleaning boy, noticed her leaving—and she was taking some of the prized silverware and a plate with her! Anyone else would have let her go, but then everyone knew her. The boy ran to the door and barred her way with his body. "Lady, I was told not to let anyone go outside with a meal. You got to go back in and eat at one of the tables."

"Little man, get out of my way!" Faydra ordered. It was said that when she was angry the look on her face could turn most people to stone. If Faydra had lived in the early nineteenth century, she would have been a gunslinger.

"Please, lady," was all he was able to get out of his mouth. Her hand snapped out so swiftly that he didn't have time to see it much less move out of the way. His body became airborne as he was lifted off the floor and crashed through the open doorway. He convulsed on the ground gasping for air. Faydra continued through the door as if she had shooed a fly away and sat on an old bench that had been part of a bus shelter. The metal uprights that once supported Plexiglas windows were all that was left of it. She ate her meal with the sun shining in her face while people poured into the building around her. Many glanced her way as they passed, but no one dared to make eye contact. When she was done, she laid the plate and spoon on the bench, got up and walked away.

The forgotten boy had managed to regain his breath, pick himself off the ground and go back in to continue his work. Things had gotten busy in the soup kitchen. Rush hour had begun. Although the cook had seen everything that happened between Faydra and the boy, he neither reprimanded nor gave sympathy to the boy. It was one of life's simple lessons. It would not be a mistake the boy would make again.

As the boy continued to work, he found excuses to walk to the door to see Faydra's progress. When he noticed her get up to leave he waited until she was out of sight before running out to grab the plate and spoon. He was responsible for maintaining the dishware at the kitchen and if they ran short of silverware or dishes, it was his job to scrounge from abandoned houses to replace or add to the supply. It seemed like more people were coming to town and using the kitchen. It was the one aspect of his job he detested the most.

After the woman left, it wasn't long before she was gone from his mind. The lunch crowd had arrived in numbers much larger than normal. There wasn't time to wash dishes while the meals were being served. That would happen after the rush was over. There was neither food nor dishes enough for all of those who came. The cook would do what he could, but the anger that was growing on his face was a bad omen for the evening to come. It was almost as bad as the beating that he had gotten from the woman.

The small kitchen crew worked through the crisis. Guests waited patiently for their meals. Eventually, the last of the patrons left the building, but the dishes needed to be washed and the room prepared for the evening meal. Usually, supper was less busy than lunch. At least there was that to look forward to. In the meantime, there was a lot of work to do. He had to move the dishes to the back area, help out where he could and make sure there were enough dishes and silverware to meet the needs for the next meal. He had to hurry if he was to have enough daylight to get the things he needed. As the crowds increased, he had to travel farther to find the things that he needed. He didn't have to be told what needed to be done. He finished his cleaning job, nodded to the cook and flew out the door. They were short plates and cups as well as silverware. He thought he might need a set of twenty. That would be heavy, maybe even two trips worth.

Chapter 53

Faydra would be damned if she was going to chase Cornwallis all over the countryside for three days, while he rode around on horseback. All three, Cornwallis, Dempsey and Bradford, would be home tonight and she would be able to find them there.

The distance between the homes was greater than she was prepared to walk. It was easier to care for, raise and feed the stock from a single stable. Most people weren't allowed horses. Feed was a valuable commodity, because it was more difficult to harvest without the help of tractors.

All of the infrastructures were free for the taking. The stables were located at a private racetrack. Most likely, the original owner couldn't handle the idea of living in poverty. No one cared. The facilities provided everything Harry needed. It was all left behind for the taking.

Faydra walked to the community stables. She wasn't expected and it didn't matter. Her rank allowed her unlimited access to any resources and she had become accustomed to taking whatever she needed. Most of the town's people knew who she was, but occasionally there was a need to educate an unfortunate peon.

She entered the stables and approached the first person she came across. *It's a rule*, she thought. *You never find the person you're looking for.*

The stable hand was a young woman in her early twenties, just some girl with a horse fascination, not even worth talking to. Faydra walked along the stalls taking the time to look at each horse she passed. The perfect horse would be the one that looked a bit scruffy, a little worse for wear and maybe a little older. She found an ancient mare with a scar that stretched from her forehead to her mouth. It would be perfect. It probably got tangled up in barbed wire somewhere along the way. There were more dilapidated fences than there were in good repair. They became booby traps for unwary animals. It was probably how this horse managed to be injured.

Enough of that, Faydra thought. *Always the analyst.* She opened the stall and took hold of the horse's halter to lead it out.

The girl came forward. She was about to protest when Faydra's menacing glare stopped her short, and she recognized the woman. She turned on her heel and slid a saddle from the sawhorse it rested on. Faydra waved her away, and picked the grungiest piece of leather she could find. The girl stepped out of the way. Another mistake could very well be her last.

As Faydra picked the tack, the girl saddled and bridled the horse expertly without further hesitation. She wanted to make sure Faydra wouldn't be back. She brought the horse out of the stall and handed over the reins. There was no appreciation in those dark cold shark's eyes, only expectations. Faydra *was* the evil queen and she played the part well.

The man in charge of the stables arrived in time to see the swishing tail of the horse leaving the stables without his permission. Glaring at the assistant, he brought the horsewhip up over his head, preparing to lash out at her.

The girl raised her hand to ward off the stinging blow saying just one word in her defense, "Faydra."

It was all that was necessary. The man lowered his hand and watched the woman ride away. If there was any anger over the theft, he didn't show it. Other horses would be returning soon and they would need to be cooled down, groomed and fed before being stabled for the night.

Chapter 54

Faydra rode to the house where Cornwallis lived. She arrived there before he did. A woman lived in the house and probably a couple of varmint kids as well, more bugs.

She tied the horse to the fence outside and walked to the top of the porch steps. She sat and waited.

Inside the house, she could hear scurrying and whispering as the woman rushed her children to safety. It was rumored that Faydra was spawned by the devil. If she had kin, it was the boogeyman. Faydra was infinitely more dangerous.

By the time Cornwallis made it home, it was dark. He had been riding all day, but the horse he was loaned was required to be turned into the stables each evening. The distance Faydra had ridden, Cornwallis walked. The man was filthy, exhausted and looked defeated, not even a challenge.

Though he slouched with exhaustion, his frame straightened the moment he recognized the figure sitting on his front steps. "Faydra!" It was not a greeting so much a startled exclamation stating the obvious.

Faydra took it as such and did not respond. Instead, she stood up and motioned Cornwallis to take a seat.

Cornwallis was well aware that he was an insignificant man in her eyes. Though he was in charge of a small group that included two other men, he was no more than a delivery boy. The deliveries were people, anyone who was a new arrival in town. There really wasn't much that could go wrong. And so far, nothing had. It was beyond Cornwallis' understanding why Harry's long arm of the law was sitting on his front step. His surprise and fear were written clearly across his face.

"Cornwallis!" Faydra called as she came to her feet. "Come up here and have a seat."

Cornwallis walked wearily toward the woman and sat down where she indicated. He was exhausted before, but now he seemed to have aged ten years since walking through his own front gate. He felt like he was walking to his own execution. And the simple fact was, he might be.

Faydra towered over Cornwallis who shook with fear. She cut directly to her point. "Cornwallis, you are so right." She finished the word "right" with a strong over pronounced tee. It was as if she was reading his mind. "It is very possible that you are already a dead man. But no matter what happens, you can make a choice. You might even be able to make a difference." She waited for him to raise his head and meet her glare head-on. She wanted to make sure that he understood and believed to his very core that his miserable excuse of a life had already come to an abrupt end.

Cornwallis sat in front of her like a child, his face blank and slack. He was about to die in front of his wife and children and he had no idea why.

"Let's talk. I want you to tell me all about everything you know about the dead men you found. Don't leave anything out."

In relief, Cornwallis exhaled. He spent the next twenty minutes telling Faydra everything she wanted to know.

When was finished talking, Faydra got up. She hadn't asked him if he'd told the truth. She hadn't threatened his life. She hadn't said that if she found out he'd lied to her that she'd be back. She walked away without looking back, untied the horse, mounted up and said to the road in front of her, "Take the day off tomorrow, Cornwallis."

Chapter 55

This was Faydra's specialty. It was her life's work and she was damned good at it. If any of the other men had fingers that needed pointing, she would have to move quickly. She couldn't allow the men an opportunity to get their stories straight. If she got to them before they got to each other, she might be able to avoid an execution or two…or three. Harry wouldn't question her judgment, but he needed as many loyal men as he could get.

It was getting dark, but she could still make it to Dempsey's house and have a little chat with him before she turned in for the night.

Chapter 56

There were candles burning in Dempsey's house. It was as she had expected it to be. Power was a precious commodity and Harry provided as little of it as he could get away with. There were power curfews and it looked like Dempsey was abiding by that law.

Faydra tethered her horse for the second time that night and strode up to the front door. She pulled her hand back as if to knock, paused, changed her mind and then opened the door as if she were entering her own house.

Dempsey sat on the sofa drinking something from a glass. It may have been beer. There were some skills that would never be lost.

Unlike Cornwallis, Dempsey lived alone. He had taken off whatever work shirt he might have worn and was now wearing a mostly brown, once-upon-a-time, white tee shirt. A pair of suspenders held up a grungy pair of pants that fit him like a sack. He revolted her.

Faydra did nothing to hide her disgust. If anything, it was a tool; one of many that she could expertly wield. The less his self-worth, the greater her power over him would be. She used it to her advantage. Dempsey was no different than any other waste of a life inhabiting this stink hole. All a bunch of mamma boys and prissy girls looking for someone to take care of them; willing to sell their souls just so someone would put a loaf of bread on their table.

Faydra approached Dempsey as he attempted to stand. She placed a boot on his chest and pushed him backwards into the sofa, an easy task while he was off balance. It required no strength but was very effective. By the look on his face, Dempsey was certainly impressed. She laid it out plain and clear for him. "Nothing but the truth so help your rotting carcass," was what her look seemed to say. Dempsey believed it too.

The conversation was short. Everything he told her matched up with Cornwallis' story. The information Faydra was looking for was absent. How could it be possible that these three men were that obtuse? Were they that stupid? It was impossible to believe.

She left Dempsey with the same advice that she had given Cornwallis. "Stay home tomorrow." The fact that he was still alive and his beer was still waiting for him was enough for Dempsey. Faydra didn't close the door when she left. Dempsey didn't get up to close it for her. He reached for his glass and swallowed what remained.

Chapter 57

Faydra had kept to the order of her predetermined list. It always started with the man that ran the crew and ended with the one with the least seniority. If there were any additions or revisions, they usually came out at the bottom. Bradford was the key. He was also the one who brought the bodies back to Harry. It was Bradford that she would break. If she discovered a story any different from the one she'd already heard, Dempsey and Cornwallis would be getting another visit.

It was late and Faydra wanted to get to Bradford before he left for work the next morning. She wouldn't say she lived there, but the house where she kept her belongings was somewhere between Bradford's and Dempsey's. She needed a little sleep.

She left the horse in the back yard which served as a temporary pen. It was enclosed with a wire-meshed fence. The area had gown up with short brush making good feed for the horse. Tomorrow she could drop down to the river and let it get something to drink. She removed the saddle, bridle and blanket, before turning the horse loose. Inside, she stripped and crawled into bed.

Faydra woke before dawn and prepared for the ride to Bradford's. She left early with the knowledge that missing him would make her job harder. She didn't believe in that, so getting up early was not a difficult thing, not a difficult thing at all.

She arrived at Bradford's front step before he was ready to step off of it. The sun had still not risen. Inside, Bradford was preparing for his day. He was in the kitchen making a lunch for his long day's ride. Faydra walked up behind Bradford as he stood at the kitchen counter. She coiled her fist and slammed it hard into his kidneys. Bradford lurched back and upward in pain, slamming his head into the cupboard. The impact cut his head and blood began to pour down his head and into his eyes.

She dragged him backwards while he was off guard and threw him into one of the kitchen chairs. The chair rocked back precariously, but he managed to check himself and balance it without falling over backwards. In nearly the same fluid motion, she grabbed a towel from the counter and threw it at him. It landed in a heap on his head covering his face.

Bradford took the towel and wadded it to staunch the flow of blood. It wasn't a particularly bad cut, but head wounds always bleed profusely. When he had pressure on the wound he looked up at the intruder fearfully.

Faydra paced back and forth in the kitchen letting his fear work on him. It always made her job easier and that was good. When she felt he waited long enough, she posed her first question. "Where is it?"

Bradford repeated the question in a bewildered, almost childish tone. "Where is it?" His voice cracked on the word "it." The question his face asked was, "Where is what?"

Not feeding him any information, she proceeded very carefully. If she had to guess, she didn't think the previous two men had scripted their stories to make sure they meshed. If they had, they were a lot craftier than they seemed. Bradford would be the weakest link. Already she could surmise that he was much less intelligent than Cornwallis. The most likely story she expected to uncover was that Bradford had swiped the gun and was hoping no one would notice.

"You know why I'm here, Bradford?"

Bradford shook his head dumbly.

"Oh come on! You know I can't believe that! You got to have some idea about why I'm here!"

Bradford's blank look held.

"Let me level with you, Bradford. Here's the simple logic. I'm here...right?"

Bradford nodded.

"And if I'm sitting in this rot hole of a kitchen, there's a pretty good chance that you won't be walking out of here when we're through. You following me?"

Bradford nodded obediently. Sweat poured down his face. *Please, God, let it be the right thing to do*, he prayed silently.

"Now here's the twist. Are you ready for it?" She didn't wait for a response. "I'm privy to a bit of important information and I'm not about to tell you what that information is. I need to decide whether you'll lie about it or not. You still with me?"

Bradford nodded, waiting for Faydra to continue.

"This is what you're going to do for me, Bradford. You're going to attempt to give me the information I want. You're going to read my mind. If I decide that you are on the up and up, you might live through this. Unfortunately, if I don't believe you're being altogether truthful…" She stopped here. There was no point continuing.

Bradford's face worked hard to try and come up with whatever it was that Faydra wanted to know. There wasn't much he could say. He often broke the power curfew. That was a worth a public flogging, but nothing more than that. Other than that, the only other serious thing that happened was taking the bodies back to Harry. It was impossible to believe that could be what she wanted to know about. He was supposed to take them to the dumpsite straight away and he did that. It was scary enough having to deal with Harry face to face. Unfortunately, Faydra was even worse than Harry.

Being careful to play it down, Bradford began to explain his illegal use of the power. "Faydra, I really didn't think it was that big of a deal. I always get home late and sometimes it's just easier to throw a light switch on than to dig up a candle. Even when I do use—"

Faydra cut him off. "I don't care one iota about the damn electricity! Tell me what else you've been getting your filthy hands into."

Bradford thought hard. Still the only thing that he could think of was the nasty business of finding the bodies on the southeast ridge. He began to tell her what he knew.

Faydra listened carefully and it didn't take Bradford long to see that this was the story she was interested in hearing. He tried hard not to place any blame on anyone else. If today was his last day, it didn't need to be anyone else's last day too.

By the time Bradford's story was finished, Faydra was convinced of two things. Firstly, Bradford was not guilty of anything…serious. Secondly, someone else had been at the site. Whoever that was, was also responsible for taking the pistol. Bradford hadn't given her this information; it became painfully obvious while he was droning on trying to provide her every detail.

226

Bradford was in mid sentence when she stood and turned to leave. The man's confused look punctuated the moment. Faydra ignored him. Passing through the door, she simply stated, "Take the day off, Bradford." The screen door bounced once against the doorjamb before the latch clicked into place.

Why would Bradford take the pistol in the first place? There were stores of weapons Harry's men had access to. Bradford would have been armed just like everyone else. On top of that, the man didn't have a clue what was going on.

What happened to the gun?

Chapter 58

There was some undercover work to do. At some point, she'd have to ditch the horse, but for now, it would be easier if she kept it. The stable master never expected to see it again anyway.

Four days had passed since the southeast outpost was decimated. Most of the clues had been destroyed, but it was the only starting place she had. The days had been warm and there had been no rain. If she could find an undisturbed section of the trail, it might tell her something.

She mounted the horse, tugged its reins and clucked it into a slow gallop towards the south. As she rode up, she ignored the men from the outpost. It was better that way anyway.

Though the hill was steep, she forced the horse to scramble up it. She hopped off and tied it to a willow. She stood examining the indent that marked the place the boulder rested.

The game trail wound around the backside of the rock. Her intuition told her that it was likely that someone had been up here. The last days were calm and sunny. There hadn't been any significant wind for more than two weeks. What would have caused the rock to tumble down on its own with nothing to act as a catalyst? The answer couldn't be found where she stood. It looked like a herd of cattle had passed through by way the ground was rooted up right down to the soil.

She had to assume that the men had being doing their job. If the intruders came from the south, they would have been spotted walking along the trail. The more plausible scenario was that they came from the north. The men from the outpost wouldn't have expected it and that would have increased the possibility they were taken by surprise. It was best to eliminate a southern approach. She moved slowly down the trail to the south scanning the ground for sign that was almost a week old. She hoped she would find none.

She eventually passed out of the area disturbed by curious workers. Being mid summer, the grass that grew in the trail was tall, dry and as she had hoped to find, undisturbed. Deer tracks in the softer soil were a good sign. It fit with what she had hoped to find, no sign of a human presence. Since they were still so clearly evident, there was hope that there might be indication of her human foe on the north side of the site. Satisfied, she turned and began to work her way north.

Once past the boulder, the disturbances in the soil became more infrequent. At last, the tracks from the last week's traffic disappeared altogether. It was exactly what Faydra had counted on. She forced herself to slow and carefully scan the ground. She watched for sign not only on the trail, but up and down the hill from it as well. How had they traveled, one behind the other, side by side? Who led? Who followed?

About two hundred feet from the bolder Faydra's patience was rewarded. A single, partial track was clearly visible in the soil. The heel of the boot left no mark, but as the person moved forward, the toe of the boot slipped and scuffed the ground. Judging from the track it was impossible to tell how big the foot was that made it. The boot left no tread mark to offer more information. That had been obliterated, but the direction was clear. Whoever made the print was traveling south at the time.

Faydra knew that the distance between the footsteps of a normal person is between one and two feet. She started to search for the next track and it wasn't long before she found it. A small patch of grass had been flattened. The plant was dry and over ripe. It did not spring back.

After her second discovery, other tracks became more obvious. She was an expert tracker and her keen senses and awareness was quickly paying off. There were two travelers. They felt unthreatened or they lacked skill. They made no effort to hide their tracks. She followed their back trail for a quarter of a kilometer before she hit the jackpot—a sandy area in the path, with little vegetation. The soil was a mix of fine sand and clay. It supported weight well, but also held the impression of the foot that fell upon it. The two had been walking side by side. They were both wearing boots of some kind. Both sets of prints were smaller than a normal man-sized boot print. There was no doubt that the tracks belonged to the boy and the woman.

Whether it was an accident that had killed Harry's crew or not, whoever these tracks belonged to held the key to the mystery. Faydra turned back to retrieve her horse.

There was only one set of tracks leading toward the outpost. Whoever made them, hadn't come back this way. Their tracks leaving the scene must have been lost among the jumble of tracks leading down the hill to the outpost. There were missing weapons, so it was safe to assume that they were armed. Would they be able to use the new weapon they possessed? Either way it was worth being cautious.

There was still a good part of the day left and there was no point back tracking to find out where they had come from. They hadn't returned that way.

The wagon trail wound down to the roadway. They had stayed clear of the road thus far, so it stood to reason that they would not be using the road, especially after the incident on the hillside. Faydra first examined one side of the road and then the other, looking for any sign that had left the road.

The sun had begun to go down, before she located what she had been looking for. Their trail did leave the road. They were headed west, up into the hills. Once she figured out where they were going, she might be able to cut them off. For now, she would have to track them. She had her starting point for the morning. It was time to turn in.

Chapter 59

Hannah was well aware they had been very lucky so far. There was no indication that they had been detected. How long could that go on? Another day was shot and now there was Elvin to contend with. It was not a stretch to think that Harry would be looking for an explanation for the deaths of his men, especially if he didn't believe that they were caused by accident. Her uneasy feeling grew.

It was obvious to Jason that Hannah was brooding. He could have waited around for her to tell him what was bothering her, but he was much more direct than that. He liked to have things out in the open. He and Hannah were peas in a pod that way. His mom had been like that. If something was on her mind, it didn't take her too long to say exactly what it was.

As Jason turned to ask her what was on her mind, she interrupted him.

"Listen, it's great and all that you named Elvin. We're not much further ahead than we were two days ago…maybe farther behind."

Jason laughed.

"Jason! This isn't funny. We're not playing a game here!"

"Of course not," said Jason. "It's just that I was just going to ask you what was bothering you. Something's on your mind and I wanted to know what it was," he finished with a smile.

Hannah returned his smile and continued. "We know that some of the prisoners harvest apples. We know that there are many more prisoners than the ones that were in the orchard, yet we have no idea where they go to and now we've missed them again."

Jason couldn't help feeling a little blamed but he understood her point nonetheless.

"Listen, Jason, all I'm saying is that we need to focus. We don't have any kind of a plan. We have some good information and haven't decided how we're going to use it. What if Harry and his men show up this morning? I don't want to be caught off guard, and I certainly don't plan to be a slave for that maniac." She hefted the rifle as if to punctuate her point.

Jason nodded his understanding. "We need to get an early night's sleep tonight and wake up before the prisoners leave. We can follow the group that doesn't go to the orchard."

Hannah breathed a sigh of relief knowing they were both on the same page. She was happy knowing they had some kind of direction to go in.

The day passed quietly while they lay low, staying out of sight. Once the prisoners were marched out in the morning, there was no movement around the prison until they returned in the evening. Hannah hoped to learn something about the prisoners' activities but by the time they returned, it was late evening and too dark to tell anything about where they had been or what they had been up to.

It was dark and if they were going to be up early enough to follow the prisoners, they would have to get some rest. Tired or not, they lay down to try and get some sleep. There was a lot to do in the morning.

Hannah's breathing was deep and rhythmic in minutes. It was more difficult for Jason to fall asleep. He was both excited and afraid of the prospects the coming dawn offered. There was a mystery to solve.

Chapter 60

Faydra drew closer. She managed to track the pair to the house they stayed at the previous night. She even slept on the same bed they'd slept on. She woke at first light, turned her horse loose to fend for itself and continued on the trail on foot.

It was easy tracking through the brush. Jason and Hannah had made no effort to conceal their trail. For an expert tracker like Faydra they may as well have paved the way. The fact that Jason and Hannah had passed this way twice made it even easier.

Faydra arrived where the creek ran into the river; she exchanged her "paved" trail for the paved road and the bridge. It would be harder to track them if they stayed to the road and that was okay too. Tracking was not about following a continuous path of signs. Tracking was all about knowing the terrain, understanding the quarry and discovering where they were going.

Her quarry was trying to avoid detection. That meant that they would be sticking close to edge of the road or would be traveling in the woods. The road to the right led back into town. The bridge led to the penitentiary and to numerous other potentially "safe" places for the fugitives. If they were on the path towards town, eventually, other security forces would likely pick them up. Faydra followed her instincts and crossed the bridge. It was still early in the day.

***

The snake slithers toward its unsuspecting prey. Silence and stealth are the tools of its trade. Its weapons are venom and fangs.

Chapter 61

Outside the prison the sun had not yet risen. There was no indication that the gates were about to open. Hannah, Jason and Elvin moved to the crossroad where the group would pass by shortly. The main group of prisoners would split at this point. At least part of the group would turn left and head to the orchards. Where the rest of the group was going was still a mystery.

The sky was starting to turn gray in the east. Stars had begun to disappear to make way for daylight. Elvin was first to notice the distant clanging that was growing in the distance. It was as if the sun was coming over the horizon accompanied by its own music, its own thunder.

The trio waited patiently. Jason took it upon himself to make sure that Elvin stayed low and out of sight. It was important he not make any noise. It would be devastating for everyone if he did. The clanging noise grew louder as it grew closer. The sound of hundreds upon hundreds of shuffling feet could now be heard clearly over the clanging of chains.

It was almost light when the group of prisoners came into view. Elvin huddled behind Jason demonstrating no particular interest. If anything, there was an air of fear behind his eyes.

Two guards led the group. A column of prisoners four wide followed them. Armed guards flanked the procession on both sides. It took several minutes for the entire group to pass by. Only a tenth of the prisoners broke away from the rest, turned to the left and walked toward the orchards.

It was difficult to make out individuals, but Jason did his best to try and get a look at the hundreds of people that passed before him. Almost beyond hope he searched to get a glimpse of his father. By the expression on Hannah's face, she was hoping to do the same.

Travis was indeed among the prisoners. He was at the rear of the group. In just a moment, he would pass by in full view of both Hannah and Jason. Elvin was the first to see him. The end of the procession came into view and he began to point and chant "Tavs, Tavs, Tavs…"

Hannah and Jason turned to him immediately. Elvin didn't have time to say more. He was suddenly smothered by the weight of his companions as Hannah and Jason pounced on him. The one thing they feared most had happened. Elvin had probably already alarmed the guards and it would be only moments before they would be dragged from their hiding place. They waited in silence. Elvin lay motionlessly beneath them. Moments ticked by, but no one seemed to notice the sudden commotion in the trees. When they stood, the last of the prisoners had already passed by.

Someone in the ranks of the procession had noticed a commotion. Travis' attention was drawn to the woods next to the road by a rustling noise. Maybe it was some kind of wild animal that had bedded too close and they had jumped up. He scanned the woods hoping to get a glimpse of a deer or a rabbit, but the moving brush had already settled. Nothing.

The trio parted the brush and stepped cautiously out onto the road after the last of the prisoners passed around the corner. They followed at a safe distance. Along the way, the groups continued to split off as they moved north along the river. Still, more than half of the total manpower continued on the road. There was no guessing where the various groups were going for the day, but for no particular reason it seemed easier to stick with the main group.

They passed all that could be considered city streets and progressed into the country. The road became windier and there were fewer turnoffs. It seemed unlikely that there would be any other smaller groups breaking off. Wherever they were going, they would be going as one large body.

There was no worry about following the prisoners too close. Each time they got to where they could see the guards bringing up the rear of the column Elvin became extremely agitated. It was quite alarming the first time it happened, but after realizing how scared Elvin was, they began to use his acute sense. He seemed to be hyper aware to the proximity of the captives. At first, his face began to light up with anxiety. His gait slowed and he began to weave from side to side. They used his keen awareness to judge their distance and were able to stay safely back. It was understandable that Elvin would not want to return the prison that he had apparently escaped from.

The captives walked for hours until they came to an intersection where a number of wagons and horses waited. The crew was swiftly loaded on the wagons in groups of ten. The horses started off at a trot. It took everything left in them for Jason and Hannah to keep up. Elvin, on the other hand, had no difficulty maintaining an easy gait that allowed him to hold his own. Jason was amazed at his level of fitness. Luckily for them, the drivers never demanded that the horses run faster than a trot.

Several kilometers later, the road ended at a large opening in the trees. Unexpectedly, the ground fell away abruptly. They were still too far away to tell what the prisoners' destination was. They stopped at the edge of the wooded area surrounding what appeared to be a canyon. The horses disappeared from sight as they descended over the ridge.

Once they were gone, Hannah and Jason moved forward. They looked back briefly to see what Elvin would do. Refusing to move, he remained cowering in the brush. That was just fine. It was safer that way anyway.

They ducked and ran stealthily towards the edge of the canyon as far as they dared and then commando crawled the remaining distance. Jason's mouth dropped open. They were staring down into the maw of an open pit mine. His reaction was not surprising. She had seen pictures in old *National Geographic* magazines years ago, but she had never seen a real open pit mine before. It looked like a giant empty, almost black, ice cream cone that was about a quarter of a kilometer deep and a kilometer wide. There was a small lake at the bottom. Hannah could only guess at how big or how deep it was. The prisoners had already become the size of ants yet they were only halfway to the bottom. No wonder it was dark when the prisoners made their way back when the journey here was so long. Hannah's heart when out to the workers who would slave away for the entire day just to be taken back and caged for the night.

She rolled on her back to face the sky. She paused there for a moment in thought before standing and walking back towards the woods where Elvin was waiting. There was nothing to hide from. The threat from the guards was gone. They were too far away to see them now.

Chapter 62

Back in the bush with Elvin, Jason casually pulled a couple of apples from his pack. They no longer tasted as good as they had two days earlier and didn't do much to hold back the pangs of hunger, but they were still better than nothing and then some. He tossed one to Elvin and expected him to drop it, but Elvin had been eyeing Jason the moment he started rummaging in his pack and caught it deftly. Hannah followed suit, and for a few minutes, all that could be heard the crunching of apples and the subsequent chewing.

"What is that?" asked Jason with a full mouth, indicating the hole in the ground.

"It's an open pit mine. They hauled all the dirt and ore away to make this big hole. But *what* are they mining is the real question." In all the pictures that Hannah had seen, they were mining for gold. What use would gold have in today's world? Gold made no sense at all. Besides, this material was black.

On the opposite side of the road, were large mountains of tailings. It would be impossible for them to get every ounce of ore out. Beyond the mountains of rock, there should be some kind of facility that would surely shed light on the mystery.

They stood ready to race across the road but the sudden appearance of a team of horses cresting the hill sent them scurrying once more into the underbrush. There was just enough time to duck back into the bushes as the team and a group of six men came into view.

It occurred to Hannah like a gunshot. Coal! Of course!

What would they be using the coal for? Wood was everywhere. It made no sense at all that the coal would be used to fuel stoves. *But,* they could use coal to fuel an electricity plant! Hannah scanned the horizon until she found a faint plume of smoke in the distance. She pointed toward it. Jason followed her finger.

"What is it?"

"I believe it's a power plant. It's the reason for hot showers and microwave ovens!" was Hannah's quick reply. Now she had a smile on her face. It didn't matter where the coal was going.

Chapter 63

Jason and Hannah weren't the only ones to get an early start that morning. Faydra had risen early as well. There was no evidence of her quarry had taken the road but she already knew they wouldn't be walking down the middle of it. Maybe it was a subconscious phenomenon, but people who traveled on foot still managed to maintain the rules of the road. They tended to stay to the right. Faydra watched carefully for signs that the two would slip into the woods to hide from an unseen or suspected danger. The grass would be trampled where they had laid low, then back onto the road. Once she passed beyond town limits, it was easier still to follow their trail. With fewer side roads for her to try to eliminate it reduced the number of possible routes the fugitives may have taken.

Faydra recognized her own need to be careful. It was possible that she might stubble upon them at any time. They did not know that they were being tracked and they might be moving slowly. Bent, broken and trampled foliage gave some good information about how long the fugitives had spent in any given spot, but making these assessments was difficult and Faydra needed the most accurate information possible. The boy and the woman might be two days ahead of her, but that didn't mean they were far away. It was much more preferable if it were she who discovered them and not the other way around. Harry wanted them alive and standing in front of him. She wasn't sure how she was going to manage it exactly, but she hoped that the solution would eventually become self-evident. In the meantime, the biggest part of her job was to locate the boy and the woman.

Faydra arrived at the prison close to noon. There was a grove of trees at the crossroads. In many ways it resembled the other places the travelers had gotten off the road and spent time in hiding. In a few significant ways, this site was different. Apple cores littered the ground. The grass was matted. The whole area reminded Faydra of a campground tucked in among the trees. They had clearly spent a great deal of time in the area. She combed the area and came to realize that there were indications that there were more than two people in the group—a new development. Who was this third person and where had he or she come from? Faydra wondered briefly, what sort of a threat this new person might turn out to be.

She examined the entire area carefully and expertly. There was a trail leading to the south and she assumed that it would eventually take her back to the outpost.

A second set of recent tracks left the underbrush and seemed to follow the direction of the prisoners. This newest set of tracks included the third member of the party. Each morning the prisoners made their own fresh set of tracks. The tracks she now followed lay on top of those most recently left by the prisoners. It wasn't difficult to surmise the woman's intent. She was probably curious about where the prisoners were going. It was possible that the woman was casing the place or she might just be curious. It didn't matter which scenario was correct. It was unfathomable that the woman and boy could be any real threat to Harry's little community.

Faydra wrestled with herself about whether to wait for them to return or to continue along their trail. After minor deliberation, she decided that it would be best to find them on their "travels" as opposed to being found in their hideout. She wanted to be welcomed into the group. It would not do to risk suspicion before she had a chance to gain trust. Besides, they might not come back.

Faydra scanned the area once more to ensure she hadn't missed any important pieces of information before picking up the trail once more.

Chapter 64

According to her calculations, Hannah estimated she had about five or six hours before the crew started back to the prison. The captives would be tired and it was likely their pace would be slower. There was a bit of an advantage in that. It would take them longer to return and that would supply Jason and her more time in their preparation. On the other hand, if things went badly, Hannah would not be able to count on the prisoners for much help. Could she expect them to rise up after a hard day's work? Regrettably, she thought not.

They wound their way back down the road toward the prison. They made good time as they walked in silence. Their progress ended abruptly when they were surprised halfway around a blind corner. Standing alone in the middle of the road was a woman. Her attire consisted of old hiking boots, faded blue jeans and an assortment of other miscellaneous items that she layered. These she topped off by a black and red checkered, wool work shirt. It was the kind loggers would have worn in the old days. Her clothing gave her away as a wandering traveler. It seemed a bit strange but she shrugged it off. There were so many strange things in the world and there was no point questioning every one of them.

Hannah's first instinct was to duck into the woods; unfortunately, it was too late for that. The woman had already seen them and to try to hide would only make them look stupid. Instead, she dropped her rifle from her shoulder and let it rest comfortably in two hands with the barrel pointing at a spot in the road near the feet of the stranger who was still thirty meters away.

It was the stranger who spoke first. "Hey," she stated in a weary tone.

Jason, who was always the more friendly of the two, returned the greeting. "Hi. Are you from around here?"

"Nah." The woman nodded toward the east.

"You're not from around here?" Jason repeated.

Hannah watched the woman's reactions carefully, but if there was anything she was trying to hide she wasn't showing it.

"No. Just traveling along, looking for a good stopping place."

"If you're looking for the main part of town, you're going in the wrong direction," Jason added.

It didn't seem to Hannah that Jason was about to give away any crucial information away, so she just let him continue the conversation as he saw fit.

The woman, on the other hand, became ecstatic. "You mean there's a town close to here? Is it a good town? Wouldn't it be great if it was a good town?"

Hannah stood her ground silently trying to sum her up. The woman seemed genuine. In all of her experience traveling, it was never good to trust anyone. Although she couldn't put her finger on it, something about the woman seemed off. Was she trying too hard?

She was feminine in some ways, but held herself with a manly stance. Her appearance didn't seem to fit with the helplessness she was trying to portrait. Hannah wondered if this was something that deserved the kind of harsh scrutiny she was giving it, or was she just trying too hard to find something wrong where everything was right. She stepped in. "Yes, there's a town. You didn't notice it?"

Again, the woman did not miss a beat. "I've been traveling on this road all summer long," indicating to the road that they now walked. Most of the towns I've passed through are completely deserted. I've been moving west trying to find somewhere that I could make up a reason to stay. Originally, I'm from Edmonton, but that place has been taken over by a bunch of thieves and cutthroats. I had no choice. It was either leave or die. I've spent the summer in the Rockies and just came through Penticton not long ago."

The woman had not answered her question and was inching closer as the conversation progressed. She now stood only about five feet away. Hannah continued to pressure the woman. There was something at the back of

Hannah's mind, something that was out of place. Was it the fact that the woman had not asked any questions of her own? Or maybe it was the fact that she was traveling alone that was bothersome. Hannah pressed the woman further. "You're traveling all by yourself?"

"Yes. I am now. My husband was killed a few weeks ago. I big cat got him. There wasn't anything I could do." Here she hung her head down as if to avoid eye contract due to the pain of the recollection. In fact, she had turned her face downward to avoid being suspected of lying. She paused there for effect before slowly lifted her head. "Are you going into town?"

"If I were you, I'd turn around and leave the same way that you came. If you're looking for a place to call home, this isn't it," Hannah stated coldly.

"I don't know if I can. I've been traveling so long..." Her voice trailed off.

The itching in the back of Hannah's mind persisted. She couldn't put her finger on it. It was Jason who noticed what it was and didn't hesitate to ask. "If you've been traveling so long, where's your pack, food and extra clothes?" He waited for a reply. What he got was a scornful smile.

"Listen, kids, if you'd have been traveling half as long as I have you'd know there are lots of places to crash. Clothes and everything else under the sun has been left behind in every little wrecked carcass of shack. All you have to do is ask the pack rats to step aside and give up a little space. They always do. All I need is this." She lifted the back of her shirt and revealed a bulging lumbar pack.

The tables were suddenly turned. Faydra recognized the opportunity and continued to force the issue. "You come up on me in the trail and you grill me like I'm dangerous. Have I done anything like that to you? Have I suggested you're less honest than you look? No, I haven't," she spat, answering her own question. "But maybe I should. You three look like the unlikeliest group I can imagine! One little boy, an old woman and a retard who looks like he graduated from Peter Pan School!"

She questioned his honesty. Jason felt his face flush. On top of that, she referred to him as a little boy. He could feel the blood boiling in his face. He hadn't realized it, but he had begun to lean menacingly forward. Elvin stayed back with a dumb half smile on his face oblivious to any of the uncomfortable feelings that had stolen the warmth from the beautiful sunny day.

Hannah, seeing Jason's temper flaring, wondered why all new meetings seemed to go the same way. They seemed to start off fine and then, invariably, something went wrong. She too, was caught off guard by the woman's sudden verbal attack. All the alarms that had been going off in her mind were suddenly forgotten. A moment ago, she wondered what the odds were that a cat had also attacked this woman's husband. Later she would feel stupid for not pressing the woman about the fact that it would have taken months to cross the Rocky Mountains and would have surely left her clothes in worse shape than they were. Did she replace all of her clothes since arriving? All of these questions would have been great questions, but the woman had disarmed her.

In truth, the stranger could have dismissed all the questions that Hannah had for her. There were a thousand reasons and explanations—all of them feasible. There *was* something wrong about this woman, but now that she was filled with guilt, Hannah was blind to it. It was exactly what Faydra had hoped and planned for.

Hannah backpedaled. "Listen, I'm sorry if it sounds like we're giving you the fifth degree. We've been through a lot too. And to tell you the truth, lady, it's a heck of a lot easier to be alone than to run into someone else. You would just complicate our lives to the nth degree if you joined us and it looks like you can take care of yourself just fine. I can't say it's been great meeting you, but we're going this way." Hannah pointed down the road beyond Faydra. "And you're going that way." She used her thumb to indicate the road behind them.

It was Faydra's turn to backpedal. She would prefer to get them back to Harry without having to force them. It was always so much more work if the captives were constantly trying to run away. The stupid looking man didn't matter. She could burry him for effect, but she hadn't reached that point yet. She still wanted to know why they were still in town and why they were heading back towards the prison, of all places.

"You're right. These are the hardest times for people and instead of being warm and friendly, the first thing we do is turn on one another. My name is Faydra and if I don't have to travel alone, if I could travel with some good company for a change, that would make my life a whole lot easier." Her tongue wasn't silver; it was pure gold and she knew it.

Hannah held her ground. "Faydra, it's been nice meeting you, but we're on a different kind of journey. We're not looking for the next wonderful town right now. In fact, there is an excellent chance that we'll be buried right here one way or another. I really don't think you want to be a part of that."

"Why don't you let me be the judge of that?" Faydra added.

Jason was still standing with a menacing look, though his features had softened somewhat. He reminded Faydra of an angry Chihuahua and the thought made her smile viciously—on the inside. On the outside, she was as soft as butter and as sweet as honey.

Having faith in people is as much a curse as it is a blessing. A person's character has a way of shining through and Faydra would prove herself in time, but would it be too late then? Hannah found her mind wandering back to the prison. Faydra had turned herself around and although uninvited, she joined the trio. Faydra kept the chatter going and by the time they got back to the thicket, it was clear, she could hold her own in terms of survival. Hannah felt less worried that Faydra would have to be one more person to baby-sit if she ended up joining the group. Part of her was looking forward to spending a little time with someone who might turn out to be a kindred spirit. It was her intention to invite Faydra to leave, but she never found the perfect moment. Eventually, she forgot about it altogether.

Another day slipped by before Hannah was able to get her thoughts back to Jason and her plan. It was still unimaginable to walk away from the town leaving hundreds of prisoners to continue to be slaves to Harry. If she could figure out how to accomplish it, she would free the slaves. It was probably not enough to stop him. He was like a spider. And as long as there were flies to be had, Harry would flourish.

The sun was sinking fast. In addition to all of the other problems she was faced with, she had to accept the fact that it was too late to employ any of her plans tonight.

The long pauses in conversation created by Hannah's deep thoughts did not inspire Jason to fill them. Since Faydra's earlier comments, he had not warmed up to the woman and had no intention to. He walked in silence maintaining his serious look. The kilometers passed beneath their feet until the lights of the prison came into view. Hannah led the group off of the road into the sanctuary of the brush.

Faydra ignored Jason's sullen attitude and pressed Hannah to find out about why she was so preoccupied. "You seem like you've got something pretty heavy on your mind. If it's not too personal, it's seems kind of strange to me that you would be hanging out in front of an old penitentiary." Darkness had fallen and the automatic lights of the prison lit up the surrounding field and provided a meager light in the thicket.

Hannah glanced up from her deep thoughts and made eye contact with Jason. He was clearly not impressed with the new companion, but she couldn't tell if it was because he was pouting over Faydra's comments from earlier or if it was something else altogether.

She turned her attention to Faydra. "Hmmm…yes…they are heavy thoughts." She smiled slightly at this. "If you want to me to tell you that this place is the perfect place to settle and rebuild your life, I can't do it. As I said, all I can do is suggest that you head south, find the first safe place you can winter at, wait till spring and then keep heading south. Since you came from Edmonton, I can tell you that there is nothing west of here. I would go south."

Jason finally perked up and added, "If you go down there" and he nodded towards the town, "you'll probably be back here by morning and we can watch you head down the road with the rest of the prisoners."

"Do you know how absolutely crazy that sounds?" Faydra gave her best look of disbelief.

"I would never have believed it myself," said Hannah. "I certainly didn't expect it. We wandered into town just like you did no more than a week ago. We're lucky we're still free."

"What happened?"

Hannah told her how they had been cornered and finally invited to dinner by Harry. She told Faydra how odd the man had seemed. She described the events of the night they escaped and the events that followed. "Maybe they thought we wouldn't try and get away…probably because all they see is a woman and a young boy. I guess it's understandable." Hannah looked over at Jason and gave him a nudge. It was enough to get a forced smile from him. Hannah felt better knowing that she had broken through his sulk.

"It's great that you got away. What keeps you around now?"

The light was now completely gone from the sky; the returning work crew interrupted their conversation. Their stomping feet and the sound of their chains were the most prominent sounds in the darkness. Moments later the first of the convoy came into view. The small party suspended their conversation until the last of the prisoners passed them. While the captives marched by Hannah looked around at her unlikely troop. Jason watched stoically as the men, women and children trudged by. Elvin's behavior had transformed from the dull detached look he normally maintained to being seemingly mesmerized. He mouthed the word "Tavs" over and over again. When the last of the prisoners were out of sight Hannah turned her attention once again to Faydra. "That's the reason why." She nodded toward the fading cloud of dust that followed the prisoners into the building. "How can I leave here knowing what's going on there? Life's barely worth living as it is, I can't bring myself to be a part of destroying it. I would be nothing if I didn't help."

"Maybe they like it this way," Faydra interjected.

"How can you even think for a second that they like it this way?" Hannah returned. Already the dust cloud was no more than a memory.

"There has always been the have and have-nots. Me? I've always been a have-not. What makes you think you're going to make a difference? Even if you release all of these people, do you think you are going to make their lives better by doing it? They have a roof over their heads and food in the bellies. That's something at least. It's something more than you have."

Hannah was appalled. "Do you really believe the crap you're trying to sell?"

Faydra began to laugh heartily at Hannah's outburst. "It doesn't matter, Hannah. What are you going to gain by getting caught? You'll get caught and that'll be it."

"Hummmph. If that was all there was to it, you might be right. But it's not just that. We're looking for someone and we think he might be here." Hannah motioned towards Jason with her head. "See that young man right there? He's the reason I'm here. I said I'd help him and I will…or…I guess I'll die trying."

"Why?" Faydra was clearly and honestly bewildered.

"I've been wondering about that myself. Each time I come up with the same answer. Family. I've only known Jason a few months, but I feel like we're connected." Again, she used her eyes to refer to Jason. "His father came this way and there's a good chance he came through here. If he's here then someone should know of him. I have to believe the key to where he is, is here."

Still, this concept was completely foreign to Faydra. It was as if she were trying to understand a different language while hearing it for the first time. The chasm between her and Hannah's perspective was too great to imagine that there could be any real meeting of minds. It seemed to Faydra that Hannah was a strange new kind of fanatic. People were always looking for something to believe in, something bigger than they are. Maybe Hannah had found something to fight for, but the fact of the matter was, it was a pipe dream and Hannah would die disappointed, at the hands of the man who had provided her last hot meal. "Alright, Hannah, you're going to find this man, free him, free the community, kill Harry…and then what?"

"Maybe you're right. I can't even imagine doing all of that. I don't have any intention of killing anyone. It does sound completely crazy. I would be very happy if we can just find Travis and get out of here."

"If he's here," Faydra finished for her.

Jason's eyes had narrowed again. He did nothing to hide his distaste for Faydra.

"This is what we're about. We'll do what we can," Hannah finished. The tone in her voice was enough to communicate that she had clearly ended that part of the conversation.

There was another long silence until once again Faydra broke it by pressing the issue again. "So what are you going to do next?"

"Maybe it's best we don't talk about it, Faydra. I can't risk that you'll talk me out of anything. We need to get some sleep anyway. You're going to have to decide what you want to do. Jason and I already know what we're going to do."

Again, Hannah left the conversation with nothing left to be said and Faydra wisely decided not to push her further.

Jason had been quiet the whole time and there was nothing that Faydra had said that moved him to want to open up. He was glad that Hannah had ended the conversation. Maybe Faydra would keep her mouth closed and there would be some peace and quiet. Turning his back to the women, he closed his eyes and tried to fall asleep. His busy mind fought him every step of the way. He resented Faydra for being such a pessimist. She did nothing to improve his feelings of confidence in his quest. It made the job before him much harder. He had never imagined that anyone could come between him and Hannah, but he had a sick unarticulated feeling that Faydra could destroy them.

Chapter 65

Hannah woke in time to watch the early morning procession wind its way along the road. The remaining guards inside would settle down for another long day of holding down the fort. An hour should be lots. When was the last time they had any security issues after all? Whoever was left at the prison was stationed there as a preventative measure and nothing more.

Hannah looked over at Faydra. Her eyes were closed and her breathing was deep. She appeared to be asleep. She was about to step out onto the road and walk towards the prison, when Jason woke up. She put her index finger to her lips indicating that he should be quiet. He sat up and tiptoed to her.

"What are you doing?" he whispered.

"Someone's got to check out the layout of the prison. I need to know more about what is going on in there…how it works," Hannah replied.

"I can do that," added Jason, his eyes lighting up.

"No, Jason, someone needs to stay behind and look after Elvin. I was counting on you to do that for me."

"What about her?" Jason queried with obvious disdain.

"I don't know. Maybe she'll move on when she wakes up. If we're lucky…" Hannah paused. "Who knows, maybe she'll be useful for something."

"Hannah, we should stay together. I don't want you to leave me behind," pleaded Jason.

"Listen, buddy, I'll be back soon."

Reluctantly Jason watched her walk up the road towards the prison. There was no indication that anyone was watching the road and the gate the prisoners departed from stood gaping open. It would remain that way until they came back in the evening.

Hannah ran through the main gate and then quickly to the wall. She stayed low and tried to keep out of the sightlines of every vantage point. She was counting on the likeliness that no one was watching, but she didn't want to end her expedition before in got started. There was no movement in or around the compound. It seemed deserted, a nice dream, but was impossible to believe. There were hundreds of prisoners. They would need to be fed. There had to be some kind of staff working there still.

In the time that Hannah and Jason had spent in the area, there had been no deliveries. Common sense told her that there had to be a staff, but it made just as much sense that there would have been regular deliveries as well. There were more questions than answers.

It was obvious where the prisoners emerged from each day. After passing through the gates, the tall fences lined with razor wire cut directly to the building making it impossible for her to skirt it. The windows were high up on the wall; too high for any man to jump and reach. They were covered with bars too close to escape through. In some places, the windows were broken and the glass was littered in the tall grass that now grew up, uncared for, around the building. *Busted from the inside out*, she thought.

There were faint sounds from the interior that seemed to come from the basement level. It made some sense that there would be a guard close by and Hannah did her best to prepare for it. She peeked around the corner. A large bay door had once sealed the entrance. At one time it would have been able to be opened and closed to secure the building, but something had happened to it a long time ago and the door was now gone. The bent and broken mechanism used to open and close it was still there. Something big and heavy had been used to do the damage. Without a functioning door, it was impossible to secure the building from that point. She passed through the large doorway and it became self-evident why it was likely that no one would be around. There was no point guarding it at this point. Inside the bay, the ceiling was at least twenty feet above her head. About halfway up the wall, a catwalk encircled the entire area. The concrete floor had begun to succumb to the elements and was a maze of deep cracks. The individual slabs of concrete had begun to heave from winter frost and plants had begun to take root wherever they could. Moss found homes in the shaded areas wherever they were able to hold on to the moisture. The only light came in from the gaping bay door.

Seeing the damage that had occurred, Hannah moved into the building with more confidence. The prison was not functioning in all of the glory that it once had. At the back of the bay was a narrow steel door. Even from ten meters away Hannah could tell that it was open. There were no other doors in or out of the bay. It was the only place the prisoners could have come from.

One of her concerns was that she would be wandering in the building for hours trying to determine from where the prisoners had come. Fortunately, their daily path was easily discernable. Apparently, it had been years since any cleaning had been done in the building, but the floors were virtually dustless where they were continuously traveled. The edges, on the other hand, were deep with dust and whatever else had blown into the building through the doorway during the years since the main bay doors had been ripped off of their hinges.

Beyond the door was a reception area of sorts, but it too was vacant. Hannah had never been in a prison before but she deduced that she was standing in the area that would have been used when the prisoners were first brought into the building. She envisioned a busload of prisoners arriving. They would have been escorted off the bus once the big bay doors were securely closed behind them. From there they would have gone single file through the steel door and waited as their belongings were checked in. They would be cleaned and then their garb exchanged for prison issue.

Hannah moved cautiously through the hallways. She passed various doors. One was marked "Supplies." The knob turned easily but the door was held tightly closed by a hydraulic closer. She pushed hard and the old stiff cylinder slowly gave, allowing the door to open. The light from the hallway provided enough illumination in the room to see that it was a custodian's closet. One wall of the small room was covered with metal shelving. The shelf held various industrial strength cleaning products. The opposite wall was lined with a number of machines that were used to clean, polish and wax the floors. Among the machines were several large buckets. Racks on the walls held mop handles. The whole place was covered in a thick layer of dust. It was obvious that no one had been in this room in years; again, probably not since the facility had been shut down. A vertical steel ladder was attached to the wall at the back of the room. It led through a square hole four feet by four feet in the ceiling, possibly leading to roof.

Hannah left the room and went back out into the hall. She wasn't particularly concerned about finding the prisoner cellblocks. The most used hallways probably led directly to them. She was more interested in discovering the whereabouts of whatever guards might be left behind. Hannah strained her ears for any movement or noise. Her efforts were rewarded almost immediately. From somewhere directly ahead came the sound of footfalls and jingling keys. She raced back to the supply room. She carefully held the door handle open and let the closer pull the door closed. She held pressure against the door so that it would make no noise when it came in contact with the doorjamb. Someone passed by and she could hear the sound of heavy boots tramping on the floor. The noise disappeared into the distance. She waited for complete silence before peering into the vacant hall.

The man was either returning from an errand or leaving to go on one. There was no point second-guessing this. Any information was good information. She walked down the hall in the direction he had gone in. The hallway was about eight feet wide and seemed to go on forever. There were various doors that led off to the right and left, but most of them were locked. Hannah rushed through the hall as quickly as she could, trying each door briefly before moving on.

At the end of the hall, the corridor teed off. It was evident that both of the hallways were used to some degree, indicated by the lack of dust.

By the looks of the prisoners she had seen so far, the laundry department was not functioning. Certainly, the kitchen should be a functioning part of the institution. She continued from one hallway to the next letting her ears do more of the guiding than her eyes. Quiet, far-off sounds were both compass and alarm.

The corridor ended abruptly with a large steal door. There was a small window high in the center of it. Thin wires crisscrossed throughout, reinforcing the glass window. It swung easily as she push on it revealing a series of steps down into a dark chamber that was lit only by the light that was now coming from the open door. Hannah stepped forward. She felt as if she were walking into the lion's den. The hallway continued, but now it was lined on both sides by small three sided compartments. The fourth side of each of the chambers consisted of a wall of bars. A portion of the barred wall was designed to slide sideways creating a doorway. The entire area reeked of damp old sweat. Hannah gagged and then began breathing through her mouth. The cells were empty. It was as she had expected to find them.

Out of curiosity, Hannah examined them. Each had been reduced to the bare essentials. If there had been working toilets they had been removed.

There were still holes and the toilet flange in the floor. The bunks that may have once existed had been taken out and never replaced. They had probably been removed because of the filth and disease they would have been home to. Hannah shivered at the thought. Having seen enough, she turned back towards the door.

She was just about to put a hand on the handle when she heard the sound of footsteps and voices coming from up the hallway. They were still far off. She walked to the top of the platform and looked out the reinforced window. She could see nothing. The sounds of heavy boots on the hard concrete grew closer. Images of guards on their way to her holding cell made her feel like a rat in a cage. There was nowhere to run, only the hallway through the door and the individual cells behind her. She moved to the hinge side of the door and stood with back to the wall. The footsteps grew louder still. Hannah closed her eyes and waited for the door to swing open.

Chapter 66

Faydra watched from the corner of her eye as Hannah walked up the hill towards the prison complex. She waited until Hannah disappeared from view before she went through the normal motions of waking.

"Good morning, Jason." She drew out the word "good" in her best I-just-woke-up voice.

Jason looked at her indifferently and nodded.

Faydra walked over to Elvin nonchalantly. Jason had already dismissed her. He was still miffed because if it hadn't been for her, he wouldn't be stuck waiting for Hannah to get back.

Though he wouldn't have put anything passed Faydra, he was caught by surprise when she slammed the heel of her hand into the bridge of Elvin's nose. Elvin dropped like a stone, unconscious. Jason recovered quickly and reached into his pack to find the pistol that lay at the bottom. He silently cursed himself for not carrying the pistol in his coat pocket. His hand found the butt of the gun with his first thrust to the bottom of the bag. He pulled it free, shaking the bag to the ground. He brought the gun up in one smooth action and was ready to fire, but he was still much too late.

Faydra had too swiftly moved from where Elvin had fallen. Her hand came down hard and grasped his. The power in her hands was astounding. She pressed hard on his fingers and smashed them into the grip of the pistol. At the same time, she stepped to the side and away from where the bullet would travel if the gun were fired. She twisted the revolver away. Jason lost his grip on the weapon instantly. With a flip of her wrist, she tossed the weapon into the woods. She continued to put pressure on his hand and twist his arm at the same time. He had no alternative but to turn his body until she had his arm pinned firmly behind his back and his hand pinned between his shoulder blades.

Although the pain robbed his knees of strength, Faydra hauled him to his feet using his arm as leverage. From her back pocket she produced a short length of cord. One end had been prepared with a loop and a slipknot. Faydra slipped the loop over Jason's free hand and pulled it tight. She added his other hand and deftly tied the two tightly together. Jason winced in pain. A wicked smile spread across Faydra's face.

By the time his hands were secured Elvin had begun to come around. He sat up rubbing the bridge of his nose. If he understood or was upset about what had happened it didn't show on his face and when Faydra began to march Jason up the hill, he dumbly followed along.

They arrived at the prison gates Faydra and walked through as if she'd been there hundreds of times before. Without hesitating, she continued through the main reception area directly to the office that doubled as a staff room for the few guards who remained behind during the day. One of those guards sat at a desk with his feet propped up on the desktop, a surface that had long since ceased to be used for its intended purpose. It had become a glorified ottoman. When Faydra came in with the boy the guard stood up immediately, almost apologetically. He ignored the prisoners that accompanied her.

Faydra explained the situation briefly and then accompanied by two guards they left the room and carried on down the hall. They passed several wings that were used to house the inmates. If Elvin recognized any part of the place, nothing on his face indicated it. At the end of the hall was a holding cell, beyond that, an interrogation room.

The bigger of the guards pushed Jason forward into a chair. The force of the push was so great that when he landed in it both he and the chair slid into the corner and toppled over. Jason's elbow slammed into the concrete wall and he stood up massaging it. He recovered in time to see the same man slam Elvin to the floor. Faydra stood in the doorway looking indifferent. To Jason none of this was in the least surprising.

He was in a small room with a door on one wall and a large mirror on another. The other two walls were barren. A metal table sat naked in the middle of the cold room. The guard said nothing as he turned to leave. The door was slammed and then locked behind them with an audible clicking sound.

Chapter 67

For Hannah, in her empty cellblock, the seconds dragged by. The blood pounded behind her eyes. The sound of her own heartbeat in her ears made it nearly impossible to focus as the guards drew nearer. She strained her ears and forced herself to calm. The sound of the footsteps was diminishing, getting farther away. Hannah moved to the window and peered down the corridor. She could see a small group of people walking down the hallway away from her. Two of them were guards. One of them was Faydra. Hannah's heart sank as she recognized Jason and Elvin as the two remaining figures. Their hands were tied firmly behind their backs. She was sadly surprised that Faydra walked freely. The truth of it was self-evident. They had been betrayed. Faydra had been a spy sent to find them.

It would only be a matter of minutes before the guards would be scouring the facility. It was safe to assume that Faydra knew her way around the facility. They would have blocked off the main entrance as soon as Faydra had come through it. That route out was most certainly out of the question.

She slipped through the door quietly and into the main hallway. As quickly and quietly as she could, she returned to the supply room. The door was equipped with a dead bolt. On the inside of the room, there was a safety knob for operating the lock. On the outside of the room, the lock could only be operated with a key. Hannah turned the bolt and locked the door. Her fears were proved valid when the quick heavy footfalls of two guards could be heard roaring down the hall. They paused briefly at each of the doors that Hannah had previously tried. They stopped at the door of her storage closet. There was a brief twist on the knob and a sudden yank. Satisfied that the door had been locked all along, the guards moved on, leaving Hannah in the dark and silence.

It was still early in the day and the main body of the prisoners was not due back for hours yet. Hannah turned a mop bucket upside down and threw a few cleaning rags on it for a cushion. She sat down to think.

Chapter 68

With the door locked and the boy behind bars, Faydra made her way back to the more comfortable office. It was up to the guards to find Hannah. She was certainly somewhere in the building and it was inconceivable that she could free herself. There were only two exits and both of those were carefully controlled. It was her turn to sit back with her feet up. A self-satisfied smile slowly spread across her face. The complex was alight with activity.

Hours later, the guards had still failed to find Hannah. Faydra's patience began to diminish. It didn't seem possible that in a near empty facility it would take so long to find a single person. Evidently, Hannah had anticipated that she would have to avoid detection, but she wouldn't have been able to evade the guards searching for her this long unless SHE knew they were looking for her. Faydra thought, *That's the answer, isn't it, you crafty wench. You already know we're looking for you.* Faydra stood up and went in search of the nearest guard.

When she found one she pulled him aside. "She knows we've got the boy."

The guard looked on stupidly. "What?"

"Listen, idiot." She spoke slowly as if the man was mentally handicapped in some way. "She's here and she knows we've got the boy and his mute friend. She's hiding in here somewhere. Find Mac and tell him to come and see me...NOW!"

She finished with a look that inspired him to run in the direction he believed Mac might have gone. It didn't really matter where he ran to, just as long as it was away from her.

Faydra went back to the office to wait.

Chapter 69

Hannah knew that there would be no stopping the search. Faydra might try to use Jason as leverage. There was no time to think about what she would have to do if that happened. If she stayed where she was, they would eventually find her. In the meantime, what had they done with Jason? Where had they taken him and what would they do to him? She couldn't move down the main hallway. A guard could appear at any time. She circled the room in frustration, searching her mind for solutions that would not present themselves.

Eventually she turned to the back of the room towards the ladder. It was the only direction to go. It was a time for action, not hiding. She wondered what she would find at the top. There was no indication of what possibilities there were. There was only a single sign beside the ladder that stated, "For Maintenance Personnel Only." It was not uncommon for structures like these to have the heating facilities placed in a rooftop room.

She placed one hand on a rung just above her head and started up. She half expected a hatch door at the ceiling level and hoped that would not be the case. She reached the ceiling, about ten feet from the floor, and passed through a rectangular opening, surrounded on three sides by a railing, waist high. She paused at the top. It was dark below, but darker still above. The only light came from the window in the custodial room and it was not enough to show any of what the loft might contain.

She climbed until her feet were level with the second floor. She stepped from the ladder to the floor. She hoped it was the furnace room, but it was too dark to tell. None of the noises one might associate with working machinery were present. Hannah felt along the wall near the opening in the floor, looking for wall switches. She finally found them only to discover that they were already in the on position. She flipped them down just to be sure. Still nothing. She would have to explore the space in the dark. Not an appealing option, but at least it was darkness she was facing and not a locked door. Starting at the switch panel Hannah felt her way around the room using one hand to feel along the wall and the other as her eyes. For the first few feet there was nothing but flat bare wall until her hand came abruptly to hard cold metal. She followed the object around to the left. She pushed against it. Although the object didn't move, the metal gave slightly. It was the typical light gage material that furnaces are often made from.

In her mind's eye, Hannah had begun to picture the room. Even in the dark, she began to visualize its dimensions and contents. It was probably not large and was most likely rectangular or square. When she reached the end of the bank of furnaces, the wall continued for a couple of feet before turning abruptly to the left once again. The next wall was about four meters long and once again bare. As expected, it turned once more to the left. She had come almost full circle and could see the faint light from below coming from the entrance about twenty feet away. She resisted the urge to hurry. She didn't want to miss anything. It was beginning to seem like she was in a dead end room. She continued along the wall.

It wasn't until she had almost reached her starting point that her progress was halted. Her shoulder slammed into a metal outcropping. It missed her face by centimeters. She backed off slightly and began to feel around more carefully. On the backside of the entryway that was yet, another set of stairs.

Hannah did not hesitate. She grabbed the nearest rung and began her assent. She stepped cautiously up. She was operating in pitch-black and the ceiling could come at any moment. She reached high above her head with each step to feel for obstacles. She had gone up about twice her own height when she came to the end of the ladder. A sealed hatch blocked her way. She felt around the edges for a latching system. Her fingers found it and she searched its shape to learn how to operate it. It was some sort of cam system attached to a twelve-inch long lever. She positioned herself so that she was secure and pulled the lever toward her. It didn't move. She gathered her resolve and pulled harder. The lever remained as if welded. Hannah feared the worst; that it was locked. Having failed her first attempt, she tried pushing on it. Again, it didn't give. She pushed harder still and it began to move. She pushed it as far as it would go.

Feeling confident that the latch was open, she took another step up and crammed her body against the door. With all of the strength in her legs, she pushed upward. At first, it was as if she was pushing against a solid wall, then ever so slowly the door began to give. Whatever had been used to seal the door against the elements had become a hard gooey substance that had eventually glued the two edges together.

The trap door opened onto the roof. The roof was not fenced in, but it didn't need to be. There was no part of the building that wasn't surrounded by the high wire fence. Even if a prisoner made it up here, the entire roof could be seen from any of the numerous towers and there was still the perimeter fence to contend with.

On the top of the roof, Hannah stood almost dead center of the entire complex. She hoped that she could find Jason and free him before reinforcements arrived and before she was discovered. There was no obvious way off the roof. There were no ladders down and the hatch she had just come through was the only one there was. Hannah returned to the ladder and resigned herself to the maintenence room.

It was bright daylight on the roof and the light from the open hatch illuminated the furnace room. Hannah took one last quick glance over the roof. Although it was still gloomy in the corners of the room, now it was easy to see everything the room had hidden from her earlier. For the most part, it was just as she thought. The place was the central furnace room for the complex. There were more than a dozen furnaces lining the wall, each with its own duct. The furnaces were separated into two groups. There was a narrow hall between the two sets. The hallway between the furnaces was one part of the room that Hannah had missed when she had traversed it the first time. Once back on the floor she walked through the gap into the second part of the room. There were actually a full twenty-four individual furnaces. The second set stood back to back with the first set in the center of a room.

Hannah looked at the furnaces more closely. Each was labeled. One said "Laundry." Another was labeled "East Cell Block." A third was labeled "Administration." Hannah looked for the one called "Interrogation Room" or something like it. If they were still maintaining the use of the various areas in the building, maybe Jason had been taken there. She continued to scour the labels. Eventually she came across one called "Conference Rooms." Maybe "conference room" was a politically correct term interrogation room. There could be something there.

Other than the silent hulks of metal, the large room was empty. Hannah took to the ladder once more and went down to the maintenance room below. Once there she went to the shelving units. The shelves were littered with piles of rags and a variety of bottles of high potency cleaning products. At the end of the shelf at about chest high was a bin. At first glance, all it contained was a bunch of junk. Hannah was running out of options. Out of curiosity and desperation, she looked closer. She discovered that most of it was not junk at all. There was a role of masking tape, a scraper of some kind, a cheap multi-screwdriver, a hammer and an old pair of pliers. There were other miscellaneous items too numerous to mention. She slid her hand through the center of the roll of tape and stuffed her pockets with various other tools. She finished her shopping spree by tucking a bundle of rags under her arm and then raced back to the furnace room.

She walked to the furnace with the words "Conference Rooms" printed on the metal tag. She could reach the top of the furnace, but she wasn't tall enough to reach the ductwork that was fastened there. Once again, she headed back down to the supply room. This time she brought back the pail she had used as a chair earlier. She turned it upside down and stood on it. It gave her the height that she needed and was able to lift her leg enough to get a knee up on top.

She scrambled to the top and stood beside the heating duct. She went to work immediately taking out the small screws that held the air duct to the top of the furnace. Once the screws were removed, she began to take out the ones that held the ninety-degree corner piece to the straight section. A half an hour later, she was wrestling the four-foot section of metal ducting to the ground.

Once back on the ground, she went to work with the rags. Using the razor blade knife, she cut the rags into strips. She used a square knot to attach each one. With each additional strip of rag, her rope grew by about eight inches. When she had finished tying the last all of the rags, her rope was about twelve feet long. She coiled it and draped it over her head like a mountain climber might.

Before hopping up onto the furnace, she returned to the hatch that led up onto the roof. It shed more light than she was comfortable with. It was highly unlikely that they would find their way up here any time soon, but there was also the possibility that the light from the outside would attract them. She pulled the door closed and began her descent.

It was more difficult making her way back through the room in the near pitch-black. She knew where she wanted to go and this time she did not pass by the opening between the furnaces and was able to get back to the duct that she had removed. She wasted no time jumping back up onto the furnace, which was easier now that the duct was not blocking the way. She worked her way into the square metal tube and began to inch her way toward the conference rooms.

It was fortunate for Hannah that the building had been built at the time when dedicated furnaces were installed to control the heat in various rooms. It meant that the heat could be precisely controlled in every part of the building. The heat could be turned down in all of the unused areas of the building. The advantage for Hannah was that the duct would lead directly to the rooms she wanted to get to.

Hannah moved undetected through the complex, crawling along with great caution. She was careful not to make scuffing noises that someone might hear.

Chapter 70

The prison was in turmoil and Faydra had still not decided to join the search. Such work was beneath her. She had brought the quarry this far. The incompetent guards could handle the rest. At least she could enjoy watching them.

There were only two exits that Hannah could escape by and guards were posted at each one. That left two other guards the task of searching the entire structure. They had already given the entire complex a quick once over. They had searched all the large rooms and hallways. Anything that was locked was ignored with the assumption that the fugitive had no keys.

The second search was much more thorough. This one was based on the possibility that she knew she was being hunted and that she had avoided them intentionally in the first search. They started from one end of the building and worked slowly through. Each room was searched carefully and thoroughly before passing on to the next. There was always the possibility of bringing in more reinforcements, but it was imperative to solve the problem without involving Harry. That would almost certainly be the worst thing that could happen. The very worst thing that could happen would be to upset Faydra. Hopefully she would enjoy her opportunity to relax knowing they would eventually capture the woman.

The hours trickled by.

Chapter 71

It was pitch-black inside the ducting and difficult to maintain a sense of time and space. She began to lose her sense of direction, and the ductwork did not lead to the "conference room" it led to conference "rooms." That meant that the piping would certainly branch off at some point. The rooms would be fairly close to one other. She continued the arduous task of inching through the metal labyrinth. She told herself over and over, *Move one knee forward and then the other, check the sides for junctions by running hands over them.* Then she repeated the whole process over again. *Move one knee forward and then the other. Slide each hand along the side to check for junctions.* The pattern repeated itself endlessly.

She made one last slide forward and when she reached her hands out to feel the sides. Nothing. She slid forward a bit and pawed at the empty space in front of her. Nothing. She continued forward until there was evidence of another single duct. With a little exploration, she was able to discover that there was now a choice of three passages ahead of her plus the one she had come from. Hannah had planned for this contingency. She had already decided that she would start from the left and explore the passages in a clockwise pattern. She removed her jacket and placed it behind her in the heating duct. It was her marker to help her find her way back.

She turned left and began to feel her way along the metal piping. This time she counted the number of times she slid forward. She might not know how far she went, but she would have some kind of measurement that would help her to gage how far she would need to go on her way back. Each time she slid her right knee forward she added one to her count. When she reached seventy-five the ducting suddenly made a sharp right turn. Hannah noticed an increase in light once she rounded the corner. The bright metal reflected the light and was shining back at her from the sides of her galvanized metal tomb.

Hannah could see the source of the light. It was no more than twenty feet in front of her. She stopped to listen. No sound came back to her ears. Jason might not have been brought this way. She forced herself to avoid the thoughts circulating in her mind; thoughts like, *He could be in any part of the building*. The building was enormous and there were twenty-four furnaces and twenty-four series of heating ducts to check. If necessary, she would check them all. She inched toward it as if guards occupied it and they were expecting her. She reached the grating and looked into the first of the conference rooms. There was a large table in the center and a large mirror on one wall. She craned her head in all directions to try and see as much of the room as she could. It was empty.

Hannah attempted to turn around. Unfortunately, although the space was large enough to crawl in, it was not large enough for her to turn around in. She began the arduous task of backing out the full distance she had just crawled forward. In took more time than it took her to get there, but eventually she made it back to the intersection and worked her way down the second of the three passages. Her experiences were the same as the first. It was made easier by the fact that there was no corner to traverse and as she moved forward the light gradually became brighter and brighter until she was squatted directly over the opening. This room was as bare as the first one. Again, she made her way back to the beginning by retracing her movements in reverse.

In the third duct, Hannah could hear the voices even before she could see faces. She moved carefully making sure she was especially quiet. There were at least two figures in the room. She could see no more than shadows from where she was perched.

Elvin was the first of the duo who came into view. She positioned herself directly over the vent and surveyed the entire room. Elvin sat at the table with his head down. Jason stood by the door looking out into the hallway through the small eight-inch square window in the center of it. Hannah needed to get Jason's attention, but she didn't want to alert anyone else to her presence. Though she crouched only feet away from those she was seeking, she too was trapped while she searched for a solution.

Chapter 72

Jason stood looking out into the hallway. The door was locked tight, but there were no guards in sight. It had been hours since he and Al had been brought to the room. He knew from the conversation between the guards and Faydra that they were looking for Hannah. The room was barren except for two chairs and the table. There was a vent in the ceiling but it was too high for Jason to reach, even on tiptoes. Elvin was no help whatsoever. He might as well have been a two-year-old.

Elvin sneezed from behind him as if to confirm his thought. Jason looked up to see what looked like fine snow pouring out of the vent above. Apparently, the dust had irritated Elvin and it had caused him to sneeze. Jason watched the downpour expecting it to lessen and then stop altogether. It did abate for a short while and then suddenly as if a new storm cloud appeared the dust came pouring out again. Jason walked closer to the vent and gazed up inside it. He took the chair and hefted it up onto the table. He jumped up to take a closer look into the vent. He could see nothing except for black. He was surprised when the vent spoke in a raspy whisper like someone trying to talk with laryngitis, "Jason!"

Though her voice was barely audible, he recognized it immediately. "Hannah!"

There was no time lost on telling stories or greeting each other. Jason knew instinctively that what little time they had was precious. He did not try to begin a conversation. Elvin looked up from his chair happily, but as usual, he said nothing.

Hannah examined the vent cover. It was held on by a series of clips. It had been pushed on from below until it snapped into place. Hinges of a sort held the other side in place. Hannah placed the screwdriver tip against the vent cover close to one of the clips. She hammered down on the handle with the palm of her hand. The clip separated from its clasp. She repeated the process on the other side and the vent swung down releasing another shower of dust.

"Step back a second, Jason," Hannah whispered. Jason backed out of the way. Hannah crawled forward through the opening so that her head was hanging down. She gripped the ledge tightly and let her body drop through the hole. It reminded her a bit of a gymnastic move called "skin the cat." She landed, not unlike a cat on the table next to Jason.

"It's so good to see you!" said Jason as he wrapped his arms around her. Hannah hugged him back, but she was already trying to devise a way out. There was no time to lose. The guards would be back eventually and there was no way of knowing how long "eventually" would be.

"Jason, I want to get us all out of here if I can, but it's going to take some doing."

"Let's do it," Jason said, clasping his fingers together to create a kind of a basket for Hannah's foot.

Hannah smiled. "Not just yet. I've got an idea."

She hopped off the table. And walked quickly around the room. She stopped at the window. She knew it was reinforced glass and they wouldn't be able to break it, but that didn't matter. She grabbed the chair that Jason had been standing on and placed it so that only two legs rested on the floor while she gripped the other two legs, one in each hand. Using all of her weight, she pressed down and forced the legs to bend. It wasn't a pretzel, but maybe she could make the damage look like it happened when the chair was bashed against the window.

Next, she shooed Elvin out of his chair and placed it up on the table. She climbed up. "Jump up here," she called to Jason. In a flash, Jason stood beside her. "Sit here, would you?" Jason obeyed her and sat on the chair. Hannah climbed first to the seat and then to the high back using Jason as a counterweight. Tiptoeing, she was able to get her head up inside the ductwork. With a small leap, she transferred her body up into the shaft and

271

wriggled in. Next, she rolled over on her back so that her feet dangled out. She sat up at an odd angle with her neck completely craned over.

"Jason, I want you to pull the table over to the window, then put the broken chair on top of it. Put all of the furniture over there."

"What for?"

"Just do it. Everything will be clear in just a minute. We don't have time for me to explain."

Jason went to work immediately. The table made a horrible scraping noise, but there was nothing he could do about that. He moved as quickly as he could. By the time he had finished, Hannah had already stretched out her homemade rope and let the coils fall down to the floor. She coiled the rope around her wrist and braced herself in the duct with her feet. The knots would help make the climb easier.

"What about Elvin? We're not going to leave him here, are we?" protested Jason.

"No! Now hurry up."

Jason grabbed hold of the rope and scurried up. There wasn't much room and he did his best to crawl over Hannah without hurting her. She tried to help him by turning to the side and cramming herself against the steel wall.

She turned her head towards Jason who was just beyond her in the dark. "Listen carefully! I'm going to try and get Elvin to climb the rope. I need you to go back the way I've come. This is important, Jason. I don't want anyone getting lost. About a hundred feet back or so there is an intersection. My coat is back there. We are going back using the left tunnel. If I can get Elvin up here, I want him between us. You need to make sure he goes down the left tunnel."

"Got it," said Jason, turning and disappearing silently into the dark.

Hannah turned her attention to Elvin. What if he didn't want to climb up the rope? He might not understand how. He might not understand her directions. If anything were going to go wrong, it would be now. "Elvin! Come now," Hannah stated simply. Elvin was no stranger to captivity and some part of him felt the urgency. A moment later, he had his full weight on the rope and was scaling it.

Hannah felt like a little like a lifeguard saving a drowning man. She knew that he would be heavier than Jason, but was surprised nonetheless. Thank God he was a scrawny man. She had wrapped the makeshift rope around her wrist several times and planted her feet firmly to support his weight and still it was all she could do to hold on. Thankfully he was quick and a moment later he was scrambling passed her and into the dark. She prayed silently that Jason would be able to lead him in the right direction.

Once Elvin had gotten out of the way, Hannah lost no time in pulling the rope up. With it out of the way, she reached down for the vent cover and slammed it home. It made a bit of a racket, but the clips snapped into place and held the grating firmly.

She rolled to her stomach and began scooting her way back towards the furnace room. When she arrived at the junction neither Jason nor Elvin was there to greet her. She felt for her jacket, but it was gone as well. Hannah could only hope that they had made it safely back to the furnace room. She strained her ears for any indication of where they went but no sound came to her. *Well, that couldn't be bad*, she thought.

Regardless of where they might have gotten to, she had no choice but to go back to the furnace room. Hopefully she would meet them there. Suddenly from far away, there came a loud clanging noise. Hannah felt the heating duct give beneath her. Her heart jumped immediately to her throat. Worrying less about the noise, she raced as quickly as she could in the direction of the furnaces.

She expected the trip back to be much shorter, especially since she was moving as quickly as she could. Although she did cover the distance in record time, it felt like it took too long. She was anxious and afraid. She stopped once or twice to listen, but the ducting was stable again and everything was silent once more.

She hurried on as quickly as she could when suddenly the ductwork took an unfamiliar sharp downward turn where it should have continued in a straight and level line instead. She stopped instantly feeling around her in all directions. A seam in the pipe had torn loose and there was a wide gaping split in the duct. It had bent down along the bottom edge. The whole thing dipped to the ground at close to a forty-five degree angle. It was impossible to judge how far it was to the floor or how much further it was to the furnace room. Hannah had not considered the possibility that it would not support the weight that she was calling upon it to bear.

She whispered as loudly as she dared, "Jason!" She waited impatiently for a reply, but got none. It seemed obvious that the conduit had collapsed under the load and that wherever it led to, that's where Jason and Elvin had gone. She realized that she might not make it back to furnace room. As silently as she could, she continued headfirst downward. She used her arms and legs to slow her descent.

She silently cursed the absolute darkness. There was no way to tell where she was or how close to Jason and Elvin she might be. There was nothing she could do but to continue.

Eventually she did reach the bottom. Her hands slid out onto cold concrete. She was on the floor, but where? "Jason?" she hoarsely whispered.

This time there was a reply. "Over here."

She moved forward in the dark, but before she had completely cleared the ducting, she banged her head against something metal. A low metallic drumming sound filled the air. Hannah reached out with her hand to feel in front of her. She followed the object both right and left. She had indeed returned to the furnace room, but the weight of Elvin and Jason in the final portion of the ducting had caused it to collapse to the floor.

She called once more in her harsh whispering voice, "Jason, where are you?"

"Over here," he repeated quietly.

They were close. She crawled on her hands and knees until she collided with something warm and soft. It was Jason's leg.

"Are you two okay?" she asked.

"I think so. Where are we?" There was a quiver in Jason's voice. He was clearly afraid that something terrible had gone wrong.

"Everything is fine, Jason. You're exactly where you need to be. It must have been a damn scary thing to be in that pipe when it came crashing down." The darkness prevented Hannah from being able to estimate Jason's state of mind or see that he nodded.

"What are we going to do now?" Jason asked.

"I've got a kind of a plan, and if it works out we should be home free. If it doesn't we're going to be in a lot of trouble."

Hannah explained where they were in the building and where the exit was by comparison. She had a pretty good feeling that if no one had come crashing down on them when the duct broke free, they probably hadn't heard it or couldn't find their way to it. There was still the fact that even though they tried to divert the guards when they left the interrogation room, there was only one escape route and they had taken it.

Hannah led the way back to the fallen piping and with Jason's help, they worked to turn it into a dead end. Using their combined weight, they were able to crush the sides over and flatten out the opening. They continued to work at it until the end was flattened. Using their combined strength, Hannah and Jason folded the flattened end up. They bent it up until the flattened section was folded, sealing off the way they had come. If anyone followed them, they would be trapped in a dead end. Hannah doubted if anyone knew where the ductwork ran. It was likely that they would experience the same disorientation that Jason had experienced only minutes earlier.

Chapter 73

Faydra was frustrated before, but it was nothing compared to what she felt when she learned that her young prisoner had escaped. She fumed silently as she listened to a variety of improbable scenarios the terribly inept guards provided. She stood up and left the room almost knocking one of the guards over as she blew passed them on her way to the cell where Jason had been held.

She stood with the door open, looking into the room that had remained as it had been found. When the guard had arrived, he found the room locked and empty. The table and chairs were stacked against the wall just below the mirror. One chair had been nearly destroyed. It appeared as though it had been used to hammer relentlessly against the bulletproof glass of the two-way mirror. The scenario made no sense whatsoever.

The obvious solution to the problem, and the only one that came to mind was that somehow, Hannah had made her way back to the cell and released the prisoners. This was the most popular scenario that had been presented to Faydra.

However, the explanation did not sit right. Hannah would have had to slip past the guards who were searching for her in a building that she had never been in before. She would have had to have stumbled onto Jason and then found a way to unlock the door or pick the lock. If she had been able to succeed, that also meant that now there were three fugitives wandering the corridors trying to avoid detection. The idiot mute was one of them. It was impossible to believe that was the only viable explanation.

Faydra pulled the one good chair from the table and sat down with the wheels in her mind turning. She let her eyes roamed the room slowly. She was accustomed to finding and decoding the minutest clues. She was rarely stumped and she was determined that this would be no exception. She looked up at the ceiling and noticed the heating vent there. She stood up and walked over to it. She stood in the middle of the room with the duct directly overhead. She stared at it for a moment.

From her new vantage point, she let her eyes roam around the entire room. Eventually her focus halted at her feet. There she pushed a small pile of dust from side to side with her toe. She casually used her toe to draw the dust together from all sides forming a small pile. Then, she spread it out absent-mindedly. She repeated the process as she considered the problem at hand. Her eyes lit up. She examined the duct with new understanding.

Faydra crossed to the table and pulled it to the center of the room. She grabbed hold of the chair and tossed it up. A moment later, she was standing on the chair. Her head was still a foot away from the ceiling, but she could easily reach the vent cover. She pulled the grate free and raised herself to her full height but still, she could not see into the ducting. She grabbed a solid hold and chinned up into the opening. From her new vantage, the signs were obvious. The surface that should have been covered with undisturbed dust was a riot of scuffing and drag marks. There were large deposits here and there where it had been pushed around. A good portion of the dust had ended up on the floor where she had discovered it.

The big oafs responsible for security would never be able to fit into the small space, but the boy, the woman and that runt of a man could. Faydra jumped down and hurried to the nearest guard. "They're in the vents. I'm going after them! Listen for my call."

She returned to the vent with one of the guards. He provided a hand up. With practiced expertise, she hoisted herself up and into the dark vent. She reached intersection and after a one failed attempt, she worked her way down the correct shaft. When she had gone thirty yards or so she stopped to listen. From far away she could hear faint voices. Knowing that she was on the right track, she hurried along silently.

She arrived at the broken section and could hear Hannah and Jason talking quietly in the dark. Everything was working out perfectly. She would catch them off guard. They didn't stand a chance. The duct made a sudden turn downhill and like a snake, she slithered down the shaft undetected. It wasn't until she reached the bottom that she realized that she had inadvertently fallen into a trap. The ducting ended abruptly. Someone had sealed off the end. Faydra tried to move backwards but the metal was much too slippery and the backward slope much too steep. She was able to make a little progress each with each effort, but when she relaxed even a little she slid back to the bottom of the shaft.

Jason was startled to hear the sound of someone in the heating duct. Who could have followed so quickly? Who would have known? The only explanation he could think of was Faydra! The three fugitives huddled against the wall silently, hoping that she had not detected them before she slid into the trap.

Faydra's struggles subsided and she ended the suspense at the same time. "I know you're there, Hannah and Jason. This little trap was very clever. I would never have expected it from you." Her voice was as sweet as honey. "Help me out of here and I'll make sure they go easy on you. I can do that you know. Harry trusts me. He and I built this town together. Help me out of here and I'll make sure that you're treated like royalty."

Hannah and Jason ignored her pleas and spoke together in hushed whispers until they made their decision. "Faydra, we could never trust you. I'm sorry, but we're going to have to leave you here. I hope your friends find you sometime soon."

Faydra responded with venom. "My friends are going to find me right now. They're waiting for me to tell them where you are." With that said she began to call loudly for help. Hannah didn't hesitate. She rushed to where Faydra was trapped. "Shhhh, Faydra. I'll help you, just be quiet."

Faydra quieted again immediately. "Move to one side so that Jason and I can free you." She waited for Faydra to follow her instructions. There was silence for a long time. She still held the screwdriver tightly. In the dark, she raised her arm slowly. Jason and Elvin sat silently in the dark a short distance away. Hannah's coat sleeve whistled as it sliced sharply through the air. Her arm came down in a swift arc with all of her weight and power behind it. The screwdriver penetrated the metal and carried on into the vent the full length of the shaft. Faydra thrashed briefly inside the metal tomb and then became still. Hannah stood up and returned to where Elvin and Jason were sitting. The screwdriver stood horizontally still embedded in the metal vent.

"Hannah! What happened?" whispered Jason.

"Nothing, Jason. Everything's fine," came her reply from the dark.

Chapter 74

The guard listened for Faydra, but it was impossible to follow the piping to where she had gone. The heating vents were placed far out of the way and sometimes ran with the hallways and sometimes they didn't. He waited patiently for what seemed like a very long time. He was about ready to give up when he heard her calling from somewhere far away. He raced in the general direction, but her calling ceased almost as soon as it had begun. He walked further in the same direction hoping to get some indication of where she might be, but nothing. He continued to wait for another hour before giving up entirely.

The only option that made any sense was to prevent the intruders from leaving the building. The easiest way to do that was to maintain patrols at both entrances. Eventually they would have to come out of hiding. As for Faydra, there was little deliberation about that. She could take care of herself. She was always coming and going as she pleased anyway.

Chapter 75

While the guards paced and kept watch, Hannah and Jason waited patiently. They took turns watching and listening for the prisoners to return. Jason was keeping watch while Hannah rested even though he knew the prisoners made so much noise coming into the building that they all could have been sleeping soundly and still they would have been woken. There was no point taking any chances.

The prisoners were brought in, fed and put to bed. From that moment she began to keep time as best they could. They would wait a few more hours before making their move.

Jason had lived through some very long nights, but for him this was the longest one ever. The hours crept by painfully. It was his job to sit watch for the first two hours. Hannah would take watch for the last two. In four hours, they would put Hannah's plan into action.

One hour of the two, or maybe only fifteen minutes had passed when Hannah stirred and spoke. "Jason, this isn't going to work for me. At least one of us should get some rest."

"I can't sleep at all," Jason replied. A sound of a deeply drawn breath filled the chamber coming from Elvin's direction. *At least one of us can*, he thought.

When the night was somewhere near half over, Hannah decided it was time to put their plan into action. The prison was as silent as a tomb and there was still a couple of hours before the prisoners would be awakened for another grueling day of work.

Jason rousted Elvin and he followed, if not eagerly, at least willingly. Hannah had left the rooftop hatch open through the night. It was too early to provide enough light to navigate by. She led the way feeling in the dark for the bank of furnaces. She found the passage through. Besides the light that was coming from the ceiling, there was still a faint glow from the opening in the floor. They moved toward it. Hannah led the way down the stairs and into the storage room. She waited for Elvin and Jason to catch up.

From what little could be seen from the small window in the door, the corridor appeared to be clear. When all three of them had assembled, Hannah turned the knob on the deadbolt and opened the door. Together they moved into the hall. Hannah turned to Jason. "Wait quietly." She tiptoed to the main entrance. She leaned around the corner as far as she dared and peered down the hall. Outside, a guard sleepily watched the main entrance. He appeared to be asleep. Not that it mattered.

She hurried back to where Jason and Elvin waited. They moved together up the hall toward the cellblock Hannah had explored the previous day. She looked to Elvin's expression to see if he recognized it, but there was no indication that he did.

Near the entrance to the cellblock was a control station used to lock down the cells. It was vacant. Once the prisoners were brought in for the night, there was no need to keep anyone at the station. The prison staff was kept to a minimum and of the various posts to be manned, apparently, this one was expendable.

Hannah walked to the console and flipped the switches that would open all of the cell doors. Then she rushed down the hall toward the cellblock. She pushed the door open and stood facing the dark room. She had expected the captives to recognize their freedom. She expected that they would already be moving out of their cells. Instead, they stood in their compartments like sheep.

Chapter 76

Travis woke with a start to the sudden clanging sound of the opening cell doors. His body clock could tell that it was hours earlier than the gates were scheduled to open. They had not yet been served the morning goop. In some of the other cells, prisoners began to stir at the unexpected sound. He had no more than gotten to his feet when the main exit door of the cellblock swung open. Instead of a burly guard, the doorway was filled with the silhouette of a woman. Slowly other prisoners came forward to stand at the gates of their cells.

The woman spoke with authority. "Do you want out of here or not?"

If the woman had a plan, she didn't take the time to share it. A number of prisoners walked out of their cells into the corridor. Travis was among them. He could see the uncertainty on their faces, although he was surprised to see so many come forward as quickly as they did.

"Who are you?" asked Travis.

***

A man spoke to Hannah. His beard was full and dirty. She cringed at the thought of what animal life it might contain. Some of her distaste was painfully evident as she hissed back, "Do you think we could discuss this later?

We need to get out of here together and we need to get out of here now!"

"What about the others? Did you free them as well?"

Hannah could barely comprehend that questions were being asked when it was action that was called for. The whole rescue idea was turning out more difficult than she had imagined. "I guess so. I opened all the cells that I could. Are you coming or not?"

Travis turned his attention to the prisoners in his block. He wanted to motivate them to move as one. He called out, "Our freedom is here! It's time to go. Stand up and leave!"

Understanding was slowly dawning for many. First, there was a quiet stirring and in moments, it grew to a low rumble.

Intuitively Travis understood that Hannah intended to overrun the guards. He called to her over the growing noise, "If you're going to make this work, you're going to need everyone."

Without hesitation, he ran past Hannah and out the door. His cellblock was not the only one in the complex. There were other blocks of cells each filled with captives. He raced from one cellblock to the next. In turn, he announced the impending freedom for all and called on someone to lead. He did not wait to find out who it might be. If he had judged these people correctly, it might be no one. He left them to their own devices and moved on.

By the time he made it to the last of the blocks, his efforts were almost unnecessary. In the last cellblock, the group was organizing and as soon as the doors opened many stepped immediately out. Travis forced his way back into the hallway where prisoners were milling about. Even in the growing ruckus, there was no indication that these people would do anything that would help their plight. In all likelihood, they would allow themselves to be rounded up and returned to their pens. They were so much like cattle.

Travis raised his voice as loudly as he could in a last ditch effort to motivate the crowd. He swung his arms madly in the air and raced through the ranks. Slowly they began to move and then just like cattle they started to stampede. The guards had realized what was happening, but it was too late. Their orders were lost in the chaos.

A pistol thundered in the dim light, but the guard that pulled the trigger was already pulled beneath the weight of the mob that flowed toward the exit like a river swollen with spring runoff. The hoard boiled down the corridor. Someone fell and was trampled beneath the mass. Travis led on. He raced past Hannah oblivious to her. Freedom was only a doorway away and it would be his.

The crazy man raced by Hannah leading the mob. The masses of prisoners were already out of control. Immediately, she recognized her opportunity and took it. She plowed in among the ranks knowing perfectly well the dangers of losing her own footing. She could see Jason huddling with Elvin in a nearby doorway, the river of bodies flowing past them.

"Hurry! Take my hand! Hurry!" she called to Elvin and Jason and she was pushed toward them.

With Elvin close by Jason leapt into the human river. He grabbed for Hannah's hand and struggled to remain on his feet. Elvin was close behind him. They were three, tethered and safe in one another's grip. Hannah held tight to Jason. She would not let him go. He could feel her hand crushing his. She willed him to follow. Jason did the same for Elvin. He squeezed tight and pulled Elvin along behind him.

Another deafening gunshot pounded in his ears. Jason didn't see where it had come from; he was focused on keeping up with the mob. A man from behind them lurched forward. There was a dramatic look of pain in his eyes. Even before his body began to crumple, deep red oozed from his chest. His arms flailed as he tried to maintain his balance. Falling forward, he grabbed onto Elvin screaming to him to help. The crowd was relentless. It pushed forward. Jason held on to him with all his might, but he could not hold the weight of Elvin and the man who pulled on him. His hand was stripped away. Elvin and the man disappeared beneath the surge of the stampede. Jason turned his attention forward. Hannah still pulled hard on him. He could see his purple fingertips poking out of her fist. The feeling was gone from them, but Hannah still held tight. They were swept away with the crowd.

When they reached the exit, the guard who had been posted there was nowhere to be seen. Bodies were strewn everywhere. The guard was probably one of them. The crowd reached the gates and raced on. When they left their cells they were a mindless mob, but now freed and angry, they ran with a purpose. They did not scatter as Hannah had expected. They swarmed toward town. As they ran, they gathered weapons picking up anything they could swing or throw, anything they could lay their hands on and carry. They wound their way down the dirt road, turned toward the bridge and into town. Hannah could imagine the rude awakening when the furry of the five hundred slammed into the slumbering village.

It only took five minutes to empty the prison and then it was returned to silence. Jason turned to Hannah. Now there was just the two of them. "Where is Elvin?" Jason asked.

They cautiously walked into the prison. There were fewer bodies than Hannah expected to see. Some prisoners did not survive, but neither had the guards. They had died bringing out the dormant fury of the captives.

In the corridor, there were even fewer casualties. The bodies of Elvin and the unfortunate prisoner lay where they had fallen. Elvin was beneath the man who had pulled him down. He had a peaceful look; no different than if he had been sleeping. Jason raced to him oblivious to the carnage. He pulled the dead man away from him. Hannah arrived and knelt, taking Elvin's hand in hers. Jason looked up with tears flowing from his eyes, expecting to see sadness in Hannah's as well, but she was concentrating, not grieving. Jason followed her gaze to Elvin's wrist and realized she was searching for a pulse. He looked up again, to read her reaction, waiting to see what she found there. The tense look on her face disappeared and was replaced with a smile. Elvin coughed and his eyes flickered open.

Hannah, Jason and Elvin were only minutes behind the main body of the hoard, but it was enough that it was like passing through a battlefield after the battle had ended. It was as if every vendetta that existed was paid in full. The mob attacked the village as one and surgically removed the cancer responsible for their pain. Not every house had been broken into, but those that had been were nearly destroyed. Windows were broken, belongings strewn in the yards. In some cases, the inhabitants lay motionless on the porch or in the grass. On one front porch, a woman wept, clutching her children. Far ahead, the crazed mob had split and passed down various streets. The town was at the mercy of the tsunami it had created.

Hannah followed with Jason and Elvin close beside. It was not necessary to track the mob. She already knew its destination. She followed it to the big house with the large tree and the tire swing in the back yard. She followed it to Harry's house.

It looked no different than the houses that had been left untouched, but there was activity going on somewhere inside. Hannah raced to the window and peered through. She was in time to see four men race through the house. Harry was given no chance to respond. The first man slammed through the kitchen door and picked up a lamp from a nearby side table. He brought it back over his head and then forward in a smooth sweep. His entire body followed through in a single graceful motion. The heavy lamp connected squarely on Harry's forehead. His feet left the floor and he curled backwards in a gymnast's arc. There was an audible cracking sound as he came down hard on the back of his head. He lay in a heap. There was no chance for him to plea his case or beg for mercy. Three others flew threw the house, destroying anything in their path. And as quickly as it started, it was over. The house stood in near perfect silence.

Suddenly, the bearded man from the prison walked casually though the door. Unlike the others, this seemed to be his destination. He walked over to Harry as if he was disappointed and bent down beside him. He reached forward and placed his thumb on the side of his neck. The look on his face indicated that where he had hoped to find a pulse there was none.

Hannah and Jason moved around the side of the house and entered through the too familiar back door. He heard the noise of their footsteps and turned on his heel to see who it was. His quick reaction reminded Hannah of a wild animal.

The man recognized Hannah as the woman who had opened the cells less than an hour earlier. "I guess I owe you my gratitude. Thank you," he said as he stood.

Hannah nodded. "You're welcome." She paused for a moment. Since there was no one else to ask and the man was a good a start as any she continued, "Actually, I'm looking for someone." She beckoned Jason to come to the foreground. "Actually, *we're* looking for someone and we think that maybe he passed through here."

The man's gaze shifted from Hannah to the boy that she had presented. It was as if he was struck with a hammer. He fell to his knees. It had been years since he had seen his son, but he recognized Jason immediately. Travis could barely contain his excitement. "Would the 'someone' you're looking for happen to be a man named Travis," he choked out.

Now it was the boy's turn to be astonished. "Yes, I am looking for Travis. He's my father."

The man approached slowly, looking deeply into Jason's eyes hoping that Jason would be able to recognize him through the beard and the filth. Although he saw no recognition, he continued nevertheless, "If you're looking for a man named Travis then that must mean that your name is…Jason."

Hannah's eyes opened wide in unabashed astonishment. The man in front of her was easily thirty pounds lighter than he had been when she first met him and the beard he sported covered most of the features that she had come to know years before.

"Dad?" Jason said no more. He was already in his father's arms.

Epilogue

It was time for Jason's life to begin again. For him, the next steps were simple. There was a family waiting to be born. His life was destroyed when his father had left him and his mother behind. It was destroyed a second time when he had to leave his mother in a grave below the house he had grown up in. Now he looked into his father's eyes with the hope that his life would be reborn. For him, in this one moment in time, there were no worries. For an instant, nothing could take that away.

Travis stood overwhelmed. He awoke this morning to freedom; a moment he barely dared to imagine. Every obstacle that had been in his path for more than four years was suddenly removed. Now, with the morning over he stood face to face with his son who had endured unimaginable hardships to be here standing with him. Tears flowed freely down his face.

It was a bittersweet moment too. In one moment, he learned his son was alive, well and standing with him. In the next, he learned that his beloved wife had been killed. Again, with no time in between, he was introduced to a woman who had done more for Jason than anyone ever could.

For Hannah, those first moments were both the sweetest and the hardest. She was filled with deep gratification to see Jason reunited with his father. The journey turned out to be worth the effort and it was over. That too was a wonderful thing. But the journey was over. Her act of being a Good Samaritan was finished and Hannah found herself stranded once more without family or home. She stood outside the circle, Elvin stood with her.

Travis turned to Jason. "Where to, son?"

Jason reached over and took a hold Hannah's hand as if it belonged in his. "I'm going wherever you two are going." He turned to Hannah and hugged her with every ounce of strength left in his body.

Travis looked at the two. Whatever had transpired between them had bound them together. Even though Travis was torn by sadness at the loss of his wife, he could see that it was no time to split hairs. Hannah had placed herself in danger's way hundreds upon hundreds of times for the sake of his son; maybe even for the sake of love. It was all, almost too much to bear.

Travis looked from Jason to Hannah. "Hannah, I can't even begin to tell you about or even show my appreciation for everything you've done for me and my son. A blind man could see how Jason feels about you and I'm not blind. If you don't mind, Hannah, I'd like to tag along with you two."

Tears welled up in Hannah's eyes as she replied, "That would be a good thing."

Printed in the United States
72864LV00004B/106-348